TALES OF THE APT

Volume 1
The Spoils of War

The Shadows of the Apt
(Tor UK)

TALES OF THE APT

Volume 1
The Spoils of War

Adrian Tchaikovsky

NewCon Press
England

First edition, published in the UK 2016 by
NewCon Press
41, Wheatsheaf Road,
Alconbury Weston,
Cambs,
PE28 4LF

NCP102 Hardback
NCP103 Softback

10 9 8 7 6 5 4 3 2 1

ISBN: 978-1-910935-20-0 (hardback)
ISBN: 978-1-910935-21-7 (softback)

Cover art by Jon Sullivan
Editorial meddling by Ian Whates
Interior layout by Storm Constantine
Cover layout by Andy Bigwood

Contents

Introduction
by the Author

Welcome to the first collection of stories set in the world of the Insect-kinden.

The tales in these pages are presented in roughly chronological order and take place before *Empire in Black and Gold*, from a piece of Collegiate history through the events of the Twelve-year War between the Empire and the Commonweal, and ending with the exploits of a certain Mantis Weaponsmaster in self-imposed exile in Helleron.

Along the way, we encounter a variety of familiar faces, both heroes and villains. For many, these stories were their first appearance before they worked their way into the novels. Other characters are seen here for the first time, but possibly not the last.

Shadows of the Apt and its associated material almost certainly represents the largest single body of work I'll ever produce, and perhaps the most detailed and wide-ranging world. For every character and location that made it into the novels there were plenty that were only hinted at, or not even that. I'm delighted to be able to work with Ian Whates and Newcon press to bring these tales of the Apt (and the Inapt) and their world to you.

Adrian Tchaikovsky,
Leeds
May 2016

Introduction
by the Publisher

When Adrian first approached me with the proposal for this series I was thrilled. The *Shadows of the Apt* books represent one of the most intriguing creationss ever to grace the field of epic fantasy. There can be no doubt that this *is* fantasy, but the stories also contain elements of steam punk, a strong grasp of entimology, and feature the sort of well-rounded characters that any long-running series needs to succeed. The idea of a world in which some races embrace and routinely employ magic but are incapable of comprehending science, while others pursue the study of science but are blind to the potential of magic proves fertile ground for a storyteller of Adrian's calibre.

The Tales of the Apt books gather together the many Apt stories that have appeared in various anthologies and online, and combine them with a wealth of new material written especially for these collections. All are arranged in chronological order, so that the reader is provided with another perspective of events alluded to or sometimes detailed in the original series. In effect, *Tales* provides an alternative history that parallels and unfolds alongside the familiar one, filling in the gaps and revealing intriguing backstories for many established characters.

Any fan of the original *Shadows of the Apt* books will, I'm sure, be as delighted and excited by this addition to the canon as I am.

Ian Whates
Cambridgeshire
June 2016

To Own the Sky

Between the years of 470 and 482, a little over fifty years before either Stenwold Maker or the Wasp Empire came to trouble Collegium, a curious contest was sponsored biannually by the artificers of the Great College itself. The challenge, extended to all comers (although in practice almost every entrant was local), was to find the heaviest self-powered flying machine.

The entrants, student engineers, professional mechanics and armchair artificers, gathered atop the cliffs east of the city, each cradling or towing his or her creation: little orthopters of a hundred different designs would be cast over the edge, to their sooner-or-later-but-certain doom, lost to the sea. College staff would be standing by, with clock and glass, to measure out the seconds, or sometimes the minutes, of each entry. The weights and the times would go into the department's books as a curio for future generations. The formal name for the challenge was the Aviation Department All-Comers Rally, but it became known in common parlance as Clifftops.

In the year 478 a maverick artificer named Cutmold Limner caused a considerable stir amongst the academics and the artificers of Collegium by turning up at the cliff edge with his *Mayfly*. It was, by some large margin, the heaviest device ever to be presented at Clifftops. Moreover, when Limner himself climbed in, it was heavier still.

The stewards of the rally were still in frantic discussion over whether such a dangerous enterprise should be allowed when Limner bid his apprentice to set the clockwork motor going. The *Mayfly* rumbled forwards, to the mingled delight, alarm and derision of the onlookers and, as it passed over the lip of the cliff, Limner threw a lever that set the wings ablur. For a moment they beat the air fiercely, and several onlookers record in their diaries that the machine seemed to rise up from the cliff's edge, hanging impossibly in the air like a living thing.

Then there was the unmistakable sound of an overstressed geartrain jumping, teeth parting company with teeth, and the vessel tilted madly in the air. Limner gesticulated wildly, his voice lost to the wind, and shortly thereafter, the sea. The *Mayfly* was well named, his detractors jeered later, or perhaps poorly named, for there was no *may* about it. It had not, and that was that.

The name of Cutmold Limner's apprentice was Lial Morless, and this is his story.

The workshop was empty. Oh, the tools, the piecework, the odds and scraps were all still there – who would bother to take them? – but Cutmold Limner would never return, and so it was empty.

Lial Morless slumped onto a stool. He felt a yawning chasm within him, as though he was falling; not that steep plunge into the unforgiving sea that Limner had taken, but falling forever, no end in sight. The diminutive forge-hand, Scop, lurked in the room's furthest reaches, a broom in his hands. He had not come to watch the Clifftops. He had said all along it would not work. He was just a forge-hand without a College education, and nobody had listened to him.

The walls of the workshop were covered with tacked-on plans: the cross-sections of wings, the corrugated backs of gear trains, skeletal sketches of the fallen flier's wood-and-canvas hull. Lial stared at them dully. *Another two years. Would that have been so hard a wait?* But for Cutmold it had seemed so. Lial's master had not been young, and he had been so *sure* of his calculations. Sure enough to cast himself off over the sea without a test flight.

Scop made a fierce spitting noise, and a moment later a bulky form blocked the sunlight from the open doorway. "My condolences, of course." A broad Beetle man in formal robes ducked in. Lial knew him well and liked him not at all. He had been a patron of old Limner's once, and later a vocal opponent. Goiter Parrymill was his name: the airship magnate. He had been keeping a narrow eye on Limner's work for a long time, had spoken against him at the Assembly, had turned potential funders and friends against him. Lial looked up at the intruder with a baleful expression.

"No need for that, lad," said Parrymill cordially. "You can't say I didn't do everything in my power to stop this happening."

Which was true, Lial supposed, from a certain standpoint. In the background Scop made a rude noise and restarted his sweeping with undue aggression, but both Beetles ignored him.

"What do you want, Master Parrymill?" Lial asked, feeling abruptly tired and wretched.

"When you're over the worst of your grief, think what you want to do with the rest of your life, lad," the magnate said, a scum of sincerity floating over the patronising tones. "Come find me, if you want. Limner always said you were a promising lad as an artificer."

Lial stood slowly. "Firstly, Master Parrymill, I am twenty-six years of age, and so don't 'lad' me, if you please. Secondly, I'll manage just fine."

"And the rent on the workshop? You have the wherewithal? Only, I know the landlord, and Limner made him scrabble for the money while the old boy was still alive." Parrymill raised his eyebrows as if in surprise at the wickedness of the world. "Alone, without commission or income, you're like to struggle."

"Good. I like struggling. Lets me know I'm still alive," Lial said flatly. It was a sentiment from some Mantis tragedy, he belatedly recalled. The plot had not ended well for the speaker.

"You know best, I'm sure," Goiter Parrymill said smoothly, and took his leave, strolling off down the street with his robes gusting behind him.

Scop stomped forwards, clutching the broom like a spear, all righteous indignation now the man had gone. His head just about came to Lial's chest: the halfbreed result of some unlikely union of Fly and Beetle parents, neither of whom had stayed around to see what their child would grow into. Formal schooling was out of the reach of a man of Scop's lineage, but he had been around artificers and their tools all his life, and made up in practicalities what he lacked in theory.

"Fat, gloating bastard," the forge-hand said. "So, what now, eh? He's right about the rent. My wages too, no doubt."

Lial opened his mouth to offer some consolation, but Scop shrugged it off. "Never mind me. I can get work anywhere. Better paying, probably. I wasn't sticking here for the money." He looked at Lial fiercely, as though expecting the Beetle to bridle at that. "You?"

"I've got two years," said Lial, flatly.

Scop stared at him, the meaning sinking in. "Master Morless, if you want to go the same way as Master Limner, the cliffs are there any day of the year. No need to wait til the next Clifftops."

"It should have flown. I checked the calculations myself."

"I *said* it wouldn't-"

"You?" Lial rounded on the little man. "What do you know about it?"

Scop put his hands on his hips, facing off Lial's greater size without flinching. "Limner couldn't fly. You can't fly. Me? I can fly, and that cursed *Mayfly* was never going to get off the ground, and a nutshell for your calculations. Too heavy. Body too heavy for the engine, wings too heavy for the joints. I *told* him." The halfbreed put down the broom and hooked a satchel from beneath the workbench.

Lial blinked in surprise and Scop nodded. "What? I knew only one of you'd be coming back. I've got work to find, to put bread on the table. Goodbye, Master Morless, and good luck."

"Lial," Lial said automatically. He had never got on with Scop, particularly, but seeing him in the doorway, pack over his shoulder, putting Limner's life and death behind him, the Beetle felt sorry to see him go.

Scop nodded soberly. In those days a halfbreed had to go a long way to be on first name terms with a College man. "You're really going to carry on the work?"

Lial nodded. In his mind there was very little else. When Limner had gone over the cliff, seven years of Lial's life had gone with him.

The halfbreed made a noncommittal noise. "We'll see," was all he said, and then he was gone.

After that, Lial needed a drink and, rather than sit in the workshop – which he knew perfectly well he would not be able to keep up – and turn gradually more inward with each bowl he drained, he decided to seek out his mentor and instead get spectacularly drunk with *her*.

She was nobody's idea of a good mentor, was Tallway. Lial didn't know how many other students she actually had. Certainly she made more of a living telling unlikely stories around the tavernas than she did actually teaching. She claimed to be an Art tutor of high repute where she came from, and when she had first arrived in Collegium she had attracted a great many impressionable people who were led on by her exotic nature. It didn't take them long to work out she was a sot.

Tallway was actually Taul We, but Collegium folk had little tolerance for trick names. She was the only individual of her kinden in the city, which seemed to suit her just fine. Freakishly tall, six foot four inches at the least, and angular every which way, she had a long, narrow face and sallow, unhealthy-looking skin. Her dark hair was tied messily back out of her eyes, usually with nothing fancier than a piece of string, accentuating her hollow eyes and hollow cheeks and a high, bony forehead. She stitched Beetle cast-offs into long coats and voluminous shirts and breeches cut to fit her gangling frame, which left her seeming always as if she had dressed in a hurry.

She was Grasshopper-kinden from the Commonweal, she said. Nobody disputed it, but then nobody could prove it, either. The Commoweal was not a welcoming place, and those Collegium merchants who had ventured the trip had come back, if they came back at all, chastised and empty-handed. A recent airship envoy from Goiter Parrymill's cartel had been met with an armed warning and turned back at the highland border. The only commodity to come out of the Commonweal, it seemed, was Tallway.

Lial had originally stayed as her student for one reason only: flight. Beetle-kinden could sometimes develop the flying Art but, unlike most other insect-kinden, it did not come easily or naturally to them, and it had so far eluded Lial. One of the few pieces of information he had got out of Tallway was that her kinden were the same: they could fly, indeed she could fly, but it was a rare and difficult Art amongst them. That qualified her as a teacher, for none of the Beetle mentors in the city professed to have mastered the Art themselves.

So far his studies had born little fruit, and indeed with Tallway as a teacher it was hardly surprising. Half the time she was absent when he came for his lessons, and half the rest of the time she was already reeling drunk before he arrived. Whatever had driven her from her far-away home, it was soluble in strong spirits. Still, a drunken Tallway was at least entertaining, as her normal talent for spinning fictions grew grander and grander the more she took on board, until she would swear that she was the world's greatest magician, the King of Sarn and the inventor of the double-reaction water-pump all at the same time. Despite his studies not progressing, Lial had grown fond of her. With Limner gone she was one of the few people he felt he could actually talk to.

In Collegium they drank wine, mostly from the local vineyards, and almost always watered. Drinking unwatered wine was for madmen and Mantids. And Tallway, when she deigned to drink anything so commonplace as wine. She was an expert in locating brands of alcohol that were as potent as they were obscure.

The stuff she foisted on Lial after Limner died was bitter on the tongue, sweet on the back of the throat and apparently some kind of nettle brandy. Where Tallway had got hold of a case of it, she wouldn't say, but they got through a remarkable quantity, with Lial brooding evermore deeply, and Tallway becoming increasingly erratic. Some time after midnight she explained to him, in great and complex detail, how she was going to go home and show "him" just how wrong he'd been, to "knock down all his people" and to "puncture his drum", whatever that meant. Lial did not try to ford the rushing torrent of her words lest he be swept away. Besides, almost everything that Tallway said was a lie, usually an obvious and entertaining one. He had no wish to find out whether the little truth left in her was all that remained after sufficient drink.

And in the small hours she looked him straight in one eye or the other and said, "So, you can't fly yet then."

"Not even the slightest bit," Lial confirmed, clinking the rim of his bowl to hers.

"Shows what a rotten teacher I am, though," she told him, slurringly earnest. "Never believe anyone who tells you they know how the Art works. Nobody does, not my lot, not your lot, not a bit of it."

"What do I pay you for, then?" Lial had been meditating under Tallway's guidance for over a year.

"This stuff costs something rotten," she explained, refilling their bowls messily. "So, you can't fly, not even with this expensive liquor inside you."

For a moment he thought, befuddled, that this was the secret, and he reached for the wings that were waiting for him in the ether, the unseen place that the Art came from, but there was nothing, and instead of leaping into the air he fell over sideways, which seemed hilarious to both of them.

"Not me," he confirmed to the floorboards.

"And your man Limner, old Cutmold Limner, he couldn't fly either," she said sadly. He cocked an eye up at her.

"It should have worked. No reason, no reason for it not to've," he told her. Long arms reached out and righted him, or tried to, and for a moment they were clinging to each other, getting tangled up with just which arm belonged to who, and she planted a nettle-flavoured kiss on his cheek. He leant into her bony armpit. "I heard the engine, though," he explained, gesturing wildly. "It was working. The wings, oh the wings were going all over the place, but then... the gears sheared. We made them strong as we could, but I heard all the teeth go on one of them, ping, ping, ping! Big old gears, but not strong enough, not for those wings. Why not? Why not fly? All the calculations worked. Master Limner had me check 'em myself."

"Nothing that big can fly," Tallway pronounced, hugging him to her one-armed, the other reaching for the bottle. "Sorry. I sorry. I sorry? Yes, I sorry, old Beetle old boy, but I say you before. Too big piece of metal belong earth, not sky, don'tcherknow?"

"I've seen bigger insects than that get off the ground," Lial muttered stubbornly. "I saw a load-beetle twice that size get airborne. Landed on a roof and went straight through it."

Tallway snickered. "No, but no, but your beetle, your beetle of whatever shape or size or what have you, you see, isn't metal. Not wood. Not *weighing*, see? Not that I know how your gears and teeth or what have you, but metal... metal belong earth not sky. Us also."

"Then I'll build it out of..." Lial frowned and slurped the last drops out of his bowl, "something that belongs sky. What belongs sky?"

"Clouds," she said, and "wind," he countered, and they continued naming the lightest, airiest things they could think of until dawn (itself named two hours before) marched from the east like a harsh and unforgiving army.

Lial slept for most of the rest of the day, and retained only two things from the entire night's work. One was a hangover of grandiose proportions, and the other was one of Tallway's suggestions for something that belonged to the sky.

Staring at the ceiling of his lodgings, knowing that the workshop was lost, his master was lost, and the entire dream was on the very point of following them, he determined that he would give it a go. What could go wrong? Or at least, what else was left, that had not already gone as wrong as could be?

He let the workshop go. He would not need one until he had fixed a great many other things, and there was no point frittering his meagre savings on it. He sold every piece of machinery in it, kept the pick of the portable tools, and let the landlord reclaim the barren room. So much for that.

That done, he began to make enquiries into supply. The commodity that Tallway had dreamt up was neither readily available nor cheap. The local stuff was legendarily poor in quality and, while the Spiderlands shipped tons of it, they charged the earth, and demand was high enough to keep prices rising in all seasons. A little came south from the Moth-kinden of Dorax, but that was through Sarn, adding both tariffs and considerable personal danger for any trader willing to risk that route. Dealing with Ant-kinden was always a dubious business, with arbitrary confiscation, imprisonment or slavery always a possibility.

After a couple of months of asking questions and trying to arrange deals, Lial began to recognise that more than simple economics were against him. Merchants saw him coming, and closed their doors. Word of his intentions preceded him, with universally negative results. For a long time he could not account for it, but then Goiter Parrymill paid him another visit.

"I was sad to hear that you'd let old Limner's workshop go," the magnate rumbled. "You're doing all right for yourself, of course?" He looked around the mould-stained walls of Lial's wretched little room, where he had turned up unannounced.

"I live," Lial told him flatly.

"And retain your ambitions, no doubt." A sharp look came into Parrymill's eye. "My friends tell me you're enquiring into the silk trade. Buying. That rang a few warning bells."

Lial sat on his sagging bed and waited, without comment.

"If you're trying to mark out a space in the airship business, lad, it isn't that easy," Parrymill said, and his avuncular jolliness was gone. "I know, I know, everyone looks up and sees the gasbags, and thinks, *that's a decent line of work, licence to mint money, I want a piece of that*. But it's not that easy, lad, and for those of us who have put in all the hard work, we don't appreciate new and inexperienced hands trying to undercut us. You're not the first young artificer to think we'll share ownership of the sky."

"So that's it," Lial said aloud. It was true, the airship trade did very well. It was the safest way to travel, the swiftest, and the bigger airships could even haul a fair weight in cargo. Over the last few decades the men who built and operated the airships had become a commercial aristocracy in Collegium, counting College Masters and Assemblers amongst their ranks.

"If you want work in the airship line, lad, there are easier ways than trying to piece together your own float and set up as a sole trader. Just ask. I'll find a place for you. For Limner's sake. He always reckoned you were a good hand." Parrymill served up his most beneficent smile.

Lial smiled back a little, and Parrymill obviously took that as an encouraging sign, but the younger Beetle shook his head.

"You needn't fear, Master Parrymill, I want none of the airship trade."

The magnate frowned. "Then why such an interest in the price of silk?"

"Because it's so very, very light," Lial told him. "Now, if you would be so kind, Master, I have an early morning in the markets."

Parrymill was actually almost through the door before he abruptly turned and stared at Lial. "You wouldn't be about the same lunacy as your master, would you?"

Lial just looked at him, pointedly waiting for him to leave.

"I don't see why I should let a gifted apprentice get himself killed by such stupidity," Parrymill snarled. "Boy, I will make it my business to ensure that you're in no position..."

"*Goodbye*, Master Parrymill," said Lial firmly, and closed the door on him. *Still*, he considered, *how very insistent. Why would Goiter Parrymill be so concerned by this?*

Does he see now what the river barge men saw, when the first airship put out and stole their trade?

And yet the doors remained closed against him. The airship cartels were the city's greatest consumers of silk, and no merchant wanted to get on the wrong side of them. Lial descended the trading hierarchy rung by rung. From the big trading houses he went to known independent dealers, then to generalist merchants who sometimes saw a little silk in their business, and then to those whose stock in trade came to them after unexpectedly parting company with its rightful owner, and still nobody would sell him the quantity of silk he required. He was making ends meet doing piecework and tinker-work around the city, saving every silver standard and ceramic bit, but no matter how much he offered, the material was not to be had.

And then, after one more dismal evening of being given the brush-off even by smugglers and fences, a Fly-kinden messenger turned up with a note, written out in blockily neat letters

Hear it's Silk now you're after. I met a Fellow has some, he says. Find the Roach's Roost on Partwell Street near the river. Party name of Terant. Looks Horrible. Probably is. Good Luck.

There was no signature, but Lial felt he had nothing to lose by then.

The *Roach's Roost* was a sagging and dilapidated hostelry that had once served the barge trade up towards Sarn. The river trade had been getting steadily poorer since Parrymill's peers had brought their airships to bear on the shipping of goods, and so he had hoped for some sympathy. Lial took a table on entering the *Roost*, and had fended off three whores and a drunken Beetle with a knife before a big man dropped easily into a seat across from him. Lial suddenly reconsidered just how capable he might be of looking after himself.

The big man was a Spider-kinden, but like no Spider Lial had ever seen. He was heavy-jawed, broad-shouldered, shockingly hairy: his arms, chest and shoulders were virtually pelted with the stuff, and a coarse, dark mane was tied back from his unshaven face. He wore nothing but a coarse cloak and a kind of leather harness, from which a knotted cudgel dangled.

"You're the naïf who's trying to become a silk merchant," the big man observed.

"And you're Terant? I just need a quantity of silk, not even very much. It's not too much to ask." Lial had his hands on the table-edge, ready to throw it up in the man's face if he needed to. He wasn't sure it would do any good. The man looked strong enough to break Lial and the table in half in one go.

"We have silk. Some," the big man said. "Your people won't trade with you, yes? Ours won't trade with us. We'll work well together. We'll make everyone hate us."

"Who's 'we'?" Lial asked, but his heart was pounding. At that point he couldn't care less who this man represented.

"Follow," said the big man, standing. He towered a full head over Lial, who was not short for a Beetle-kinden.

Lial was led to a private house in a poor district, and by that time his initial enthusiasm had begun to wear off. He kept a hand to his knife-hilt and tried to reassure himself by considering that, had the big man wanted to do him harm, then precious little could have prevented it already, they were so mismatched. This proved less reassurance with every step he took.

Then the man was pushing open a door in a tall, narrow house of very poor repair, looking back to give Lial a grin that showed one missing tooth. "Followed me this far, did you? Stout Beetle. Come in."

It was clear that only a couple of rooms had been made liveable: cheap rugs for the floor, a table, a couch. The bare walls had been covered over with hangings that glimmered darkly in the gloom. Lial reached to examine one, and felt a sudden rush when his fingers encountered the unmistakeable filmy smoothness of silk.

When he looked back to Terant, they had been joined by a woman, or perhaps she had always been there, shrouded by shadow and Art.

She was short and slight of build, a Spider-kinden of more conventional aspect. Her robes were also silk, pale in the dimness. "A lantern for our guest, Terant," she said, her voice soft. "You forget, he does not have our eyes, for the dark." There was something cradled in her arms and he took it for a child, and then for a lumpy bag of valuables.

Terant took out an ancient-looking oil lamp and then started fumbling with flint and steel. Automatically, Lial said, "Let me," and came forward with his steel lighter, producing a flame on the third turn of the wheel and setting up a subdued glow from the lamp. He looked at his hostess, and froze, trying desperately to fix his face in a polite smile.

She wore a half-mask and it was a beautiful thing, a lattice of gold filigree and black lacquer about a many-faceted ruby that sat neatly over her left eyesocket. For material and craftsmanship that mask could have bought Lial Morless many times, and would have put a dent in even Goiter Parrymill's accounts. What froze him in place was how the mask had been made: not what it concealed, but what it revealed. It was open-lattice and sat like a spider's web over half her face, and hid not at all the fact that someone had done a great deal of work, over a considerable period of time, to ruin her. The scar-lines filled in the detail of the mask's web, so that between them, artifice and injury, she was complete.

He swallowed any retort and managed to straighten up from the lamp and hold himself still.

"Terant, our hospitality," the woman said, and her – what? Servant, slave, friend? – fished a jug and some clay goblets from a table. The wine was brackish and cheap. Tallway would have turned her nose up at it. While the big man served, the Spider-kinden woman hugged her bundle to her, an uneven, sagging thing of knots and loose ends.

Lial racked his mind for all he knew of Spiders and their cohorts. "He is of your cadre?" he asked her, nodded towards Terant.

"He is almost all the cadre I have left," the woman replied. A cadre was the close personal retinue of a Spider lady or lord, the most trusted, most capable and most valued of her staff. Lial was looking at someone who had lost out in the politics of the Spider dance, fallen far and hard.

"My name is Lial Morless, artificer," he told her.

"And you may call me Gryssa." The way she said it made it clear that it was a name of convenience. "You want silk, and nobody will sell to you. That's what Terant tells me."

"He's right," Lial admitted.

"I want to invest, but nobody will trade with me. Any reputable merchant of this city knows me as someone who has enemies. They consider me a bad risk. I, on the other hand, have access to a small supply of silk." She was watching him carefully. "Not enough to make an airship of, but I'm told that is not your intent."

Told by whom? But at the same time Lial had no other offers. "I need silk, yes. I'll gladly deal with you, if I can meet your price. But I don't understand. If nobody will trade with you, how are you bringing the goods into the city?"

She just looked at him, pale living eye and rich ruby in tandem, and a moment later he realised she had shifted her bundle, trying to proffer it for his inspection. It clung to her, though, like a child, clung to her with its thin, sharp-elbowed legs. The lantern-light caught a glitter across the scatter of its eyes.

"I have one other in my cadre, save Terant," she told him, but she was looking down at her burden now, doting, and the spider in her arms looked back, linked to her by some communion of her Art. Lial shuddered uncontrollably, for although any venomous beasts of such size were long driven far from Collegium's walls, there were still houses where the nursery windows were barred to keep them out, and you still heard *stories*…

But he had no options, and they needed each other, and despite the thing in her arms, or because of it, they reached an agreement.

"Now do you remember old Cutmold Limner," grated out the iron magnate, Torqwell Glassey, as a servant topped up his wine.

Goiter Parrymill nodded almost fondly. "Oh yes. The heavier-than-air flying machine. Well, we saw where that went, sure enough."

"Down," another wit suggested, to general amusement. Parrymill was dining with some of his peers, a very comfortable affair. He had not thought of old Limner in months.

"Why drag him out?" he asked. "The old fellow was a good artificer in his day. You'll not be disrespectful, I hope."

"One of my people ran into a chap that used to be his apprentice," Glassey explained. "Reminded me, is all."

"Reader's rights! *That* boy?" Parrymill shook his head. "And would you believe I offered him a perfectly decent place working on the airships, and he wouldn't take it. So what's he up to now?"

"Same business as the old man, from what my fellow could gather. Buying up all sorts of odds and ends in the machine parts way of things," Glassey explained.

Parrymill had gone very still. "You're surely mistaken," he said softly. "I made clear to the young man months ago that Limner's line of speculation was leading nowhere. Besides, last I heard, nobody would deal with him. He was trying to elbow into the silk trade." *And,* the unspoken thought, *I made cursed sure that he'd not get the first foothold there, to build his flying machine. It's been so long. I assumed he'd left the city or something. Has he just been* planning *all this time?*

"Putting together something for Clifftops in his bedroom, is he?" he asked carefully.

"Fellow's got a workshop," Glassey said, all apparent innocence, but there was a part of him watching Parrymill with great amusement. "Fellow's *serious,* Goiter. He's set up on Shallowacre. Go take a look at him, if you want."

Parrymill made every pretence of politeness, but as soon as he could he was out of the door and heading for Shallowacre as fast as was dignified.

Then, as now, Shallowacre was not a wealthy part of the city, but a street of artisans at the bottom of their trade, whose customers were the working poor. There were three or four artificer's workshops, but discrete questions by Parrymill's servants showed that a Beetle of Lial's description was indeed frequenting one such, although he did not appear to be the owner. Parrymill descended on the luckless place in great pomp, and recoiled when he came face to face with an Ant-kinden, a Sarnesh.

Now in those days matters between Sarn and Collegium were far from settled. Indeed the statesman Jons Pathawl, whose words would soon after forge a lasting peace between the two cities, was then a great thorn in the side of the Assembly and would preach about Sarn in Collegium's parks to whoever would listen. However, he had yet to turn his speeches into action and Sarn remained a militaristic northern neighbour that gave many a Collegiate citizen sleepless nights. A Sarnesh Ant was not a common sight, and here was one – no, three! – in the middle of the city. Rogues, therefore, Parrymill deduced: renegades from their city, come here for reasons of their own to set up some shabby business enterprise.

They were looking at him suspiciously; the usual Ant-kinden paranoia when presented with someone whose mind they could not read. How they got any custom was beyond Parrymill, but he forced himself to sweep into their little shop, servants in tow.

"I am looking for a friend of mine," he informed them imperiously. "I'm told he visits here sometimes." He looked about the cluttered room, three worktables crammed into a space devoid of elbow-room. Only Ant-kinden could work so, in each other's' hair and treading on each other's' feet. The pieces on the nearby tables seemed reasonable domestic, he noted: gas lanterns, well pumps, disarticulated pieces of cheap forge machinery. "What work do you do here?" he asked the Ants.

"Machine repairs. Factory and forge, agricultural, automotive," the nearest one rattled off, devoid of inflection. "You have work?"

Not that I'd trust to such as you, Parrymill thought, and shook his head with a pleasant smile. "Just mending pots and kettles then, so to speak. Well, perhaps I was misinformed." His eyes drifted to the furthest table. One of the Ants was standing there a little defensively, and Parrymill frowned, seeing unfolded plans, proper artificer's work. *Surely even Ants don't need schematics to repair a steam pump.*

Some part of the design, so glimpsed, did look remarkably like a wing. Parrymill was about to lunge forwards for a better look, and he could see the Ant tense to fold the thing away, when a familiar voice caught him.

"Well, Master Parrymill. It's been some while."

He turned to see none other than Lial Morless, standing familiarly in the workshop doorway. From the way the Ants relaxed at his presence it was clear their association was not a new one.

"Lial, I hope you're not doing something foolish with these..." One beringed hand indicated the Ants, but Parrymill left the sentence unfinished.

"They are doing something foolish for me," Lial replied flatly, and then, to leave no doubt, "Clifftops next year, Master Parrymill. Not so very long now, I think. I'll see you there, no doubt."

He stepped back pointedly, leaving room for Parrymill's exit, and leaving no doubt that he had no more to say. Parrymill managed a polite smile and a nod of the head before stalking away.

The workshop and the three Ants, had come to Lial by the same way as Gryssa and her silk-spider. He had finally got to the point where his plans were sufficiently advanced to need facilities, and Gryssa had accumulated sufficient silk to work with, and he had started doing the rounds, looking for somewhere that would lend him some space for the very little coin he had. His name was still familiar, though, to the artificers of Collegium. He had several offers that were withdrawn hastily when he tried to call on them, and he spent most of a month traipsing round the city, gradually lowering his expectations, trying to find anywhere that had the tools and the space for his work.

He had complained to Tallway, seeing the hand of Parrymill in this. "The old maggot's done his work well. After the silk business, nobody'll deal with me," he had explained, and the Grasshopper woman had frowned.

"Why should he care? Sky's full of insects and people," They had been up on the low roof of a little shack overlooking the river, although not too close to the edge as Tallway had once pushed him off a similar ledge in an impromptu attempt to stimulate his Art. She had her arm around him companionably, and they had been sharing a bottle of something tooth-jarringly sharp made from, if she was to be believed, radishes.

Lial had taken a moment to formulate his answer. "Insects get tired. People get tired. Machines work harder, faster, longer. That's what artifice is about. It doesn't matter how well you do things. There's always a way to do it better, and it's our duty to find that way. Men like Parrymill, though, they care more about money than progress. They're onto a good thing and they don't want anyone to come up with a better way to do it."

He had seen that the urgent and irrefutable logic of the Apt world had passed her by, and then she had replied, "So sell it to Parrymill. If ' doing it 'is the thing. Sell your work to him, and then he'll help you and not stop you." She had smiled a little sadly at his instant outrage. "Or is the doing it not the point, after all?"

He had opened his mouth to protest, and she had pushed him off the roof.

Later that night he had limped home with a sprained ankle, which had been the only result of his abrupt descent, and found another note waiting for him.

Shallowacre. New workshop. The Brothers Workwell. Don't stare at them, Treat them like Citizens, and they'll Suit you Well.

The writing had been the same and, when he went to Shallowacre, there the place had been. The Sarnesh renegades gave him no believable names, probably for fear that word of them might reach their abandoned home. Instead they had scrabbled around for a good, decent Collegiate-sounding moniker, and come up with Workwell. All three used it, apparently interchangeably. They were not aware of Lial's tainted reputation, and were more than happy to rent out a worktable and tools. Once they understood what he was working on they became very excited, and he learned that they had been military engineers back in Sarn, artillery-builders. His plans acquired a number of improvements based on their knowledge of stresses, tolerance and the recalcitrance of moving parts.

A tenday or so later saw Goiter Parrymill hosting guests in his townhouse: not Beetle magnates but two Fly-kinden, the foremost of whom was a slight woman with greying hair and hard features who was well known in Collegium society. She had sat through his explanation and now she shrugged, lighting a small pipe with deft fingers.

"So it's your obsession," she told him.

"We had this conversation over Limner," he reminded her.

"So we did, and we looked at Limner, and we knew he'd fail. Why should the apprentice outdo the master? Let him hurl himself off as many cliffs as he wants."

"And if it flies?"

"A dozen good artificer-magnates assure me a heavier-than-air flying machine that carries a man is quite impossible," she said, but something in her tone lacked conviction.

"And you trust that implicitly do you, Sulle?" Parrymill pressed.

"Goiter, flying machines are your business. If this boy builds a better one, that would therefore be your problem."

Goiter stared out of the window, hands behind his back, like a tactician considering the disposition of his troops. "Your messengers enjoy riding on my airships, Sulle. They get good rates."

"And that's why they ride on *your* airships, rather than your competitors'," she told the small of his back, unmoved.

"And if Lial Morless's machine flies, covers the miles faster than my airships? And if your customers realise their packages and notes and letters can get where they're going that much faster? And how much will Morless charge you? And will he want to build a machine that will take him *and* your messenger, or will he calmly suggest you hand over your solemn trust to him, and he'll drop it from the skies over the recipient's house when he flaps over?"

For a long moment Sulle regarded him. "So?" she said at last.

"So we have to know," Parrymill stated. "Like last time. Send your man in." He jabbed a thick finger at the third occupant of his parlour, an ageing, stocky Fly-kinden who had been sitting, quiet and still, in one corner. He wore clothes of dark and slightly shabby canvas, and an artificer's toolstrip was bandoliered across his chest.

Sulle made the sort of face she always did at unavoidable expense. "Master Turlo," she named him, "You understand what is required of you? Just like last time, yes?"

The Fly man nodded. Collegium bred an odd crop of experts, and Turlo was a particular specialist. Most accredited artificers from the College found roles in the daylight business of designing, building and mending machines. Turlo had turned his tools and his hands to less legitimate ends. With wings and lockpicks and an impeccable sense of order, there was barely a house in Collegium he could not enter, search through, and leave without the owner ever knowing he had been there. For all that, he disdained theft, despite the reputation his kinden had for it. He was an artificer, a professional. His front business was in thief-proofing but his meat and drink was professional rivalry within the trade, and many a jealous engineer had paid his considerable fees to know just what a competitor was working on.

He nodded politely to his two patrons, and went about his business.

Only two days later he returned a detailed report concluding that the machine that Lial Morless was attempting to build at the Workwell workshop could not work, with itemised reasons why.

And, a few tendays after that, the entire report, scrupulously copied, was left in the Workwell workshop, together with a simple note, in handwriting now more than familiar to Lial Morless: *Read this. If you're going to do this then get it Right.*

Lial sat down with the Workwell brothers and they went through Turlo's points one by one. Each was valid, each was something Lial had not considered. A master artificer had crept into the workshop, undetected and unheralded, and concluded that Lial's flying machine would never get off the ground, and had been sufficiently proud of his knowledge, or conscientious about the services he was providing, to go into explicit detail. Months, perhaps years of frustration had just been taken from Lial's back by someone who very plainly did not have his best interests at heart.

"Someone working for Parrymill, or one of his friends," he concluded to Tallway, later. He still got drunk with her, when she wasn't trying to push him off things. Sometimes she tried to scare him, too, leaping out on him from around corners, wearing grotesque masks. None of it had got him off the ground.

"Your contest thing is a long way off," she said dubiously. If he wants to stop you before then, he'll get plenty of chances. Set the workshop on fire, I would."

"Three Ant-kinden in a strange city don't all sleep at the same time. There's always one of them around the workshop. That's the problem. Whoever is dropping these letters off knows them, but they'll not tell me anything. Someone's stringing me along like a puppet."

But by that time Tallway had located another bottle, and was far more interested in its contents than Lial's fears.

Some tendays went by and the airship trade picked up, and Goiter Parrymill was more concerned with his own business than with Lial's. Clifftops was still a year off, and Lial was keeping his head down. Still, he and the Ant brothers had got past the theoretical, and had begun making parts and pieces, just one at a time at first, and then a few together, hinges and gear trains. The Ants made a clockwork motor of their own design, that was as light and compact as they could get it, and then tested the motor until they destroyed it, and then started again, experimenting with how much they could punch and cut from the gears, and precisely where, without sacrificing the all-important strength. Lial remembered all too well the way the gears on Limner's *Mayfly* had gone. His flier would be lighter, half the weight or even less, but he would be in it, and he only had the one life to risk. Clifftops was still over a year away and he had no intention of angling for a spectacular public death the way that Limner had. *A test flight*, which meant that of course he had to build the wretched machine, and where could that be accomplished within the cramped confines of the Workwell place? In the end it was the Ants themselves who had the solution. They were used to a city that neither liked them nor trusted them. When they had a problem they solved it themselves rather than going to others for help. When there was no space left inside they took everything up to the roof. Like most buildings in Collegium, their workshop had a flat top, where Lial and Tallway had already spent a few hazy evenings watching the sunset and talking philosophy. Now the roof became an extension of the workshop, cluttered with pieces, with the frame of the machine beginning to sketch itself out in disjointed rods and spars. The numerous children of a neighbouring Fly-kinden baker were paid a meagre stipend to keep watch over the whole and warn of thieves or vandals.

None of this escaped Goiter Parrymill's attention for long. Once the skeletal frame of wood and hollowed metal started to monopolise the Workwell roof, people began to talk, and Parrymill had a man who went to look at the place every month, and whose usually barren reports were suddenly ignited by the spectral shape taking piecemeal life over the little businesses of Shallowacre.

Sulle, when he called her, was decidedly put out.

"Turlo said so. It won't fly. On that basis, let him build a hundred of them."

But Parrymill was troubled. "I want Turlo to take another look."

Sulle had her miniscule hands on her hips, utterly out of patience. "Goiter, you're a leading magnate of the city, and Morless is a fool apprentice, so how is it that you're looking more and more the fool, and making him into some great and important threat to life and freedom? Turlo's expensive —"

"I'll pay. I don't care," Parrymill growled, cutting her off. "If you can't see the danger you're in, then too bad. I was an artificer before I was a merchant, Sulle. I have a sense for these things." He turned to glower at her, but her steel stare was a match for him.

"Tell me," she said flatly. "Give me the missing piece."

Parrymill's face sagged. "When I was at the College, there was a band of us wanted to gain the skies. Airships. Airships won out, and every one of us is a rich man in his own right now, and not just a rich man's hired tinker. But we looked at the problem all ways. We did our calculations. There is no reason why a heavy self-powered flyer shouldn't work. And then we looked at the numbers and we wrote a great big paper saying how heavier-than-air flight just wasn't feasible. We knew we could put an airship up right then, you see, and corner the market, own the sky. We couldn't have put a heavy flier up. Ten years of development and research and we could have done so, but by then we'd be just one among many. The mechanics of it said one thing, but the money said another."

"You pulled the wool over on the whole College?" Sulle said, half-impressed and half-derisive.

"Did we?" came Parrymill's bitter response. "Then why Clifftops? Why Limner, and a half-dozen before him I could name that still tried their hand at it. Every year I'm having to bring my influence to bear to discourage someone else. Every year a new challenger!" His face, just then, was a man driven to guilty treason. "It can be done. It will be done. If not Morless then some other. But I'd go be a fisherman before I let Limner's apprentice take my empire from me. Get me Turlo. Tell him to take another look."

Sulle sighed, but nodded.

Two nights later Turlo found the Fly children keeping watch, and paid them somewhat more coin than their regular wage to render him invisible to their eyes, on the proviso that he didn't break anything or steal anything, for they had an odd remnant honesty about them. He pored over the half-built machine for over an hour, making notes and sketches. He was assisted by the advanced stage of the project, which had come on with almost prescient leaps and bounds since he had last viewed it. The winged construction he was examining seemed on the very point of metaphorphosis into a complete and finished form. In his artificer's soul, which was as pure as any College master's, he professed himself impressed.

The report he left with Parrymill was exhaustive, but on the front page he had written three emphatic words. *It will fly.*

When the next message arrived, Lial was half-expecting it. He had gone some months now without contact from his mysterious patron, but he had kept each of the little notes, the handwriting of the puppeteer who was guiding his hands. He should be glad, he knew. He would be nowhere if not for that unasked aid. If it had been in Lial's nature to go with the prevailing winds, though, he would not currently be trying to put a heavier-than-air flier into the sky. His reliance on his unseen benefactor rankled and he was waiting for the scales to swing the other way, for the price to be demanded from him.

The message was waiting by his worktop, weighed down by a pouch. It read:

You've done Well. Celebrate. Invite Everybody.

There was money in the pouch, silver Standards of Helleron mint, all of which had seen a fair round of use since they came off the dies.

"Who brought this in?" Lial demanded, but the Ants just said that it had been a messenger, some Fly perhaps. They had a fine line in sullen Ant silences when he pressed them too far, and he was well aware that he was living very much on their good graces.

Celebrate. There was no reason he should. There were plenty of other places where the money was actually needed. He stared at the words, though. If they had a little get-together, here at the workshop, would his patron step from the shadows?

And it had been a long time since he had last thrown a party, his College days, in fact. It had been a good three tendays since his last drunken stint with Tallway, even.

"Me, the three of you," he told the Workwell brothers. "Gryssa and Terant. Tallway. Lanzo's family," meaning their Fly-kinden watchers.

"Can we fit all of that in here? All of that plus one more, maybe?"

And the Ant-kinden could fold everything away, of course. They were used to a military life, of travelling compactly and usually on foot. There would be a party.

He gave some of the money to Lanzo, to procure food, and more for Lanzo's middle cousin, who could play the lyre quite well. He took Tallway's recommendations regarding the pick of Collegium's cheap-but-drinkable, although he made those purchases himself, as experience had taught him that Tallway could not be trusted to purchase alcohol without consuming the bulk of it before delivery.

Three nights later they all came: the Spiders, the Grasshopper exile, the swarm of Fly-kinden. It was a confused and awkward gathering at first, but Tallway took the edge of that, regaling them with the kind of rambling story that she made most of her livelihood by, where even the digressions had digressions of their own. After that, when she had most of them laughing, and had even drawn a smile from Gryssa's butchered face, tensions eased, and the motley outcasts' assembly got to work on the wine.

It was near to midnight when the knock came, at the door. Tallway was inexplicably succeeding in teaching the Workwell brothers some Commonwealer dance, and Lial had ended up sitting on the roof-edge with Terant, the big Spider-kinden, who said little but listened well. When Lial saw a diminutive figure approach the door, his words dried up and he felt his heart skip, but when one of the Ants opened up, the lamplight from inside illuminated only one of Lanzo's brood, home late from whatever employment she had managed to scrounge. A moment later, though, Tallway had bounded up onto the roof, drink and her Art almost springing her over the edge before she could regain her balance. "Lial! Come see!" she exclaimed, grinning madly. Lial realised that the music had died down below, and the talk also. If Tallway hadn't found whatever it was so hilarious, he would have been reaching for his knife.

There were mixed expressions downstairs. Lanzo's family seemed to share Tallway's point of view but Gryssa was looking haughtily offended, and the Ant-kinden were, for once, openly bewildered.

"What is it?" he asked the room at large. Tallway fished a pamphlet from a little stack that had presumably been brought in by the latecoming Fly-kinden.

It was what they called a 'polemic', merry little satires usually put about to lampoon and ridicule the great and good. Lial started at the crude illustration on the frontpiece, and read out the title. "*Big Beetle Learns to Fly,*" he murmured.

"It's wonderful!" Tallway jostled him. "Look, I'm in it. I jump!"

Lial flicked through the pages. The feeling that came over him took him way back, to when he was a child at school, with some calculation or piece of logic gone awry and the other children laughing at him. Someone was laughing at him. Possibly the whole city was laughing at him. His work, his great work, the death of his mentor and his lofty ideals, had been laid bare for the derision of the masses.

What am I doing here? he wondered bitterly. *I should have listened to Parrymill when I had the chance.* He let the polemic's few badly-printed pages flutter open, seeing little caricatures: a grasshopper, two spiders, some ants, and all through it the clumsy, foolish beetle who wanted to fly.

He frowned. "So who's 'Small Helpful Beetle?' Do they mean Lanzo?" It seemed unlikely that the anonymous author did. At that moment there came another knock at the door.

Everyone turned, corpse-silent. Lial put down the polemic softly, as though even the sound of rustled paper would trigger some calamity, and lifted the latch.

His hopes died immediately. A short and grubby figure was thrusting forwards a folded paper. No great confrontation, then: just another note.

In a few days the Workshop will be Attacked. They will be Watchmen suborned by Parrymill. Be ready to Defend what you have Built.

Lial swore, and he sensed the others changing the way they stood, from at ease to readied. *When did I become their leader?*

He realised the messenger was still there and automatically fumbled in his pouch for a coin, but when he proffered the little ceramic bit, the Fly would not take it.

"Lial Morless," he said instead, and Lial blinked, looking again, seeing not a bulky Fly, but a man of mixed blood, Fly and Beetle both, wrapped in a threadbare long-coat, and with a woollen cap on his head, but no less familiar for all of that.

"Scop?" he said hoarsely. It had been a good year since Cutmold Limner's forge-hand had walked out, and his path and Lial's had never crossed since then. Or so Lial had believed.

31

"Lial," Scop said, and walked in, looking from face to face, seeing offence and uncertainty and, in Tallway's case, barely-contained giggling.

"We have preparations to make," he told them all, and Lial felt his briefly assumed leadership evaporate in the face of the halfbreed's utter certainty.

"You've done well," Scop said. As if the Ant-kinden mindlink had briefly expanded to include everyone except him and Lial, all the others had returned to the wine and the food with a will, and given over the roof for more private matters. Lial watched with a mixture of bafflement and resentment as the halfbreed studied the lines of the half-completed flying machine.

"You know," Scop added after a moment, "when I left Limner's place, I didn't think you meant what you said. I thought it was any apprentice's mad dream, that it would be forgotten in a tenday, and you'd find another position and end up somewhere comfortable and unambitious, like most artificers in this city. When I heard you'd got as far as shopping for silk, I knew I was wrong. I'm glad of that. This is good work."

He was not the man Lial remembered: Limner's deferential, humble forge hand. Scop was filled with an iron purpose. "How did you find out?" Lial demanded of him. "What business is this of yours?"

Scop turned to him, and the lanterns cast his face without sympathy in it. "I found out because by then I'd got myself new work, Lial, a new master."

"Who?"

"Goiter Parrymill."

Lial stared at him. Each time he tried to assemble the pieces, the picture made less sense. "He hired you? Because you used to work for…?"

"He has no idea who I am. He's never met me. His steward hired me, because Parrymill's such a tight bastard that he can't ever keep decent staff, respectable staff, not for the filthy jobs: only foreigners and debtors, and halfbreeds. I'm the man that shines the shoes of his better servants, Lial. I'm the man that cleans out his privy. And because I'm mixed-blood, the other servants take advantage of me. I do all sorts of other people's' jobs, when the steward's not looking. I go everywhere in Parrymill's townhouse. I read all his letters. I don't think they realise I can." The speech was delivered in flat, hard words that had a lot of pent-up anger beaten into them. "When Parrymill was warned not to deal with a fallen Spider Arista, I passed her onto you. When the other servants were taking Parrymill's goods to be fixed by Ant-kinden, because the housekeeping monies were pitiful and the Ants were cheap, I passed them onto you too. And when Parrymill got worried enough about you to commission a report on your machine, well, you know the rest."

Lial shook his head. There was no real affection for him in Scop's eyes, only the pride of a smith who has made a sword that will slay emperors. "Is this just to get at Parrymill for the work he makes you do?" he tried. "Why are you doing all of this?"

"Why are you?" Scop turned on him.

"Because I was Cutmold Limner's apprentice, and he had a dream!" Lial shouted at him. "And that means something!"

"Yes, it does," Scop confirmed. "And I was his forge hand, Lial." He used the personal name as if he were hammering in nails with it. "Think, for a moment, what I am now. Ten years around machines, and I know as much as most who have their College accredits, but I'm the man who cleans the privies because nobody wants a halfbreed artificer. Limner was different. He didn't care about the blood. For that, I'll make you fly."

Lial had nothing to say to that. From below came the sounds of Tallway launching into another tangled tale. "The money for the party..." he managed weakly.

"Some of what I'd saved. I never did have much of a taste for indulging myself. The rest went on the polemics."

A jolt of undirected rage went through Lial at the very mention. "You...? But why do all that, just to knock us all down...?"

Scop shook his head. "Lial, the polemics are all over the city by now. Collegium loves a good satire with a few funny drawings. Everyone *knows*, Lial. This isn't some secret that Parrymill can do away with and throw a cloak over. Whether they're laughing at you or not, people are waiting for you to try your wings."

For a long while Lial looked at the little halfbreed. He searched his heart and realised that, in the last ten minutes, he had become afraid of Scop. He abruptly had no idea what the man might not be capable of.

"Which leads us to my most recent note. You've not forgotten, I trust?" Scop prompted.

In a few days the workshop will be attacked, Lial remembered. "They're really going to come here…?"

"Parrymill's terrified that you might reduce the value of his airship empire by three parts in a hundred," Scop confirmed, "and for that he's gone to a watch officer friend of his and told him about the dangerous treasons that you're plotting with all manner of foreigners. You'll get a couple of nights in the cells before they decide it was all a mistake, but in the meantime the machine will be destroyed, your charts and notes confiscated, everything wrecked.."

"Then what do we do?" Lial asked, and as he said it he realised that he had given in at last. He had accepted Scop's authority over him, accepted that every success of the last year was a gift of the halfbreed's hand. "Look at them down there: renegade Sarnesh, rogue Spider-kinden. They'd all face exile if they so much as raised a hand to a watchman."

"You have perhaps three days, and the nights that go with them," Scop said. "Thanks to the polemic the city is watching, and I hope that may stay Parrymill's hand long enough."

"Long enough for what?" demanded Lial.

"Finish the machine," Scop told him.

The city watch of Collegium was not comprised of redeployed army men, as in Ant cities, nor was it the foreign mercenaries and house guard of the Spiderlands or the partisan, privately hired militia of Helleron. Collegium's watch was engaged by the Assembly on behalf of the city, and for the most part did its duty well enough. Human nature was a rock on which many good intentions had foundered, though, and so enter Maxel Rodder, fifty years of plodding watch officer, whose priorities were for the comfort of his anticipated retirement. If so much of a man as Goiter Parrymill assured him that the Workwell workshop was a nest of crime and double-dealing then he needed no further prompting, and so it was that he and a half-dozen watchmen marched through the streets of Collegium towards Shallowacre.

The influx of outlanders was a common topic of debate in those years, being brought before the Assembly at least once a month. In time, and especially after the settling of matters with Sarn, calmer heads would prevail, but at that moment there were many Beetles in Collegium who fretted about the number of other kinden on their streets, and what they might be up to. So it was that a watch officer like Rodder could feel justified in utilising a heavy hand against, say, a gang of rogue Sarnesh who had irked one of the great and good.

He was preceded into Shallowacre by a flurry of Fly-kinden children, scooting ahead of him at gutter-height, but that was a common-enough thing, Fly-kinden being forever curious for spectacle, and so he paid it no heed. Instead he spotted the Ant workshop ahead and slowed his pace, deciding that his years merited the 'awful majesty of the law' approach, rather than the more exerting 'catch them at it' rush that younger men might have tried.

Indeed, the Ant-kinden appeared to be waiting for him. At the back of his mind had been a worry that Ant-kinden were habitually violent and of poor judgment, and that this might actually turn ugly. His men had come weighed down with chainmail, helm and breastplate, and they had maces, crossbows and round shields. Greater than those was the partisan aegis of Collegium law, which would look extremely narrowly on any foreigner that raised a hand against its own. Still, that would be poor solace for the man who ended up with an Ant dagger in his eye.

However, the scene that met him was as peaceable as any in the city. The three near-identical Ants stood, as if on parade, before a workshop whose small dimensions were utterly crammed with worktables and pieces of disassembled artifice. Rodder had been briefed by Master Parrymill as to what he was looking for: plans, part-complete mechanisms of some kind of flying automotive, and of course the item itself, which he knew to be above on the roof. He had anticipated sweeping in, confiscating everything that looked pertinent, and sorting it out later. Seeing the true state of things, he realised that he should have brought a score more men just to carry everything out.

"Where are the plans for the flying machine?" he demanded of the Ants, optimistically. They stared at him without expression. Rodder was aware that a crowd was slowly accumulating, other residents and artisans of Shallowacre taking in a free piece of street theatre.

Rodder was no artificer, but he was a Collegium Beetle and had a good idea what he was looking for. Searching through the Workwell's piled junk would be the work of a tenday, though, and Parrymill had stressed the urgency of the task. "The roof," he snapped, and did his best to shoulder past the Ants to the stairs. The Ants themselves, the model of civic obedience, stepped meekly aside. The clutter of their workshop did not. There was not space for an armoured Beetle-kinden to make any headway at all, and for a moment Rodder was stalled by sheer logistics.

He ordered the Ants to clear a path to the stairs. They looked at him blankly, as if to say 'whyever for?' He told them to get the workbenches out of the way. They began painstakingly unloading the tables, piece by piece. Nothing of them indicated defiance. There was not the slightest rough edge that Rodder could use as a trigger for justifiable arrest or persecution. He was acutely aware of the several dozen spectators, a good half of whom, given Shallowacre's low rents, were also foreigners.

But on the other hand, Parrymill would be waiting for his report. With a snarl of frustration Maxel Rodder took hold of the nearest workbench and upended it, spilling parts and tools, papers and piecework across the floor. "Clear that up, you Ant bastard," he snapped, halfway hoping for some supporting murmur from the crowd. Instead the silence behind him was stony. Still, he was committed now, and forged ahead to the foot of the stairs, flinging everything out of his way.

He was just about to ascend, his men after him, when one of the Ants spoke up.

"Excuse me, but we do not use the stairs. Possibly they are unsafe," one of the Workwells informed him.

"I know you work on the roof," Rodder levelled at him. The man shrugged.

"We go up the outside wall if we need to. Our Art, you understand."

"Likely," snorted Rodder, and went up the stairs on the double.

The growing crowd of onlookers was treated to a brief but memorable duet for metal armour and cursing, and Rodder and most of his men reappeared at the bottom of the stairs. For a moment it was unclear what had transpired, but then it became apparent that several of them were in some way attached to one another, and that at least one of the watch remained stuck halfway up. What had seemed originally to be dust covering them was revealed as strands of silken web, of a particularly adhesive kind, and precious minutes were wasted in the watchmen disentangling themselves.

"We do not use the stairs," the Ant repeated. "We believe there is a spider." His hands indicated a beast of variable but alarming size.

After that there was nothing for it: Rodder and his men went up with maces at the ready, using lighter-flames to burn through such webs as they found, and cautiously at that because a fair proportion of Shallowacre was flammable. Their ascent to the roof of the Workwell workshop became as difficult and painstaking as mountaineering.

But at last, because he was nothing if not determined, Rodder cleared the roof, and there he saw it.

It was an unlovely thing. Even silk stretched over a skeleton of wood and steel can be ugly, and this machine was a triumph of practicality over aesthetics. The front end looked too broad and heavy, angular and lumpy like a spider's cocooned victim, cupped about the single bare seat and the few sticks that served as the vessel's meagre controls. The back end tapered off into a two-pronged rudder, seeming too fragile. The ribbed wings themselves were half-closed, up and back, at an unnatural angle. Nothing that flew in life would have held itself so.

There were three people up on the roof, Rodder saw. A small Fly – no, some Fly halfbreed – and some lanky, sallow foreign woman were watching him as he clambered out into the air. The third was a Beetle-kinden man, and he was working at the machine.

At that moment Rodder saw how he had been made a fool of, what all the stalling had been for. The Beetle was not mending it, or building it. He was *winding* it, priming an engine.

"Right, you bastard, you're under arrest!" Rodder shouted. "You stop that right now."

The artificer stopped, indeed, straightening up and looking back at Rodder. Then, in one movement, he had swung himself over the side and was sitting in the machine.

Rodder lunged for him, even as his watchmen were pulling themselves up onto the roof. The artificer was reaching for the controls, but Rodder reckoned that if he could get a hand onto any part of that unwieldy looking machine then it wasn't going anywhere.

Lial swore, seeing the watch officer lunge. The lever that engaged the clockwork was stiff. He hauled on it. The man's hand clawed for the unnamed flier's hull.

He heard a whoop from Tallway, who had been reeling drunk from before dawn, and a moment later the watch officer was receding backwards at twice the speed, because the Grasshopper-kinden had *kicked* him hard enough to put the imprint of her bare foot in the steel of his breastplate.

He struck the rest of his men, knocking at least one back down the stairs, and then they had to help him get his armour off, because the dent was stopping him drawing breath, and Tallway turned to Lial and grinned like a maniac.

The lever slipped free at last, and the wings slammed down with a clap like thunder. Tallway and Scop leapt into the air with their own Art wings, and one of the watchmen ended up hanging off the edge of the building, which further inconvenienced his fellows.

The machine leapt skywards with a drunken lurch that Tallway would have been proud of, the rhythm of the engine's gears rattling every spar. The wings were thundering, a blur of silk, and Lial heard the engine complaining. In his mind was the fatal sound of Cutmold Limner's own machine, when the gears had come apart.

The nose tilted downwards. He had spent evenings arguing with the Workwells about that nose, the precise distribution of weight. On the ground they had been able to balance the machine on a point but, with the wings flailing, the weight was constantly shifting forwards and back, and abruptly the flier was pitching and dropping.

And Lial took a deep breath, bracing his knees against the hull, and opened his own wings.

It had been last night. It was the reason that Tallway was even more sodden than usual. Looking at his creation, knowing that on the morrow he would fly or fail, Lial had been struck by a sudden moment of utter revelation. The sky was his now, the limitations of artifice had failed to hold him back and, in that moment, the shackles of Art had likewise given way.

And the flying machine was as light as they could possibly construe, and its own wings were doing their best. All it needed was a little extra lift.

Lial felt some part of him that he had never owned to before wrench and strain, and his Art guttered and waxed, the shimmering of his wings there one moment, gone the next, but the nose came up; the nose was up and he was skimming the rooftops of Shallowacre before casting himself and his machine over Collegium, startling Fly-kinden with the beat of his artificial wings, and with such a clatter of engine that every citizen below looked up.

By the time he reached the better parts of the city he could feel the engine winding down, and when he came in to land it was at a glide, the wings barely moving. He landed before the gates to the Great College, though, with a hundred scholars and students as his witnesses.

The next year at Clifftops Lial brought his machine, but there were already two manned competitors waiting to contest with him. Two years later, manned, heavier-than-air fliers were sufficiently commonplace that the College officials brought the competition to an end.

Lial himself became one of the youngest ever College Masters. Although his precise influence on the matter is unknown, during his tenure the first ever halfbreed student was accepted into the College.

Although Lial Morless was to be one of the great heroes of artificing, more level-headed historians now play down his influence. It was clear, they say, that manned orthopters would have been achieved within a few years of his maiden flight, by someone else if not by him. Besides, the airship trade continued blissfully unaffected by the introduction of heavier-than-air fliers, as airships had a greater range, and could carry vastly more cargo, although the Messenger's Guild was forced to adapt considerably. Professional opinion continued to play down the import of orthophers and other heavy fliers right up until the year 538, when the Wasp Empire commenced its invasion, and the character of the skies changed forever.

This is an odd one to start with, taking place so long before the beginning of Empire. It's a look at a Collegium the novels don't show – not just before Stenwold, but also, while the city of Empire isn't perfect, it has, at least, improved since Lial Morless's day. This is Totho's story, in a way. Scop is his spiritual ancestor, paving the way to get Totho into the Academy, while not quite disarming the Collegiate's prejudices towards halfbreeds, and from those two things, of course, a great deal follows.

Ironclads

"Tell me again." Varmen could feel himself getting angry, which was never a good thing.

"No sign." The little Fly-kinden kept his distance, for all the good that would do against a Wasp. "Not a single soldier of them. Nothing, Sergeant."

"They said –" Varmen bit the words off. He was keeping his hands clenched very deliberately because, if he opened them, the fire within would turn this small man into ash.

"They said they'd be right behind us," said Pellric from behind him, sounding as amused as always. "Didn't say how far."

"Right behind us," Varmen growled. He stomped back to the downed flying machine. The heliopter had been a great big boxy piece of ironmongery when it was whole. When it struck the ground the wood and metal had split on two sides. What roof was left, shorn of its rotors, would barely keep the rain off. A rubble of crates and boxes had spilled out of it, some of them impacting hard enough to make little ruins of their own.

The pilot had not lived through the crash, and nor had two of the passengers. Lieutenant Landren was, in Varmen's opinion, wishing that he was in the same position. The bones of his leg were pushing five different ways, and there was precious little anyone could do with them.

"Oh we love the Imperial scouts, we do," Varmen muttered. "Bonny boys the lot of them."

"You should have seen what hit him," the Fly said. The tiny man, barely up to Varmen's waist, was supposedly a sergeant as well, but he was happy to hand the whole mess back to the Wasp-kinden. "Cursed thing came right down on the props like it was in love." The corpse of the dragonfly was in smashed pieces around them, along with what was left of the rider. *Did he know?* Varmen wondered. *Did he bring them down deliberately? Probably the stupid bastard thought he could fly straight through, 'cos the rotors were going so fast he couldn't see 'em.*

The ground around here was as up-and-down as anyone could wish not to be holed up in. The Dragonfly-kinden could be anywhere, and probably were. The red tint to everything told Varmen that the sun was going down. The unwelcoming hill country around them was about to get more unwelcoming in spades.

"Where are they?"

"I said —"

"Not our lot, *them.*"

"Oh, right." The Fly's face took on a haggard look. "Oh they're right all around us, Sergeant. They cleared out when you got here, but for sure, they're still watching us. You can bet, if we know the Sixth Army isn't coming, then so do they."

"Get fires going," Varmen heard Pellrec saying. Pellrec wasn't a sergeant, but Varmen wasn't a planner. They had an arrangement. "The Commonwealers see cursed well in the dark. Tserro, your little maggots are on watch."

The Fly sergeant's face went even sourer but he nodded. *Tserro, that was his name.* Names were not a strong point of Varmen's.

Stupid place to end up, frankly. For the cream of the Imperial military, the spearhead of the Sixth Army, the very striking hammer of the Wasp invasion of the Commonweal, he had hoped for better. It had all seemed such a good idea. Varmen was a professional soldier after all. He was used to sniffing out dung-smelling errands and dodging them. This had carried all the marks of little risk and high praise. *I'm such a sucker for the praise...* Scouts have got into trouble again — *like they always do* — A squad of Fly-kinden irregulars and a heliopter suddenly stranded. Go hold their hands until the army picks up the pieces. Sixth is heading that way anyway, won't be a day, even. *So off we trot with a little iron to give the scouts some backbone. Five sentinels and a dozen medium infantry slogging ahead of the advance in all our armour. Because we knew the rest were right behind us. They told us they were coming, after all. How can a whole army lie to you?*

"Get all the luggage into some kind of front wall," Pellrec snapped out, getting the infantry moving. "One man in three with a shield at the front, the rest keep under cover and be ready to shoot out. Tserro —?"

"Here." The little sergeant was obviously still weighing who was supposed to be giving orders, and where the chain of command ran. He clearly took the fact that Varmen had not countermanded anything as his casting vote. "Where do you want us?"

"Space your men so they can keep watch over every approach," Pellrec told him. "Bows and crossbows, whatever you have. When they appear, get in under the heliopter's hull."

Wings bloomed from the Fly's shoulders and he skipped off to order his men. Pellrec leant close to Varmen. He was a proper Wasp-kinden beauty, was Pellrec: fair-haired and handsome and a favourite with any ladies they met that the army hadn't already slapped chains on. Compared to him, Varmen was a thug, dark-haired and heavy-jawed and five-inches taller. The two of them had come through a lot in the vanguard of the Sixth Army. Seeing Varmen's expression Pellrec laughed and said, "So, glad you signed up?"

"Enough of that," Varmen snarled. "We're the Pride of the Sixth. Who are we?"

The one sentinel close enough to hear said, instinctively, "The Pride!" and even Pellrec mouthed the words, grinning.

"Sentinels, boys," Varmen said, louder, in his battle voice. The words carried across and past the wreck of the downed heliopter. "The pit-cursed best there is." He hoped that the Commonweal soldiers out there could hear him.

He stalked into the shelter of the downed flying machine to check on the man who was nominally in charge. Lieutenant Landren was conscious, just now. The Fly-kinden quack the scouts had brought crouched by him, changing the dressings on his mangled leg.

"What's it look like, Sergeant?" Landren's voice was ragged enough that Varmen knew there would be no help from him.

"Seen worse, sir," he said dutifully. "We'll get through. Sixth is on its way, sure as eggs."

"We've made contact?"

A little sharper than I reckoned, after all. "Not so much, sir, but when we set out, they were right behind us. What's going to have happened to them?" *And what in the pit has happened to them?*

"Good, good. Carry on, Sergeant."

"Will do, sir." Varmen grimaced as soon as he had turned away from the man. His eyes met those of Tserro, the scouts' own sergeant. The man was perched up under the heliopter's fractured ceiling, stringing a bow with automatic motions, not even looking at it. His stare was made of accusation. Varmen scowled at him.

"Three of my men I sent to the Sixth," the Fly hissed as the sentinel passed him. "One got far enough to know the Sixth ain't coming. Two didn't come back. Why'd the first man live to get through, Sergeant Varmen? You think perhaps they want us to know we're stuffed?"

"Shut it, you," Varmen growled at him. "Pell, how's it coming?"

"Oh, it's arrived, Varmo," Pellrec told him. "Or at least, as much of it as we're likely to get." He had made the best job of turning the crashed machine into a defensible position, with the broken sides of the heliopter to fend against airborne assault, and a rabble of crates and sacks to turn aside arrows.

"Arken!" Varmen snapped. The man he'd put in charge of the medium infantry clattered up instantly. From his privileged position at the front, Varmen had always regarded the medium infantry as a bit of a botched compromise: armour too heavy to fly in, and yet not heavy enough to hurl into the breach without losing more than you kept. Varmen's chief memory of men like Arken was as a froth of shields and spears either side of the sentinel wedge as the thrust of the Imperial assault went home. He never seemed to see the same men in charge of the medium infantry twice.

"All right, here's the plan," Varmen told him, and loud enough for everyone nearby to hear. "What them out there don't realise is that we're exactly the right men for this job. Screw flying about like racking moths and Fly-kinden. We're the armour-boys. We don't need to go dancing all over the sky. We just need to stand and hold. Me and the lads will take the front. I want your lot in a line behind us. Sting-shot at anything that tries to come in above us. Anything that gets past us, or that attacks the scouts, take them on – sword and spear."

"Right you are, Sarge," Arken said.

I always remember the names, with the medium infantry, Varmen thought. *Odd that. A dozen men in a dozen fights and I always know which name to yell, and I can have a commanding officer for two years and still get it wrong.*

"Sentinels!" he shouted. "Get your racking kit on!"

They had hauled it all the way here, each man's mail spread between three of the sweating medium infantry as well as the man himself. This was the pride of the sixth, the elite of the Imperial army, the honour so many soldiers aimed at, and fell short. The sentinels, the mailed fist. Let the light airborne rule the skies. Let the engineers hurl forth their machines and their artillery. When it came to where the metal met, you sent in the sentinels. Worst job, best kit, best training. None of Arken's men could have stood wearing Varmen's armour.

He helped Pellrec with his, first: the long chainmail hauberk first, shrugged over the head in a moment of oil-and-metal claustrophobia; breast and back-plates strapped sight at the side, the anchor for everything that came later; double-leaved pauldrons for the shoulders; articulated tassets that covered from waist to knee. Armoured boots and greaves from knee to foot; bracers and gauntlets from elbow to hand. Each piece was spotless, the black and gold paint lovingly restored after each fight until not a chip remained. Each curve of metal slid over its neighbours until what was left was not a man but more a great insect, a carapace of armour over armour.

Moving swiftly and surely in his mail, Pellrec returned the favour, putting in place by practised motions the barrier that kept Varmen and the world decently separate. The other three sentinels were similarly clad now, hulking ironclads in Imperial livery, their heads looking too small for their bodies. *Easy to fix that.* Varmen slung his arming cap on, tied it beneath his chin. The coif slid over that, lopsided at first until he tugged it into place. Last came the helm, cutting down the world into a manageable slot, to be dealt with a slice at a time. The senses he had built up in training were already starting to speak to him, to tell him where the others were, where was a wall, where was open space, without having to look around like some backwoods farmer come to the capital for the first time.

He held his hands out. His shield was buckled to one, and the other received the weight of his broadsword. There was no standard weapon for a sentinel. The man who could wear this armour was fit to make that decision for himself. Varmen's sword was a cavalry piece, weighted towards the tip for a crushing downward blow. Pellrec fought with a Bee-kinden axe, short-hafted and massive-headed. He made a habit of breaking down doors with it, or sometimes flimsy walls. The others had their favourites: a halberd, a broad-headed spear, a pair of brutal maces. Varmen let his narrowed gaze pass over them, seeing metal and more metal, his faceless soldiers. Beyond them, the men of the medium infantry were looking slightly awed.

"Pride of the Sixth!" he shouted, his voice hollow and metallic in his own ears, drowning out their answering cry.

Getting dark out there. And they would come when it was dark. Dragonfly-kinden eyes were good. The fires that Pellrec had ordered lit barely held back the darkness a spear's length. Beyond that he had to trust to Tserro's scouts. *Craven little bastards, the lot of them, but they know they'll die right alongside us.* No doubt the Fly-kinden were itching to take wing and abandon the armoured Wasps to their fate, but this war had taught them that the Commonwealers were just as swift in the air as they were. Any Fly that tried the air would end up on an arrow in no time.

"Movement," one of Tserro's men spat out. Varmen's heart picked up, that old feeling that had been fear, when he was a raw recruit, but was now no more than anticipation. He and his fellow sentinels readied themselves, waiting for the onslaught. The darkness was thick with unseen spears and bows. Behind their metal-clad line, Arken's men waited. They had their short-bladed swords drawn, but their free hands out, fingers spread. In their palms waited the golden fire that was the Wasp sting, that searing piece of Art that made their kinden so deadly as warriors. Tserro's scouts nocked arrows, shuffling uneasily on their perches.

"Coming in now," one of them said.

"How many?" Varmen braced himself.

"Just... Two, just two."

"*What?*" But the guttering firelight touched on movement now. "Hold your shot," he snapped out, and even as he spoke one of the Flies let loose an arrow. "I *said* –" he started, but then he saw what happened to the lone missile, and he swore, "Bloody guts and knives..." One of the approaching Dragonflies had caught it, snatched it out of mid-air. It was a neat party-trick, he had to acknowledge. *Like to see them do it with sting-shot, though. That'd burn their pretty hands a treat.*

"What's going on," he rumbled.

"Maybe they want to surrender?" Pellrec murmured from beside him. Varmen chuckled despite himself.

"Close enough," he called out, clanging the flat of his blade against his shield to make his point. "Here to surrender are you?" It was always easier using Pellrec's words. Pellrec was so much better at speaking than he was. A rattle of sour laughter came from the Wasps at his back.

The two Dragonflies were lightly armoured in leather and chitin scales. They were slight of build compared to a Wasp, but they moved with a careful grace. On the left was a man who looked younger than Varmen's five-and-twenty years, wearing a crested helm. An unstrung bow and quiver of arrows jutted over his shoulder. The shaft the Fly-kinden had sent at him dangled in one hand like a toy.

Varmen's eyes turned to the other one and he grunted in surprise. A woman. Of course the Dragonfly women fought alongside their men, but when there was actual fighting to be done he tended to blank it out, seeing them all as just more faceless enemies. The firelight turned her skin to red, but he knew it would be golden. Her head was bare, dark hair worn short in a soldier's cut. She held a sword lightly in one hand. It was a good four feet long, most of her own height, but half that was the long hatched haft. Varmen found himself grinning in the privacy of his helm, when her eyes met his. The only women he had seen recently had already been claimed by the Slave Corps, or by some officer or other. This one might want to kill him, but she was still a sight for the eyes.

"Who speaks for you?" the man asked, to Varmen's disappointment. *Don't we get to hear her voice, then?* He could imagine it, light and graceful as she was, sly and dancing. He swallowed abruptly.

"Lieutenant awake?" he called back.

"Not just now, Sergeant," Arken reported.

"Then I reckon I do," he stated. *Is it a trick? Is this to get us off guard before they storm us?* He looked at Pellrec, saw the man's pauldrons shrug up and down.

To the pit with it... He took a couple of steps forward and thrust his sword down into the earth for easy retrieval. "You want something, do you?" he asked them.

"We offer you the chance to surrender," said the woman. Varmen stared, Her voice was exactly as he had imagined. He had always had a thing for women with good voices. After a moment he realised that the awkward pause in the conversation was him.

"Go on," he stated, mostly to get her to keep talking.

"You think that –" the Dragonfly man started but Varmen cut him off with an angry motion of his gauntlet. "Not you, her. Don't interrupt the lady."

The angry, injured-pride expression on the man's face made it almost worth being stuck out here about to fight off the hordes. *Shame he can't see me grinning right now,* the Wasp thought. *Oh I'd make him look sour, all right.*

"You believe your army is coming to save you," the woman said. Varmen tilted his head up a little, listening. *Music, like music.* He'd not had a Dragonfly woman yet, was probably one of the few men of the

Sixth who hadn't. It wasn't as though the Slave Corps hadn't been touting a sorry collection of Commonwealer whores about the camps, but Varmen had no taste for women who wept, or cursed him, or tried to kill him. *Well-made man like me shouldn't need to rent it from the Slavers.*

She had stopped speaking, and he realised he had been nodding along without actually absorbing any of the words. "I suppose you think that scares me," he hazarded.

"You have this one chance to cast your weapons down," the man snapped, icy-voiced. "I suggest you take it."

Yeah, I thought it was something like that. "Nothing doing," Varmen said, talking to her and not to him. "Sorry, girl, but the first thing they teach you when you put on his armour is not to go knock-kneed with fear, 'cos of how everyone can hear you." *Was that a bit of a smile? I think it was. Shame we all have to kill each other now, really. We were getting along famously.*

"Bring your worst," he finished.

"Oh we shall," the Dragonfly man promised. Varmen could see him raging inside, desperate to bring the fight to the Wasps. *And you with a bow on your shoulder. Angry men make rotten archers, I know that much.*

"Bring your worst!" Varmen repeated, "'Cos we're the best. Pride of the Sixth!"

The words rose up from behind him in a chorus of Imperial solidarity.

The man stalked away, and Varmen was mildly surprised that one of the Fly-kinden didn't put an arrow in his oh-so-inviting back. The woman regarded him for a moment more, that very-nearly-almost-amused look still on her face, and then followed after. Varmen carefully stepped backwards until he could see Pellrec from the very corner of his visor.

"How'd I do?" he muttered.

"Oh I'm amazed the Emperor didn't come round and hand out medals," the other sentinel told him. "What now?"

"We fight."

"And when the Sixth doesn't come, like she said?"

"Feh." Varmen shrugged. "And why won't they come?"

"Well…" There was a pained pause, but Varmen wouldn't look at him, so Pellrec went on, "There was the little thing about the whole Grand Army of three principalities currently beating on the Sixth like a man with a sick slave."

There was, was there? "And you believed it?" Varmen raised his voice to carry to the men around them. "Of course they're going to tell us that. Why even come here to ask for surrender, unless they were scared of us, eh?"

He heard a subdued rustle of laughter as his tone rescued a little morale. Pellrec wasn't fooled. Pellrec never was. Still, Pellrec would stand and fight alongside him whether he believed it or not. Sentinels didn't break. "Pride of the Sixth," Varmen murmured to himself.

"And here they come," Tserro said, and to his credit his voice was steady. Varmen dropped into his fighting stance, keeping his shield up, and the arrows began to arc into the firelight. He felt an impact on his shoulder, two or three on his shield. A sharp rap knocked his head to one side but he brought it back, waiting. The gash in the crashed heliopter was mostly filled with Varmen and his sentinels, and it would be a fine archer who could spin an arrow into a narrow eyeslit or up under an armpit at the range they were shooting at. Varmen heard a shout of pain from behind him, an errant missile catching one of the Fly-kinden in the leg after clipping Pellrec's pauldron. Another splintered on a sentinel's halberd blade.

"Spears now," Tserro said. He must have been crouched high just behind and beside Varmen's head.

"Brace!" Varmen shouted. Arrows began to dance the other way, the short shafts that the scouts used. Fly-kinden weren't good for much, in Varmen's estimation, but they were decent shots when their nerve held.

The firelight caught movement, and then the Commonwealer soldiers were on them. They came running: lithe spearmen with thin leather cuirasses, archers in amongst them with arrows to the string, a rushing rabble of golden-skinned faces. Even as they hit the firelight half of them were airborne, the wings of their Art flaring from their backs and shoulders, launching them up and forwards. Their arrows kept coming, loosed on the run or on the wing. One struck Pellrec's breastplate and bounded up into the mail under his chin, sticking and hanging there like a beard. Varmen heard several cries behind him as the missiles punched through the banded armour of Arken's medium infantry. The Wasps were returning shot for shot. The light arrows of the scouts were cut through with crackling bolts of gold fire. Varmen saw a half-dozen of the Commonwealers go straight down. *No decent armour and not a shield amongst them*, he thought. The Dragonflies did have a few decent military traditions, but most of their army was levy like this.

"*Pride of the Sixth!*" he called out and stepped forward just as the first spearman got to him. The Commonwealer's wings flashed as he charged and the spear slammed into Varmen's shield hard enough to stop both of them in their tracks. Varmen's sword flashed down, knowing where the spear-shaft would be through the surface of the shield, hacking the head clean off. The Dragonfly reached for a dagger but one of the Fly-kinden arrows lanced him through the throat and he dropped. Another two spears were coming in but Varmen's shield was dancing on its own, his reflexes keeping it moving, covering throat and groin. An arrow clipped his helm and a spearhead was briefly lodged between the plates of his tassets. He swung his sword, tireless as an automaton, breaking spears and keeping them back while their friends tried to push forwards, and the Wasps behind him launched their sting-shot over his shoulders. It was an archer's war. The sentinels stood as firm as a wall, and everyone else died at range, not even seeing the face of their killers. If Varmen and his fellows had fallen back it would all have been over, the mob of Dragonfly levy swirling forwards to run each Wasp and Fly onto a pike. They held against the ground forces, though, and those that tried to force through between the sentinels' flashing weapons and the jagged edge of the heliopter's top wall were picked off by the men behind.

Abruptly as they had come, the Dragonflies broke off the attack, disappearing into the darkness chased by a few hopeful arrows. Varmen made a quick count and saw a score of bodies. *No counting how many dead and wounded they took away with them.* "What's our losses?" he called back.

"Two scouts, one infantry," came Arken's dutiful voice. "Two others wounded."

"They'll be back," Pellrec said.

"Oh surely." Varmen shrugged his shoulders, settling the plates back into place. Pellrec murmured to him and he added, "They'll take a few shots at us now, hope we've forgotten about them. Stay sharp."

"Sergeant…" Something in Arken's tone promised complications.

Varmen sighed. "Watch the front," he told Pellrec and ducked into the wrecked heliopter. "What? What now?"

Arken said nothing, but he was stepping back from the prone form of Lieutenant Landren.

"Don't suppose we're lucky enough that he died in his sleep?" Varmen said. There was an awkward pause, several seconds' worth, before he noticed the arrow.

"Ah, right." He knelt by the body: dead, all right, no mistaking that. It was dim, back there, too dim to get a look at the wound, not that it would have told him much. But he could feel a tension behind him. *Sounds like he was alive and well when Arken did his count the first time round.* "You must have missed him in the dark," Varmen said absently.

There was a distinct pause before the "Yes, Sergeant."

"Go get some of your men to back up my sentinels," Varmen told him. "Sergeant Tserro, a word."

The Fly approached doing a fine impression of nothing-wrong-here. Varmen nodded amiably and then lunged for him. He had been going for the throat, but the fly's reflexes were good enough to foul his aim. The heliopter was a cramped cage, though, and Varmen got a fistful of tunic and hauled the man in. He was aware that several of the other Fly scouts had arrows abruptly nocked to the bow. "Go on," he growled softly. "See if your little sticks're any better than the Commonwealers'."

Tserro waved a hand frantically at them, still trying for a calm face. "Something – something wrong, Sergeant?"

"You stabbed him," Varmen said quietly. He was aware that all this was taking people's attention off the real fight, but then a scatter of arrows came in to rattle from the sentinels' plate, and that took up most people's minds. "And then you stuck an arrow in," he added. "Or maybe you stuck him with an arrow first. What's going on?"

Tserro's face twisted, and for a moment he was going to keep up the act, but Varmen shook him hard enough to loosen his teeth, and finally the truth broke loose.

"Who d'you think was going to get the blame for this?" the Fly hissed.

"Him," Varmen pointed out. "Or were you saving him the long walk to the captain's tent to explain himself?"

"Fool, nothing would have landed on his shoulders," Tserro snapped. "Landren was Rekef. We all knew it."

The mere mention of the name made Varmen feel uncomfortable, feel *watched*. The Imperial secret police, the Rekef, the thing that men of the Empire feared more than any external enemy. "And killing him helps, does it?"

"A dead man's got no reputation to maintain," Tserro stated. "You're Wasp-kinden, what could you know? It's easy to blame us, and nobody cares if we end up on crossed pikes to protect some Rekef man's career."

Varmen threw him down, seeing the flash of wings as Tserro caught himself. "This isn't over," he promised. "But in case you hadn't noticed, they're trying to kill us. If we get out of this, we're going to have words."

"Oh for sure," said Tserro, half-mocking, but with fear still underneath it.

"And in case you get any daft ideas, you just remember who's standing between you and the Commonweal."

The rest of the night passed in light showers of arrows: long, elegant shafts that broke off the sentinels' armour or rattled against the ruined coping of the heliopter. One of Varmen's men took a hit to the elbow, the arrowhead lodging through the delicate articulation of his mail and digging three inches into the joint. He let Tserro's field surgeon remove the missile, the Fly doctor's hands tiny as they investigated the wound, and had his arm strapped up. In just over an hour he was back in place, wielding a single mace in his left hand. Another arrow, arcing overhead, resulted in one of Arken's men officially dying of bad luck, as it came from nowhere to spit him through the eye. There were no other casualties. By mid-afternoon the next day it had become plain to all sides that this occasional sniping was getting nowhere. The Dragonfly-kinden mounted another sally.

That they had been reinforced was unwelcome and immediately obvious news. After a fierce volley of more arrows, one of which came in hard enough to put its point through the inside of Varmen's shield, the first wave out of the trees were not Dragonflies but a rabble of Grasshopper-kinden. They were lean, sallow men and women without armour, wielding spears and long knives, clearly a levy sent to the front from some wretched peasant farmland somewhere. They were very quick, rushing and bounding towards the heliopter in no kind of order, but nimble on their feet. Several had slings that they were able to loose whilst running. A stone dented Pellrec's helm over his forehead, staggering him, and for a moment Varmen was bracing himself for a real fight to hold them, but then Arken's voice was shouting to aim and loose, and a concentrated lash of short arrows and the golden fire of sting-shot ripped through them. Varmen reckoned that almost a score of them went over in that first moment, and the others scattered instinctively, no trained soldiers they. Arken called to shoot at will and another score of the Grasshoppers were picked off as they tried to get away. There was precious little left of them but a crowd of frightened farmhands by the time they lost themselves in the trees.

"Good work," Varmen called back. "Now let's have some proper fighting."

The Dragonflies themselves had massed. Varmen guessed they had expected to ride the wave of their Grasshopper levy and break up an Imperial line already engaged. There was a pause now while they re-evaluated their tactics. Varmen tried to see if he could make out either of the envoys, the woman especially, but when they stood shoulder to shoulder they were all too alike.

"Here they come," muttered Pellrec, and they came. Again there was a mass of spearmen in the vanguard, and the individual archers, the Dragonfly nobles and their retainers, vaulted up into the air, Art-spawned wings glittering, to slice down shafts at the Wasps. The sentinel line braced, arrows and sting-fire lancing past and between them from behind. Although they were no more professional soldiers than the Grasshopper-kinden had been, the Dragonflies weathered the volley without breaking and smashed against the thin line of black and gold armour that held the entryway to the crashed heliopter.

The fighting was fiercer this time. Varmen took a dozen strikes to his mail in the first few moments, each one sliding off to the armourer's design. There were a lot of them, jabbing and stabbing furiously at him and his men. He had the uncomfortable realisation that if they had been Ant-kinden or even Bees, used to fighting in solid shoulder-to-shoulder blocks, then the fight would be halfway over by then. The Dragonflies were used to mobile, skirmishing wars, though, and although the Wasps could match them in that, the locals had nothing to meet the hard core of an Imperial battle formation, the core that Varmen had drawn up in miniature here. The Commonweal spearheads were long, narrow, but narrowing only very close to the tip, not the needle-point lances that Varmen would use against heavy armour.

These Dragonflies were summer soldiers, their first love and training in some peaceful trade, mostly farming. They had neither the mindset, training, nor gear for this war. Every Wasp-kinden man of the Empire was foremost a soldier. The slaves and the subject races did the tedious business of actually making the Empire run.

He saw it only in retrospect. One of the Commonweal archers had been scorched out of the sky even as he dived in for a shot. He came skidding into the mass of spears, bowling a couple of peasants over, still trying to stand with feebly flickering wings even as he ended up at the very feet of the sentinel line. His chest and side was a crisped mass of failed leather and chitin armour, and boiled flesh beneath. His arrow was still to the string.

Varmen raised his sword point-downwards to spit him, and the man's fingers twitched, the arrow spearing upwards. From the limited window of his eyeslit Varmen did not actually see Pellrec struck, nor did he hear him cry out. Even as his broadsword chopped solidly into the archer's chest his honed senses were telling him of the gap to his right, the abrupt absence.

The worst was that he could not turn, could not look to see what had happened to his friend, whether the man was even living. He stood his ground. He kept his shield high, and redoubled his sword-work to make up for the gap, the man on his right doing the same. For Varmen-the-man it was loss and horror but for Sergeant Varmen it was a change to the tactical situation.

The Commonwealers kept the assault up for another twenty savage minutes before the back of their offensive was broken and they made a messy retreat under the fire of Arken's stings. Varmen forced himself to watch them go, to be sure that they would not suddenly rally and return. The very moment he was assured of it, he turned, barking the name, "Pellrec!"

The man lay prostrate, but the field surgeon had his helm off. The sight made Varmen's innards squirm. The arrow had pierced the mail under Pellrec's chin, lancing up into his jaw. One corner of the arrowhead glinted out of his left cheek.

"Report," Varmen got out.

The surgeon looked up resentfully, and Varmen spared a brief moment, only a brief one, to acknowledge that a good eight more men were wounded or dead around them to the Commonwealer arrows.

"He lives," the surgeon said. "Whether he'll live much longer —"

"Make him live," Varmen snapped, further endearing himself by spitting, "He's worth ten of the others." *And I need Pellrec around to stop me saying things like that.*

"No guarantees." The little Fly-kinden seemed to be watching the steam-dial of Varmen's temper, knowing how essential his skills were. "I need to find how deep the tip's gone. Then I need to take it out." Pellrec's eyes were staring, unfocused. Varmen guessed the surgeon had already forced something on him to strip the pain away. The wounded man's breathing was skipping, ragged. There was a scream there waiting for its moment.

"Do it."

"No guarantees."

"*Do it!* If he —" *dies I'll kill every last one of you midget bastards*, but he managed to bite down on that one. "What can be done, to help?"

The surgeon shook his head disgustedly, glanced sidelong at Tserro, beside him. The sergeant of scouts had a clumsily-tied bandage about his forehead, a narrow line of blood blotting through.

Varmen stalked to them. "If he lives then nobody cares how Landren died," he promised.

The surgeon's eyes were haunted. "Listen, Sergeant, I will do all I can, but men die easy from wounds like this. Ain't nothing you could do, unless you reckon you could talk the Commonwealers into pissing off to give me some quiet."

"Right," Varmen said, and walked back to the other sentinels. They were awaiting him patiently, looking only outwards towards the hidden enemy.

"What's going on, Sergeant?" The worried tones were Arken's, the infantryman stepping up behind him.

"Ah, well," said Varmen. He glanced out at the trees, at the waiting Commonwealers watching every move. "Sometimes I do some pretty stupid things, soldier," he explained. "Only normally, see, there's Pellrec telling me not to, to keep me in line. You'd think it'd be the other way, what with me a sergeant and him not, but that's just the way it turned out."

Arken looked back to where the surgeon was stripping off Pellrec's breastplate. "Sergeant...?"

"I'm going to do a stupid thing now," Varmen announced, loud enough for the sentinels to hear as well. "You've got a good enough head on you. If this goes arse-upwards you're in charge. Do what you can with what I've left you and just hope the Sixth pulls its finger out before it's too late."

Arken's look was bleak, but he said nothing. Varmen shouldered past the sentinel line, now only three men, and one of them wounded. *Nothing's going to change anything, at this point*, he knew, but at the same time a voice was hammering inside his head: *Pellrec can't die, not now, not ever!* Too many years together, under the mail. There was a sick, horrified feeling inside him, waiting for him to indulge it, but a soldier's habits meant he could leave it down there unrequited.

"Sergeant," one of the other sentinels murmured, and Varmen strode out into the open and waited, drawing his sword.

He expected a few arrows on the instant, just Dragonfly-kinden reflexes at work, but none came. Perhaps he had startled them as much as he had alarmed his own men. He waited, letting the weight of his armour settle comfortably about him.

They should kill him, he knew. He was a perfect target. One of their archers could be sighting carefully on his eyeslit, the fine mail at his throat. He just kept on standing there, as though daring them to do it.

There was movement, now, amongst the trees. Suddenly seeing the part of the plan he had missed, Varmen snapped out, "Hold your shot! Nobody so much as sneezes!" to stop his own followers killing his idea stone dead.

One of the Commonwealers was coming out to him, just one. It was the woman, of course. She had her long, recurved bow strung, an arrow nocked and half drawn-back, picking her way towards him uncertainly. It must take courage, he decided, but he already knew she had that. She looked very young to him, but she must be one of their nobility, some prince's by-blow.

"Are you surrendering?" She had stopped well out of sword-reach.

"No," he called back.

"Are you..." She slackened tension on the bowstring, just a bit. "What *are* you doing? Are you asking for permission to relieve yourself? It must be hard, in all that metal."

The soldier's joke, coming from her, surprised a laugh out of him. "You have no idea," he told her. He had forgotten just how pleasant her voice sounded. "I'm challenging you."

"You're *what?*" She was staring at him with a faint smile, as though he was quite mad, but in a mildly entertaining way.

"I heard," he said, trying to dredge up precisely what he had heard, and who from, "that your lot do duels and single combats and that."

"We're at war," she said flatly. "It's a little late for that."

"Come on, now." Trying to gently cajole her into it, with Pellrec being cut open somewhere behind him, felt unreal. "Me against your champion. If we win, you go home."

"We are home," she said, and left the words hanging there for a moment before adding, "You may have noticed a large movement of soldiers from your lands onto ours. We call that an invasion."

And she's probably lost family, and she's certainly lost followers, even today, and she's still out here talking to me, despite that, and she's interested, and...

"And what would we get, if we won?" she threw in. "Your men will throw down their weapons and bare their throats? I don't think so."

"You get me dead," Varmen said. "You've seen me fight. Take me out of the line, you'll win that much sooner. Don't think the Sixth's going to be forever finding us."

She looked at him for a long time, and eventually he thought he saw something like sympathy in her dark eyes. "I have more recent news than you, Wasp, whatever your name is." He could see the rudeness of it bothered her, even here, between enemies. *Such a delicate lot, these...*

"Varmen, Sergeant of Sentinels, Imperial Sixth Army, known as 'The Cutters'," he said, automatically. "And you, soldier?"

"Princess Minor Felipe Daless," she told him. He did not know enough about the Commonweal hierarchy to say whether 'princess minor' was a great deal, or just fine words. "Sergeant Varmen, word has come back that our Grand Army has scattered your people, killed a great many. They are hunting the survivors even now. Our little conflict here is being repeated a dozen times, just a few miles away. The army that will find us here will not be flying the black-and-yellow."

"Sounds like you've got nothing to lose then," he said. She was caught unawares by it, staring.

"Doesn't that bother you?" she pressed.

Pellrec is dying. Even now he may be dying. "Not my command, Princess Daless. This is my command. Your man going to fight me or not?"

"We can't let you go," she said. He sieved for genuine regret and found it there. "I'm sorry. We are at war."

"What can you give me?" he asked, using honesty as a weapon, taking advantage of a better nature he knew was in there. *And if this were reversed? No Imperial officer would think twice before killing anyone pulling this kind of trick.*

"A day's grace," she said. "After all, our numbers will only increase. I shall take your challenge, Sergeant Varmen. You are an extraordinary man of your kinden."

It tasted like victory, even if it was nothing of the sort. The fact that Pellrec, that all of them, would die in any event, win or lose, did not impact on him. Instead he just knew that the surgeon would have his time.

"Bring it on," he said.

"You have called out a formal challenge, have you not?" she asked him. "Do you not wish to prepare yourself, before the duel?"

He almost said no before realising that she was giving him time for free. "Of course," he said. "How long?"

"An hour would be fitting." She was still trying to work him out, no doubt seeing wheels within wheels when all that faced her was a simple soldier with an injured friend. At last she put a hand out to him, open and empty. He dropped halfway into his fighting stance, bringing his shield up, before he overrode the instinct. *Clasping hands, that's right. Forgot they did that.* He levered his helmet off, feeling the cold air on his face.

"Human after all," she said. "How easy it is to forget." Her hand was still out, and he clasped, wrist to wrist, awkwardly.

"Amongst my people, an open hand means you're about to kill someone," he explained, meaning the energy of the Wasp sting that seared out from the palm. Her hand, on the wrist of the gauntlet, was unfelt, weighing nothing.

"How sad," she said, and stepped back. "One hour, Sergeant Varmen."

Just Varmen, Princess. He felt a lot of things, just then: his anguish for Pellrec; his knowledge that he was extorting a grace from the Commonwealers that he was in no way entitled to; and his utter, earthy admiration of Felipe Daless.

He returned to his men, and Arken's questioning look. "Going to be about an hour," Varmen told him. "Then you and the lads get some entertainment."

"You know what you're doing, Sergeant," Arken said, not quite making it a question.

An hour. He had not considered what he would do with himself, for that hour. A glance told him the surgeon was still at work. He could not watch that. In a small but keen way he was a squeamish man. He could not watch butchers at their trade, even had it not been a friend under the knife. He took some scant comfort from the fact the man *was* still working.

There was a sound, a choking gurgle. *Herbs are wearing off.* Varmen turned away, his stomach twitching. His gaze passed across the mutinous Fly-kinden, Arken's dispirited medium infantry, the remaining sentinels still at their post.

"Stand down, lads," he told the armoured men. "Take a rest." He found he trusted Felipe Daless instinctively, which he really should not do. "Be easy,"

"Hold him! More sedative!" the surgeon snapped, and Pellrec groaned, with a raw edge to the sound. Varmen shuddered and stepped out into the open again.

Nothing to do but wait. How was the Princess Minor spending her time? Some mindless ritual, no doubt. They were a superstitious lot, these Commonwealers. They believed in all sorts of nonsense and magic. It had proved no answer for good battle order, automotives and artillery. He wondered now if it helped them in some other way. He would subscribe to anything that simply helped calm the mind, just now.

He carefully let himself down to his knees. He could not sit in the armour, but it was padded out to let him kneel indefinitely. He thrust his sword into the earth. He would wait for her like that, and try not to hear the increasingly agonised sounds from behind him. He took up his helm, looking at the curve of his reflection in it. *Ugly-looking bastard. Wouldn't lend him a tin bar piece.*

A succession of bitter thoughts occupied his mind then: the argument with his father the last time he had returned to the family farm; a girl he had left in Volena; the time he had been in his rage, and killed an old slave with one blow – not something a Wasp should regret, but he had always felt it ignoble.

What time had gone by he could not have said, but when he looked up she was standing before him: Felipe Daless. She had an open-faced helm on now, and a breastplate, moulded in three bands that could slide over one another: breasts, ribs, navel. She had bracers and greaves. Little of it was metal: these Commonwealers were good with it, but sparing. Their armour was lacquered and shaped chitin, mostly, over horse-leather. They had a knack, though, to shine it up until the best pieces glowed with colour like mother-of-pearl. Her armour was like that, brilliant and shimmering. Varmen had seen such armour throw back the fire of a Wasp's sting without the wearer even feeling the warmth of it.

Against swords it could not compare to Imperial steel.

"Time, is it?" he asked. She nodded.

"Go send for your champion then," he said, with faint hope.

"She stands before you," Daless told him.

"Thought she might." Varmen levered himself to his feet. *I knew it would be, surely I did. Not my fault that we're the only kinden sane enough to keep our women from war. How're you going to get next year's soldiers, with this year's women all dead, sword in hand?* It was a strength of the Empire, of course, and a weakness shared by almost all its enemies, but he had not regretted it more than when Felipe Daless stood before him in her gleaming mail.

To his eyes, a veteran's eyes, she looked small and young and brave.

"You are not like the rest of your kinden," she observed.

"Nothing special, me," he countered.

Pellrec screamed, a full-throated shriek of agony, from nothing. Varmen did not flinch, just raised his helm to don it. In the moment before his world shrank to a slot he saw her expression. She knew. In that instant she understood everything about him, why he was doing what he did, what he sought to gain.

She had only sympathy and understanding for him, as she drew her blade. It was one of the good old Commonwealer swords, that their best people carried: four feet long, slender and arrow-straight, but half of the length was hilt, making it almost something like a spear. She gripped it with both hands, but he knew it would be light enough to swing with one, if she needed.

He shrugged, settling his pauldrons properly, took up shield and sword, and nodded.

She was at him, and Pellrec screamed again at the same time, so that it seemed the sound came from her mouth as she leapt. Her wings flashed and flared from her back, feet leaving the ground even as her blade came for him. He swayed slightly, letting the tip draw a line in the paint of his breastplate. His mind followed the arc of her flight even if his eyes could not. His shield took the next blow, raised sightlessly to shadow her, and the third struck his shoulder as he turned, glancing off the metal. His sword was already lunging for where he guessed she'd be, but he had misjudged that. She was a flicker of movement off to his left, getting under his guard. He heard her real voice then, a triumphant yell as her blade scythed at his head.

It struck. There was no way he could have ducked it. All he had time for was to hunch his shoulders and cant his head away from the blow. He felt the impact like a punch in the head, but the cutting edge of her blade slid from the curve of his helmet, clipped the top and was clear.

He took two steps back and found her again. She was staring, wide-eyed. *She has never fought a sentinel before.* He felt sorry for her, then, as though he was cheating somehow. *Not just armour, girl, not the waste-of-time tinpot stuff the light airborne wear; not even the plate and chain that Arken's people slog about in. This is padding under leather under fine-link four-way chain under double-thickness plate that the best Beetle-kinden smiths forged to my every measurement, and nobody who's not trained for it could even walk in it.*

He went for her. He had to, cutting in under his own shield to gut her. It helped her get over her surprise. Her wings flashed her back, ten feet out of reach. He could wait. It wasn't as though she was going anywhere.

She should have started running rings just then, making him turn, taking advantage of his narrow view, but she could not see the world as he saw it. She attacked head on. Her wings opened again, a brief sheen in the air that launched her at him. Her sword was a blur in both hands. He braced behind his shield.

He did not see the blows, just felt the impact. The shield, moved to his best guess, took two. One slammed him in the side, denting breast and back where they came together. A fourth struck the plates of his upper arm, barely hard enough to make a mark. The strikes told him where she was as well as eyes could have done. His sword was swifter than she thought, not quite as swift as she was. Dragonfly-kinden were fast like that. He felt the faintest scrape where he had nicked some part of her own mail, and even as she fell back her blade scored a fifth strike on him, bouncing back from one of his greaves. He stepped back again and let his eyeslit find her.

Her face was very set. She had appreciated the rules of the game now. *Not first hit, Princess, not first blood even. You have to hit me until this skin of steel gives way.*

Varmen was a strong man made stronger by the weight of metal he had lived with these ten years. He would only have to hit her once.

Her wings fluttered, shimmers of light and motion, there for a moment, now gone. She had not moved. She kept her sword between them but would not come to him. *Fair enough. My turn I reckon.*

He set himself to motion. There was an art to fighting in full mail that was every bit as hard-learned as all her duelling fancy. It was a study in momentum and interia, and Varmen had been years mastering it. He was slow when he started moving, and her wings fluttered again, sword held out towards him, but then he was hitting his speed, and she saw that he would slam straight through any parry she put up. He drove in with sword and shield, always leading with the blade, great cleaving strokes that never stopped, just curved on into more and more blows at her. Oh it was no difficulty for her to step or fly out of the way, but he made her move. He drove her back and forth like a wind with a leaf. Each small move of his birthed a greater move of hers. He was a miracle of economy. She attacked back, sometimes, saw where his strike was going and laid her sword on him, on the shoulder, on the side, on his shield as it met her ripostes even as she made them. He could see it in her face, though. He did not need to dance. She could not cut through his steel. He would run her, and run her, until she had no more run left in her. Already she was backing against the trees. He was driving her like an animal.

She shrieked at him and exploded in a flurry of blurred blows. He took a solid whack across the helm, three on the shield again, one into the mail where his neck met his shoulder. If that had been her strongest she might have set him back, with that, but her strength was leaching from her, step by step, as he forced her ahead of him. There would be a bruise, but there and then he did not even slow for her.

She was over his head, wings a blue and green blur. He turned with her, felt his sword clip something. She was within the view of his eyeslit once more, sword drawn back.

She stabbed. With all that length of sword she stabbed for his eyes. It was a good move, but he tilted his head as the lunge came in and the blade grated along the side of his helm and accomplished nothing. She was within his sword's reach, was close enough, almost, to embrace. The edge of his shield smashed across her face, shattering part of her helm and dropping her to the floor.

Her sword had spun from her hands, she crouched before him, bloody-mouthed and defiant, and he held his blade point-down over her.

There had been a sound, these last minutes, only he had not noted it. Her head snapped up to look at something, and he saw that she, too, had been so taken with the fight she'd missed it.

The ugly box-shape of the Imperial heliopter thundered overhead a moment later, impossible to ignore now. As it passed over the trees he saw the glint of what they threw from its belly, and the fire a moment later, grenades shivering tree-trunks and shrapnelling through the forest. Then there were men in the air, not the nimble Commonwealers but the good old familiar sight of the light airborne: Wasp-kinden men in their stripped-down armour, landing all around with sting-fire and the sword.

Felipe Daless was still crouched before him, her face a mask of battered bitterness. Varmen lowered his sword. She could not see his expression, but she would have seen his helm nod, once. She took flight, not up but straight away, into the trees. *I am too soft*, he knew, but *it would not have sat well, silencing that voice.*

He turned back to the crashed flying machine. There were already a couple of the airborne there, one of them with lieutenant's insignia. Varmen trudged over, feeling abruptly exhausted, as he always did when the fighting spirit bled away from him.

He saw Tserro there, and Arken. They had sour looks on them, and he asked, "What's the stone in your shoe? They came, didn't they? We're rescued."

"If you can call it that," Arken said sullenly, and then, when Varmen did not see. "It's not our people, Sergeant, not the Sixth. These bastards are the Gears, the pissing *Second.*"

The main body of the Imperial Sixth had been caught unawares by the

Grand Army of the Commonweal and almost completely wiped out, save for such detachments as had been sent away for other duties. It was the Commonweal's only significant victory of the war, and the Sixth's remnants, dug in and stubborn, held the Dragonflies long enough for Imperial relief forces to put the Commonwealers to flight.

Pellrec survived his wound, and of matters such as a dead Rekef lieutenant and the perfidy of Fly-kinden scouts, nothing was ever said. If the Rekef took any interest in the matter, Varmen never found out. He recommended Arken for sergeant, but nothing came of that, either. His superiors knew too well how much his recommendations were worth.

Pellrec would die later, outside Mian Lae, in what would turn out to be practically the last large engagement of the Twelve Year War. Varmen would survive to march on the Lowlands with the newly reconstituted Sixth under General Praetor. All that was to come, though.

After the Second Army's intervention, and after the subsequent brutal assault on every Commonweal village and position within ten miles of the heliopter crash, Varmen toured the slave markets. He had the time, while the Sixth was in shreds. He saw every female Dragonfly the Slave Corps had taken, every prisoner of war awaiting disposal or execution.

He never did find Felipe Daless.

The Twelve-year War is the focus of most of the stories in this volume: the cataclysmic battle in which the Commonweal ceased to be the inviolable closed state it was for 'To Own the Sky' and lost half its land, hundreds of thousands of its people and its pride to the Empire. This was one of the very first shorts I wrote for Shadows *and Varmen stuck with me – to a second story 'The Last Ironclad' and then to his appearance as a major character in* Heirs of the Blade *where the events of this story still haunt him.*

Spoils of War

"You know, Yot, this is particularly fine wine," the Wasp-kinden officer said, swilling the dregs round in his bowl. Sfayot obediently leant forwards to pour him another before setting the jug back on the upturned barrel that served them as a table.

"The Thorn Bugs make it, in the North-Empire," he explained.

The Wasp man gave a surprised snort. "Who'd have thought a people so ugly could make something so pleasant." He leant back in his seat, an elaborate thing of cane and dyed wicker that had presumably been some Commonweal noble's pride and joy before it became spoils of war. The hut they were in, the Empire's makeshift clearing house for its plunder, was piled high with all manner of goods that the Commonwealers had once held dear, some of it already boxed up and some of it loose: silks and fine cloth, rolled artwork, statuary, books and scrolls. Only the gold was missing. The gold was being sent back to the Empire as a priority, to pay for the ongoing war.

"You came with a cart, Yot," the Wasp noted, "filled with jars. Of wine, one imagines?"

"The Imperial army is thirsty," Sfayot observed. He was used to Wasps cutting his name short for their convenience.

"One might wonder why the Imperial army should not simply appropriate your cart, wine and all, rather than pay good silver." The Wasp raised an eyebrow.

"Why, then I would not be in a position to bring more excellent wine next month," Sfayot explained with great remorse.

"And...?"

"And make a gift of wine to my good friend Lieutenant Malic who was so helpful to me when I was here before."

Malic smiled at that. He was a factor for the Consortium of the Honest, the mercantile branch of the Wasp army. The role bred greed like a corpse bred flies, but Malic was a plain-dealing rogue of a man. "You know," he said, "I've a farm in the north-east Empire. Wife, too.

Years since I last saw either of 'em, mind. Your lot, Roach-kinden, are all over there. A right curse, you are." He said it almost fondly. "Steal anything that's not nailed down, always shifting from place to place. Drive the customs lads half mad." He took another mouthful of wine and his smile widened. "Not to say you don't have your uses. This is truly fine, Yot. Don't get me wrong, we're taking enough liquor from the "Wealers to drown the Fourth Army, but it's good to get a taste of home. The men will appreciate it."

Sfayot nodded, taking a moment to plan his attack. "There is a matter…"

"I thought there might be. Speak now, while I'm in a mellow mood."

"I wish to travel west, and not be put in irons. Perhaps some papers, licence to trade…"

"Towards the front?" Malic was frowning. "That's not wise."

"I am aware of that."

"There's a market, certainly, but it's ugly." The Wasp's eyes narrowed. "But it's not just for profits, is it Yot? Or you'd unload here and head back east. What's going on?" He had a hand on the barrel-table between them, an implicit threat: every man of the Wasps could spit fire from his hands. Their sting, they called it.

"You know how we Roach-kinden live," Sfayot said carefully. "How we travel with our families, and meet, and trade."

"And get moved on," Malic added. "And steal, and sometimes exhaust the patience of the local garrison."

"It is just as you say," Sfayot confirmed mildly. "My family were travelling near here, travelling and trading. One of our number was unwise, she wandered from our camp. I have heard she was taken up."

Malic looked at him for a long while. "I remember a white-haired girl," he said at last. "That Slave Corps man had her with him, Sergeant Ban, his name was. You know this much, I take it."

The Roach-kinden nodded. He was white-haired as well, although in his case it could pass for age. It was a mark of the Roach-kinden: white hair and tan skin and restless feet. Sfayot was old for it, though, too old for the journey that he was considering. Lean and snow-bearded, dressed in shabby, patched clothes of green and brown and grey, he knew he looked like a beggar before this well-dressed Wasp, whose black and gold tunic was worn over looted Dragonfly satins.

"My daughter," Sfayot said softly, watching the other man's face. "She is but thirteen years."

Malic nodded, taking a little more wine, and his face was not without sympathy. "Then yes, Ban's gone west to pick up another chain. Seems like every Slave Corps man is headed that way, and I hear they still have more prisoners than they know what to do with. I'd guess he saw your lass and took a shine to her. Slave Corps," he added, with faint disgust. "You understand, in the Empire even the worst have a role to play, and the slavers are that role. I remember she was a pretty enough lass, for a Roach."

Sfayot said nothing.

"Means she's more likely to stay whole on the trip," Malic noted. "Unless she catches the eye of some officer on the road, he'll want to get her back to the good markets, back home. At this end we're glutted with slaves, you can't give them away. What will you do when you find Ban?" The question was thrown in without warning and Malic was regarding him keenly.

"Offer him a good price," Sfayot said without hesitation. "I am not a Wasp. My people do not fight or demand vengeance or harbour grudges. We cannot afford such luxuries."

Malic's face had a strange look on it, almost a sad one. "I'll give you papers to trade," he said abruptly, "and to travel. I wish you luck, Yot. I hope you find her, and I hope she's not too damaged when you do." There was something about his manner to suggest that he might have done as much even without the wine. Greedy, corrupt men, as opposed to upright, honest soldiers, had more leeway for spontaneous kindnesses as well as private evils.

Sfayot watched him sign the scroll, sealing the papers with black wax and the Consortium's imprint.

He had lied to Malic, of course, but only a little, details that would have complicated matters. The girl had not simply wandered off: Roach-kinden knew better than that. Their roving lifestyle, across the Empire and the Commonweal both, was to avoid the persecutions of government. In the Empire it didn't do to stay too much in one place, lest someone decided that made you property. You stuck with your family because they were all you could rely on.

Sfayot's family had been in the little village of Nalfers, when something had gone wrong. Nalfers was an occupied town with a garrison, but the Wasps had apparently decided it needed sacking anyway. Perhaps orders had been misunderstood, perhaps the local troops had got drunk and leery. In any event, nobody would be visiting Nalfers any more, and when Sfayot's family had finally regrouped the next morning, within sight of the rising smoke, he discovered that a cousin and a nephew were dead, and that his daughter was missing. A niece had seen her dragged off by a slaver, the man's trade made unmistakable by his full-face helm.

His family had begged him not to go looking for her, for it soon became clear where the slaver was headed. The Roach families did not go near the warfront. There was nothing for them there. The advancing plough-blade of war was a steel barrier they could not cross, and what was left exposed on the upturned earth behind it was rumoured to be worse than the fighting itself. The Wasps were a hard, wild people. Their army forced them to obey orders when they were on duty, and so when they were released from it they became monsters.

But Sfayot had left his younger brother to take the caravan east, and had set off in slow pursuit. He was old, and it had seemed unlikely he would ever achieve any great thing in his life. Perhaps retrieving his daughter could be that thing. Certainly if he died, and he accepted this was likely, then the loss to his family would not be severe: one less mouth to feed in a harsh season.

The roads to the front were clogged with soldiers and army transports: reinforcements heading for the front, slaves and plunder being escorted home again. Sfayot passed smoke-belching automotives with cages full of thin, dispirited Dragonfly and Grasshopper-kinden, men and women bound to feed the Empire's infinite capacity for human servitude. He did not approach the slavers, for there was room enough in those cages for an inquisitive old Roach-kinden, but he asked many questions of others about a white-haired girl, and sometimes he got answers.

He found a military camp a few nights later, and peddled his wine to the Wasp officers, showing them his papers. Malic had been better than his word, it seemed. The conduct passes were faultless, and he was neither robbed nor beaten, more than a Roach-kinden would normally expect from Wasps anywhere. Eventually he fell in with a squad of Bee-kinden Auxillians from Vesserett in the East Empire, who were surely hundreds of miles further from home than anyone else. The Bees of Vesserett had a proud and embattled history, and at one time had looked to be in a position to destroy the burgeoning Wasp Empire almost before it began. These men, though, short and dark and weather-beaten, were simply tired. When Sfayot spoke of their homeland, that he had seen more recently than they, they let him into their circle and drank his health. After his questions had gone around the fire someone called over a tiny Fly-kinden man because "Ferro knows everything." Ferro was not in uniform, and Sfayot understood he was a freelance hunter engaged in tracking down fugitive Dragonfly nobles. The Empire had determined that certain Commonweal bloodlines must be terminated without scion, and so professionals like Ferro were making a healthy living.

Ferro was as good as his reputation. He had seen such a girl, and he named Sergeant Ban without prompting. They had gone to Shona, he said, Shon Aeres as had been, and maybe Ban was going to fill his string of slaves there. A bad place, Shona, Ferro confided, did Sfayot know it?

"Only before the war," the Roach replied guardedly.

Ferro nodded, abruptly nostalgic. "Ah, before the war this was a beautiful country. I stayed at the castles of the nobility, at their summer retreats. I tracked brigands for them." He drank more of Sfayot's wine with the expression of a connoisseur. "Now it is those nobles I hunt down like animals, so the Wasps can put them on crossed pikes. So the wheel turns." It was clear that Ferro's sense of balance enabled him to walk that wheel as it ground over those less fortunate.

Sfayot set out for Shona the next morning. Ferro's talk of the Dragonfly nobility had stirred no nostalgia in his breast. There were plenty of times his family had been moved on by the lords of the Commonweal, and some when they had been punished, too: whipped, beaten, lectured, put to work. The Commonwealers did not have the cruelty and savagery of the Wasps, but they did not like a people who wandered where they would and did not fit in. Sfayot himself had been hauled before some headman or prince enough times, and seen in those aristocratic eyes a keen loathing of a man who was neither servant nor master.

The road to Shona was many days towards the front, and Sfayot could only guess as to how much faster Ban and his captive were travelling. He examined keenly every slaver that passed back towards the Empire, seeking a head of white hair. Slaves a-plenty there were, and a few dozen of his kinden, but none were his daughter.

Shon Aeres as was had been torn up by the roots. Not a sign of any Dragonfly buildings remained, and the fields had been churned up by war and marching feet. Now there was a veritable city of tents and shacks and lean-to's. A large proportion of the Imperial Third was currently billeted there, either waiting to take the few days' march to the current fighting, or taking a rest from the front. Shona was no simple soldiers' camp but a Consortium town, it quickly became clear. Here the Empire's merchants set about the business of fleecing its soldiers of their pay and their booty. It was growing dark by the time that Sfayot arrived at the tent-town's edge, but he had been able to hear Shona for miles: the sound of an army off duty and riotous with it. The guards that stopped him had the surly, miserable expressions of men on punishment detail, and a gratis jug of wine bought more ready admittance than all the papers in the world.

He saw three fights before he had gone thirty yards, all of them between Wasps and one of them fatal. The makeshift, mud-rutted street he walked down was lined with taverns, gaming houses and brothels, or so the signs outside various tents advertised. Soldiers were everywhere, most out of armour, but Wasps were never unarmed. Their expressions were almost desperate: determined to lose themselves in any vice rather than think about what tomorrow might bring.

Further progress with the cart would be impossible, Sfayot saw. He sold it and most of his remaining stock to a taverner, and for a price that told him just how much the soldiers were being overcharged. He retained as many jugs as he could safely string from his belt or hide in his pack, because his bribing work was surely not done.

He made for the centre of Shona, adopting a careful, skulking walk that put him beyond the notice of the rowdy Wasps. Sfayot's Roach-kinden people had a knack for hiding born of long years of spite from most other races.

He could see (for Roach eyes were good in the dark) that the centre of Shona, perhaps the entire original area occupied by Shon Aeres, was an open square, and that there was some manner of entertainment there. Vague, wild strains of music drifted to him, and he followed them around the edge of a crowd until he saw a set of Grasshopper-kinden minstrels plucking and piping as best they could, enduring the occasional kick and missile from the jostling crowd. The square boasted a series of raised wooden platforms, Sfayot saw, and on the nearest there were women dancing. They wore rags only, and he soon saw why: when any of them got too close to the crowd, hands reached for them, to tear off whatever remained. An old, bald Wasp with a pike kept watch, and jabbed at the dancers when they clustered too close to the centre. They were Dragonfly-kinden, all, with that people's slender grace and elegance, and they wept and shook and went on dancing, unfettered and with the wide sky above them. For a long time Sfayot could not understand why they did not simply manifest the wings their Art gave them, fly free and risk the Wasp stings.

He saw, at last. At one edge of the platform sat an unexpected rank of the audience: a dozen children cross-legged there, some crying, some stony-faced and blank eyed. They watched, he saw. They watched their mothers or sisters humiliated for the pleasure of their captors. They would be too young to have learned that airborne Art. Their presence held their relatives in captivity more surely than locks and chains. Sfayot felt ill and shouldered on past the spectacle. Other platforms boasted fighters, men and women hobbled, bound together, forced to fight each other, or to fight beasts. He saw a nine-foot dragonfly, its wings mere broken stubs, slicing savagely into a pair of unarmed Grasshopper women with its razor mandibles. He saw a tethered, raging Mantis-kinden, one eye out and the rest of her face a mask of blood, killing slave after slave in a heedless, mindless frenzy, carving each up with the spines of her arms until an officer flew from the crowd and seared her with the bright fire of his sting. The expression on the officer's face as he killed her was the only compassion Sfayot was to see that night.

Eventually he could take no more. He found a Consortium counting house and took refuge in it, buying his tenure with wine. He was shaking, he found. His family had been right. He was losing all hope of seeing his errant daughter again, or whatever the war had left of her.

The clerk left minding the coffers whilst his master revelled was a young Beetle-kinden man named Noles Mender, obviously not long from home and not at ease with the Wasps. He and Sfayot diced for pittance coins, which Sfayot let him win, and by then Noles was happy enough to answer a few questions. Did he know Sergeant Ban? No. Did he know about slavers? Yes. Shona was not fair game for slavers, he explained. Everyone here was for the army's pleasure, not the slavers' profit. The army loathed the slavers, and would rough them up and throw them out if they tried anything. Slavers were being sent hotfoot to the front, where there was enough spare flesh to fill all the quotas of the Empire.

Noles was heading there too, quite against his will, as a confidential messenger to more enterprising Consortium factors. He would have an escort of soldiers, but he would be more than happy to have any company that could maintain an educated conversation. He was a stout, dark-skinned, bookish youth, and it was plain that military life did not suit him. Like a lot of Beetles, he had no difficulty with Sfayot's kinden. Beetles in the Empire tended to judge a man on his moment-to-moment usefulness, not his race.

Noles travelled by mule, with Sfayot and the half-dozen soldiers on foot. The front was not far, he said. He'd heard that there was some central depot that slaves, and slavers, were being sent to, but he wasn't sure where it was. When they reached his destination he would surely be able to find out. The escort obviously disliked Noles almost as much as they disliked Sfayot, but the bonds of rank held them: Noles was, youth notwithstanding, a sergeant, and despite provocation they took no action against him. Sfayot was willing to bet that matters would have been different if Noles had been carrying much of value.

Noles was explaining how the fighting had been close to here for some while: some Dragonfly prince or other had amassed a big army, and there had been several inconclusive engagements, all quite bloody. Probably they were fighting even now, Noles opined, in the airy tones of one who considers himself a military expert.

He might have been exactly right. Certainly the battlefield they found two days later looked to be about two days old.

The smell got to them before they saw it, and then they started being approached by scouts, Fly- and Wasp-kinden both, all of whom pored carefully over Noles' papers, and Sfayot's. Then they came out of a stand of trees and saw where the Dragonfly general had made his stand.

The battle had been partly within a wood, and that section was mercifully hidden, but it had spilled out across several acres of low, rolling fields. Sfayot was no military man, but he suspected that such a man would have been able to read the history of that battle in the dispositions of the dead. True, most of the Imperial dead had been claimed by now, taken off for identification, recording and cremation. The Commonweal dead had been left there, probably because there were neither hands nor will enough in the victorious army to do otherwise. Drifts of peasant levy lay like snow, like earthworks, in a welter of broken spears and staves. Mounds of Grasshopper- and Dragonfly-kinden who had been sent off to war with nothing but the clothes on their back and a knife tied to a broom-shaft; they lay five, ten deep, there in their scores where the Wasps had halted them. They were sting-burned, stuck with crossbow bolts, impaled on spears, hacked by swords, broken by artillery, crushed beneath the tracks of war-automotives in their hundreds, in their many hundreds. Here and there the dead wore the pearlescent sheen of Dragonfly-crafted armour: hard chitin and harder steel layered together into a surface that would turn a blade or a sting-bolt with equal fortitude. Here they lay, each little knot of dead a noble's retinue, their mail broken, their long-hafted swords and bows and spears all awash with blood where they had been plucked from the sky or made their last stand over the body of their fallen lord. Scavengers, the lowest camp-slaves and Auxillians, picked over them for anything of value, and their expressions were of such hardened sobriety that it seemed they were performing some funereal duty rather than seeking their own profit.

Noles Mender had gone quiet, was staring straight ahead with his lips pressed tightly together, but Sfayot could not drag his ravaged gaze away. He saw face after face, the men and women of the Commonweal, each locked in a final expression of fear, shock, pain or grief. He saw Mantis-kinden and Dragonfly swordsmen lying dead, the stained, clear earth about them speaking all that needed to be said about their last moments. He saw the broken, husk-like bodies of insects: saddled dragonflies with shattered wings; the curled bodies of wasps riddled with arrow-shafts; fighting mantids with spread limbs, their gorgeous, glittering eyes caved in, their killing claws broken. In the field's centre a burnt-out automotive smouldered still. A small team of engineers, faces swathed with scarves against the reek, laboured over it, trying to salvage anything of value. And everywhere there were the flies: the finger-long, torpid black flies that coated the dead like tar and arose as Noles' party passed, in glutted, blood-addled clouds.

Once they had passed the battlefield they found the army camp where Noles' contact was. The Beetle was obviously anxious to deliver his message and be gone, and the soldiers were likewise keen to return to the delights of Shona. Sfayot bid them farewell and took his last few jugs of wine to see what they might buy.

He had expected fierce celebration, Shona in miniature, but there was none. The battle was too recent, too many men were in no fit state to cheer. He guessed that much of the army must be off routing the remaining Commonweal forces, for fully half the tents in that camp were crammed with the Imperial wounded. Battlefield surgeons, Wasp men with lined faces and steady hands, were working their way through them with fatalistic patience. Elsewhere stood tents of the Mercy's Daughters, caring for those that the surgeons had not reached yet, or had given up on. The women of that unofficial order – Wasps and of a dozen other kinden - were often the last sight and comfort that a wounded soldier could hope for. Their faces, as they went from pallet to pallet, were calm and fixed, their voices low. Around them the wounded cried out, or begged, wept, slept or died.

Sfayot spilled a lot of time and wine finding someone who had the knowledge he needed. In the end he found a half-dozen Thorn Bug-kinden auxillians at the back of one of the Daughters' tents. They were engineers, he understood, and from the shiny burns and scars, they had caught the rough end of their trade. He had the impression that the greater part of their company was dead. They were hateful, hideous, spiky creatures, crook-backed and hook-nosed, and the Empire regarded them with as little love as it did Sfayot's own people. He produced for them his last jug of wine, though, and they passed it around in solemn silence. For them it was a taste of distant, distant home, that briar-riddled place that the Empire ruled only loosely, but tightly enough to conscript luckless men such as they. From their wounds, at least half would likely never return there.

Two of them knew Sergeant Ban, in no uncertain terms. The sergeant was a gambling man, but not insofar as it extended to paying debts owed to lesser kinden. Sfayot guessed that Ban had been gaming with the Thorn Bugs because nobody else would take his marker. They knew him, yes. Had he been through here? Yes, twice.

"Twice?" Sfayot frowned.

"Once out, once back, with a full string of Dragonfly-kinden slaves, good ones too, all decent-looking women." A Thorn Bug leer has no equal.

"All Dragonfly-kinden?" Sfayot pressed, dismayed that he had managed to miss Ban entirely. "There was one, perhaps, a woman of my kinden? White hair."

They shook their malformed heads. They had got a good look at those women, yes they had. They would remember if one of them had been something as lowly as a Roach. Dragonfly princesses, the lot of them, all fit to fetch a good price back in the Empire.

"A higher price than any Roach-kinden, of course," Sfayot said softly. Of course, they agreed, almost laughing at the thought, the last dregs of the jug making their rounds. Who would buy Roach-flesh when that beautiful golden Dragonfly skin was so cheap these days.

And where was this place to which all the slaves were going? They weren't sure, but they knew which road the slavers always took, and it could only lead there.

Sfayot spent much of the night in thought, and by dawn he believed he understood, for all the bitter taste it left in his mouth. Ban had a quota, and no doubt the Slave Corps set limits on how many charges any given slaver could mind. Sfayot's daughter, stolen from him on a brutal whim in Nalfers, had been held up to the light and judged unworthy. She had been cast off in favour of the extra coin that Dragonfly women might buy.

She might be dead, therefore. She might have been used and cast, throat slit, into a trench without another thought on the part of whatever Wasp slaver or soldier had done it. Or she might have fallen into that great melting pot of unclaimed slaves he was hearing of, and still be there. Having come this far, what choice did he have?

He set off that morning. He had some coin in his pocket, little enough after giving away most of his stock, and he sensed that Malic's papers would not hold much weight this far out. A lone Roach-kinden had no legitimate business in these places. He would most likely be executed as a spy if they caught him.

He saw more signs of war, on the road, but he felt as though his sensibilities had begun to erode under the relentless storm of trauma. Dead men and women, dead children, dead animals, his eyes slid off them. He had no more room for horror. So he thought.

But he found it. He found where the slaves, the myriad captives of war, were going, and he discovered that there was a little room left, after all, for a kind of horror that a connoisseur might savour as Malic had savoured his wine.

The Wasps had built a cage, and the cage was like a honeycomb, and the honeycomb was vast, eight-score cells at least, all wooden-slatted walls and a hatch at the top. There had been a wood here, before, but it had been hacked back for half a mile in all directions, the felled wood going towards this abomination,

There were plenty of Wasps here: some were arriving and departing with strings of slaves, others were plainly the custodians of the place. All of them wore the tunics and full helms of the Slave Corps. There was not a regular soldier, not a Consortium factor or clerk or artificer to be seen, but of the slavers there were dozens, stalking about the perimeter of the thing they had built, or walking atop it, looking down on their massed charges. Sfayot waited until twilight and crept closer, trying to find a vantage to see into the wooden cells.

The sheer size of the construction awed him. They had built cells, and then built more and more, each one borrowing a wall from the last and, as more slaves had come, they had built and built, their labour becoming as mindless and instinctive as that of their insect namesakes. The cells looked to be designed for perhaps four prisoners. Sfayot guessed that none had fewer than eight, and many had more. The stench put the battlefield to shame. That was a smell of death; This was life, the most wasted, pitiful dregs of life: a sour, stomach-clutching stink of sweat and excrement, fear and despair. The slaves went in, he saw, and if they were lucky some slaver came and took them out. Otherwise, they stayed and some were fed and others starved or grew fevered from wounds, and eventually, he saw, some of them had died, and still their remains endured, because the slavers were working all the time bringing more people *in*. Every cell he could peer into had at least one collapsed form that did not move.

He saw one slaver take his helm off, just the once. The man's face was hollow-cheeked, haunted. He looked away from the slave pens as though he would rather be a slave himself elsewhere than a master here. They had built something too large to manage, even with the force of slavers present. They had lost control, not to their prisoners, but to entropy.

Sfayot was absolutely sure that he could not simply walk up and offer them money for a Roach girl. They would take his money and throw him in one of those cells, because men who could do this could have no possible shred of civilisation left in them. No papers or promises or appeals would move them. He would have to go about this a more direct way.

Sfayot waited until it grew properly dark, and then he crept forwards. The slavers had set a watch, but it was a desultory one. They were expecting no retribution. The war-front had moved on. He reached the outside edge of the pens, peering in and seeing Dragonfly-kinden bundled together, leaning on one another, without enough room to lie or even sit properly. Some slept, some just stared. None saw him. With creeping care Sfayot ascended, using his Art to scale the wooden wall until he was atop the pens. The stench assailed him anew here, rising up from below almost as a solid thing. He was Roach-kinden, though. His were a hardy people who could survive a great deal. Methodically he began to search.

Sometimes there were slavers up there with him, landing in a shimmer of wings to give the prisoners a look over. And looking for *what?* Sfayot wondered, because it surely could not have been to check on their well-being. At these times he crouched low and called on his Art to hide him from their view. In truth, they were so careless in their examinations that he barely needed to.

He searched and searched, as the hours of the night dragged away. Even with his good eyes it was hard, peering between the slats and trying to see how many were in there, who lay atop whom, what kinden they were. Towards the centre was a knot of around a dozen cells whose occupants were all dead, every one. Sfayot was growing desperate. He began to move faster, glancing in at each hatch for a glimpse of white hair.

A voice hailed him softly and he froze, unsure where it had come from. When it spoke again he realised that it was from below. A Dragonfly man was looking up at him from out of a tangle of his fellows.

"They tell me that Roach-kinden get everywhere," said the man, sounding, despite everything, quietly amused. "Now I see it's true."

"Please..." murmured Sfayot, horribly aware of all the Wasp slavers, of how close they all were.

"What are you scavenging after, Roach-kinden?" the Dragonfly asked. His voice was cultured, elegant, suited for polite conversation over music. He was around Sfayot's own age, the Roach saw. The others in his cell were awake now, eyes glinting in the dark.

"Please, sir," Sfayot said hoarsely. "My daughter. They took my daughter." He realised how pathetic the plea would sound, to people already in cells.

"Mine too," the Dragonfly told him. "Although she is out of this place at least. It seems strange to say that the life of a slave in the Empire may be the best she could have hoped for, having come here." He sounded infinitely calm and Sfayot wondered if he was mad.

"Please," he said again, but then the Dragonfly said, "I know you, I think."

In the dark, Sfayot could not have placed the man for any money, but Dragonfly eyes were always keen. He just crouched there above while the prisoner studied him, and at last decided, "Yes. I remember, you were a thief, I think. A vagrant and a thief, like all your kind. You were brought before me. I sentenced you to work in the fields, but your family rescued you. It was a long time ago now, but I remember."

Sfayot felt like weeping, clutching at the slats with crooked fingers. *Now?* he asked the heedless world. *This man, now?* In truth he had no idea whether it was true. It could have been some other Roach. It was not so uncommon a sequence of events.

"I had thought we were all from the battle, or from the villages hereabouts," the Dragonfly said abstractly. "Do we have a Roach-kinden girl among us?" He did not raise his voice, but Sfayot numbly heard the word being passed back and forth between those who were still awake until at last some reply must have been passed back, for the Dragonfly informed Sfayot, "five cells away, in the direction that I am pointing, is a Roach-kinden girl. May I take it that you intend to remove her from here?"

For a mad moment Sfayot thought the man, in this reeking, hideous place, was objecting to sharing captivity with a Roach. The Dragonfly's face was sublimely serious, though.

"I shall try."

"You have the means to get her out?"

The hatches were all secured with padlocks, something the slavers had apparently possessed in abundance, but the fittings themselves were wood. "I do," Sfayot said. "But it will take time." He was frowning. "What do you intend?"

"Tell me," the Dragonfly- the Dragonfly nobleman, Sfayot assumed- asked him. "Were you really a thief, when I tried you?"

Instant easy answers, normally his first line of defence, did not seem to have followed Sfayot when he mounted up here. It seemed impossible to tell anything but the truth to that calm, doomed face. "I can't recall," Sfayot whispered. "Sometimes I was. Sometimes I wasn't. I cannot remember."

"Ah, well." The answer had apparently been satisfactory in some way. He turned to a man in the next cell. "Kindly pass this on until it reaches my master of arms, if you would. Tell him that it is fit, after all, that he dies in battle."

The low-spoken word passed from mouth to mouth in the opposite direction, until all was dark and silence, and then the noble said, "I should stand ready, if I were you."

Sfayot obediently crawled over to the given cell. Peering in he saw – yes – a flash of white. He called her name, softly, urgently, and again, and at the third time she stirred.

She was half-starved, filthy, bruised and scabbed, but her face was beautiful when she saw that he had come for her.

The padlock holding the hatch shut was solid. The wood, though, was a different matter. His people had an Art that meant they would never starve, that they could live anywhere, on anything.

There was a cry from the far side of the cells, except that the word did not do justice to it. It was a long, howling yell, dragged straight from the pits of someone's being, a maniac's death-cry. It went on and on, and Sfayot heard the sounds of someone battering and kicking at the wood, screaming curses and oaths, and it seemed that every Wasp in the area was running that way or flying overhead.

Sfayot set to work, bringing his head low to the foul wood of the cage. He got his teeth to the slat the lock was secured to, and began to chew. His stomach roiled, but then his Art overruled it, and his jaws worked, grinding and grinding away, tearing off splinters and jagged mouthfuls of the cell.

Wasp slavers were in motion from all around, pitching into the air and casting over the labyrinth of cells towards the commotion. Sfayot glanced up, jaws working fiercely, as one of them levered open the lid on that cell, hand extended. Instantly there was a man leaping up from it, Art-born wings flaring: a Dragonfly-kinden, rich clothes reduced to nothing but rags, but there was a brooch, some golden brooch, proudly displayed on his chest now, that surely the slavers would have taken if they had found it. From nowhere, from thin air, a sword was in his hands, long-hafted, straight-bladed. Still keening that dreadful, agonised shriek he laid into the Wasps, cutting two of the surprised slavers down on the instant before the rest descended upon him with sword and sting.

Sfayot bent down and fixed his teeth in the wood again, wrenching and rending until the lock was abruptly holding nothing at all and the hatch swung open when he pulled.

They passed her up to him. That was what he remembered most. The other prisoners, Grasshoppers and Dragonflies, passed her up first.

He looked round. There was still a commotion at the far extent of the cells, and he saw the flash of sting-fire. The howling cry had stopped, but somehow the Dragonfly master at arms was still fighting. It could not be for long: the distraction was coming to its fatal conclusion.

While he looked, the cell beneath him had emptied, Grasshoppers clearing the hatchway in a standing jump, Dragonflies crawling out and summoning up their wings. Sfayot took his daughter in his arms and huddled back to the nobleman's cell.

"I cannot free you, sir," he said, almost in tears. "I would, but –""

"Take your child," came the reply. "You can do nothing for us except remember."

And Sfayot fled, with his daughter clinging to him, and never looked back.

Another early story, and another exploration of the Twelve-Year War, showcasing the absolute worst it has to offer. The choice of the Roach-kinden's totem reflects the unreasonable prejudice shown to them by almost everyone, a people without a home, constantly being moved on, and now caught in the middle of a war they have nothing to do with. Sfayot and his daughter (Syale, though not named here) cross the path of the novels in Dragonfly Falling *and, from those humble beginnings, go on to carve out quite a career for themselves.*

Camouflage

I'll start from when I got called up in front of Old Mercy – which was a journey of two days from the Sel'yon where I was stationed. You always got called to Mercy. He was not a soldier's soldier. He didn't go out to the battlefront to walk amongst the men, or even to giving his underperforming subordinates a dressing down.

Major Tancrev, that was his real name. He had a reputation, though: everyone knew that Old Mercy never had a man killed, no matter what: Captured enemies or those juniors he was disappointed in, he was meticulous in preserving their lives, often far beyond the point that even a skilled surgeon would have given them over. You understand, then, that his was not a *soft* reputation.

I was going, because Captain Kanen, who had been put in charge of the Sel'yon, had opened his eyes one morning and seen the sharp end of an arrow approaching at some speed. It was a common complaint just then. You'll not read about the Sel'yon in any of the histories of the war. It was a heavily wooded armpit on the map of the Commonweal, important to nobody save the wretched, stubborn, sneaky bastards who lived there.

Old Mercy was not even very old: a middle-aged man, strong-shouldered, square-jawed and fair-haired, quite the ladies' favourite. The more sedentary life of a tactical major was starting to show about his middle, but not as much as you might think. He held court at Yos, that had been Iose before we took it, and there he summoned the luckless sods like me who weren't doing well enough.

I found myself standing to attention in his office, whilst he reclined on a couch like some Spiderlands grandee. A Fly-kinden slave threw a scroll at my feet, and he beckoned for me to take it up.

"Casualty figures for your command, Lieutenant," hesaid. I knew it all already, of course, but he liked making his point. "Why are these savages still troubling the Empire?"

This wasn't the first time someone from the Sel'yon detachment had stood before him. He knew full well what the problem was. Still, I trotted it out: "Sir, the Sel'yon is heavily forested, and we lack the troops to make a decisive strike against the natives."

"Your orders aren't even to strike, Lieutenant, just to *hold*, and yet you're losing men hand over fist."

"The local Dragonfly clan has holed up with a Mantis hold. They know the woods and the surrounding land very well, and that, along with their Art, makes them difficult to *hold* anywhere, sir. Our troops there aren't ideal for this sort of operation, sir. Give me another two hundred light airborne and —"

"Cannot be spared, Lieutenant. Not for something as insignificant as these woodsmen of yours. Lieutenant, had it been Captain Kanen standing here now, no doubt I would be having orders written giving you command of the detachment in his prolonged absence, together with my fervent wishes that you stabilise the situation before I have to request your presence personally. As Kanen has managed to evade true punishment for his incompetence, I will give you a fair chance to prove that you are more able than he. One chance, Lieutenant."

Standing there before his iron stare I was closer to deserting than at any other time during the war. "Sir, I need more troops to hold the line at Sel'yon," I got out, staring straight ahead now because I could no longer meet his stare.

He made some dismissive gesture that I saw the shadow of from the corner of my eye. "I've sent you some pioneers. It's all that can be spared. You had best use them wisely, I think. On your way, Lieutenant, and have better news for me soon."

There were probably only between a hundred-fifty and two-hundred fighting men within the Se'yon, half the numbers we had. They were Mantis-kinden woodsmen and warriors, though, led by a Dragonfly headman and his family, and it would take more than two-to-one odds to clean them out. Instead, as the man said, our orders were simply to keep them bottled up. Had the headman been reasonable then we could have settled in for a relatively peaceful few months. Instead, the locals were holding a grudge, and were quite capable of making us pay for it. Scarcely a tenday went by without some scattering of Mantis-kinden creeping invisibly past our sentries and killing some of ours, double the guard as we might. We lost provisions, tents were burned down, and then Captain Kanen himself had been shot dead one morning from *within* the camp, in broad daylight. I wanted the manpower to move in and crush them, or perhaps some incendiaries to burn the entire Sel'yon to ash, but at this point the Empire had other hives to raid, and so we were being whittled down, and there was nothing we could do about it.

The quality of my troops was also less than inspiring. About a third were light airborne: keen, skilled, swift and just the sort of soldier needed to crack this particular nut. The balance, though, were auxillians from Sonn. The Beetles of Sonn had done well out of the Empire and won, or stolen, a great many concessions, but they were still obliged to put up troops for the army, same as everyone else. As it wouldn't do for the sons of Consortium magnates and factors to live in terror of conscription, the city elders' practice was to send the army their criminals, which meant a scattering of thieves and a great many debtors. So it was that the men lined up to defend against the ravages of the Sel'yon were tradesmen, factory workers, artisans, clerks and small-time merchants, and military training sat uneasily on them. They were equipped with chainmail hauberks, shields and maces, which would have given them some clout in a field battle, if their nerve held, but for a contested advance through tangled woodland they were just about the worst-suited men one could have asked for.

When I got back to the camp I sent for Sergeant Wanton, whose greatest contribution to the war effort was to never once find anything amusing in his own name. "Old Mercy says we should be expecting some pioneers," I told him.

"Yes, sir. They've arrived."

"How many?"

"Ten, sir."

I had hoped for a few more, but given Old Mercy's habitual generosity I'd not have been too surprised at the pioneers turning out to be two scruffy Fly-kinden. Ten was better than nothing, if they were any good.

Pioneers were an odd lot, and their position in army hierarchy was vague. Officially they were right at the bottom, beneath regular soldiers, on a par with unskilled auxillians like my Beetle-kinden, just above slaves. Unofficially, those that lasted for any time at all tended to be good enough at what they did that the army handled them carefully.

They were not quite soldiers, not quite mercenaries, not slaves but not entirely free. Their work required them to be out of reach of orders and officers most of the time, so they had more liberty than almost anyone in the army. At the same time, they were always suspect, and if they slipped up then the Rekef would take them, with glee.

I had them lined up for inspection. They were a motley band. Half were Wasps – four tough-looking men, out of uniform, wearing armour of leather and dulled chitin under capes or long coats, not a piece of black and gold to be seen. There was also one woman, apparently the partner of one of the men. I groaned at that – setting one woman down in a camp of army soldiers was always trouble. Even Beetle-kinden get the itch after a few years of campaigning, as plenty of Commonweal girls had found out. Of the balance, four were Fly-kinden, who tended to make the best pioneers – fast, sneaky, good shots and they could see well at night, at least as well as the Commonwealers they would be up again. Most Flies avoid physical danger as keenly as they do paying taxes, but I knew full well that when a Fly-kinden gets put through the mill enough you get a vicious little bastard at the end of the process.

The last of the pioneers stopped me dead, because Thorn Bug-kinden'll do that to you, and this one was uglier than most. The top of his head came about to my shoulder, but his back peaked a few inches higher, and of course there were the thorns on top of that. He was bundled in layers of ragged tunic and coat, a tattered scarf snagged about his neck, and a cloak over that, and every garment was patched and darned and then torn through again. What little I could see of his skin was shiny and nut-brown, but the thorns grew out every which way, twisted and irregular. A lot of them were truncated, with the stumps sprouting a half-dozen smaller spikes like new shoots growing from a tree-stump, so that I wondered whether the creature had some uniquely Thorn Bug disease. The face was the worst. Even behind the stubble of small and large spines he was a nasty-looking member of the breed, long nose broken and reset crooked, with his pointed chin slanting the other way in a perverse kind of balance.

"And who in the pits are you?" I demanded, all military propriety slapped from me by the very sight.

"Auxillian soldier Cari, sir."

The creature's voice was low and husky, and undeniably a woman's. Nothing else in that bundle of rags and thorns suggested the feminine, most certainly not the face.

"Cari," I said weakly. "A Thorn Bug pioneer?"

"Try me, sir," Her eyes, in amongst all of that hideousness, were green and lively.

I didn't shrug, because imperial officers did not show that kind of casual weakness before their men. "It'll be the Commonwealers trying you, not me," was what I said, albeit a beat too late to be a proper riposte.

Our little slice of war started to change from that day. The pioneers knew their business. *Cari* knew hers, certainly.

Within two tendays, one of the Fly-kinden and two of the Wasp pioneers were dead. The main force's deaths to the knives of the Sel'yon insurgents were just two, rather than the ten or so I'd have expected, and one of those two had been incautiously relieving himself outside the camp edge at night. The distrust and contempt that my light airborne and auxillians felt for the shabby pioneers was replaced by a wary respect. The female Wasp had not yet been raped or assaulted. And there was Cari.

She vanished for the first tenday, and everyone assumed she had deserted. I, on the other hand, had the sense to talk to the other pioneers. No, no, they assured me, she was out there. They didn't see her, not so much, but they found traces. They were just intercepting the Commonwealers as they tried to sneak past our pickets and cause mischief. Cari was in the deep Sel'yon, *hunting*.

One morning, a tenday and a half from when she arrived, I awoke to find she'd left me a present.

Enemy casualties were hard to estimate. Pioneer accounts were contradictory, and the forest swallowed bodies. That morning, though, I was treated to a unique audience as I left my tent, yawning and rubbing my eyes. I nearly choked on my own yawn, I'll say, and my body slave screamed and bolted back inside. He was a twitchy little Grasshopper from the East-Empire, and he never did have much nerve.

There were heads: nine of them, on poles, neat as you like. One was Dragonfly, the rest were Mantis. They watched me with glassy disinterest.

Sergeant Wanton explained. "She pitched up before dawn, sir, with a sack. Had all these set up by first light and off again."

"Did it occur to you I might not *want* to see a lot of severed heads first thing in the morning, Sergeant?"

Wanton had assiduously practiced a sergeant's proper lack of expression. "No sir, it did not."

I dismissed him, and strode down the line of decapitation. Strangely enough, the more I looked on those slack, drained faces, with the day's first flies bumbling about them, the more I *did* like them. I had been fighting a losing war for too long. It was about time I had proof that the blood being shed wasn't all ours.

"Glad you approve, sir," came the voice. I stopped dead, only then realising that I had been grinning back at the dead heads. There was nobody about.

There was. I only saw her because she moved. The Sel'yon was a fecund place, and though we were on its edge, and had trampled our campsite flat besides, there were always nettles and ferns and cane springing up, growing at appalling rates. What I had taken as a stand of bracken had shuffled a place closer. Armed with that, I saw her.

She had foliage all over, knotted and twined about her into a meshed cape of green and fading brown. Her shape, that had always been at the edge of a human figure anyway, was lost in it. The eye passed over her and consigned her to the static and the vegetable. There was more to it than that, of course. I knew all too well how some kinden could call on their Art to hide them, for the Mantids of the Sel'yon were keen practitioners of it. I had not realised that Thorn Bugs owned to the same Art. Only now, seeing her afresh, did I note the crossbow over her shoulder. The dead Commonwealers had eyes better than mine, but they must never have seen her coming.

Glad she's on our side, I thought, *and never so glad as when she appeared out of nowhere.* "Auxillian," I acknowledged her, with admirably steady tones.

She was watching me with a direct stare unbecoming of an auxillian, but then it was hard to actually look her in the eyes without flinching at the knotted carnage that surrounded them. I recovered my professional bearing.

"Who do these represent?"

"The Dragonfly lad there's a nephew of the headman. The Mantids... Whoever I could catch. They're getting a mite less happy about just jaunting off into the woods."

"And you took the heads why?"

"You don't need to ask that, surely, sir?"

I wanted to slap her down for impertinence, but slapping down a Thorn Bug is always a self-destructive activity. She was standing just the other side of the row of posts now.

"You know how superstitious these Commonwealers are, sir," she said, her voice just a whisper coming from between those twisted teeth. "Does no harm to make them fear."

I sent to Old Mercy with reports of our progress in holding the line, hoping for a quiet life, and perhaps a minor commendation. What I did get proves that a little success can be worse for your health than any amount of failure, because Mercy decided that he wanted us to take the Sel'yon, or at least start making inroads into it. Was he sending us more men? A dozen heavy infantry arrived with his message, not sufficient to make any difference and yet arrogant and argumentative enough to start really getting on the backs of the Auxillians.

I had my orders, which I knew were a bad idea. There was no way we were going to catch them much by surprise, for all that I had the pioneers sweeping the forest fringe for their scouts before we formed up. I put the Beetles on the wings, the newly-arrived heavies in the centre, made our front as broad as I dared, mostly only two men deep, and we moved in. The airborne ranged on either side and ahead, but the trees denied them their wings half the time. Still, they were used to fighting in skirmishing order, at range or in close as the situation demanded. If my whole force had been airborne I'd have cleared out the Sel'yon myself long before.

The Commonwealers had our number and no mistake. They started putting arrows at us from ten yards in, a nuisance at first, a menace pretty soon after. The heavies and the Auxillians were decently armoured, but those Commonweal bows were like nothing I've ever seen in the hands of the Inapt. A clean shot could go through mail and still leave enough punch in the arrow to make a mess of the man inside. The Commonwealers didn't stand still, but they knew the woods better than we did and they could move faster. They were behind us soon enough, as well. If we held together we were slow and they picked at us. When the airborne, or individual maniples of the heavier troops, rose to the bait and went for them, then the Commonwealers were always there in force to make them regret it.

I had a decision then, to push on as per orders, or to fall back and bare my throat for Old Mercy's knife. I ordered the advance, such as it was, to continue. I was not one of my more inspired moments, but I was only a lieutenant, and more used to relaying tactical decisions than actually originating them.

Things went to pieces pretty soon after that. Our line was broken up courtesy of some precise strikes by parties of Commonwealers, mostly Mantis-kinden, appearing from the trees and getting to blade range before anyone was the wiser. The arrows followed hard on them, once the Beetles' shields were in disarray. I sent messengers up and down the line with instructions to keep it together, but the Commonwealers had a habit of picking the messengers off, and the entire advance turned into a series of skirmishes, with most isolated groups independently deciding to pull back out of the forest. Goes to show that soldiers have more sense than their officers, sometimes.

I was with the Wasp heavies when they came in for their battering. There was a feint at us by a half dozen Mantis-kinden with spears and swords, whilst a larger force assailed the Beetles down the line. Then it turned out *that* was the feint, while we were suddenly up to our ears in Mantis-kinden. The enemy were unarmoured but swift and very good. The heavies did their best, but they were beset from all sides. I ordered the retreat and we began to back out, hoping that we'd run into some of the Auxillians we might have outstripped. Then I got an arrow through the leg and went down.

I lay there, expecting to find a Mantis about to cut my throat at any moment – don't believe all that rot you hear about their vaunted bloody honour, they'll gut you without a second thought, any chance they get. Either they had followed up the retreating heavies or they were off fighting someone else. I was left with a few corpses for company and a long shaft gone right through my thigh.

I couldn't muster my wings at all. Having a shaft through you like that will play hob with your Art. I tried crawling, but the arrow stuck out too far both ways, and each time I snagged it on something I nearly passed out. The same applied when I tried to snap the head off, which is what you're supposed to do, I've heard. Also, there was surprisingly little blood, and pulling the arrow out might change that in radical and unwelcome ways. I lay there, feeling my life creep slowly out from what, on a properly ordered battlefield, would not be a serious injury. The night was coming on, I knew, and Commonweal nights are cold.

I would like to say that I took this all very philosophically, knowing that it was my own failure as an officer that had got me in that predicament, but frankly I was cursing Old Mercy every which way. If you ever needed to prove to some Moth or Commonwealer that all that magic stuff doesn't work, then take me as evidence. If it was even slightly possible to put a curse on someone then Old Mercy would have burned up on the spot with the fire I was spitting about him inside my head.

Then there was someone stepping very near me and I stopped even those thoughts, as if they might somehow have betrayed me, led an enemy to me. I looked about, but for a moment I saw nobody. Then I realised that the nobody I saw was Cari. She was crouching right by me, festooned with greenery, blending in with skill and Art. Within the cocoon of her stolen foliage I saw her crossbow. She was scanning the trees around us.

"What are you doing here, soldier?" I got out, though my voice (so fierce in my head when I was biting at Old Mercy) was just a croak.

"When you didn't come back, sir, I thought I'd see if I could find your body. Didn't want them to, you know..." She made a chopping motion with her off hand.

"Get me out of here," I rasped at her.

She considered me dubiously. "Dark now, sir, and you can bet they'll be hunting. Bastards for the dark, Mantis-kinden. No way I could keep quiet with you over my shoulder. Besides..." I thought I saw her grin, "Don't reckon you'd survive my carrying you anywhere. Now, come morning the other pioneers are going to come out and look for me, and we'll get you out of the woods. I reckon you and I'd better keep company here 'til then." After a pointed pause she added, "Sir."

I wanted to be angry with her, and to assert an officer's authority, but I was cold and weak and probably the first person in the Empire's history who's actually been glad to see a Thorn Bug. I said – I could not stop myself – "You'll stay with me." It was a wretched, whining thing to say, and said in a whining way.

"As much as I can, sir," she said softly.

I kept losing her in the dark, with nothing of the human in her outline. Then she was kneeling right by me, close enough that a couple of her spikes grated on my armour. "Got something for you to drink, sir. It'll take the pain off a bit."

Of course, as an officer you never drink anything a soldier offers you, whatever their kinden. Notwithstanding, I gulped it down and, true enough, everything seemed a great deal less urgent shortly thereafter. Lying there in the forest, surrounded by dead soldiers and with a nightmare vision as my ministering guardian, suddenly felt almost idyllic.

I muttered something to that effect, but Cari was busying herself about my let, and taking long enough that eventually I propped myself up on my elbows to have a look. The moon was up by then, and fighting its way through the trees with as much difficulty as we had done in the daytime. She had snapped the arrowhead off – because I could see it lying beside my leg – and as I watched she yanked the shaft free. No amount of numbing potion could quite cover that, and I yelped. Instantly she was still, her crossbow back to hand, waiting and watching. After a long pause she set to bandaging, and I stared at the spectacle, utterly absorbed by it. I had never seen anyone make such hard work of the task, nor had I seen Cari quite so awkward at anything. The simply act of wrapping a bandage three times about my leg and then tying it took her forever, as the cloth continually snagged and caught on her. I had a feeling that she must have left a fair few scratches on my hide, too, but it didn't seem of pressing concern just then.

"Must make life awkward, all those spikes," I told her, finding the words slightly hard to get out. "Must be all sorts of things you can't do."

She went still, but not in the same way as before. It was like a flinch, that stillness. Something retreated inside her, where all those sharp points could keep it safe.

"Mind you," I went on, because the words, once started, seemed to have a life of their own, "you've got it worse, you've got that, whatever-it-is you've got. I've seen you. Some kind of disease of the spikies. All of them gone wrong, eh? Sorry, I'm sorry for that. You're a good soldier. Shame, really."

Slowly she started on the dressing again. "It's not a disease," she said.

"Well what is it?" I have no idea why I cared, but it seemed to matter a great deal at the time. "You people, Thorn Bug-people, you're born all spickly anyway, but you were born even *more* spickly? Is that what is it?"

"We're not born like this. The world is not quite as cruel to our mothers as all that. It's an Art that develops early, though." She was whispering, scanning the darkness yet again. "But this isn't the way I was born, sir."

"Oh no? So tell me, soldier. That's an order."

There was a long silence, long enough that I forgot whether I had actually said the words or not, but at last she spoke.

"When I was just a slave, and not an auxillian, sir... when I was just a slave, a man decided he wanted to know what it was like to lie with one of my kind. Obviously there were... challenges involved. We are not easily raped, sir." She shifted position slightly. "I understand it was for a bet, or maybe some kind of game. It took the artificers hours to file me down to something vulnerable enough that he could have his fun. In truth, I don't think he enjoyed it much. More than me, though."

I had about a hundred rejoinders swimming about in my head, most of which would be standard army issue, concerning slaves, free men and lesser kinden. I didn't say any of them.

"I got into the army soon after. Better Auxillian than civilian, right?" she went on, her voice quiet and brittle, but just reaching me. "Pioneers suit me. Don't see many people, in Pioneer Corps. Can be your own officer, most of the time."

"You're very good at it." I don't know why, even in my state, I thought that weak praise was what the situation needed.

"I like blending in."

I laughed, just a coughing chuckle. I couldn't stop myself.

She shrugged, a soft rustle of greenery. "Sometimes it's a blessing to look like something else, lose your outline, be overlooked. And besides, there's no better way of getting close to your prey. You can't deny me that."

"I wouldn't want to." My leg was starting to throb as her draft began to wear off. There was still a fair amount of the night to go. I was considering whether it befit an officer of the imperial army to beg more potion from an Auxillian when there was a clack, and a choked gasp from between the trees. It took me a moment to realise that Cari had loosed her crossbow. A moment later she was gone from my side, though I couldn't have told you where she went.

There were sounds in the dark. I hunched myself partway to sitting, a shaking hand directed out at the night. I saw nothing.

Then, just as I was about to collapse back down, someone jumped me. I got a knee to me chest punching the breath from me, and my hand was struck aside. I had a glimpse of a lean, angular Mantis woman with her dagger already drawn back, her face utterly expressionless. The only sound I made was a panicked inhalation.

Then she was thrown off me by an invisible hand, rolling over to lie still, all with barely a sound herself. In the moonlight the moth-scale fletchings of the crossbow bolt stood proud of her body.

Cari was back with me shortly after that. "Got them all, sir," she reported. "Just three of them come to look over the bodies. Maybe take a few trophies, hey?"

I refrained from saying that using an officer as bait was generally frowned upon in the army. I was suddenly extremely away that if she, who clearly had few fond memories of the Empire or the Wasps, chose to make me one more casualty of war, there would be little I could do about it.

"Don't worry, sir," she told me, still staring off into the darkness. "I'll watch over you."

Old Mercy was not much pleased by the affair, as you can imagine. It was only because of the Beetles that I was able to salvage any of it. We lost about one in three of the regular Wasp-kinden, but the Beetle Auxillians got out with less than one in ten casualties, thanks to a combination of durability and common sense. I was thus able to dress the whole disaster up as a scouting exercise and repeat my doomed requests for a stronger force with which to make the assault.

A tenday later, enter three hundred light airborne.

I was as surprised as anyone, but there they were, spoiling for a fight. Apparently Old Mercy had decided to smash the Sel'yon once and for all, and our 'progress', which existed almost entirely within my reports, was enough for him to secure the release of troops who had been idling elsewhere. My orders were for a swift, merciless raid, leave no opposition alive. With the new troops I reckoned we could give it a decent try.

I conferred with my sergeants, old and new, and laid out an order of battle to make best use of our new resources. The Commonwealers would know we had been reinforced, so no sense waiting around. We would allow the new arrivals two days to rest up and get their bearings, and then we'd be back into the trees.

After I'd packed the sergeants off with their orders, I did not call Cari into my tent. One of the Wasp-kinden pioneers, the one with the wife, had already been given orders. It would not be fitting for me to consult with a mere unranked Auxillian.

No, so instead I sought her out, which was easier said than done. I limped all over camp looking for her, and at the last she obviously heard about it, because she found me.

"You've heard." I wasn't quite looking at her, just standing there gazing over the camp. Anyone watching me would not have seen me conferring with a subordinate. Perhaps they would not have seen Cari at all. "What do you think?"

"Have the pioneers sent ahead of the line. We'll break up their positions, spoil their ambushes. Before we came, sir, the 'Wealers had a lot of home ground advantage, but we've been chipping away at that, and with the men you've got now..."

"You think it'll work?" A Lieutenant of the imperial army seeking assurance from a shabby little Thorn Bug wench. "You know Mantis-kinden..."

"I do, and they'll go down fighting to the last one of them, no doubt; but, sir, there are perhaps sixty of them, maybe less. Send the pioneers ahead. Let the airborne get stuck in everywhere the enemy appear, mop up with the Auxillians."

After that, I thought for a while and then sent for the leader of the pioneers, to amend his orders.

We went in on schedule, stings blazing. I had the light airborne set a punishing pace, which was easy for me to say since I wasn't capable of keeping up with them. I went in with the Auxillians, but I told Sergeant Wanton not to stop until he was in sight of the Sel'yon fort. I felt I was being somewhat optimistic, in this, but once the orders were given and the men sent off, it was out of my hands.

My experience of that battle was basically a gruelling march through a wood, at the best pace I and the Beetles could set. We didn't see a single live enemy all the way, and everything I know I gleaned from reports. The short story is that the imperial army excelled itself, admittedly with odds heavily in its favour. The light airborne attacked in force, swarming the enemy every time they showed themselves, taking losses but not letting up. The slightly longer story is that those enemy were usually visible to be swarmed because one or other of the pioneers had already stirred them up. We lost three more pioneers in that action, but they did their job, the job that Cari had set out for them. They were the only soldiers we had who could meet the enemy on the Commonwealers' terms, spoil their ambushes and draw our airborne to them.

Two hours later my Auxillians and I drew up alongside Wanton's airborne, and the fort was indeed within our view. I was exhausted and, although I stepped out to greet Wanton on my own two feet, I had been leaning on Beetle shoulders for a lot of the way. Strange how sometimes we feel we have to make more of a show for our own people than for the Auxillians.

As ordered, the airborne had halted their advance to allow the heavies to catch up. Indeed, the pace of the airborne had been such that they had been in time to see the fort gates closing as they arrived. Wanton reckoned there couldn't be many people left in the fort, given how many of the Mantis-kinden had gone down during the advance – never easily, but stings and numbers will deal with most things. The Dragonfly noble who was at the heart of this, however, was unaccounted for, so he and his family and closest retainers were likely still holed up there.

The fort itself was nothing worthy of the name, a thing of slanted wooden walls and mounded earth, all built up around and between three trees. The base was broad, the top narrow and ringed with spikes of splintered cane, and there were plenty of arrowslits. Not a joy to take over ground or air, therefore, but such places are only as good as their defenders. It was time for the Auxillians to get their hands dirty.

Sporadic arrow-shot met us as we stormed the gates, but the Beetles had come with big shields, and the airborne put enough stingfire into the walls to dissuade any sharpshooters. One of the Auxillian company artificers set a simple petard against the gates and then they made their hasty retreat. No doubt the Commonwealers thought they'd driven us off and were celebrating, because precious few shafts were sent after the Beetles. Shortly after that there was a muted boom, the metal pot of the petard flew off into the trees, and, when the smoke cleared, the gates were punched in as though some giant foot had stamped on them.

In went the airborne, and there was a brief, vicious skirmish: a half-dozen Mantis-kinden dead for nine of ours. Any enemy left had retreated to an inner bailey, another slanted wooden box with arrowslits. At this point I was considering just burning them out, but Sergeant Wanton pointed out that there were no arrows coming at us.

"Maybe there are no archers inside?" I wondered, and then, "Maybe they want to surrender." Certainly the list of possible outcomes that saw any of the defenders remaining alive was growing slim. "You're sure nobody escaped by air after we got here?"

"Absolutely, sir."

"Sir!" one of the other airborne shouted. The gates were opening.

The Dragonfly nobles had indeed fled into their fort, at the end, I later discovered, although they had left their Mantis-kinden followers outside to die. However, even as they closed the door on our troops, they had not known that they were already infiltrated.

Standing in the gateway was a familiar figure, all over spikes and stripped of her usual cloak of leaves. In the crook of one arm she held her crossbow, and the other hand was lifting a head high. I could not know for sure, but I was willing to lay odds that the twisted features were those of the Dragonfly noble who had made the Sel'yon such a miniscule thorn in the Empire's side.

We cheered her then, first the Auxillians and the soldiers of my original command, but soon enough the newer arrivals too.

What impact any of this had on the war as a whole I can't say. I don't imagine that Commonwealer princes were running up and down the halls of their palaces, decrying the loss of the Sel'yon. Old Mercy, though, was very pleased indeed. After my detailed report I received, by return, a terse note informing me that he would be taking the unprecedented step of actually coming over to inspect the troops and congratulate them. He wanted them ready for the parade ground within two days, which was not going to endear him to them, and he particularly wanted to see the Pioneer Corps, of whom I had spoken so highly.

I had them ready for his inspection. He came with a sizeable escort of his own: medium infantry and a few sentinels, as though he was expecting a Commonweal resurgence at any point. As I say, his usual style was to demand people came to him, not actually go visit them. Possibly he'd forgotten what the outside world looked like.

I'd got my men into some semblance of order. The Beetles polished up nicely, although the airborne are never easy to keep in line. I had Sergeant Wanton stalking between the ranks with a stick, ready to belabour anyone joking with their neighbour, but even so there was a fair amount of shifting and shuffling going on. Major Tancrev, Old Mercy, had billetted his own men, and now he made his appearance, dressed in enamelled mail with a cloak gusting behind him. I met him, and followed him down the ranks, just a step behind him, answering his occasional question about the troops. Despite his promise of congratulations, his praise was sparse, but at least he didn't actually have anyone mutilated for having dirty boots, so I was counting the whole exercise as a success.

Then we got to the pioneers, those that were left. They were not parade ground material, but they stared straight ahead as the major inspected them: the Wasp-kinden, the Flies, then Cari.

"Well, Thorn Bug, eh?" he said, with that higher officer's infallible knack of stating the obvious. I had praised her in my report, because I've got at least that much decency, but Old Mercy did not personally commend lesser kinden, and so we passed on. Just as we were about to look at the Auxillians, though, he remarked to me, "I had a Thorn Bug once..." with a curl of his lip. I knew then. From his tone it could just have meant that he'd had one serving under his command, but I *knew*.

I could have done something. The whole business was in my hands and at my discretion. As a lieutenant in the imperial army I had a duty.

That night, after everyone had turned in, I got drunk enough that I didn't have to think about what the morning would bring, what I *knew* it would inevitably bring, barring any action from me.

She was gone before dawn, of course, and I never heard tell of her since, but who keeps track of Thorn Bugs, honestly? Old Mercy's people turned the camp upside down looking for him, but I didn't help. I played the ignorant card and bumbled about getting in their way. Only towards noon did one of them realise that the number of Cari's grisly trophies was up by one on the day before, a new post added to her collection. The rest of him we never found.

Thorn Bug-kinden feature a few times in the novels, primarily in the form of Scuto, Stenwold's Helleron agent. Cari has little common ground with Scuto, though. In 'Camouflage' we see more of the Wasp-Dragonfly war, this time just a little backwater part of it. Cari has no repeat appearance (though she really deserves one) but the Pioneers themselves have a part to play in War Master's Gate and their ramshackle training and diversity come straight out of this story.

The Shadows of Their Lamps

The Commonweal's Grand Army – the flower of its nobility, its gallant cavalry, the unnumbered host of its infantry – had met the Wasp Empire's forces in the field. The warriors of the Commonweal had possessed a vast numerical superiority, but more than that, they had been heroes; their hearts had sung a ballad of honour and glory; they had *right* on their side, defending their hearths and their homeland.

The Imperial armies had war machines, automotives, repeating crossbows and artillery. In a single day they had mown down tens of thousands of Commonwealer Dragonfly-kinden, over a hundred thousand left dead on the field in all. All those noblemen and women in their glittering mail with their thousand-year-old sword and archery traditions; all that massed host of terrified peasant spearmen: the Wasps had made no allowance for social class. Born in a castle or a byre, the machines and ordered soldiers of the Empire had not cared. In the end, the broken shreds of the Commonweal army had fled in all directions, and those nobles who had survived had run for their stone walls to hide. And of course, the Empire's artillerists were good with stone walls. Before their might, the ancient architecture of the Commonweal was so many children's wooden blocks.

And yet Prince Serge Esselente did not know the meaning of dismay. He had withdrawn the remnants of his forces to his mountain stronghold, up the steep paths where the war machines could not follow. He had forced the Wasps to invest his fortress with their infantry and their airborne soldiers, and he had held out. And winter was on its way, that the mountains would make a rod of iron for the natives, but a murderous terror for the invader.

Serge Esselente was a noble of the old school. He was not just glitter and glory and a heedless disregard for the lives of his own followers; he was a seer. Through the lenses of his eyes, the strands of an infinite future were strung. From the tallest tower of his castle blazed a beacon that was called Light Eternal, a reminder of his family's history as champions of justice and truth. He took the rostrum for his people daily, telling them that the shining light of the Commonweal, that had fought many darknesses back in the Days of Lore, would triumph yet over these machine-handed Wasp-kinden. After the winter, he told them, they would retake what was theirs.

He would have been flattered to discover that the Wasps shared his beliefs. Not about the magic; the Wasps had no belief in magic. They had a hard-learned respect for Commonweal winters, though, and had no intention of keeping a mountain siege going once the ice set in. That was why Prince Serge Esselente, preparing to go before his people once more, had his throat cut by a woman wearing the face of his wife.

After she had done that, Scyla took his shape, donning the face and mannerisms of the prince as easily as she would a slightly ill-fitting coat. The magic, the meagre magic that was yet all the magic she had ever learned, was almost second nature to her now. She was a scion of an ancient mystery, its last and least. The masters of her masters had spun webs of intrigue between great houses and mage-lords and scholars of the unseen; and here she was, a mercenary infiltrator for the grubby-handed Wasps.

She went out to Esselente's people wearing his skin, and told them that the omens favoured their cause; that they must throw open the gates and surge down the slopes, that the Light Eternal would send the Wasps stumbling bloodied back to their far home. She told them in his voice, with his precise patterns of conviction and passion, and they ate it up. They loved it. This was what they had been waiting for.

And they opened the gates and sallied forth and were destroyed: many killed, many more captured, none understanding how it was that they had been betrayed.

The Dragonfly-kinden of the Commonweal were a graceful and elegant people, gold-skinned and delicate. Surrounded by the Wasps – big, pale men with hard eyes and broad shoulders – they seemed like something of another world, something that would break at a touch. And many of them would break. They had made the Empire work hard to conquer them. There would be reprisals.

Scyla presented herself before her paymaster. Only with him did she drop most of the masks. She was no Dragonfly, no Wasp, nobody from this corner of the world at all: an exiled renegade casting her lot in with the winning side. The face she showed him was that of a slender man, sharp-featured, fair-haired, but showing the features of her Spiderlands home of the far south. It might have been her brother's face, had she ever had a brother – always better to be a man, to deal with the Wasp-kinden. As for the woman's face she had been born with, she had no cause to don that any more. She had left it behind like a bad debt.

Scyla had been working with Captain Thalric for some years now. She had been in a prime position to watch him being corrupted by his work. When she first offered her services to him, he had been a bluff young officer, a patriot, a hero. Then he made the mistake of being too successful. He had been noticed by his superiors, dragged up the chain of command. Now he worked for the Rekef, the Empire's intelligencers and secret police. He had gained the world and lost all his friends.

"You've done well, you and your tricks," he told her. "Nobody wanted to be sitting outside these walls when the snow came."

Her tricks, because that was what he could cope with. He would not admit to magic. Show him a hundred proofs and he would contrive some way of explaining it in terms of suggestion and sleight of hand. Looking into his eyes she felt a chill sweep through her like the first wind of winter. *I am the only magician in the Imperial advance,* she thought. *And where we have trodden: nothing, the earth swept clean of magic and wonder, trampled down by their machines.*

He paid her wage, heavy coin in exchange for the ancient mysteries of her order. Her teachers would have despised her for selling herself to these grim, small-minded people, but she had never been a good student.

Back in the castle they were securing the prisoners, waiting for the Slave Corps to come take them away. Long chains of them, bound at the neck, coiled dispiritedly through the halls of Prince Esselente's castle. Wearing the face of a Wasp, she walked amongst them, cuffing and swearing at them because that was what Wasps did.

And there she saw him.

The Wasps had been stringing their lamps about the castle. They could not abide the dark and their eyes were pitiful compared to those of the Commonwealers or Scyla's own. Wherever they went, they beat the night back with lamps that burned chemicals or noxious gas.

Everywhere they made their own was lit up by a cold, dead flame a world away from torches and hearths.

When the radiance struck her, she thought it was their lamps, so fierce and blinding was it, but it was him: his beauty and his power. She had not realised the boy had survived.

The late Prince Esselente and his slightly later wife had one child, a youth of barely eighteen. Serge Volante he was named, and he was beautiful. His father had been a seer for many decades, but the son had already been overtaking him. Those slanted violet eyes could see forever: truths and lies, pasts and futures. He was a natural talent such as Scyla had never known – such as the Commonweal had not known for a hundred years.

Esselente had prophesied that his son would bring back the great days, the Days of Lore; that Serge Volante would be the hope of a new generation of magic. Instead of which, the Apt forces of the Empire had brought their armies and their scoffing disbelief and swept them all away. All except Volante himself.

Nobody else would see that glorious golden aura about him. It was for her eyes only. His perfect face hurt her deep inside. And he was young, and she had surely been young within living memory.

All at once she decided that the Wasps were not paying her enough, and that *this* would be a just recompense for her skills.

And then his eyes met hers and they flashed wide as she cut through the mill of busy soldiers to him.

"You…" he said. "I see you." Behind the glow he was haggard, bruised, stained with blood. "You're not like the others. You shine."

Her heart, an organ from which she had been estranged these last ten years, stuttered.

"I see the magic about you," said Serge Volente. "I see your face."

A sense of panic flooded through Scyla, her mind a blank. *What face? Which face?* Did he look past this stolen Wasp visage, with its brutal jaw and narrow eyes? Did he look past the male Spider-kinden mask she donned to speak to Captain Thalric, to fool him into thinking she was being honest with him. Did Volente see all the way back to the face she had been born with, the face that she never used anymore?

In that moment, she searched her memories and found that she could not remember what that face had ever looked like.

He was reaching out to her, and one of the guards smacked a

cudgel across his arm with a snarl. Still, Serge Volante's eyes did not leave her. There was a pleading in those eyes. If there had been a promise, she would have freed him then and there, if she'd had to borrow Captain Thalric's face to do it. But he was golden and beautiful and noble. Such as he did not make promises to a broken renegade like her.

I will have you, she told him silently. *But I will have to break you first.*

She retreated from him to make plans. No point asking for him as a gift from Captain Thalric. The moment the Rekef man's attention was drawn to Volante, the boy's death warrant would be signed. There was a standing order to exterminate all of the Commonweal noble bloodlines, to deny any uprising a focus. It was Thalric's special mission, and he was nothing if not dutiful.

Is it time I parted company with the Empire? But it would not come to that. She was fond enough of her own cleverness to decide that she could have it all: Volente and the Empire's gold. She was all the magic there was, in this latter-day world; all the magic after the Light Eternal was put out and the great magician-lords of the Commonweal fell under the wheels of the Empire's progress. The Wasps had no magic, nor any way to believe in it, and that made her a secret lord of their world.

Plans made, she left the castle, slipping out of the gates and passing unseen through the Empire's camp there. The officers and their cronies had commandeered the walls but there were plenty of the lesser soldiery left to huddle in their tents still. They had not wasted any time making themselves at home. There were many locals there too, some prisoners, some simply starving and willing to serve their oppressors in exchange for the scraps from their table. The air filled with the clamour of soldiers who weren't going to have to fight in the morning.

There was one strange moment, though. She was leaving the camp, having appropriated a horse that could pass as an Imperial messenger's, when there was a man. For just a fractured instant, in all the camp there was only that one man that mattered. He was not a Wasp, not a Wasp's male whore or servant. He looked like a beggar, a shabby creature in ragged, dark robes holding out a stick-thin hand for alms. And she thought, *You're out of luck* because, of all kinden, one did not go to the Wasps for charity. And then she met his eyes, those protuberant red eyes that pressed out from his gaunt, ashen face, and the world stopped for a single heartbeat.

He was gone after that, and she shook herself and went on with the plan. It had been a long war and she had been put to find many inventive uses for her training. Perhaps she needed a rest from it: enough murder and treachery would start to wear on anybody.

She chose her face from the packed shelves within her mind. Her magic gave her a major's rank badge, a uniform creased and stained from travel. She turned up at the gates on the very horse she had just led through them and nobody spotted it.

They took her to Thalric, of course, and she played her part perfectly, simultaneously the major looking down at the captain and the regular officer wary of the Rekef man. She told him she had a remit to look for some specific prisoners wanted for questioning. She had no papers but it was a routine request and she was good at her job. She talked him round and laughed at him silently all the while.

And of course she went down the ranks of prisoners, and Volante's eyes were on her. She stopped by him and murmured, "How would you thank me if I freed you, little princeling?"

The rush of gratitude, of hope; these things she did not see.

"What has been done to you?" he asked her. "You are like a stunted tree."

A shock of hurt fury went through her, so that for a moment she almost lost her false face and shape. *How dare he, prisoner that he was? How dare he play the lord with her?* And she was going to walk away then, and leave him to his fate; she was going to inform on him to Thalric and have him executed on the crossed pikes. But no: *No, I'll take him. I'll break him. I'll make him thank me. I'll show him the way the world has turned.*

And in her clipped major's voice, with its heart-of-the-Empire accent, she ordered that he be released into her custody. Did she need an escort? She poured scorn on them. She was a strong soldier of the Empire and Volente was barely more than a child.

And she led him out of the Empire's camp as easily as if she had bought him at auction, her golden boy.

She had already chosen her spot to let him down from the horse. They were still within sight of his father's castle: let that symbol of defeat be right in the forefront of his mind. She had a whole itinerary planned for him, but this desolate stretch of road and rocks would serve for now.

He stood, thin and shivering, and made no attempt to flee. He had nowhere to go.

"What is to become of me?" he asked her.

She regarded him with a mocking smile fixed to a face she had chosen specially. She was a woman of the Spider-kinden once more, but with as much allure and grace as her skills could stitch together. Still, she was in his shadow, and all the work she had put into her features and her frame passed him by.

"Tell me, princeling," she addressed him, "what would you do, if you had the freedom for it?"

His eyes met hers; again the sheer exotic wonder of them struck her, the perfection of his golden skin. "My father saw many futures," he told her. "He said I would bring a new dawn. Let me bring that dawn. Let me fulfil my destiny." Abruptly a passion entered his voice. "You – whatever you are, however you have fallen, you are a creature of magic as I am. You are not one of *them*," and he thrust a hand towards the conquered castle.

"You have no idea what I am," she told him derisively.

"I see through your faces. I have read of your order in the tales of my people. It was once a calling of honour and skill." And his eyes searched the face she showed him, as though he really thought he would find some dormant spark of all that in her. There was such yearning in his expression, in that moment, that she shrank back from him. She knew that he could search there a year, dig through all the layers of her, and find no grain of what he sought. His disappointment cut her, because for a moment he had thought she was something more than she was. If she had been capable, she would have been that, for him.

Then she had him by the chin, yanking his head about, forcing the confrontation onto her terms. "Even in my homeland, my teachers were nothing more than pawns of the Aristoi, and our magic just the tool of princes. Servants and mercenaries, that is all we are. Your shining past was dead long before the Empire came. They're just throwing its body onto the pyre."

"I will not believe it," he said calmly. "My father –"

"Is dead," and she almost said, *I killed him wearing your mother's face,* because she wanted to hurt him. She wanted to take his pride and self-possession and crumble them to pieces in her hands. She had seen herself through his eyes now – *a stunted tree*. It made her want him all the more but, if she was to have him, he must be broken. Only then would he give himself to what he had seen in her.

But all she said was, "Come with me," and she got him back on the horse and then led the beast down the road towards lower ground.

Two days before, there had been a battle here. A force of Commonwealers had turned up at the rear of Thalric's men, either sent to relieve the castle or just very lost. The Empire's response had been swift and predictable.

Serge Volente stood and looked out at it all, and she saw him tremble. Her secret heart exalted at it.

"Behold," she told him, "the glorious field of valour. Here did the gilded lords and ladies of the Commonweal bring their righteous battle against the craven brutes of the Wasp Empire."

She was exaggerating, of course: courage was one thing the soldiers of the Empire never lacked. She was telling him the story as the old tales were told, though, where the heroes of those days had walked through a world that bled superlatives.

The Wasps had removed their own dead for cremation, of course. What was left was the history of the Wasp-Commonweal war in miniature: dead Dragonfly-kinden and their allies, strewn and abandoned.

"Here, these were noble retainers," she went on, picking her way forwards and drawing him with her. "See how their bright armour gleams." *Where it isn't shattered.* "See the swords and bows and lances, the tools of their ancient and exquisite skills." *Broken now, fallen from lifeless hands.* "And here, the great and loyal populace of their farms and fields, banded together in the loyal service of their masters," she went on, showing him where the peasant levy had been mown down, hacked down, crushed beneath the grinding wheels of the war automotives. "And here –" but for a moment even her jibes failed her, staring at the cracked and half-dismembered carcass of a praying mantis twelve feet long, killing arms splayed and twisted. Around it, the spined corpses of Mantis-kinden lay where they had fallen, the most feared killers of the old days brought down by crossbow bolts and stingshot.

"Stop," whispered Serge Volente, although she already had. And then, "but who are these that have come here." He was clutching desperately for hope. "Have they come to honour the fallen?"

106

There were a score or so tattered and hunched figures, creeping sidelong across the field of ruin like crabs. At his assessment of them she laughed.

"Oh my princeling, my poor innocent, they have come to rob the dead of what little dignity remains. They are the carrion-pickers, here for rings and broaches, treasured keepsakes, ancestral heirlooms. Because trinkets are the only things of value left to your people." She was going to laugh again, but for a moment one of those shabby ring-cutters was looking at her, and she thought she saw red, bulging eyes beneath its cowl.

"How can you be on their side, the ones who have done this?" Volante's voice brought her back to herself. "You're one of us."

And he was clutching at her arm: even her support was better than no support at all. He was pressing close to her because the alternative was the dead or their parasites.

She took him by the shoulders, feeling him shiver. "There is you and me," she told him, with all the gentleness she could scrape together, "but there is no *us*. There is no great age of magic for you to inherit. All the futures your father saw were lies." And tears came to his eyes at last, as though he had only just understood his parents were dead, "The engines of the Wasps grind forwards," she explained, "and leave *this* in their wake: this is all that is left of magic now – its corpse."

"Then what are you?" he asked her desperately.

"I am a maggot in that corpse," she told him. "But, if you let go all your foolish futures and give yourself to me, I will save you."

His face clenched, and the sobs took hold of him and shook him. Scyla gathered him in her arms, let him bury his face in her shoulder. He was not hers, not quite: he had not stepped through the doorway of that gilded world he had been born to, but the door was open. All she had to do was wait.

She took him to a sheltered dell: within sight of the high castle, close enough to the battlefield that the air bore a faint scent of festering decay. She was stage-managing Volante's fall from grace expertly. She got a fire going, while he sat on the hard ground and stared up at the glittering and cheerless constellation that the Wasps had made of his home. Their little artificial lights were out in force, burning with their acrid, unnatural flames and lighting the way for the Wasps' poor, dull eyes. Eyes that could not see the wonder of the world as Volante's could. Eyes that saw only mundane and pragmatic things, like profit and victory.

"What do you want with me?" His voice was thin, still ragged with weeping.

"You know what." She drew him to her; they sat shoulder to shoulder, hip to hip, her arm about him, and yet the last of that distance still remained.

"But I don't," he complained. "You want this flesh? You want this face, to add to your collection? And then what? How will I live, then?"

"At least you will live," she told him. "You'll live like me. And I will teach you my mystery." As she said the words, it was as though she were a seer herself: the future unfolded before her. "And we will walk together through the lives of others. I will teach you how to live as a maggot, princeling, if you will learn it of me. If you will step down from your broken throne to stand in the dirt with me. For I am all that is left. The Wasps pillage your home of its treasures, and you are what I carry away from the wreck. But you must surrender to me. You must be mine."

And he stood at the threshold, trembling at this new world she offered him. It was a world of bones and dust, but it was all the world there was.

Then a new voice came to them from beyond the reach of their fire. "In the old days," it said, sepulchral and sharp, "there were many paths to magic."

She had her knife in her hand, but when the newcomer showed himself she could not attack him. His eyes reflected the light back red, and his skin took no life from the flames. His forehead bore a birthmark or a blotchy scar, save that it shifted like liquid beneath the translucence of his skin.

"Who are you?" Scyla demanded.

"You make an eloquent case," he said softly, folding himself crossed-legged across the fire from her.

"What do you want?" As though there could be any doubt.

"Young prince," the newcomer whispered to Volante, "your father had high hopes for you."

The boy was staring at him, rigid with fear.

"In the old days, men lived in fear," the ragged man went on. "Tell me of your histories, young prince. Tell me your oldest tales." But Volente would not speak, and so he continued, "They huddled about fires like this, and they looked out at the darkness. And the darkness held many terrors: the magics of night, and death, and blood." And he smiled slightly, and his lips showed needle teeth, thin and sharp as a fish's.

"Go," Scyla spat out, drawing that crimson gaze to herself.

"But you have been so good as to bring the prince out here to meet me," the creature told her.

"He's *mine*." *Almost. Almost he was mine.*

"The Prince of the Golden Future," the old man breathed. "But now the Wasps have stolen your gold, and what future have you left?"

"I will give him a future!" Scyla snapped.

Again that serrated smile. "One where he will bring about a new age of magic?"

"There is no age of magic." Volente sounded like a dying man. "The Light Eternal has gone out, all across the Commonweal. Why should I not be a ghost in this woman's dead world?"

And a fierce shout of joy boiled up within Scyla but, before she could give voice to it, the old man spoke again.

"Oh, young prince, how could you think such a thing? Or course there is a new age of magic. We stand on its very brink."

The silence that followed his words was like a well without end.

"In the beginning there was night, and death, and blood," and a ribbon of tongue touched across the tips of those needle teeth. "And then the first Monarch of the Commonweal gathered all that was bright and glorious about her, and cast back the darkness, and swore that her nation of light and joy would endure for a thousand years." He laughed softly. "But a thousand years have been and gone, my prince, and province after province falls beneath the boots of the Wasps, who know no light but the sun and that which their artifice makes. And so the light of your people, that has been guttering these many years, is put out like a candle." He mimed it, withered lips pursing to blow. "But even the Wasps know what happens when you put out a light," he added with a hungry glee. "Even the Wasps know to fear the darkness."

Scyla's hand was tight about her knife-hilt, but she couldn't move.

"And your people have forgotten the battles they fought, all those years ago," the old man stated. "You forget that night, blood and death are magic too, and though your high-burning fires banished them to the edges of the world, what will happen, now those fires are out? Let the Wasps light as many lamps as they can. All they achieve is to cast more shadows."

"What are you saying?" Volente asked him, voice raw.

"A new age is coming, boy." The ragged apparition hunched forwards towards him, the firelight reflecting in his eyes. "A terrible age, of horror, of despair. An age of suffering and fear to spark nightmares from the Wasps and their victims alike. But it shall be an age of magic for all that. Not your fading fires, but magic nonetheless."

The old man gestured derisively at Scyla. "You can diminish, and become a husk of a thousand faces, none of them your own, picking over corpses until you are no more than a corpse yourself, inside. Like this one." And he spared her a look at last, from those blood-coloured eyes. "Or you can realise the destiny your father saw in you. You can give up your power to feed a new age of magic. Not a new dawn, perhaps, but a new dusk."

She felt Volente tremble in her arms and tried to hold tight to him. The distance between them, that had always been there, only grew greater and greater until he was standing before the ragged man, so deep in his shadow that the firelight barely reached him at all.

"My father..." he got out: a plaintive, lost cry.

"Your father was so blinded by his own light, he could not see," the old man whispered. "He could not see how dark the path is that you will walk."

"Wait." Scyla was on her feet, useless knife still in hand. "Wait, Volente, princeling, please..." And she wished, she dearly wished that somewhere inside her was even the slightest spark of that light magic his people had espoused. Even the faintest gleam of it would have driven the haggard creature away, and made Volente hers.

When those violet eyes turned on her, she saw herself, her true face, in them: her true face as it would be, if she had worn it for all the mean and bloody things she had done. The sight had her cringing back, hand thrown up to blot it out.

And they were gone, when she next dared look. Her golden boy was lost to the shadows. He would rather let his life's blood feed the dark, than stay with her. *But how will I live?* he had asked, and now the question echoed in her ears, in her own voice, and it occurred to her that, whatever it was she had been doing these last ten years or more, it had not been living.

Sympathy for the devil? Three major villains of the early books turn up here, but in the novels Scyla never quite gets the moments of redemption that Thalric, and even Uctebri, are allowed. This story goes some little way to making up for that. And the war, of course, goes on. The great battle at the start of this story breaks the back of the Commonweal resistance and it's all downhill from there. What remains, then? The renewed age of magic that Uctebri predicts. For those who reach the end of Seal of the Worm, *you decide.*

The Dreams of Avaris

Roven was a tough guy and Merric was a killer and Skessi was just an annoyance, and they were the bad part of the deal, but me and my partner had been in Wasp cells at the time, and finding a couple of Wasps willing to go absent without leave for a private errand had been all the luck we could scrape together. It was better than slavery. I'd been born poor in Siennis, way down south, and I know everything that one Spider-kinden can teach another about slavery. I was bought and sold from when my mother had parted with me at age five to when I'd cut the throat of the latest merchant to offer me for sale, and I fled the Spiderlands after that because the merchant was an Aristoi man. Back then the Commonweal had seemed a nice peaceful place to pull a few scams and get rich. That was right before the Wasp Empire got the same idea, only on a much larger scale.

From that point, the Dragonfly Commonweal had become an overly exciting place, and I'd have made tracks south, or north, or anywhere, if not for the money. There was money in other peoples' suffering. The Wasps were chewing up great tracts of Commonweal land, scooping up whole villages' worth of slaves, winning hard-fought battles, enduring the keen Commonweal winters. They were men, those Wasp soldiers, and men had needs. A light-footed trader in certain luxuries could make a living out of drink and whores and second-hand Dragonfly souvenirs. If I watched my step: watching one's step was a difficult proposition even for a Spider-born. The Wasp officers had short tempers. Every so often a trader in dubious goods would be taken up, stock confiscated and leg-irons applied with professional speed and care. There was no appeal. The Wasps accorded other kinden no rights, nor even the status of a human being. Everyone else was fair prey.

My name's Avaris, and I've never stayed still long enough to have to change it. My partner was a lean old Dragonfly called Gatre Fael who'd been robbing his kinsmen up and down the roads and canals since long before the Wasps took an interest. Our game was black guild trading and a lot of different versions of selling the Monarch's Crown to people, which makes sense when you know there's no such thing, but you'd be amazed how many people don't know. We'd been working together three years now: my mouth and his knowledge of the land, until we landed up in the north-eastern end of the Principality of Sial Men, and in irons, and in trouble.

We'd done a fair trade, and had missed just one step. We'd passed through the Wasp camps peddling our seedy wares, bringing flesh and firewater to bitter, bloodied soldiers who had been fighting, some of them, a full ten years without seeing their homes and wives. It was not that the war was going badly: to the generals and the folks back home it was stride after stride of victory for the legions of Black and Gold. To the soldiers it was fighting a numberless and fiercely determined enemy, bringing Imperial rule to village after village of bitter, surly peasants, months of trail rations and harsh discipline, the bite of each year's snow and ice, the red-washed memories of what war had made them do. Even Wasp-kinden started to feel the bloodstains, after ten years without mercy.

We never knew what it was that had seen us taken up, stripped of our goods and slung into slave-cells. It was simply one of those things that happened to people, that you heard about, and this time the people it happened to were us. We had planned for this, though. Gatre Fael had a caper, a good one we had been waiting months to spring, and with slavery our only other option, why not spring it now? *Riches beyond riches*, Fael had said. Riches beyond riches indeed, but our target was behind Wasp lines, now, and somehow it had never seemed worth the journey.

"It'll be worth the journey," I had explained to Roven and Merric. "It's a fair step, but riches, Sergeant, riches. They used to bury them well-heeled back in the bad old days."

It helped that Roven, the sergeant, had heard something of this. He opined, offhand, that some officer in the engineers he knew had struck old gold excavating some Commonweal lord's broken-up castle. "Vaults of it, he said," Roven explained. "Just bodies and gold." Merric had looked interested.

"I don't know, though," Gatre Fael had said, his lean face twisting, the colour of gold itself. "Disturbing the dead."

"Disturbing the dead what?" Roven had grunted.

The Dragonfly had shrugged. "They say... bad things happen, when you open the oldest tombs. The makers protected their wealth with curses, and the dead aren't always that dead."

And the Wasps had jeered at that, and the seed was planted in their minds.

I could talk forever and Fael knew the land, and that got both of us sprung from the cells and travelling overland north, heading for the mountains. Roven and Merric were sick of campaigning, they said, or of campaigning places where there was too much risk and not enough gold. Both of them were swearing blind they wished they'd signed on with the Slave Corps. Who cared if everyone hated you when you were that rich? Money bought back all the respect that a slaver's uniform lost you, was the way they put it. As for Skessi, he just turned up when we were two days out. Skessi was Fly-kinden, a scout attached to the Fourth and a nosy bastard by anyone's book. He'd heard somehow that Roven and Merric had something on, and he turned up threatening to shop them to their officers unless he was dealt in. Nobody much liked that, but Skessi could fly faster even than Gatre, and he was a wary little sod, and it didn't seem we had much choice. It was odds on whether the officers would declare Roven deserter anyway, especially after he'd had it away with four horses and a pack-beetle, but if he came back rich, well, that would smooth over a lot of rough waters. Besides, there were just so *many* Wasps forging west even as winter came on that it seemed possible that two soldiers could slip off on a frolic of their own and just claim to have got left behind. That was what Roven was counting on. As for Merric, he was happy enough to follow along, and if he got the chance to open my or Fael's throat, well, that would be a bonus. Merric was like that, and he liked that. He was a simple man with simple pleasures, and would have been a perfect Wasp soldier if he'd had the slightest interest in listening to orders.

The plan, when me and Fael had first made the plan, had been to hightail it over here on our twosome, but it turned out our friends from the army were worth something after all. We ran into trouble twice. The first was with the Slave Corps, but Roven straightened that out. The second was with brigands, who had been having a field day since the Commonweal soldiers gave up these lands without a fight. About a dozen lean, ragged Grasshopper-kinden swept down on us from a tree-clogged ridge, with two Mantis warriors in the vanguard. Roven's sting picked off one in a flash of golden fire, and Merric killed the other. He killed the Mantis sword to sword, too, with the Mantis blade near twice as long as his, and that gave me and Fael plenty to think about. The Grasshoppers had leapt and flown and run as soon as their leaders were down.

Still, the plan didn't call to split the loot five ways, and on the journey me and Fael had been given plenty of chance to talk about just what to do about that. "High stakes, high risk," Fael had said, but it turned out it was just one of our usual stock in trade scams after all, only played taut as a bowstring, and for real.

So that, and two tendays' sullen travel through the cold crisp air and the occasional flurry of early snow, put us here, looking at the castle. This was an old one, and like a lot of them it had been left to rot a long time ago. No Wasp army had been forced to besiege this place. The walls were crumbling, their tops gappy and uneven like broken teeth. One face had come down entirely, leaving three tottering sides of uneven stones, internal architecture laid out in sheared floors, traceries of fallen walls, windows and doorways gaping like dead eyes.

"Don't know why you people bothered with these things," Roven spat, jabbing Fael. "Half-dozen trebuchet and a leadshotter, and they come down a treat."

How strange a thought, I remember thinking, having one of my philosophical fits on me, *that sufficient Wasp artillery can do the work of centuries. Is there a precise exchange rate, a year-value one can assign to a catapult? How many decades wear is a solid ball from a leadshotter worth?*

"We didn't build them," Fael said, which prompted a reflective pause. It was news to me too. The Commonweal was dotted with these castles, tall stone keeps and towers, inward-leaning at the top to defend against aerial attackers. The Dragonflies had made much use of them as strong-points during the war, although Roven's assessment of their longevity was a fair one. Everyone knew that the structures were very old, and these days the Dragonflies built flimsy stuff out of wood and screens that looked like a strong wind would blow it away. This was the first suggestion I'd heard that the castles were not originally *theirs* though.

"Grew like mushrooms, did they?" Skessi jeered, winging close for a moment. Fly-kinden flew, it was true, but Skessi seemed to have unlimited reserves of Art to call on. He was in the air almost every waking moment.

"We were not the first," Fael said airily, "to call these places home. Especially here near the mountains. There were ancient powers who taught us our ways and blessed the first Monarch and bade us found the Commonweal, but they were not our kinden. They were great masters, whose magic could reshape the world, command the skies. They had the castles built, for while they lived amongst us, they loved to dwell in cold stone." By now I'd figured what he was doing, and just nodded along.

"Right, whatever," said Roven, but uneasily. The great broken edifice before us had a forlorn, tragic feel to it. Evening had fallen by that point, and Merric chose that moment to start setting up camp. Nobody suggested plumbing the place at night.

"Where's this loot of yours?" Roven would ask, though, by moonlight. "Can't see there's much left of any treasury."

"Crypts," I explained blithely. "It's the loot of the dead. The family that ruled here in yesteryear laid out its dead in state, and in gold and jewels."

"And maybe those from before are laid out here as well," Fael muttered in dark tones. "The ancient nameless ones. They can lie in the earth forever, they say, and yet wake again, if they must."

"Enough of that talk. We're not superstitious savages like your lot," Roven growled. Merric's fire shadowed his face, but the corner of Skessi's mouth was twitching, and Merric himself had his sword held close, as if for comfort. The gutted castle loomed impartial over all, black against a darkening sky.

We went in next morning, once dawn and a bottle of war-loot wine had emboldened the Wasps. Fael would go first, with Skessi hovering at his shoulder, and then the Wasps with me in arm's reach, in case of funny business. The Imperials had a couple of hissing gas lanterns, one of which was forced on me. If it had been just the two of them, matters would have been easier, but Skessi's eyes were as good in the dark as mine.

Still, after some searching and shifting, the plan proved its worth by providing a passage into the earth that was only partially choked with fallen stones. It was a sheer drop, but Fael's wings carried him down there easily enough. Skessi didn't look keen to follow, but a dirty look from Roven convinced him, and he fluttered down after.

"Where'd you and he hear about this place?" Roven growled, one ear cocked for a report.

"We turned over a castle crypt where your lot had been. Good business: Empire doesn't know that's where the good stuff is, half the time. Only we found clues, there. The nobles had a branch lived over here, 'til they died out. Rich as rich, Fael reckoned, and who's been here to dig it up, but us?"

"Local boys didn't seem so shy," Roven pointed out. "How'd you know they've not had it all?"

"Oh, you won't find any locals willing to go into a noble family's crypts," I told him lightly. "Not with the curses."

"You don't believe that," nothing but a growl deep in Roven's throat.

"Oh we're all civilised sorts from the Spiderlands," I said. "Still, makes you think, doesn't it?"

"Come on down," came Skessi's distant call, and we did so, the Wasps lowered on spread wings, and me hand over hand down the wall. The gaslamps threw guttering shadows across walls made of irregular stones that still fit into each other so tight you'd not get a blade in.

"This is never just for the dead," Roven spat. "Too much work. Burn 'em or bury 'em, but not all this digging and masonry."

"Reckon they took their dead seriously, back then," I put in. Fael and Skessi were already ahead, but it was so pitchy down there that even they had so stay in the edge of the lantern light. I wasn't sure then that this wasn't just some kind of grain store. Fael was leading strong, but it wouldn't have done to show we weren't sure. I was as much in the dark as Roven right then.

I'd have been able to pacify the Wasps, I think, had we turned up nothing but a few jars of rice that first day, but some kind of luck was with us - good or bad, your call - because Fael found some gold.

It was in some niches in the wall, and there wasn't much, but it was enough to make us look good. No bodies, mind, just a little trinketry: broaches, rings. I caught Fael's eye, because of the two plans we were running right then, the first one - the get rich one - had turned out sunny. That stuff we'd read in that other old castle looked to have been true after all, just like I told Roven. Of course, the second plan, the new one, would need a bit of work.

Roven and Merric confiscated all that glittered, although I'd bet Skessi pocketed a handful as well, and then there was nothing for it but for Fael to press on. Every so often there was a niche, and sometimes there was a piece of loot there, and sometimes there wasn't. Then Fael had yelled out, his wings taking him up so fast he bounced off the ceiling and ended up scrabbling away on his backside as something reared up over him. The Wasps' stings flashed, blinding bright down here, and then things went quiet. I helped Fael get to his feet, and he looked shaken. It had been a centipede, and living proof of how well you can live eating roaches and pillbugs and silverfish: ten feet long if it was an inch. Not a man-eater, but the poison in those fangs would have finished Fael for sure, and, anyway, centipedes are bad luck in the Commonweal, because of old history.

We went on a bit slower after that. The roof was lower, for a start, and the walls had become oddly slick and nasty to touch. The floor was slippery, and sloping too, and the lanterns didn't seem to be giving out enough light even for me. I could hear the two Wasps breathing harsh and hoarse in my ear, and a lot of other little scuttlings and scrabblings as well. Nobody was much looking forward to stepping on the next centipede, or whatever other venomous residents we might disturb. You didn't get scorpions so much, not in the Commonweal, but my little spider brothers certainly put in an appearance and I didn't have the Art to warn them off. Skessi was sticking close to the light, now. He might not have the fear of the dark that the Wasps had, but he was somewhere he couldn't make much use of his wings. In the Lowlands the Fly-kinden love little tunnels. Their warrens are mazes of chambers and narrow vertical drops and the like that make it impossible for any bigger kinden to get around. I think Imperial Fly-kinden don't like being enclosed so much. Certainly Skessi wasn't at all fond of the experience.

Then came the bad news. The whole thing led to a wall: a dead end.

We argued then, or at least the Wasps threw accusations and we tried to defend ourselves. The loot we'd found already might as well not have been there. They wanted the big haul, worth absconding from the army for. Harsh words were spoken, a free and frank exchange of views, until Merric got free and frank enough to shoot at Fael. His sting went wide, from poor light and Fael throwing himself flat, but it knocked a chunk out of that wall, a chunk the size of your hand.

I won't swear something moved, past that gap, but Skessi was shouting that it had, and then a great deal was moving all at once because the tunnel saw fit to collapse.

Not all of it, and not all at once, but Fael just pitched forwards into what was suddenly quite a big hole, too many stones and stuff in the air to use his wings. I felt the earth beneath me shift and I scrabbled back and back, Art-clinging from stone to stone and feeling each one move as I trusted it. One of the lanterns smashed and the other one went out, and it was all suddenly very black and everyone was shouting.

We got to a stage when the only noise was us, though, and all the stone that was going anywhere had gone. Roven had somehow shielded his dead lantern with his body to save the glass, and now he coaxed a little light from it. The place had undergone severe redecoration. We counted the two Wasps and me, and Skessi had got clear of course because his kind always do.

"Fael?" I called. I had no idea what shape the plan was in, just then. The plan needed Fael, for starters.

"Here," came a weak voice, and then, "Down here, quick!" with extreme urgency.

I started forwards and Roven came with me, lantern out. The first thing we saw was that the place was crawling with critters. There were little centipedes, finger-length, and worms and slugs and some kind of palm-wide albino cricket that just looked bad to touch. The tunnel we were in had just gone, a few feet ahead, but it had *gone* into a lower level that none of us had guessed at. Roven tried to get some light down there, and the first thing we saw were the bodies.

I hadn't thought Fael was telling the truth, perhaps he hadn't either. There hadn't been bodies in the other place, just a little loot and the writing that put us onto this one. There were bodies here though. Before the stones had fallen on them they had been standing up in armour, and one of them was still on its feet, propped up in an alcove with its bony hands about a sword-hilt. The rest were in pieces, and the dried skulls seemed to leer and scream out at us when the lantern-light hit them. There was plenty else to catch the light, though, and it was mostly gold. Fael was lying there surrounded by a Monarch's ransom. The armour the corpses had been wearing was all precious metals and enamel and gems, and there were other pieces: jewellery, masks, inscribed tablets, and all of it enough for any two of us to live on till the end of our days. No coins, of course, because even these days the Commonweal runs off barter and goodwill, but there were lots of these little ingots of gold, all the same, that I'd never seen before. There were weapons, too, fine ones, and some pieces of gilded armour that were big enough for one of the giant Mole Cricket-kinden to wear, and were surely just for show. There were spread quivers of white-shafted arrows with elegant, pearl-hafted bows and dragon-swords with inscribed blades.

"Start passing it up," Roven snapped, a barbarian at heart, and he signalled for Merric to go down to help. Merric was having none of it, though. He was staying well back from the edge. Something had spooked him. I thought it was just the danger of another collapse, at the time.

"I don't think I can fly, not with any weight," Fael said. He was sitting up, and I couldn't see any obvious hurt. I got it: this was part of the plan.

"I'll go down and help," I said, but Roven pushed me back, grabbing Skessi by the collar before the fly could scoot away.

"Starting shifting it up here," he said, virtually throwing the Fly down the pit. Fael was already kneeling by then, gathering stuff up into a sack. The Fly ended up hovering above the room's centre, and in a rasping voice asking, "What's through there?"

There was an archway, you see. The pit Fael had fallen into wasn't just on its own. It must connect to some other set of tunnels. The archway was big, ten feet at the keystone. The whole chamber was big for that matter. It dwarfed the dead guardsmen someone had set down there.

"Forget through there," Roven snapped. "Just bring up the treasure."

Skessi grabbed the first sack, and very nearly couldn't get it airborne. With a supreme flurry of wings he lifted it to where Roven could snag it, and then Roven would have tilted head-forwards into the pit if Merric hadn't grabbed him. By that time Fael had a second sack of loot just about ready, but he was doing a lot of looking about and twitching, and I took that as plan two, part two.

"Did you hear that?" he called out abruptly. Skessi dropped the sack he'd just been passed and vaulted into the air again.

"There was nothing!" Roven bawled. "Bring the loot up you little pin-sucking bastard!"

"I heard it!" Skessi squeaked. "Something's coming." He was fumbling for the sack.

"Nothing's coming!" Roven shouted back. I thought he was shouting so loud to block out anything that he *might* hear. Merric had retreated a good ten feet back down the tunnel, eyes wide. He'd have run, I think, if the lantern hadn't still been by Roven's feet.

Skessi got airborne again, straining furiously to lift the sack up to us. Behind him, Fael gave out a dreadful shriek.

"Avaris!" he cried. "Run! Just run! Leave the loot and run!"

That was my cue. I followed his exclamation with a blood-curdling wail and just bolted, and to my glee Merric was already outpacing me to the exit. It was pitch dark, but there was only one way to go, and we went. Skessi overtook me before I hit daylight, keening like a madman. I heard Roven behind, lumbering and cursing and bouncing off the walls. The last we heard from Fael was a high, rending scream, wordless and filled with horror. I could barely stop grinning.

It was still daylight outside, of course, and that put a little bravery back into them. We rendezvoused at the camp, where the hobbled horses were skittish and the beetle was practically dancing with anxiety, and I saw that the plan hadn't quite worked.

I had to hand it to Roven for utter single-mindedness. He had fled just as we had fled, but he'd had both the self-possession and the sheer Art-fired strength to drag both sacks of treasure along with him. We were out and we were rich, which was all good for the Wasps, and not much fun for me. I had no illusions that they'd give me any kind of share.

We stayed and watched the opening for some time, but there was no sign of Fael of course. The other two looked to Roven for ideas, and they were relieved as anything when he said, "We move out. We've got what we came for." Merric broke camp, and we loaded up the beetle. It was a plodding old thing, that beetle. It could keep up with the horses walking but not at a gallop. There was no chance of using it as a quick getaway, not laden like that.

However, Fael and I, we'd talked about this. The plan could survive a few knocks. It just meant it was going to be difficult, and we'd have to do some things we might regret, but I was ready for that. I'd regretted most of my life so far, save hitching up with Gatre Fael, so why should this caper be any different? Skessi was already doing my work for me, as though he was in on it. "I saw them," he was insisting, mostly because it meant he was getting out of doing any work. "I saw them coming for us. The white shapes. White shapes with grey wings."

"You saw nothing," Roven told him disgustedly. When Skessi went to say more, Roven put an open palm his way, and the Fly shut up. The Wasp looked at me next. "You see anything, Spider-born?"

"I see the weather's turned," I told him mildly, and it had. The sky was scudding white clouds, not the white of light weather but heavy with snow. I thought of the path back to Roven's army, twenty days of hills and forests and solitude. We might pull it off yet.

We mounted up. Skessi preferred to stay airborne, letting Fael's horse trudge behind mine as mute testimony to our losses. We made poor time that day. The wind was against us, cutting coldly and keenly enough that the horses didn't want to walk straight into it and would veer off every time they could. The snow came shortly after midday, first a light feathering of big, slow flakes, then flurrying and blowing into our faces until we could see nothing of the road, barely anything of our horses' heads. The beetle was leashed to Roven's horse, and a dozen times I thought of trying to cut the traces, to lead the thing off into the snow. It was going slower than ever in the colder weather, though, and I was too worried about getting lost myself. I could freeze to death as easily as the next man, and the Wasps were better equipped to get a fire going.

We stopped before nightfall because Merric had found a wooded hollow that would keep the fire's heat in. The wind was really up, then, and when it hit the trees it made all kinds of sounds: my cue again. When we were all sitting round the best fire Merric could make I jumped up all of a sudden, meaning so did they, swords out and palms clear.

"Did you hear that?" I called over the wind.

"What?" Roven snarled at me.

"Voices!"

His look was all belligerence on the surface, but that surface was thin ice. "Whose?"

"They were calling my name!" I insisted.

"Your Dragonfly?" Roven demanded. I just shook my head dumbly. He tried out a disgusted expression, but I could tell they were all listening. The problem was, once you've said a thing like that, well, the wind makes all kinds of noises, out there in the wilds. I just hunched closer to the fire and told myself in no uncertain terms that *under no circumstances could I really hear my name in the wind.* I've always had an active imagination and it's never done me much good.

Then it was Roven's turn to jump up, sword out, and we repeated the whole pantomime. This time, when he insisted he'd seen a shape out there, everyone was supposed to believe him.

"Bandits," he snapped out. "Got to be. They've seen the fire." Nobody objected to this, although I think you'd have had to be within burning distance to do it. "Merric, go scout. You find anyone, kill them."

Merric didn't look happy about that, but Roven was a sergeant, and he was just a soldier, and they beat that into the Wasp army with big lead hammers. This, too, was the plan, but it was that part of the plan we hadn't really talked much about.

Merric bundled himself up in a cloak, a grey-white garment that would hide him nicely in this weather. He had his shortsword drawn but he led with his offhand, palm-out. Crouched low to the ground he went, with one backward glance at Roven.

He didn't come back. By the time that was clear, the night was well and truly upon us and nobody was going to search for him. The three of us, Wasp, Fly and Spider, just looked at each other mutely over the fire and listen to the storm call off its roster.

Merric was still absent the next morning when we set off, trailing two horses now, and with the snow much decreased. We caught up with the man soon enough, though. He was waiting for us, in a way.

It was a long time before Roven spoke. I don't know how long he'd known Merric or what he felt about him, but he took a good, long look at what had been laid out for us. It made me wish for more snow.

He was strung between two trees, held there by some tying of the whip-like branches themselves, arms and legs spread out at unnatural angles. The pieces of his armour, the plates of the Light Airborne, were hanging off, scratched and dented. He had been quite hollowed out. You could see his spine through his belly. His eyes were gone too, and his tongue. His head was back, his mouth was open, and you could almost hear the scream in your mind. It was a real professional job. The Wasps themselves seldom put that much effort into stringing up a corpse. It's just crossed pikes and leave them to sag, most of the time.

Skessi was swearing under his breath now, almost constantly. "On," Roven said at last, and kicked at his horse even though it needed no real encouragement. I followed right along, feeling absent eyes watch me go. This was the plan, but the details had turned my stomach. I knew the reasoning, but still, there's such a thing as going too far. Of course, Merric would have been dead before all that window-dressing happened, but even so...

We made better time that day, although the ruin was still on the horizon when we stopped to camp, The wind was picking up again, and I tried to block my ears. "Avaris! Run!" it called, but the wind will say all sorts of things if you let it. After dark the snow crept back too, shrouding the world beyond the firelight in a blur of gusting white, not as fierce as yesterday, but it cut us off from the world, severed us from it totally. As the wind formed words, so the snow was apt to make shapes, and it wasn't long before I stopped looking.

Skessi was near breaking. He'd been high-strung even before we found Merric, and around the fire that night he ran out of brave.

"I want my share!" he burst out with. Roven gave him a long, level look.

"What's that?"

"Give me my share of the loot, now," Skessi insisted. "I'm not crawling along here like this. Give me mine, and I'm out of here."

"You'll keep pace, soldier," Sergeant Roven told him. Skessi was shaking his head very fast.

"Oh no," he got out. "Not a hope. You're going to die. They're going to catch you. Not me. I'm fast. Give me my share."

"A whole third of what we've got?" said Roven, grinning. "Little man, that'd weigh more than you do."

"Give me what I can carry. Keep the rest."

"How generous." Roven stood, still trying for casual, but Skessi skipped back a few steps and abruptly his sword was out.

"You cross me, Roven, I'll tell! I'll tell your lieutenant about what you've been up to. I'll tell them you killed Merric." The Fly was in the air now, wings a-blur, and I heard the wind call, "Skessi! Skessi!"

Roven shot, but Skessi was faster, the bolt of fire streaking past him. The Fly launched for the campsite's edge, towards the dark where Roven would not be able to track him, but he tumbled from the air even as he did so, ending up a crumpled heap at the edge of the firelight.

Roven, for whom the edge of the firelight was a good deal closer, lit his lantern with patient care. When he stood he had a hand facing me. I spread my own, showing that I had nothing. He jerked his head the way Skessi had gone.

The arrow that had transfixed the Fly was dead white, both the shaft and the fletchings, that were made from shimmering moth scales. I knew where I'd seen arrows just like that, not so long ago. So did Roven.

"I get it." He'd grabbed me before I could step back, snagged a hand about my collar and hauled me close. His face was uglier than ever up close, and his breath stank. "I get it," he repeated, shaking me for emphasis. "Your mate, the turncoat 'Wealer."

I shook my head, but he was shaking it for me pretty hard so he probably didn't see. "I don't know how he killed Merric," Roven growled, "but he surely won't get me, *or* the treasure." With contemptuous strength he threw me to the ground and fixed me in place with the threat of his open palm. "And as for you," he said.

And stopped. He made a sound then I never heard from a Wasp: a little, broken sound deep in his throat.

He turned from me and ran for the animals, stumbling and almost falling into the fire. He got to the beetle even as I struggled to my feet. He was wrenching at the animal but it dug all six legs in and would not move. I could just hear Roven's voice shrieking at it, see his mouth opening and closing. At last he just wrenched at the sacks. One of them tore open, spilling the wealth of ages over the trampled ground of the campsite. The other came away whole and he shouldered it with a supreme effort and was gone, obliterated by the snow, lurching away under his priceless burden.

I crawled back to the campsite, for the fire's warmth more than anything else. Even before I got there I heard him scream. And scream. It went on for some short while. I just took the time to gather my wits. The plan seemed to be going ahead full tilt, but in ways I hadn't really imagined.

When I looked up, he was there: Galtre Fael in a cloak of blown snow across the fire from me. I nodded wearily and reached to start gathering up the spilt loot.

"Stop," he said. "Avaris, listen to me. Do not touch the treasure, not even one piece of it. Just go, Avaris, go. Please listen to me."

A cold feeling came to me, but it was disappointment, not fear. I stood slowly, sensing the end of what little good times I had known. "Fael," I told him, "Don't." I reached down for a piece of treasure, a broach worked into the shape of a beetle with spread wings.

"Avaris!" he insisted. "Not one piece! Please!"

"Don't play it on me," I told him. "Fael, I practically invented the ghost scam. There's enough for both of us to live like Princes Major. Don't try it on me. There's no need." But I felt sad because, whether he tried it on me or not, we couldn't trust each other now. Our partnership had just been killed as sure as Merric.

"Avaris," Fael said despairingly, and his friends turned up.

Pale shapes with grey wings, but I can do better than that. Ancient armour, hollow eyes, the military prime of the Commonweal's early glories, pearly bows and white arrows, crescent-headed glaives and long-hafted swords with inscribed blades. Behind them, and mercifully half-lost in the snow, some taller thing, some greater figure, man-shaped but pale and regal and ten feet tall, armoured in mail that would put to shame a sentinel for bulk and a merchant-lord for precious stones.

"Fael." I remember very clearly my voice, then, how it shook and twisted.

"It's too late for me," Fael said, "But they have let me intercede for you, for they were of my kinden once." His gesture took in the gaunt-faced warriors about him, most definitely not the looming shadow behind.

And I fled, then. I fled without ever having touched the smallest part of the greatest hoard I have ever seen, and I never saw Galtre Fael again, nor heard any word of him.

And I wonder, now… well, at this remove, I'm sure you can guess what I wonder. I wonder whether my friend truly spent his last free moments, facing absolute annihilation, bartering for my continued life and health, and if so, I cannot measure what I owe him in all the world's riches.

But I wonder, too, whether the second plan, the plan Fael and I had that contained the first plan we explained to Roven and the others, I wonder whether that second plan might not have been part of a third plan, known only to Fael.

And I will never know.

"They loved to dwell in cold stone..." People do ask how much I planned Shadows of the Apt *out in advance, and really I should just point them at this story. This was written with 'Ironclads' and 'Spoils of War' at around the time* Empire *was published, and anyone who's read* The Scarab Path *will be able to make a stab at what's going on in the background and who the armoured giant is. Moreover, the business with the Centipede is absolutely pointing at the revelations from the last few books. As a side note, Avaris turns up in* Heirs of the Blade *as one of Dal Arche's brigands, and he tells this very story to his fellows to entertain them. So perhaps it is just a campfire ghost story after all...*

The Prince

There were two other men in Cordwick's cell. One was dead and the other was showing far too many signs of life

When the Wasp-kinden had taken Maille Castle from the Dragonfly-kinden they had taken it mostly intact, and Cordwick was given to understand that the task of turning Commonweal fortification into imperial garrison had fallen to the engineering corps. He gleaned this by what the Wasps had done to the cellars, which spoke volumes of the lengths artificers would go to to stave off boredom.

They had converted the cellars into a prison, being Wasps. Their technical difficulty was that Maille Castle was constructed over a subterranean river. The ancient stones of the fort above formed an arch straddling nothing, a bridge over nowhere, each end soundly founded in the rock, and the middle suspended over the hidden watercourse. Architecturally, it was a piece of genius. Defensively it had been less than useless, and the Imperial Sixth had captured it in just a day. Now the war, which they were calling the Twelve Year War, was done, and the border of the Empire had swept on far from Maille. The place had become a storehouse and a prison and a staging post for the Slave Corps.

The aforementioned cellars were a great vaulted space buried beneath the castle's arch, and floored only with dark water, where the river plunged ten feet into a roiling pool before coursing on between the rocks. Denied a conventional oubliette to store their captives in, the engineers of the Sixth had become ingenious.

Of the men in Cordwick's cell, the dead one, had been Dragonfly-kinden. He had been wounded before he was lowered in and had died shortly after and, despite Cordwick's vocal complaints, none of the guards had seen fit to remove him. The third man was the problem. The third man had been brought in bound, wrist and ankle, spitting death and vengeance. His legs were already free, and he was slowly working at the leather thongs pinning his hands, wearing them away against the rough iron of the bars, gnawing at them with his teeth. His eyes were fighting mad. He was itching to kill someone. The barbed spines of his arms, that had made such short work of his ankle-bonds, were twitching and fretting, demanding to be slaked with blood. The problem was that the cell itself was shackled shut, an impediment that was never going to yield to spines and teeth. The further problem was that the cell they were in was an open lattice cage suspended over the inky waters of the pool below by a mere rope, which rope was attached to, by Cordwick's estimate, a particularly fine example of a Shewner version 5 winding engine. The *real* problem was that the only blood available for the raging, very-close-to-escaping prisoner to paint the bars with was Cordwick's. Having done so, the prisoner would be free to do nothing but, by dint of some effort, sever the rope and send himself and the two corpses -- one older, one fresher -- hurtling to a watery tomb. The fact that Cordwick Scosser, fellow prisoner, soon-to-be-fresher-corpse and failed thief, would already be dead by this point did not rob the thought of its horror. Death by drowning was a terror to him, even at such a remove.

Cordwick knew Mantis-kinden, or he'd thought he did. He knew the Lowlander Mantids, from closer to home, as brooding, sullen, backward thugs, and that was fine. He had thought that the Commonweal breed was different: quiet, ceremonial, unflappable and usually in service to some Dragonfly noble or other. His cell-mate was a Commonweal local but he seemed to be the exception to the rule. To be blunt, he seemed the sort of mad killer that even the Lowlanders would have felt was overdoing it.

"Look, you Mantis-kinden like stories, don't you? I know a hundred of them, heroic and tragic as you like," he tried. The Mantis prisoner continued to worry away at his bonds, which were looking alarmingly frayed. Other conversational gambits that he had rebuffed included "Those Wasps are bastards, aren't they?" and "So, what are you in for?"

My mother always said it would end like this. It was an assertion that did not bear too much scrutiny. In telling the young Cordwick, on the occasion of his precipitate leaving of home, "You'll come to a bad end, you'll never amount to anything," the old dear probably hadn't been envisaging quite these circumstances, but Cordwick was willing to bet that she'd take the credit for prophecy if she ever found out.

There was a taut little sound that was leather giving way under great pressure, following by one that was a Beetle-kinden thief whimpering. He had tried calling for the guards several times already. Now he opened his mouth one last time as the Mantis turned to him, his hands free and on his face an expression of morbid delight. Cordwick's voice died in his throat.

A second later he screamed with fright and released tension as someone landed atop the cage. The Mantis lunged upwards instantly and had the newcomer been an incautious Wasp then things might have gone badly. As it was she was a Fly-kinden and four feet up the rope on the instant, leaving the Mantis clutching at empty air.

She was a neat little thing in a tunic that the hanging lanterns showed as black and gold. Her hair was cut short like a soldier's, too, but something about her had already given the lie to that. Cordwick was good at reading people nine times out of ten. Of course, the tenth time was always the important one...

"Enough of that," she snapped at the Mantis. "Evandter, yes?"

The Mantis crouched below her, poised to spring as though there were not solid iron bars between them. "I am Evandter. Kill me or die, Fly, or go. You are of no interest to me."

The Fly-kinden studied him. "You're the famous Evandter, are you? Scourge of a dozen principalities? Rogue and kidnapper, murderer, enemy of princes? Who'd have thought you'd end up in here, eh? I heard you were drunk when they brought you in. Drinking toasts to your own health, was it? Celebrating the fall of the Commonweal?"

A shudder went through Evandter that Cordwick identified as sheer penned rage. *Don't antagonise the bastard!* he thought frantically, but that would be stoking a fire that was already roaring.

"My master has an offer for you," the Fly said.

"I want nothing from your master, Rekef bitch," the Mantis hissed. Cordwick considered this, and decided he agreed. A cocky female Fly-kinden in imperial colours almost certainly led to the Rekef eventually.

"He offers death by the sword," she went on. "I won't say it'll give you a chance to regain your ancestors' approval, because from what I gather you pissed on that a long time ago, but he reckoned you'd rather die fighting than on crossed pikes."

"And what do the Rekef –?"

"He's not Rekef, neither," the Fly said sharply, and then, more softly, "Piss on the Rekef, I say. I'll have naught to do with them."

There was a pause in which her words echoed in the vaulted space. Cordwick craned about, seeking out the single doorway that led up to the castle proper. There were two guards there, always. They had been the object of his desperate pleas since Evandter had started on his bonds. Now they were gone, vanished away.

Evandter's gaze had obviously followed Cordwick's because the Fly said, "Oh they think I'm Rekef right enough. They're not expecting trouble, and I'm good with pieces of paper. When I call them back, they'll come with the keys and you and I will walk out of Maille like old friends, Evandter. What do you say?"

Cordwick saw the Mantis grin death up at her. "Call them," Evandter said. "Set me free."

"Swear, first," the Fly told him, calm as you please. "Swear by the health and life of Nysse Ceann that you will serve my master, not as slave but as sworn bonds warrior."

Evandter had gone utterly still as the name – a Dragonfly woman's name, Cordwick assumed – was uttered. "So," was all the Mantis said.

"Swear," the Fly repeated, "or I go, and you stay."

"You name me murderer and enemy of princes," Evandter growled softly, "and yet you set your life by my word."

"I name you kidnapper, and my master says that by *her* name even your word is good, though it would not be worth a hair else," she replied.

"Then I so swear, and may you and your master regret it all the days of your lives."

"Good enough for me", the Fly said, almost cheerily, and she dropped down to the cage. Evandter made no attempt to strike at her.

"What about me?" Cordwick asked. There was a moment of bewildered silence as Fly and Mantis regarded him.

"Who the spit are you?" the Fly asked eventually.

"Cordwick Scosser of Helleron, procurer," he told her, mustering what dignity he could in a cage too low to stand up in.

"That mean pimp or thief where you come from?" she asked him.

"Procurer of *goods*," he stressed, as if pressing a claim to the aristocracy.

"Well, thief, you're not in my brief. You stay here."

Cordwick, who a moment ago would have been happy enough to share the cage with nothing more threatening than a corpse, suddenly felt the yawning chasm of dark water below him. "Please, you can't just leave me here."

"Doing good deeds for the sake of it got put on hold after the Empire invaded," the Fly told him, without sympathy.

"But I'll be executed, or enslaved!" Cordwick insisted.

"You'll be in good company. It's very fashonable these days. Everybody's doing it." She stood as tall as she could and called out "All right, Sergeant!" in a voice that rolled and resounded across the cavern until the waters claimed it.

"No no," Cordwick said hurriedly. "Look, I don't know what your master's about or who he is or if he's the Rekef or what, but I'm useful, I'm a good thief. I can get in just about anywhere, talking or lock-breaking."

"Yet you're the one on the wrong side of the bars," she pointed out. A Wasp with a lantern had appeared at the portal above.

"*One mistake!* Don't let me rot here just because I slipped up once. Please, I'll serve your master 'til my dying day, please, please don't leave me in here. Don't leave me to the Wasps." A sudden inspiration struck him. "You're Inapt, or you'd have brought the keys yourself. The Mantis is Inapt. Your master, I bet he's Inapt. Locks, machines, door-catches, incendiaries – you want them? I'm your man. Come on now, give me a chance."

Her solemn eyes regarded him, a weight of doubt that seemed too great for her small shoulders to carry. "If I say kill him, will you kill him?" she asked, even as the guard above took wing to come down to them.

"I'll kill him even if you don't, like as not," Evandter said lazily. "Better to tell me if you *don't* want him dead."

The Wasp's wings brought him up on the cage's very edge, as far from Evandter as he could manage. "You're done?"

"I'll take them both," she confirmed and Cordwick felt like weeping in relief.

"Papers only said the Mantis," the Wasp muttered stubbornly, but it was clear he believed her Rekef credentials because he was already fumbling for the keys. Cordwick had never tried to pass himself off as Rekef but he had met a few of the Outlander recently, as he set about his one-man mission to get rich from the Commonweal invasion, and he knew that the regular army held them in utter dread.

"You fly, Beetle?" the woman asked him, as he ended up crouched atop the cage, gripping the bars. She and the Mantis and their jailer were standing there quite happily, heedless of the drop and the water. Cordwick shook his head and saw a suffering expression come to her face, already regretting springing him. Still, if she changed her mind now it would look odd to the Wasps. *Just get me out of the castle,* Cordwick thought, *and then you never need see me again.*

"I'll call for the winch," said the jailer, clearly amused.

There was nothing in the world so lovely as the sun, Cordwick decided as he was led out into it. Even in the stockade that the Wasps had bound about one arm of Maille, where men and machines and beasts jostled for space, the air was cool and fresh, the freedom and space intoxicating. He took deep breaths, turning his face to the sky and squinting against the light.

When he next looked, the Fly was regarding him dubiously, seeing him in good light as a Beetle-kinden man in ragged clothes, just the right side of young, just the wrong side of thin – which still made him relatively slender for his kind – short, slope-shouldered, a mild, dark face and thinning hair. Beside him, Evandter looked like some Bad Old Days personification of death, his dark hair worn long and half-shrouding his lean, angular face, his pale skin laced with random scars. The jagged barbs flexed and jutted from his forearms as though possessed of their own bloodlust, entirely separate from their owner's.

"Lieutenant." A Wasp bustled up, followed by a Grasshopper slave who set down a little table with quill and ink. The Fly-kinden made her mark on a few pieces of paper and the Wasp nodded. "You're sure you're safe with him," he asked, nodding at Evandter and ignoring Cordwick entirely. "I can detail you some guards if you want." He seemed genuinely concerned, but perhaps it was just that he wanted to do right by the Rekef.

"Him?" she scoffed. "Have you heard how many nobles he gutted, the banditry, the raids? He's done more harm to the Commonweal than half the fighting Seventh." She didn't quite claim that Evandter was a Rekef agent all along, but the implication hung in the air clear enough.

When they had trekked far enough for the slopes of the Commonweal countryside to put them out of sight of Maille, the Fly-kinden turned to Cordwick. "You really can't fly?" she asked him.

"My people aren't known for it," he replied, in understatement.

"Then let your feet take you where they will, thief. I can't see you're much use,"

A wave of glad relief washed through Cordwick, only to crash against the intractable wall that was Evandter.

"No," the Mantis said And when the Fly quizzed him he explained, with relish, "The Beetle paid the same price I did for his freedom. If he walks free, then so do I. Otherwise he's bound to the Prince's purpose as I am. Or I'll open his throat now, if you don't want him slowing us down." He had Cordwick's collar instantly, without his arm seeming to move, dragging the Beetle close and putting razor-edged spines to his neck. For a horrifying moment the Fly hesitated, then: "We walk," she said, disgusted either at the Mantis, Cordwick or her own soft-heartedness.

After they had gone a mile or so in stony silence Cordwick judged that her ill temper had ebbed sufficient for him to prompt, "I'm Cordwick Scosser, of Helleron, by the way."

"Yes, you said." She frowned as Cordwick pointedly stretched the silence. "Tesse," she told him shortly.

"And you work for some prince, the Mantis said," he proceeded carefully. Evandter snorted with derision.

This time Tesse's look at him was cruel. "Prince Lowre Darien," she pronounced carefully, and, "Heard of him, I take it?" as Cordwick choked.

Lowre Darien was a name known to a lot of people, mostly imperial soldiers, but the stories had filtered down even to lowly thieves trying to filch war-plunder from its rightful conquerors. Prince Lowre Darien, who had led the coalition of principalities that had smashed the Sixth Army, and who had fought the Empire to a brief standstill outside Shan Real. In a war that was a catalogue of defeats and retreats he was one of the only Commonweal leaders to boast even a halfway success. More stories were told of his personal courage than his military acumen, though. He was the man who could walk in and out of imperial camps like the wind. He freed slaves and killed enemy officers, and Rekef men, especially Rekef men. The Empire had been after him forever, assassins and freelance hunters and the cream of the Outlander, but his name refused to go away and, even now the war was over, word of his exploits kept coming. The Monarch had signed the

Treaty of Pearl in craven surrender but Prince Lowre Darien had not been a signatory and for him the war was still raging.

From death sentence to death sentence, thought Cordwick, because anywhere near Lowre Darien – or even someone pretending to be Lowre Darien – sounded like a mighty unhealthy place to be, but at the back of his mind was a spark of curiosity. To set eyes on the Wasp-killer, the hero of Masaki, the man who stung back: that would be worth a little risk. That would be something to regale his fat, rich friends with, when he was fat and rich himself, and stealing like a merchant steals, rather than like a poor and honest thief.

Whatever Cordwick was expecting, the army of enamel-armoured Mercers, the castle hidden in a wood, the golden splendour of a Commonweal warrior-lord, none of it was there. The tangled stretch of trees that Tesse led them to was in a hollow so rocky that even the locals hadn't tried to step it and plough it, let alone build a secret fort there. Instead of a hundred sworn champions ready to drive the Wasps from Commonweal soil in fulfillment of their destiny, there was one man and one woman, and Cordwick looked at the man two or three times before realising that this was *it*. This was the man himself.

Prince Lowre Darien was lean and slight of frame, like most Commonwealers, although perhaps a little taller than most. His dark hair was raggedly cut, as by a man with a knife and a mirror, and Cordwick reckoned he could see a little grey over the ears. His golden skin was smeared with grime, making him seem older. Instead of a Mercer's scintillating armour or the gold-heavy robes of a nobleman, he was dressed like a successful bandit, hardwearing leather backed with coarse silk that was either dirty or dyed mottled, with a long hauberk of cloth-backed chitin scales and shoulder-guards of the same. Beside him, on the rock he sat on, lay a worn pack and a quiver of arrows. The bow was in his hand, a servicable recurved shortbow, not the elaborate man-high weapon of a noble but that of a bandit who must fight and run. His eyes were the only part of him that convinced Cordwick of who he was. They were the colour of amber, and they held all the noble fire and mastery that every other part of him had been stripped of.

His companion, whoever she was, was not this Nysse woman the Mantis had sworn on. She was a surprise for Cordwick, because she no more belonged in the Commonweal than he did: a slender Moth-

136

kinden, grey-skinned and blank-white-eyed, dark hair intricately plaited into a braid that fell to past her waist. She wore a tunic, breeches and sandals, in the style of the Commonwealers, and they looked strange on her. Her face was inward, clouded with secrets, but in Cordwick's experience that was true of Moths whether they had any secrets or not.

Seeing the Fly-kinden and her baggage approach, Lowre Darien stood like a man readying himself for a fight. Evandter's progress towards him slowed and stopped and the two men regarded one another coolly.

"Prince Darien," Tesse said, but very quietly, and he did not glance at her. Nobody paid any attention whatsoever to Cordwick.

"So you've lost her," Evandter stated flatly. "Seems a shame, after you went to so much trouble to take her back from me."

"The Wasps have her at Del Halle," Darien confirmed. His expression, gazing on the Mantis, was utterly without love. "Well guarded."

"A trap," Evandter said.

Darien nodded. "For me," he agreed, "and yet she is mine, and I must free her."

"And for this you come to me? If she is *yours* why should I help you regain her?"

"Did he swear himself to me?" Darien asked Tesse lightly, and she nodded, too caught up in the tension between the two men to speak.

Evandter sneered. "To the pits with swearing and oaths. Why should I?"

"Because your oath holds only to when we have freed her. If you will cross swords with me then, I will oblige you," Darien told him.

The words transformed the Mantis, just for a moment. In that brief second his mocking expression, all the slouching despite of his stance, had vanished away, and Cordwick had a brief show of a younger man, a brighter one: some Evandter that might have been, had the world not been so very wicked and taught him so well. Then the old snarl was back but the Mantis was nodding. "Lead me, my prince," he invited, with a curl of his lip.

"And who is this?" At last those amber eyes pinned Cordwick through, and the Beetle stammered out his name.

"He's a thief. Cordwick Scosser. Evandter wants to kill him or keep him about. Send him away, I would," Tesse explained, "or let the

Mantis have him."

"Cordwick Scosser." Darien pronounced the Lowlander name carefully. "You understand what we're about, here?"

"Off to rescue some noblewoman," Cordwick replied guardedly.

"To rescue Nysse Ceann, because she and I are promised, because it is my duty, and because I love her," Darien confirmed. "Did you swear yourself to me?"

Did I? Even as he wondered, Cordwick had opened his mouth for the instictive denial, but Evandter said "Yes" before he could say "No."

The Mantis grinned coldly. "Oh he didn't say it as an oath, but his kind never do. Your Fly let him out because he said he would help. 'Serve you to his dying day,' were the words, I think. Free him and I'll kill him as an oathbreaker."

"What is he to you?" Darien asked.

"He talks too much and I want to kill him," Evandter replied. Cordwick looked between the two of them: relics from an age that industry and the Empire were scouring from the face of the world, and yet here he was caught between a prince's duty and a Mantis' bloodlust.

"If it's all the same to you," Cordwick said faintly, "I'll help in the rescue, if that's all right. How far to Del Halle?"

They moved across the face of the Commonweal like fugitives, far from any princely procession that Cordwick had imagined. Then he brought to mind the fact that this countryside, the ditches and the copses, the untilled fields and the hollow, abandoned villages, none of this was the Commonweal any more. The Empire had, after considerable choking and gnawing, swallowed it all. Prince Lowre Darien was dethroned and in the shadow of his enemy. These were the captured principalities, taken in blood, sealed in ink when the Monarch signed the Treaty of Pearl.

They moved more by night than by day, avoided any human contact. Darien hunted for them, his bow bringing down stoneflies or goats gone feral. He moved through the grown-wild land as though he had lived under the stars all his life. Evandter was seldom seen, ranging ahead or dragging behind or off murdering children for all Cordwick knew. Still, whenever they paused or rested or started a sheltered fire, there he was, the professional brigand emerging from the landscape.

The Moth woman was seldom absent from Darien's side and he

conferred with her often. Cordwick understood that she was some manner of advisor, and then that she was some manner of magician, who told Darien where to find game and had found for him the whereabouts of his lost love. Her name was Philomaea, he learned from Tesse, and she had been in Darien's retinue since before the war. If she had dressed for it, she would have been beautiful, but it took Cordwick a while to realise this because she had that quiet, drab look that most Moth-kinden had, all in-looking and severe. He saw what she could be in the rare moments when her face truly came to life, and that was only when she looked directly at Lowre Darien, which was only when he was not looking at her. This was so guttingly tragic that Cordwick, who was used to having people to talk to, wanted to discuss it. As Darien scared him, Philomaea ignored him and Evandter actively wanted to kill him, he was left with Tesse, and he could not talk to Tesse about *that* because, when she stole glimpses of Lowre Darien, her expression was the same.

She was a tough and prickly little thing but she needed to talk too and, although she ventured the occasional lighthearted banter with Darien, there was too much bottled up within her to keep that going. Philomaea ignored her, too, and if Evandter hadn't got as far as threatening her life, he was still not much of a conversationalist. So it was that, when they stopped to rest out the noon hours, under cover and hidden away, she spent her words on Cordwick. They were derisory words, mostly, but it was better than hostile silence. Mostly she mocked his credentials as a thief. How could a Beetle-kinden possibly survive on what those thick fingers could pilfer? This allowed him to ask about her own pedigree. She was Imperial Fly-kinden, as he'd guessed, and she told him she'd done five years as a Consortium clerk, in which time she learned to fake official documents with great precision. Then she'd left to pursue her chosen career, taking with her several hundred gold imperials originally slated as Slave Corps back pay. What was her chosen career? Cordwick asked her.

"*Thea repa*," she replied mysteriously, on the basis that he would certainly never have heard of it. Cordwick was a people person, though, and fond of street entertainment, specifically as an opportunity for his thick fingers to do as much pilfering as humanly possible, and his face split into an incredulous smile.

"What? Little Miss Superior is a street-dancer? Ribbons and knives and that? *And* a thief, and who knows what else you've had to do, when prancing about in the air wouldn't pay your way! Why we're well met, Miss Tesse, all thieves together."

"Is that why the Wasps caught you, Beetle? Your big mouth?" she demanded. To his surprise her hard shell was cracked; she seemed almost on the verge of tears.

"Pretty much," he said pointedly turning the conversational lamp onto himself. "I was dressed as a Consortium factor and talking my way into the big war loot depository in Shoal Acer, only I got carried away with my life story and someone saw the holes."

She looked at him cautiously, gauging his willingness to let the previous subject sink out of sight, and even then she snatched a quick glance at Darien, sleeping just then with Philomaea watching over him. *I see*, Cordwick understood. *Not good enough for him, is it? He's a prince and you're just a rover and a thief, but you're doing your absolutely tiny best to be the prince's right hand woman, capable and loyal and utterly professional.* She was younger than he'd thought, too, perhaps no more than twenty. She would have been a mere child when the war started, not even on her ill-fated apprenticeship at the Consortium.

"So..." He glanced about, seeing a conspicuous absence, and ventured. "The prince and Evandter, then," getting the stress on the Mantis' awkward Commonwealer name wrong. "They go back a ways."

"Oh they tried to kill one another a good ten times before ever the Wasps came," she confirmed. "Darien was a great bringer of justice, a Mercer and a magistrate, and Evandter was the man he never quite caught. And he was a bad one, certainly. A confirmed killer, for sheer love of blood, and a brigand leader who abandoned his men to save his own skin. He was the greatest villain of three principalities, and Darien was always after him. There are songs, even, stories of when they clashed. They fought, oh, half a dozen times, they say."

"This is because the prince stole his woman?"

Tesse goggled at him for a moment. "No! Idiot Beetle. Nysse was betrothed to Darien, and to get at Darien Evandter stole her away. Kidnapped her, holed up with some cutthroats in a cave somewhere, set an ambush. You've never heard this story?"

"I prefer making them up to hearing them," he told her.

"Must be the strain of listening to someone else's voice for so long," she sniped at him. "Well, Darien turned up and killed the cutthroats, and Evandter turned up and met him at the cave mouth, and probably Darien thought that the Mantis had laid the girl open and cut her up, you know. But the story goes that Evandter just told him he was a lucky man, and fled, and Nysse was untouched." She smiled, and for once it was an expression that fit with her age. "Didn't believe a word of it, until Himself sent me to fetch the Mantis out of Maille. They say she charmed him, used magic, used her Art, but you know what? That doesn't last, not like that. You saw how he was when I said her name."

"And he's good for his word, you think?" Cordwick pressed. "I mean Mantis oaths normally, yes, but even then only if they respect you, and this one..." but Tesse's expression had changed, and Cordwick hurriedly changed the subject, understanding from her look that Evandter had rejoined them. *Still*, he thought, *maybe Evandter respects the prince, and so maybe his word will hold.* The thought carried on, though, to darker waters, because it was just as evident that Evandter hated Lowre Darien as no man had ever hated man, the gall-bitter, vitriolic hate that the envious have-nots reserve for those that have. When they had rescued Nysse Ceann there would be blood. The two old enemies would fight their last.

It would have been a little under a tenday's clear run to Del Halle. There were Wasps about, but they were still consolidating their vast gains from the war, spread thin and lording it over the populace only because they had killed off every noble or leader that they could catch, leaving the dispirited peasantry to trudge back to ruined fields and broken villages. Avoiding Wasp scouts, messengers and soldiers on the march would have been child's play to any of the travelers.

Then they came across the slavers: two great automotives grinding their way over the hilly landscape, the rear sections made into cages into which perhaps two hundred Commonwealers were crammed. The vehicles, overburdened, moved at a walking pace, and most of the twenty or so Slave Corps guards walked alongside, only their officers and artificer-drivers riding.

Lying along a hill crest, lost in the long grass, Lowre Darien watched.

"No," cautioned Philomaea, when he returned to them. "This is not your quest."

"We will free the slaves," the prince announced to them all. "It will be simple."

Evandter snorted derisively, a sound that was becoming far too familiar. "You mean we kill the Wasps and release the others. That *is* simple."

"You've lost your taste for blood?" Darien asked him archly.

"I'd happily finish the slaves as well, for the crime of being stupid and weak enough to be caught," Evandter said lazily. "Let's be at it."

"You make your entrance," Darien instructed him. "Kill all the Wasp-kinden you wish. I will slay those who goad the machines." He turned to Tesse and Philomaea. "Take up your bows and make a good accounting of yourselves." Those amber eyes turned on Cordwick. "You are a thief, you say? Steal the slaves from those machines."

This isn't theft was Cordwick's mantra as he made his way to the abruptly halted slave wagons. Theft, for him, was an exercise in being clever, in getting in, getting the goods and getting out without anybody being the wiser. Theft was also more definitely nothing to do with hurting people. Scosser Cordwick had a terror of hurting people that was born from a childhood understanding that people would hurt him back twice as hard if he did. This wretched circus, therefore, was not theft.

Darien kicked off the festivities by flying straight at the driver's bench of the lead automotive. He had two small punch-swords, like glorified brass knuckles only with foot-long blades projecting from them and little pearly round shields to cover the backs of his hands. He had cut apart the two Wasps he found there almost instantly and was away even as the slavers realised they were under attack, dodging and arcing in the air to come about for the other vehicle as the crackle and snap of sting-fire lanced the air around him. By that time Evandter had made himself known.

The prince's retinue was low on armaments. The two women had a tatty shortbow each and a varied selection of arrows. Darien had his swords. There had been nothing left to arm the Mantis but Evandter had not complained. As Cordwick ran in, utterly unremarked, he saw why. Evandter was killing the slavers. He raced through them with an erratic, zig-zagging swiftness, never staying still for longer than it took him to strike a blow. Each time he crossed Cordwick's eyeline he had something different: a club, a shortsword, a spear, all ripped from the hands of the Wasps and turned on them without mercy. Between these chance acquisitions, taken up and cast down without care, his barbed arms spoke for him. He fought close up, tearing throats, ramming his spines through eyeslits, ripping at groins and armpits and guts, wherever the blood was easiest to get to. Then Darien was back, killing off the driver and officer in the other cab even as they tried to follow Evandter's red progress. Added to the mix, sporadic arrow-shot came from beyond the edge of the fray, catching the Wasps off guard as their attention was monopolised by the killers in their midst.

Cordwick reached the first automotive unspotted, less by any great stealth on his part than that he had become the least conspicuous thing in the locality by some margin. The locks securing the heavy bars were solid and unsophisticated. He had already manufactured some new picks from discarded military surplus on the road, a securing pin and some stout wire becoming the tools of his trade. They were makeshift poor tools, but it was a clumsy lock and he had its measure, springing it in half a minute and passing on to the next.

All the while he was aware of Darien and Evandter fighting. As they circled around the fixed point of the wagons, on the ground and in the air, he understood that they were working as a matched pair, driving the Wasps into each other's path, herding and dividing them. It was as though they had worked together for years, or were linked mind to mind as the Ant-kinden were. *Or,* Cordwick thought, *it's as though they really, really want to duel one another, and have just expanded the killing space between them until all the Wasps fit into it.*

The second lock took longer, more for lack of repair than greater complexity. By the time he had tripped its tumblers the fight was done and Evandter was stalking from body to body, either extinguishing any remnant sign of life or mutilating the corpses, it was unclear which.

The prisoners had formed an uncertain, awkward mob between the two machines, looking about them at the devastation. As a mass, they spelled out the words, "What now?" Cordwick agreed with them. All very well for Darien to come down and shed some blood to save his conscience, but would he feed them? Would he take them someplace safe? Cordwick freely admitted that the Prince and the Mantis had produced a skilled piece of bloody-handed performance art, but in his eyes there was nothing that clearly defined the supposed hero from the admitted villain. Killing people, even wicked people, was hardly a skill confined to the virtuous.

He glanced at Evandter and saw his thoughts mirrored in the man's sneer. It was clear the Mantis would happily butcher the prisoners as well, and solve their problems with his characteristic finality.

"Listen to me," Darien said. He had hopped up onto the top of one of the automotives. Despite the grimy clothes, the bandit's mail, he had an undeniable authority about him. He did not have their trust, but he had their attention.

"If any one of you wishes to remain in the hands of the Empire, stay with the machines and they will find you. Tell them our descriptions, tell them you could not prevent us. It may help. I speak now to those who will venture a little for their freedom."

They had quieted entirely but their stare remained suspicious, waiting for him to name his price.

"Who among you has any woodcraft? Hunters, woodcutters, poachers, bandits even. I will not judge you. Step out and make yourselves known."

Cordwick wouldn't have moved, but almost a score did, stepping to form their own small band away from the rest, until Darien asked them to separate, to each stand alone.

"Now, you others, take yourselves to these men and women, so that each one has followers." Darien made no attempt to organise or divide them and the result was uneven, some of the self-professed woodsmen having a few, others having more than a dozen. The Prince nodded approvingly nonetheless.

"Perhaps a tenday's travel from here to the west is the border between the free Commonweal and the captive principalities, newly drawn. Hear me: make for that. Avoid towns and villages. Avoid the roads. Travel by night where you can: our eyes are better than theirs. Each group of you must move alone. The border itself is not secured, not yet. The Wasps will make it a line of forts and watchposts soon enough but for now their numbers are spread across all their stolen lands, and they have not the hands to bar the door to those who have a will to escape them. Head west, and do not stop until you are free."

"And if they catch us?" one of them asked bitterly.

"Then say nothing of this, nor of being prisoners. Say only that you were turned off some distant village somewhere. You will be no worse, I hope, than you were before I came. If you are caught by any other than the Slave Corps then no doubt you will be better. The Wasps need men and women to labour in what are now their fields. You may simply be made their serfs, and not taken away as their slaves." His voice was mild, clear and kind, and it loaned them confidence, enough to start out where before they might just have crouched in the ruin of their former slavery until new masters arrived.

Not one stayed behind. The little bands of Dragonfly-kinden and Grasshopper-kinden trekked off away from the fight, and soon they were lost to sight, each on its own private mission, each with the blessing of Prince Lowre Darien.

When the Prince's retinue set off again, Cordwick put himself next to Tesse. She was looking at Darien's back, and the only word for her expression was adoration. When she caught the Beetle looking at her she scowled, but then said, "Do you see?"

"I'm beginning to," admitted Cordwick. What he actually felt was mild resentment. As a man in his chosen line of work he lived off his firm belief that he was simply cleverer than most people, and that most people were rogues who deserved to be robbed. Lowre Darien was a thorn in his ideology.

Del Halle was another of the old Commonweal castles that had been built in some previous age and which the Commonwealers themselves had scant use for before the invasion. When the Wasps had rolled in, however, the locals had rallied to their ancient fortifications to muster against the invader, and the leadshotters, the incendiaries, the rams and the trebuchets of the imperial armies had brought them down or cleaned them out, one after another. The old stones did more service to the Wasps themselves, who used them as seats for their new governors, re-edified and strengthened and fitted with artillery. Such was Del Halle. The town it overlooked was thoroughly occupied and while the townsfolk, whose exchange of serfdom for imperial slavery had not markedly altered their lot, went back to the fields to repair the damage that a dozen years of war will inflict on careful agriculture, there was a Consortium office set up in what was once the headman's house, and drafted auxillian soldiers, Bee-kinden from some forsaken part of the east-Empire, patrolled the streets.

The castle itself was not the spanning marvel that was Maille, of unfond memory. The original structure had been a four-storey square tower, but the Wasps had been busy, installing a large ground floor and a smaller floor above, making the whole thing look like a makeshift cousin of the ziggurats they favoured back home. It stood on a rise, with a good view of many miles of newly imperialised coutryside, and must be the garrison commander's pride and joy. Looking up at it, Cordwick's professionalism was piqued. He saw at once that this had been a lynch-pin of the Imperial advance, every window narrowed down to a slit, every hatch reinforced, and the top of the tower roofed over with plenty of slots from which defenders could shoot flying attackers.

Prince Lowre Darien looked on the castle of Del Halle with nothing but determination. If he considered the defences, it was merely to acknowledge that the Wasps were taking the value of their prisoner seriously.

That evening found them on a bluff that overlooked the village but was still beneath the watch of the fortress. Darien and Evandter had both taken up posts where they could study the Wasps' refortification of Del Halle, and Cordwick knew exactly the kind of entrance both were thinking about. Not a frontal assault, for not even Lowre Darien's legend included taking castles single-handedly, but denied the chance to be forthright the old Inapt kinden always fell back on the same kind of skulking business. Stealth and creeping, prying a way in, stalking corridors, silent murder. He understood the Commonweal had boasted some limited success with this tactic, but of course the Wasps had been *outside* the castles in those days, not inside having had plenty of opportunity to update the place with locked shutters. Even Cordwick's eyes, which were half-blind compared to Darien's, could see that there were no conveniently open windows for a sneak to make his entrance. *If I were here to rob the place, I wouldn't risk it.* Levering open shutters was a fool's game in a place so obviously well-stocked with soldiers.

But it was plain that Lowre Darien's legend also failed to include giving up and going away.

Time to let him hang himself? Looks like the Empire's given him more than enough rope. And Cordwick laughed at the thought, because it reminded him of a joke he used to make. Everyone looked at him in annoyance. Darien was liaising with Philomaea now. Whatever counsel she was giving him, it was not what he wanted to hear.

"But you're sure she's there," he insisted, breaking from his whispering.

"I..." The Moth woman's face twisted. "Yes. I think. All the signs say yes."

"Then I will go there and I will bring her back," Darien said simply. "I defy prophecy."

"My prince, *please*..." the Moth hissed desperately, and Cordwick saw she was almost in tears. "You will die."

She was a seer, and Darien was one of those superstitious people who believed in that sort of thing. His face had a desolate, despairing caste then, perhaps for the first time in his life. "I cannot leave her." The 'cannot' was said as though it referred to some absolutely insuperable physical barrier.

"Oi," said Cordwick quietly, and prodded Tesse in the ribs. She scowled at him, her attention briefly wrested from Darien. "What?"

"You want him to live?"

"What sort of stupid question is that?"

"You want him to go to Del Halle?" he asked. "You're sane enough that you know the best way for him to live is to leave."

"He won't leave," she said, and he saw that she understood. Whether it was the seer's doom or just common sense, she knew the odds.

"It was your idea, how you got Evandter out, right? Darien was all for storming in?" When she nodded he went on: "Will you back me? I have a plan."

He put on his most confidence-inspiring expression, that had robbed several men and women of their valuables almost by itself, and she gave him a tiny, distrustful nod.

"Lord Prince, your highness," said Cordwick Scosser the proletarian, loud enough to break through whatever impasse had grown between Dragonfly and Moth, "we have a saying, where I come from."

Darien regarded him, and while the Moth glared and the Mantis sneered, he waited for Cordwick's next words.

"Give a man enough rope, he'll hang himself," the Beetle explained. "Give him too much, he'll make a hammock." Seeing that the Prince did not understand he elaborated. "There's a whole load of swords and armour in that place. They could hold off an army *and* they could keep out a single thief or assassin, and it's a rare place that can do both. They must have sentries and patrols and all manner of fun going on inside.

Your lass is in there, and you want her, and they know it. They're ready to take you, is how I see it. It's like a trap, sprung and tensed to snap down the moment you put your hand into the jaws." He saw that his Apt metaphor had lost his audience a little, but the meaning was plain.

"All this I know," Darien told him. "And yet I must go."

"The thing about traps," went on Cordwick as casually as he could, building his courage, "is that if you know they're there, you can disarm them, step round them. They know you. They know the stories. They know precisely how you'd do things. What they don't know about is Tesse, or me."

"What could you possibly be good for?" Evandter growled disgustedly. "And don't say locks. I could break any lock faster than you could undo it."

"Though not quieter,"said Cordwick mildly. "But I don't mean locks. I mean that we're a Fly and a Beetle, such as throng the Empire's supply corps, and Tesse does a fair hand in pass papers, and we'll just turn up at their door and they'll let us in." As he spoke he let matters fall into place in his mind. "Then, when the opportunity presents itself, some time late tonight, we'll open up one of those shuttered windows, and you three can flit in like shadows. Simple as that, if you trust me."

"And if they kill you instead?" Evandter snorted.

"Then you'll be saved the bother," Cordwick told him. "And if they come out to find you, then you can kill them and even the odds a little. What do you say?" He turned away from the Mantis pointedly, appealing directly to the Prince.

Tesse opened out her calligraphy set and took a blank sheet of blue-white imperial paper. It had always amused Cordwick that such a fiercely martial people had a monopoly on the best paper in the world.

"Make use of this while you can," she warned him. "Now the war's over they'll be back with doing things the long way, machine-stamped passes and all sorts of other things I can't fake."

Cordwick nodded almost nostalgically. During the war, with thousands of imperial servants in constant motion, imperial writ was made out, stamped and signed by hand, which was a gift to the opportunistic rogue. Soon enough would come the time when people like Tesse and Cordwick would no longer be able to slip through the imperial net as easily. *And even then I got caught...*

"So," she said, "what's it to be? A pair of Rekef agents, yes?"

"No!" Cordwick snapped immediately. "Rekef? I don't know how you're still alive, waltzing about pretending to be the Rekef."

She shrugged. "So what? Everyone's scared of the Rekef. They'll do whatever you ask, *and* the Outlander employs lots of non-Wasps."

"Until you meet the real thing. And I reckon the Rekef reserve their worst for people who take advantage of their good name. No, no Rekef. Do me out papers for a Consortium agent, nothing too ambitious, just a lieutenant maybe. There are hundreds of imperial factors and agents on a roaming brief just now, taking census and working out what everything they fought for is really worth." He savoured the next words greatly. "And you'll be my slave."

"You jest," she said crisply, with a smile as sharp as a razor.

"Not a bit of it," he confirmed.

"You're a lieutenant, I'm a lieutenant. Or maybe a captain."

"You're my Fly-kinden clerk and slave, as evidenced by your superior handwriting."

She shook her head, trying to pretend good humour, but failing at it. "Listen, Beetle, I'm being nobody's slave, not even for an act, and especially not for *you*. Why should I?"

He told her, outlining the plan that he was still fleshing out in his mind. After that she bucked, refused, complained and threatened him, but at last her eyes were drawn to Darien, the man all of this was in aid of, and she bit her lip and nodded.

So it was that Lieutenant Cardwic Scotawl arrived at the gates of Del Halle with his Fly-kinden slave in tow. The name followed Cordwick's recent practice after one job on which he had failed to recognise the grandiose moniker he had given himself, leading to an inevitable degree of mistrust amongst those he was attempting to mislead.

The village that the fortress lorded over had been cowed and quiet, and if there had been a warfront it would have been far from here, but the surly sentry who received them had to wait some time before the gates were unbarred and unlocked, whilst suspicious eyes watched them from arrowslits. Cordwick and Tesse exchanged glances, because there was only one cause they could see for all the security, and even then the Wasps seemed to be going a bit far. *All this just for his Lordship?* Cordwick wondered, but then he recalled just how much of a legend

Darien had built about himself. His appearing over a hilltop with a thousand Commonwealer spearmen was not entirely impossible.

For an intinerant Consortium agent, however, the doors were opened, and Tesse's draftsmanship bore the weight of the gate-guards' scrutiny. With as little difficulty as that they entered Del Halle.

Once inside, there were a few more hoops to fly through, of course. There was the hoop of kicking their heels in a barren antechamber while someone was found to deal with them. There was the hoop of explaining to the duty officer the exact same business that they had given over to the gate guards. Then there was the fortress quartermaster, who was all fat-man joviality on the surface whilst being viciously suspicious about someone trying to pry into whatever rackets he had going. Cordwick had done it all before. He had the imperial speech off perfectly, not quite an accent so much as a rhythm to the words: attack and defence, now pushing his own importance, then giving way to authority: the perfect picture of an ambitious Beetle in a Wasp's world.

After that they got the governor. The man was mid-supper when they were ushered in. Cordwick had timed their arrival for the appetisers, but the quartermaster had been more suspicious than expected. The governor himself was an old soldier, as the place merited: a battlefield major jumped up to colonel for the post. He was broad-shouldered, just starting to thicken at the waist, and he wore bracers and a gorget even eating in his own hall. His greying hair was short and neat and there was a sword slung over the back of his chair, as though he was prepared for an attack on the very heart of his power. Cordwick saw it, and saw that this was not the general readiness of the fortress but the man's personal campaign to cling to his younger days of beloved strife.

"Colonel Borden," he was named, and Cordwick, as Cardwic, saluted him.

Borden's gaze passed over him, finding nothing of interest. He continued eating, something highly spiced and with plenty of meat, from the smell and look of it, letting his visitors stew for a while before grunting, "What do you want?"

"Well, sir, I'm conducting a survey of this principality for my factor..." Cordwick started, anticipating the interruption.

"Who?" Borden snapped.

150

"Obden Bellowern, sir," came the prompt, prepared reply. Whether there was an Obden of that family, Cordwick had no idea, but the Bellowerns were a Big Noise in the Consortium, a name to conjure with.

Borden inclined his head, sullen but satisfied. "By survey you mean seeing what's not nailed down," he asserted.

"One man's theft is another man's conquest," Cordwick agreed, philosophically. The recently-occupied Commonweal territories were awash with agents of the various Consortium magnates wrestling for control of the new opportunities the invasion had turned up. The fact that Borden disapproved was noted and filed.

"Any special brief?" the colonel asked suspiciously.

"Agriculture, if you can believe it," Cordwick told him. "I don't know if you've heard, but the East-Empire harvests weren't so great, the last two years."

It was a sufficiently innocuous and plausible proposition that Borden just nodded along. "And you want what from me?" he demanded.

"From you, sir? Why nothing, As I'm going to be underfoot, so to speak, I thought I should take the courtesy of introducing myself."

That drew a few beats of calculating silence from the man, as Cordwick held his breath and hoped he'd got his appraisal right. Then the office nodded again, less abruptly. "That's more courtesy than most Consortium men show," he noted. "Most of your lot come and go without so much as a word, but you can imagine the fuss when two or three of them get strung up as smugglers because nobody knew."

Good. This was a story Cordwick had heard before, enough times to guess that it was probably apocryphal, a soldier's joke. That was fine because Borden was a soldier's soldier who didn't like the presumption of the Consortium merchants. Cordwick had now presented himself as respectful and polite, and it was no surprise when the governor gestured at a chair. Cordwick sat at the colonel's table, implicitly *in*.

A scattering of other officers were present, most of them looking as though they had been pried from their armour only reluctantly. Borden surrounded himself with like-minded men. Cordwick nodded carefully to them, measuring each until he came to the discordant note: a man as bald as a stone, sour faced as though whatever he was eating had been laced with lemons. A man, more to the point, with a vacant chair to either side of him. *Not one of us*, that said, but at the same time he was there, and within two seats of the governor. To Cordwick, that said *Rekef* as clear as if it had been branded on the man's forehead. Had circumstances allowed, he would have shot an I-told-you-so at Tesse, currently fidgeting behind his chair. As it was, he just gave the bald man the same polite acknowledgement as the rest. It was not returned.

"You'll want a roof over your head, while you're surveying," Borden dropped in.

"If possible, for myself and my slave," Cordwick said.

"Knew you'd want something from me." Borden nodded at Tesse. "She's all you have, no escort? So you'll be wanting guards and the like also?"

"Colonel, on my way here I saw a score of dead Slave corps men who'd run into some kind of local trouble. Travelling light and out of colours and, if you'll forgive me, with no pale Wasp faces to catch attention, is the safest thing for me."

Borden smiled at that, for the first time. "Prudent," he noted, and then ate for a while. A bowl and wooden spoon was placed before Cordwick, and he took a few mouthfuls of some kind of stew, so spicy as to be flavourless.

"You've done a fair job of turning this place into a civilised fortress," he commented at last.

"More than you know," Borden told him, chewing. "I had to defend Del Halle twice during the war." The hook was there, and Cordwick made his eyes wide with a non-combatant's earnest admiration.

"I never got to see any of the fighting," he prompted, and Borden obediently responded with, "I'll show you where we threw them back, then."

Throughout the whole meal, the bald man said nothing, was not introduced or even much looked at. His silent, brooding presence was as pointedly evident as a stone in a shoe.

Then came the grand tour, which Cordwick had been angling for. Borden, now sufficiently convinced of the credentials of his fresh audience, had a chance to tell his war stories, and as such stories relied on a knowledge of Del Halle, Cordwick and Tesse were guided through its halls and rooms, able to remark at their leisure just how the place was laid out, and how well it was secured.

Well, was the answer to that, and there were a lot of guards at their posts, far more than peacetime would normally mandate. Borden even dropped an offhand hint that they were "expecting a little bother right about now." Cordwick managed to exchange a look with Tesse. *They are ready for Darien.* Not for nothing had Philomaea led them here. Specifically, there were more than sufficient guards on the two downward stairs that they passed. The cellars were not just for wine, and Cordwick could only hope that the arrangements down there were less convoluted than those at Maille.

Then Borden took them to the central light-well of the castle, and Cordwick breathed an inward sigh of relief. The place had been so heavily refortified that this original Commonwealer feature might easily have been cluttered up, but here it was: a column of empty space in the centre of the castle reaching from the ground to the roof-space, with plenty of openings and doors up and down its length, the swiftest road through the building for anyone with wings. Most of these old Commonweal forts had them, and there, at the top, were what had been portals to the outside. They were shuttered and barred now, but Cordwick recalled what he had seen of the exterior, matching up window for window and door for door.

"I say, colonel," Cordwick said, as the man came to the end of one of his military anecdontes, "seeing this space here... Have you ever heard of *thea rappa?*"

Borden's look suggested that he assumed it was some piece of martial artifice that he hadn't yet encountered.

"It's an entertainment, a Commonweal dance form," said Cordwick, in his best 'oh-what-silly-things-these-primitives-do' sort of voice. "My slave's a fair hand at it, in fact. I only mention it because it's a sword-dance, a fighting dance, almost. As a soldier, I thought you might enjoy it."

Borden glanced back at his officers, gauging their mood. They had been waiting for Darien for a while, Cordwick guessed, because the idea of some fresh amusement obviously appealed to them. The colonel nodded. "Proceed."

"I will need a sword," Tesse said, and then, "*Master,*" with what sounded to Cordwick like undue sarcasm.

The Wasps exchanged looks, Borden's officers instantly suspicious, but Borden growled at them, "What's she going to do? This is nothing.

This is nothing to do with *him.*"

Cordwick kept his face carefully straight, watching as the colonel drew his own shortsword and passed it to Tesse hilt-first. She bowed gracefully and took up her station in the centre of the space, beneath that far-off roof. The original plan had been to use her *thea rappa* for a distraction, allowing Cordwick free rein to make his inspection. This would be better, though, provided the Fly had understood what he required of her.

She stamped on the stone floor, and in the echo of it was airborne, wings shimmering and flickering about her shoulders. She had a red ribbon in one hand, its end weighted with a bead of lead, and the sword dragging at her other side, and she spiralled up until she was halfway to the far ceiling. Cordwick hoped that she was as good as her boast. If nothing else, bad *thea rappa* could be a hazard for the spectators, and if she clipped one of Borden's general staff, things would not go well.

She let go of the sword. Even as the Wasps were spreading out in alarm she had caught it up again, the ribbon trailing like blood, casting the blade up towards high shuttered windows. Instantly she was after it, spinning and gyring about it, catching and lifting the weapon with tiny touches, making it spin in a glitter of steel that the high sconces caught. She moved in swift loops about it, making it seem that the blade was nearly still, that she was orbiting it as a moth about a flame. The streamer of red that followed her spelled out the corkscrew of her path in brief letters as she flew.

She was adequate, Cordwick decided. His interest in such displays was purely for their tendancy to distract people from their valuables, and in this he judged her adequate. The Wasps seemed more appreciative, supporting his suspicion that decent entertainment was at a premium out here.

After she had landed, with the sword repatriated to its owner, Borden grunted his approval.

"How much for her?"

Cordwick's innards lurched but his mouth was already working. "Alas, Colonel, I can't, much as I'd like to sometimes. Not only is she my clerk as well as my dancer, her papers are in the Bellowern name and not mine to dispose of."

"Well, perhaps she can entertain us again tomorrow," Borden said, pragmatic as any field officer. "Find the lieutenant quarters," he directed one of his underlings. "Until tomorrow, Lieutenant."

Once they had been decanted to a spartanly appointed guest room, with barred boards over the windows, and once he had made an exhaustive investigation to ensure that nobody was nearby and eavesdropping, Cordwick sat on the hard-mattressed bed and said, "Well?"

"Well, I'm going to kill you, some day soon," Tesse informed him.

"You sound like Evandter," the Beetle noted drily.

"You think I like performing for Wasps like some kind of trained cricket?" she demanded in a fierce whisper.

Cordwick held his hands up. "Please, please tell me that you took a look at those high windows."

She looked surly for a moment, but then nodded.

"And you can go out tonight and pop one open for Himself?"

Tesse shook her head. "Shuttered, secured. Same as that one, in fact." She indicated the bars of their own chamber. "But they're definitely the outside ones at the top, that we were talking about."

Cordwick looked at their own window. The thick wooden shutters were backed by a solid metal bar secured at each end with a lock. Darien and Evandter could have spent all night hacking with axes before they made any serious dent in the castle's security. "Be thankful for the Engineering Corps' love of order," he told Tesse, "because they make these locks by the hundred in Sonn, and I can spring them easy as breathing." He met her gaze, finding her small face so crammed full of determination that he almost laughed at her.

"If we let Darien and the others in, then they're going to start killing people," Cordwick noted soberly.

"Wasps," Tesse responded, three foot six inches of disdain.

"People," he corrected absently. "All I'm saying is that, once they're in, our part in this is done. We can walk away."

"Coward."

"Yes. Also, bloodshed was never really part of my way of doing things. And what about you? Darien storms in here, kills some Wasps, frees his sweetheart, kills Evandter, probably, and they live happily until the Wasps finally track them down? Where does that leave you, or the Moth for that matter?"

"I don't know what you're talking about," she snapped.

"You do, but I can't be bothered to set out the proofs. Anyway, you're not my business any more than the prince is, once he's in. I'm just saying, going elbow-deep in blood so that someone else can have the story-book ending is no recipe for happiness."

For a moment he thought she would crack, that the conflicting, boiling, wretched feelings inside her would spill out and admit to fallibility, but then she just shook her head. "Let's do it," she instructed.

"Fine. You go out, as my slave, talk to some guards, ask for some food, some decent wine. Flirt a bit, if you want. Dance for them, if they ask. Word will have spread, and they seem easily pleased here." He caught her glare and spread his hands theatrically. "What? You think you're *that* good? Just be glad they're bored. You do all that, and I'll be up top, Art and shadows, springing the locks on one of the windows. All good. Then I'll go do the rounds, chat to the guards, maybe flirt a little." He looked for a smile, and didn't find it. "Meanwhile, you take a lantern or something, hang it outside the window I've cracked, so the others know we've done it. After that it's up to them. How's my plan?"

"Just be glad they're stupid here," she shot back acidly.

Cordwick's preference would have been to wait in his room, to sleep even, until the shouting started, and then to take his exit by whatever window or door looked most promising. Tesse, however, was a most unpromising partner in crime. She was going to meet Darien on his entrance, no matter what. She said it was her duty to him, and Cordwick knew that it was because she wanted a pat on the head from her idol.

"You stay here then," she told him. "You save your own hide. Probably Evandter won't care enough to come after you."

"Come after me for *what?*" Cordwick objected. "I've done my part. I've got them in."

"I'm sure he'll see it that way," she told him sweetly, and stepped out.

"House of my *father!*" Cordwick swore. It was a good oath. He saved it for special occasions. After the echo of it had returned to him he got off the bed and followed the errant Fly-kinden.

There were still guards patrolling, and the guard on the entry to the cellars had been doubled since Cordwick had last seen it. His credentials were obviously well-known enough that he received just respectful nods and the occasional salute from the men who passed him. In the great central chamber of the castle, however, he and Tesse were alone. Patrols would come and go, he knew, but Borden had not seen fit to keep a permanent watch here in the heart of his castle. Wasps were daylight creatures and even soldiers had to sleep, and so the night sentries would be concentrated at the gates, and down below.

Down below where Darien must go. Well, that was surely Darien's problem, and anyone fool enough to follow him. No reason why it should fall on Cordwick's shoulders. *And yet here I am.*

The castle was lit mostly by wall-hung oil-lamps, which filled the place with shadows. The colonel's dining hall had been gaslit, the modern lighting fussing and spitting in its glass bowls, but such enterprise was costly and occasionally dangerous, and the imperial engineers had left most of the castle with little more than its original Commonwealer owners would have used. Sitting in the gloom, hidden from the occasional guard that passed, Cordwick and Tesse did not have to wait long.

Above them, the shutters were silently opened, and three forms slipped in, feathering down on wings of Art. Cordwick expected them to spring into action instantly, but instead the two men were watching Philomaea as the Moth woman looked about them. The grey-skinned woman held up her hand. "Wait, my lord..."

Darien frowned at her. "Philomaea? She is here, is she not? You have traced her here?"

"Yes, but..." The Moth bared her teeth. "Something is wrong. I cannot... The Wasps and their machines. It is hard for me to concentrate."

"It is a trap, I know that," Darien confirmed. "We are prepared for them."

"There are guards all over, below us," Tesse put in. "She must be there."

"Then that is where we will go," Darien said simply. Cordwick caught a glimpse of Philomaea's agonised expression and guessed suddenly that it was not just the readiness of the Wasps that had her by the throat. Some other wrongness had hold of her but she could not put it into any words, let alone words strong enough to sway Prince Lowre Darien from his purpose.

"Patrol coming," Tesse said abruptly.

"Everyone be still," the Moth snapped instantly. Cordwick, who was already back into the shadows, leant back against the wall and all but held his breath. To his eyes, the others were painfully obvious, standing in shadows but not even attempting to hide. He heard the bootsteps then, and a pair of Wasp soldiers walked in, one of them laughing behind his hand at something his comrade had said. Philomaea was staring at them, her hands curled into claws. Under that blank-eyed gaze the two soldiers passed by, somehow failing to see any of then, Moth or Mantis or Dragonfly prince. They went almost in arm's reach of Darien himself, ignoring him as though he was just some piece of long-familiar statuary, and carried on their round, oblivious.

Then Evandter was abruptly behind them, taking a dagger from the belt of one of the Wasps and ripping it, in two brutally economic passes, across their throats. There was no cry from them, just a choking gurgle that made Cordwick sick to the stomach, and then they were on the ground, kicking out their last. Bloody blade in hand, the Mantis regarded his fellows.

"Why?" Cordwick hissed at him, made bold by horror. "Why do that? They were about to go!"

"Because I willed it," Evandter told him coldly. "Now, do we have a rescue to undertake, or shall we wait here for the next two? I could kill the whole garrison pair by pair if you prefer."

"Tesse, which way to the cellars?" Darien directed, after shooting the Mantis a look of disgust.

"Follow," the Fly said. "There are guards..."

"Philomaea shall let us pass them. We shall leave them *alive.*" Darien glared at Evandter. "That way, when these poor wretches are discovered, thety shall not think that we have gone that way."

"Pass them? Six of them are at the very door," Cordwick objected.

"You understand nothing," the Moth told him disdainfully.

Cordwick, veteran of a hundred confidence schemes, did indeed have to confess that he understood nothing. There were ways he knew of getting past guards. They involved talking to them, or creeping riskily behind them, or causing some distraction.

Philomaea did none of these things, not quite. No words were exchanged, the guards had their backs to the door to prevent just such creeping, and there was no distraction that Cordwick could see or hear. Nonetheless, once they were in sight of the cellar door, something spooked the guards. One drew his sword, another held a hand out, palm open. Something in the shadows had their attention, and the whole pack of them hunched cautiously forwards, caught between waiting to sound an alarm and fear of ridicule in case it was nothing. Eventually one of them forged ahead a dozen steps, the rest half of the way with them. Behind them, as they peered into the gloom, the intruders went neatly through the door.

No lock, Cordwick noted. It was still the original Dragonfly piece, secured by a hook-and-cord arrangement. *I'd have put a lock on the cellar door, if I were keeping prisoners down there.* He filed the thought for later, absently.

There were stone-flagged stairs, then. These old castles always had a complex piece of business beneath them, Maille being an extreme example. As Dragonfly-kinden were a people of air and sunlight, it had always puzzled Cordwick, but he guessed now was not the time to bring it up. Beneath them they could hear more Wasps, the sound of a few voices in idle, grumbling conversation. As they reached the stairs' end Cordiwck could identify a handful of soldiers, the rattle of dice. The gaming table was set up immediately where the stairs came out, and Cordwick saw a half-dozen Wasps idling there. Philomaea held up a hand for silence and led the way. The shadows seemed to gather about her and Cordwick shuddered, feeling abruptly chilled more than the stone around him could account for. Not one of the Wasps looked round, not *one*. Instead, the Moth seemed to trail a cloak of night behind her, that each of her companions partook of.

I am involved with something I want no part of, Cordwick told himself, but that was nothing new. What *was* new was the gaslamps and pipes bolted to the walls. Here, where the darkness could never be relieved by the sun, the Wasps had set up a patchwork of modern lighting, but perhaps it was still being installed or out of service, for intruders and guards both had only the meagre oil lamps to rely on.

There was a maze of chambers down there, cellars beyond cellars, low corridors and low rooms, and stairs that went to lower cellars still. The walls had been marked, at some stage, but time and crawling lichen had sufficed to obscure the markings, and they seemed meaningless little squiggles to Cordwick, wherever he could make them out. Still, Philomaea led them in fits and starts, stopping every so often with that uncertain, suspicious look, her worry ebbing and returning. Each time she only had to look back at the trusting, expectant face of Lowre Darien to reassure her, and she was leading them off again.

Their progress was a series of stops and starts, shadow to shadow, and every step brought more Wasps: the cellars were crawling with them and the bulk of them in armour and ready for battle. This was the trap, then. The serrated jaws trembled on all sides and yet Philomaea led them step by step and not a single soldier marked them.

Cordwick was reminded of certain war stories he had heard from Imperial soldiers. The Commonweal lost battles, on the whole: it lost them gloriously and with colossal waste of life, so that the Monarch would have been better served executing a significant percentage of the population in the conquered principalities, and then just signing over the devastated remains. The Commonweal lost battles, but the Empire lost officers. The stories were too circumstantial to be mere fiction. Commonweal mercers and assassins had walked into command tents, into colonel's quarters, into the sanctums of the Empire's finest, and left neat corpses to attest to their presence, followed shortly after by harsh discipline for the sentries and guards involved. *And is this it? Did they breeze in, invisible as air, like this?* Cordwick had no answers.

They paused at a crossroads, the Moth looking from one dark passageway to the other. The guttering oil lamps were their friends, for the Wasps clustered close to them, blind to the darkness. The intruders' impossible progress had taken them deep into the heart of the castle's underside.

"Which way?" murmured Darien, on a knife-edge of anticipation.

"I..." Cordwick could not make out the Moth's expression but her voice trembled. "This way, I think..." One hand indicated a direction indistinctly. "Something is wrong. I am unsure." All around them the clatter and chatter of three score of imperial soldiers was constant, putting Cordwick in mind of the hum of a hive that any moment might erupt in stinging wings.

"I smell something," Tesse whispered, and the Beetle realised that he did, too, a familiar chemical scent of...

And then the lights came on. The automatic strikers wheeled sparks in the sconces, and a moment after there were tall flames leaping behind glass all throughout the cellars, banishing night with an artificial dawn.

Philomaea cried out, just a desperate denial of what had happened, but whatever veil she had carried with her was banished with the darkness and a dozen Wasps had already spotted the intruders, leaping up with exclamations of surprise and alarm.

Cordwick dropped, falling to his knees and dragging Tesse to him just as she was about to take wing. He saw a soldier's palm flash fire and Philomaea was punched off her feet, a blackened circle smoking beneath her throat. Tesse was fighting him, kicking and struggling, but then Evandter and Darien were in motion and she stopped, just watching.

Golden stingshot danced about them, but they were neither of them hit, though the stone above Cordiwck's head was scorched and charred. Then Darien had his swords into two of his enemy, and the Mantis was butchering the other way, taking and discarding the swords of his foes as he chose. For a few packed seconds there was no pattern to it, Cordwick's eyes could not follow the swift exchange. Then both fighters were gone. Neither had taken the way that Philomaea had indicated, each letting the tide of the fight determine their most efficient path to more of the foe.

"Oh – oh –" Tesse crawled over two dead Wasps to get to Philomaea, but the Moth was quite dead.

"They knew," Cordwick said quietly. "Whatever she was doing, they knew it. They let us get so far, and no further."

"Shut up," Tesse spat at him. "We're going to rescue her."

"What?"

"Nysse Ceann. She's this way, Philo said. Darien will be coming for her, the Mantis too. We'll go there."

"We?"

"I need you for the locks!" she hissed. "And if you run now, and if Evandter doesn't hunt you down, I swear, you craven lump, I'll kill you myself!" Her teeth were bared, her eyes flaring. She was a quarter of his size and yet he thought she would leap on him and try for his throat with her teeth.

They seemed momentarily beneath the notice of the Empire. However many soldiers Borden had stowed down here, they were all engaged in trying to contain Darien and Evandter.

"Let's go," Cordwick agreed, and the two of the scuttled off, their path brightly lit by the sear of the gaslamps.

They came to another cellar almost immediately, cluttered with barrels that were patched with mildew, some old Commonweal stash that nobody had got round to dealing with. The gaslamps were fewer here, and Cordwick was grimly certain that they had been in the very epicentre of the modern lighting when the lamps had been struck up. Two further halls led off, and for a moment they dithered, unsure which way to go. Then from their left, Evandter stalked in.

He was red to the elbows with other peoples' blood and grinning like a skull. He barely glanced at his two former comrades. He seemed to know exactly where he was going, and there was anticipation writ in every line of him. *He's going to get to her first,* Cordiwck realised. *He's going to spirit her away and leave Darien to the Empire.*

Then there were soldiers, a squad of eight or so dashing in behind him, and Evandter turned smoothly on his heel, dropping back into a fighting crouch with his spines levelled. In the centre of the newcomers was Colonel Borden himself.

There was a moment's pause, the soldiers awaiting the order, the Mantis like a drawn bow, ready to loose at any instant.

"I know you," Borden said. Distant, echoing, were the sounds of fighting, the cries of the injured, but here it was very quiet. "You are Evandter, the murderer, the brigand-king. I have seen your likeness."

The Mantis sketched a slight bow without breaking his stance.

"They put me here to kill Lowre Darien, the hero," Borden stated slowly. "Orders are orders, but I'd not want to be the man remembered for *that* deed. Ridding the world of *you*, however, is fit matter for a man of honour." The colonel drew his sword, the one he had lent Tesse for her dance.

Something had soured in Evandter's face with the Wasp's words. Even as Borden's sword cleared its scabbard he was in motion, leaping almost onto their blades' points. He felled two of them, jagged spines lashing left and right, stingfire flying wide, and then he had carried them backwards, dancing through their midst, and the knot of fighting men swept from the cellar and back the way they had all come.

"On!" decided Tesse, and almost dragged Cordwick the other way. The hall was shorter than they had thought, though, and the room beyond lit only with two low oil lanterns, one hung beside each of the soldiers stationed there. Tesse and Cordwick shrank back but the men had not seen them. Nor had they left their post to investigate the fighting, sounds of which had now almost entirely died away.

Between them, her hands tied before her, was a Dragonfly-kinden woman in the rags of what had once been a very fine robe indeed. Her head was down, a cascade of dark hair hiding her face. Tesse's hand tightened on Cordwick's arm.

Even as they were creeping back towards the barrel-filled cellar someone passed them, unheralded and almost silent. Darien.

He did not glance at them. His eyes were for Nysse Ceann only. He barely glanced at the two Wasps as their stings flashed at him, as their swords clashed against his own. They were skilled, those two, hand-picked for the job, but he killed them nonetheless and barely noted them.

He spoke the woman's name, and her head lifted. Cordwick was struck, even in the poor light, by how plainly-writ there was the quality that had captivated Darien and Evandter both.

The prince cut her bonds, kneeling to sever the ropes and then raise her to her feet. Tesse was trembling, clutching at the Beetle's sleeve, but Cordwick made an abruptly puzzled sound despite himself. "I'd've locked her up in one of these cellars, myself," he muttered philosophically, watching the two Dragonflies together.

And she stabbed him. In a single move, perfect in its power, speed and precision, the woman had rammed a blade hilt-deep under Darien's armpit. In the moment of shock that followed, she dragged it out and plunged it, two-handed, past his collarbone. Darien's mouth was wide, head thrown back, and his hands clawed briefly at the air as though trying to out-wrestle fate. He collapsed to his knees without a sound, toppled sideways, from hero to carrion without ever understanding what had befallen him.

Tesse twitched, and Cordwick grappled her, dragging her back, pulling her away and into the room with the barrels. He could feel her trying to scream, her body racked by silent convulsions, her mouth gaping like a drowning woman's. Cordwick barely got her down behind the barrels before Nysse Ceann had walked in.

But it was not Ceann – or it was in the instant she stepped from the low, dark, hall, but then there was a man there, a Spider-kinden man no less, tearing the rags of a ruined robe from himself to reveal loose-fitting clothes beneath, such as an acrobat or actor might wear. The man's hair was dark, but not the flowing mane Cordwick knew he had seen, and that face had nothing in it that recalled the prisoner-turnedmurdereress. Yet it had been that woman who entered, and this man who now stood in her place.

Cordwick did his best, just then, to find a way to lie to himself about what he had seen, Later still, he would know that he had been mistaken, that wigs and makeup and mumming and poor light had fooled him, but just then he knew it was not so: he had seen what he had seen.

The sound of boots heralded the arrival of the bald, humourless man who had haunted the colonel's table: the Rekef man.

"Captain," the Spider acknowledged, cleaning his blade on the remains of the robe.

"Scylis," the Rekef man nodded. "Where...?"

The Spider indicated the room he had just left with a jerk of his head. "I take it you did not include Colonel Borden in your plans, Captain?"

"How could I have explained matters to his satisfaction?" The Rekef man had taken one look into the further room, and was clearly satisfied. "One more enemy of the Empire done with. You'll get your pay, Scylis, and a commendation."

"So kind," the Spider, Scylis, remarked. "And Nysse Ceann? I'll find her at that place in Kalla Rae, I take it?"

"What of it?"

The Spider's smile was only affable. "It was suggested that I could kill the precious bitch, after I'd done for her lover."

The Rekef man shook his head. "She might yet be useful, as bait, or to keep some Commonweal hotheads in line. Forget her. There's call for you in Helleron, I hear."

Scylis shrugged. "You'll want her dead some day, and my rates for ridding the world of spoilt princesses are surprisingly reasonable. Now, shall we collect my fee?"

And they were gone, walking companionably off, the killer and his paymaster. Only then did Cordwick realise that he had been holding his breath.

Tesse insisted on seeing Darien's body at first, but when they reached the entrance to that room her nerve failed her and she would not look. Instead, she let Cordwick guide her away, weaving carefully through the nest of cellars. Wherever the live Wasps were gathered or searching, they changed path, went into the dark and found a way round through the interconnecting passages.

And later, as they crouched in the shadows whilst Wasp surgeons and their slaves hunted for wounded that could be saved, Cordwick stated, "We can do it."

Tesse looked at him mutely, locking eyes with him until, somehow, his meaning seeped into her.

"Nysse Ceann?" she breathed.

"Kalla Rae," Cordwick confirmed.

"And why?" she pressed him, "Why would you? Where's your profit, thief?"

Cordwick just held her gaze, and at last said, "Just because I am Apt, and a Beetle, and make free with the goods of others, do not think I know nothing of doing what is right. If it can be done, without great risk, without loss. Besides, there might be profit in it. Some Commonweal family would pay well, to have her. No reason why a man can't be mercenary and still do right."

She gave him a sharp look. By that time they had been left alone some time, and she crept out from their hiding place, forcing him to follow. They chose their path almost at random, avoiding any hint of movement, until they found the bodies.

Not the first bodies they had seen, of course: Darien's assault had wreaked a costly ruin on so many of the Wasps. Cordwick recognized a face, though, in the flaring gaslight. Colonel Borden stared up at the ceiling, his face slack and his stomach opened. His dead men lay around him in a clutter of limbs and blades and riven armour. Looking down at them, Cordwick felt a sudden spur of anger at Lowre Darien.

"Bloody Dragonflies," he said through his teeth, and at Tesse's angry look he added, "Had to do things the old fashioned way, didn't he? You and me, we could have got the woman out, if she'd even been here. We'd have got her out without spilling a drop of anyone's blood."

And a hoarse, faint voice answered him, "And where would be the fun in that?"

The two of them started, only then seeing the man who sat at a shadowed corner of the room, leaning back against the stones, his clothes gored and blood-streaked, his face wealed with burn-scar. Evandter.

Borden had done his best, Cordwick could see, to make an end to the infamous killer. The Mantis had been stabbed three times, not one of them mortal but enough to bring him down. Too late for Borden, though. Too late for his followers.

The eyes of Evandter glittered in the light. "So," he asked them, the pain telling just a little in his conversational tone, "What now, eh?"

The garrison of Del Halle had been torn apart, and the reason for its existence was gone, too, though none of the Wasps seemed to know just what had happened to their vaunted prisoner. Still, in licking their wounds and with nobody to give them orders, they kept no special watch for any that might wish to further break in to the fortress, still less for those who only wished to get out.

And in the morning three set out for Kalla Rae.

So the Twelve-Year war is over now, and we're just dealing with the after-effects, such as Lowre Darien. His father, Lowre Cean (the male version of Nysse Ceann's name, of course), the mastermind behind Darien's crushing of the Sixth (the army that fails to come for Varmen in 'Ironclads') makes a showing in the story 'The Sun in the Morning' (to be found in Newcon's Feast and Famine *collection) and then in* Heirs of the Blade, *still mourning the loss of his son. Cordwick Scosser, by the way, is absolutely inspired by Michael Keating's character Vila from* Blake's Seven...

Shadow Hunters

Should never have taken this job, was Gaved's thought on seeing the forest. He was a man who preferred to trust his instincts, but he also preferred to eat. Being a freelance Wasp-kinden in an occupied land where every other man of your people wore the uniform made it hard to find work. Patrons were scarce when you were hated by the locals and despised by the invaders.

Then he had met the Moth, tucked quietly in the corner of a raucous army drinking tent full of off-duty soldiers, half of them still in their black and gold armour. That one corner had been an oasis of stillness and quiet, and there was the Moth. They were a relic of another land's mystical past, the Moth-kinden, eking out a living on the edges of the Apt world. Like all the Inapt – like the Dragonfly-kinden that the Wasp army had recently bludgeoned into surrender – the Moths were a people who could not grasp the principles of machines, of logistics, of the modern world. They were the last tattered scraps of the past.

This man of the Moth: grey skin, blank white eyes, slender enough that a burly Wasp like Gaved could have broken him in half, yet somehow his soft voice had slid past all the rowdy jabber of the drinkers. "I have work for you."

And here Gaved was, following the only employment he had been able to find, doing the bidding of one Moth by hunting down another. Somewhere in this tangle of thorn-barked trees there was a second man of that grey kinden, and Gaved was tasked with bringing him out.

Or kill him, the instructions had gone. *Tell him it is better to be dead, than to be what he is.*

Gaved had trawled for rumours about the forest his quarry had holed up in. A dark place, he was told; a bad place. The locals never went there, the army had not needed to fight there. Probably it was somewhere the Dragonflies thought was magic, not that a Wasp would care about that. More recently it was a haunt of bandits, because the war had left a lot of armed men with nothing to do,

Gaved didn't mind bandits. He preferred them to soldiers, most of the time.

They ran into him at the same moment he ran into them, both sides freezing in surprise. Gaved had his hands out instantly, his palms warming with the Wasp Art. A thought from him and golden fire would spit from between his fingers, showing these locals just why his people were feared.

He saw a man and a woman, both Dragonflies, lean and golden-skinned. The woman wore a few pieces of iridescent armour, no doubt prised from a dead noble's body. She had a sword, and perched on one wrist was the hunting insect of her kinden, a dragonfly two feet long with a carapace of glittering metallic blue, huge eyes regarding him and all the world impartially.

The man wore a ragged greatcoat and he had a short bow in his hands, which concerned Gaved far more than the sword or the insect.

"Good day, fellow travellers," he said, one hand covering each of them. He tried a smile, but his smiles were seldom reassuring. He was one of the dreaded invaders, after all: a big, pale man with the red weal of a burn-scar about his neck and chin, from when he had finally decided to leave the army and go freelance.

"What do you want here, Wasp?" the woman demanded.

"I've come looking for someone." Better not to say *hunting*. It had so many negative connotations.

Gaved saw the archer's hands twitch, saw a moment's glance pass between them, and then the Dragonfly man said, "He's after the Moth."

It was plain that 'the Moth' was no friend of theirs. The tension leached out of the moment.

The woman's name was Eriss, the man was Kael. They never used the word 'bandit' but that was plainly what they were. More, they'd another dozen friends who plied the same trade. Or they had, before coming to this forest.

"Because the army wouldn't be here," Kael grumbled. "Even the Empire can't make the trees pay taxes."

"But *he* was here already," Eriss added. "We didn't realize at first. We'd made camp. But there was something…"

"Nobody slept," Kael took up the story. "Not well. We started to

168

see… shadows, ghosts. Then he came to our fire. A Moth. A magician."

Gaved raised a doubting eyebrow.

"Scoff all you want," Eriss snapped. "He walked in and told us we were his, and our chief couldn't speak, not one word. Kael and me, we got out, just slipped away. We thought the others'd follow us when they could. Nobody did."

"This is a place of evil magic from the old days," Kael added. "A death-place. We should never have come here. Your people wouldn't understand."

They were going back to find their friends. Gaved was going to face down their enemy. Common cause was made.

The Art of the insect-kinden gave many gifts. It let the Ant-kinden speak to each other, mind to mind, and allowed the Wasps to sting; to each race its own blessings. Gaved could fly a little, too, the shimmer of wings materialising from his back when called on. The Dragonflies were better, born to the air.

The forest was dense, the interlaced branches of the canopy a fortress that even the Imperial army had not fancied bringing down. The bandits' preferred road was the high one, from bough to bough, making short hops through the uppermost fingers of the trees.

Eriss had sent her dragonfly ahead to scout, the agile insect hovering and darting over the dense foliage. When it returned to her, she would speak with it, gleaning what it had seen from its simple mind; another gift of the Art.

The first two times she sent the insect out, it had found traces of the other bandits' progress through the woods, heading for the very heart of the place. The third time it had been on the way back when the canopy came alive and. In sight of its mistress, what had seemed just green leaves and branches unfurled toothed arms and clawed for the insect. Gaved saw a triangular head with bulbous, gleaming orbs for eyes and mandibles beneath that resembled scissor blades: a mantis, one of the great forest mantids, and this one surely fifteen feet long.

For a long moment they stared at one another: the three humans and the monstrous insect, with the dragonfly waiting on above. Then the mantis cocked its head at them and let itself drop, vanishing into the gloom of the forest below.

They thought like men, Gaved had heard it said. They hunted and planned and held grudges. And sometimes, said the old tales, they served magicians.

Soon after, they found the rest of the bandits.

They were in a clearing, sitting in a circle as though they had decided to stop for some conference of thieves. Except they were dead. Except they were splinted up, propped on bloody, jagged shards of cane and wood. Some even had arms spiked out as though caught mid-gesture. Some had open mouths, and Gaved could see the splinters that had been driven in, to keep their jaws in place. It was a ghoulish tableau, and what was worse was the empty place. All those dead eyes, all that arrested body language, led the eye to one spot about the circle, as though some chairman of the damned had only that moment stepped away.

Kael and Eriss were frozen, staring. Gaved himself was watching for the Moth, because a man with this sense of showmanship would not miss his entrance.

And sure enough, there he was: stepping in to take his place at the circle, the grey-faced man of slender build, bundled in a threadbare robe. His blind-looking eyes took in his visitors and he smiled.

The Moth. The same Moth. The same man that had sent Gaved here; there was no mistaking.

Then Kael had his bowstring back with a shout of fury, and Gaved was already moving, running around that grisly circle, hands out, but holding off –

His forbearance made Kael the target, so that when the mantis' strike lashed out of the shadows it was the archer who was snatched away, gone in a heartbeat and a cry. The huge insect loomed above them, from shadow to killer like a trick of the light. Its razor mouthparts were working busily as it chewed at the stump of Kael's neck.

Eriss should have run, then, but she shrieked and hacked at its nearest leg, her dragonfly spiralling up and away overhead. Gaved saw her blade smash one of the mantis's stilt-like limbs, and it raised its killing arms in threat, Kael's remains still dangling.

Gaved's hands flashed, his sting searing across the clearing. One bolt charred across the creature's thorax, another crackled past the creature's head, even as Eriss lunged forwards and sunk her blade up to the crosspiece into the insect's abdomen.

And it was shadows; it had only been shadows. Gaved stared, seeing the patterns between the trees that had looked as though a monstrous mantis was there, wondering how he could have been fooled by it. And yet Kael was dead and dismembered, and Eriss's sword was gone...

Gaved saw the Moth already beside her, reaching out. One thin grey hand caught her collar and the other drew a dagger across her throat with a butcher's economic skill.

Then those white eyes turned to Gaved, who unleashed his sting.

Or he had meant to. There had been no other thought than that, before the burning gaze caught him. Moths had their own Art, and abruptly this one was in Gaved's mind, holding him rigid, trapping his will as the thin figure picked its way towards him, bloody blade held reverently.

"Why have you come to this place of power, little Wasp-kinden?"

He could not be sure whether the voice was in his ears, or just in his head.

"This place of magic – and there are so few left any more. The iron armies of your people trample and trample, your machines and your progress and the brightness of your lamps. A poor scholar must travel a long way to find somewhere that has even a vestige of the old days about it. And who can say what the quality of such a place might be?" The Moth was right before him now, the wet coldness of the blade resting on his cheek. "And yet we must make accommodations. We magicians cannot be choosy, in this latter age..."

The Moth turned the blade, so that the thin, hard line of its edge was against Gaved's burn-scarred throat,

Then the dragonfly stooped, glittering wings battering madly at the grey face as it tried to avenge its fallen mistress. The magician staggered away, clutching at it, shielding his eyes, and abruptly Gaved could move again.

He sent a sting-shot at the robed figure, only catching the Moth a glancing blow, even as the man snatched the dragonfly from the air, crushing its delicate wings between his fingers and tearing them from the insect's body.

Those white eyes were on him again, and although he had a hand out, he could not loose his sting. But the Moth's hold was imperfect: he could speak.

"You sent me!" he got out. "You came to me and sent me here! You told me, 'Tell him it is better to be dead, than to be what he is.'"

The words struck the Moth hard. For a brief moment there was realization on that grey face. Those blank eyes took in the scene around them: the gruesome parliament, the utter bloody madness of what had been done under the forest's influence. No wonder some part of him had rebelled, seeking what little help could be found in this occupied land.

Then Gaved's hands blazed again, and this time he struck true, and just in time. He had seen the twist of cruelty coming back to the man's face, the moment of truth already passing.

Standing there, with nothing but that conclave of the dead for company, he felt a tired emptiness inside him.

With a wary eye out, in case that mantis had been real and not just shadows, he set about relieving the corpses of their valuables. One thing was certain: he wasn't getting paid for this job.

The character of Gaved originated in Dragonfly Falling *and went on to have quite a chequered career in and out of the novels and in these stories. He was inspired by a sketch I drew back when* Shadows *was just an RPG setting, of a somewhat roguish Wasp, and for some reason he held my imagination far more than a minor character should have, levering himself a significant role in the novels while always trying to get clear of them.*

Sword and Circle

They were shouting for her. At first she thought she heard her name in the tulmult: "Ineskae! Ineskae!" but that was her sodden imagination. The roar was a wordless demand that she turn up and bleed for them. Out there was a makeshift amphitheatre, just a hollow in the ground. Its uneven sides were lined with a raucous, leery crowd who wanted to be entertained by her death.

There were almost no Wasp-kinden amongst the spectators, that was the shame of it. The Commonweal had possessed a tradition, once, of stately and mannered duels between skilled masters. Like so much, it had not survived the war. What the Wasps had brought with them was a taste for blood and brutal violence, and these conquered locals were latching onto imported ideas with a will. Why not try to emulate the winning side, after all? Centuries-old traditions had not stopped the armies of the Black and Gold.

She drained the jug, harsh grain spirit searing her throat. The sound of individual voices blurred in her ears so that the mob of them, gamblers, brigands, fugitives and deserters, became like a wave of the sea that ebbed and flowed in its own living rhythm.

"You need to go!" someone shouted in her ear.

"I need to drink!" She was already swaying: a wizened woman of the Mantis-kinden, lean and leathery as dried meat, every feature withered as a prune. Her wild white hair floated about her head like a cloud, and her eyes were red-rimmed. Her people had a reputation as peerless killers. It was a reputation she was trying hard to undo, but so far it had proved insoluble in alcohol.

When she took a step forwards, she stumbled, then wheeled around glowering as though someone had tripped her. Had it not been for that accursed badge, nobody would have taken her seriously.

They were not taking her seriously. They were laughing at her. She realised she had lurched forwards just enough to be nominally before her opponent. She was supposed to be fighting.

173

"Grandmother." Her opposite number was a broad-shouldered man of the Dragonfly and he had one of their long-handled swords down by his side. "Perhaps you have come to the wrong place. This is a fighting circle. For fighters."

Hoots, jeers. Had her badge lost its power at last? Was that why they were so deservingly derisive?

No. She realized that her dishevelled, stained robes were hiding it. With a convulsive twitch of one hand she freed it from the folds, presenting the device to her enemy and to the mob. The sword within the circle blazed in gold from left breast and the catcalls and mockery died in patches. She turned one way and the other, feeling the world swim and the ground tilt beneath her feet.

"Yes!" she shouted out. "Look at it! It's right there!" She tried to point, but ended up jabbing herself painfully in the chest.

"How dare you?" came the voice of her opponent, the nameless Dragonfly warrior. "How dare you steal such a thing and defile it?" He had been in the war, she guessed. To him, the Weaponsmasters' order was an ideal that had somehow survived his people's defeat.

She deserved every drop of his contempt, but still she slurred out, "Didn't steal it." The charge of defiling she did not bother to defend.

Then he was at her, just a simple cleaving stroke aimed at ridding the world of this offence to dignity. She tried, she really *tried* to stand and take it, but the badge was a harsh master. The badge would not let her.

She had come to the circle without a blade, but it was in her hands even as her enemy swung, the grip familiar as breathing: a Commonweal sword like his, five feet from point to pommel, and half of that haft.

She struck halfway through his swing, the blade dragging her tired old arms with it, no messing about with ripostes, but making the parry itself an attack. She ended in a high guard, commanding the middle line, point jabbing at his face. Convulsively, he tried to force her sword aside, because he was far bigger and stronger than she. It took the slightest rotation of her wrists to angle her blade inside his own and, in pushing her sword across himself, he cut his own throat. It was a miserable death for him, a miserable show for the audience, a wretched failure for an old woman who wanted only to die.

Die with dignity, she reminded herself, but that ship had sailed long before, carried off on a tide of cheap spirits.

Later, sitting with a bowl of something clear as water and harsh as defeat, she sensed someone approach her from behind. There had been a time, shortly after the war, when she had put her back to corners to deny the assassins their due. These days she sat with her back to open doors whenever she could. Surely *somewhere* there was a killer competent enough to rid the world of her?

Not this one, though, and she turned and rose in one smooth motion, holding the drink up at arm's length, bringing the blade down in a smooth strike to bisect her enemy's left side from his right. Except the sword was not in her hands, or anywhere in evidence. *Always the fucking thing knows best.* She was left in a guard as perfect as an illustration from a manual, save that her hands were empty. The boy she faced was barely twelve. He had a name, she recalled.

Eshe: a malnourished Dragonfly-kinden child, hollow-cheeked and hollow-eyed. She could not remember where she had got him from, or why. He had just been there, one morning, getting the fire going when she woke on the cold ground. He was just another of the ten thousand orphans the war had churned out.

"Please, Weaponsmaster, we must go." He was so deferential to her. It was as though he saw someone else before him, someone who still possessed an echo of that pre-war golden glory.

"Winnings," she got out. The bowl was empty. She had no idea if she had drunk it or spilled it.

"I have them, Weaponsmaster. We must go. I have had word. There were men asking for you."

"Let them ask it to my face."

There was a rod of iron in this one that somehow the Wasps had not broken. "They are hunting you, Weaponsmaster."

She just blinked at him blearily. Slowly, muscle by muscle, her perfect form collapsed until she was sitting on the floor again, her stained robes spread out about her.

"Fine. Go tell them where I am. There might be a reward."

But that was too cruel and his face showed it. She hated Eshe, sometimes. She had never asked to be responsible for him. She had tried to drive him off. He had not gone. She had refused to feed him. He had proved more than able to scrounge food for both of them. And these days, he kept hold of the money.

"Bad men," he insisted. "Killers. They will not care who dies, what burns, to get at you." He was shuffling from one foot to the other. "Please."

Why should I care? But the badge cared. The sword and the oh-so-honourable circle of the doomed order of Weaponsmasters, they cared, and they hauled her to her feet. *Will I seek them out?* she wondered. Apparently, she would not. Instead, she left town hurriedly – this place in the heart of the occupied Commonweal whose name she couldn't even recall. She made sure people saw which way she had gone.

Once she had staggered a sufficient distance, with the alcohol evaporating off her like mist, she covered her trail and doubled back. She wanted to look at her pursuers. Perhaps one of them would be good enough to kill her. There was always hope.

Sober, she could be stealthy as a shadow. An old, old shadow, it was true, but then all shadows were old. They were the only things in the world that even the rising sun could not renew but must either destroy or leave in hiding. Creeping like a creak-jointed thief back into that village, hiding and lurking, she felt in bitter need of destruction.

Eshe, she had told to stay away, out in the fields. No doubt he would ignore her, as he always did, but he was at least half shadow himself, and who would notice one more starving Dragonfly child in a land that the Wasp armies had chewed their way through?

She remembered the war: the one that had so recently ended. Back then she had been a prince's champion and her badge a source of pride. Sword to sword, she'd had no equal, and this in the Commonweal, where the art of the duel had been perfected centuries before. When the Wasp Empire brought their challenge she had laughed, they all had. Oh, certainly the Wasps had always been a hostile presence on the Commonweal's eastern border, but they were savages, soon riled and soon slapped down.

Those few merchants and vagrants who warned that the Empire had changed in the last generation were ignored. The Monarch of the Commonweal commanded a nobility unparalleled with sword and lance and bow, and a levy of peasants vast enough to swallow the Empire a hundred times over. The outcome of the war was never in doubt.

Of all their predictions, only that last had been true.

A fugitive in her own country, she crouched and spied on these men who had come to take her. There was no mistaking them: not soldiers but some band of trackers sniffing after the bounty the Empire would pay for her head. There were more than a score of them, men who had been peasants, and then soldiers, and were now just survivors. She saw Dragonfly and Grasshopper-kinden amongst them, and a handful of Wasps who were probably deserters. It was their leader who caught Ineskae's attention, though.

It wasn't that you didn't see Wasp-kinden women. They came with the army, but as slaves and kept women and whores. The Wasps had a firm idea of where women belonged in their Empire. And yet here was one of their delicate maidens out on her own, and in command of a pack of killers. This one had seen better times, it was true. She was lean and angular, and wore a knee-length brigandine that had been ill-used and stitched back together. Her fair hair was hacked short, and she carried herself with every bit as much belligerence as a man of her people. Across her back was the same style of Commonwealer sword that Ineskae herself carried.

What, then...? the old Mantis asked herself. *What does this one want? And what do I do about it?* The answer to that one came readily enough. *I suppose I kill her. That's how this usually goes.*

Yet there was something disturbing about her, impossible to define, impossible to ignore. Ineskae reached out for her sword – not an act of the body, but of the mind – and yet her hand remained empty. Something was wrong.

She was too old and too sick of her own existence to know fear. More, there was nothing about this tatty-looking mercenary to strike awe into her. This was just some runaway with a Dragonfly blade, some hunter for hire. There was *nothing*.

But still her sword avoided her grasp and she slunk away. There would be a clean death in some other place. Better to die crossing swords with some ignorant brigand or fighting beasts in a Wasp pit. So many better ways to die.

Two nights later, and Ineskae could not even find herself a fight.

This was some wretched little village, barely a half-dozen wooden huts and some animal pens. She was not welcome. The locals feared her. She had been rattling at their doors demanding drink this last hour, but each family had closed and shuttered their homes, just as they would if the fierce winter wind were crying outside. Eshe had stood in the centre of the village, the still point she was orbiting around, watching her sadly.

She had no wish to be sober. Sobriety brought memory in its wake like a leprous beggar. Outside, under the keen and starless sky, Ineskae took her sword in both hands, but this was an enemy she could not fight.

Past midnight, feverish and trembling, the last veil of her drunkenness was stripped away and she could not stop herself remembering Aleth Rael.

Weaponsmasters were supposed to pass on their skills, but in all her long life she had trained only the one student: Aleth Rael, the swift, the laughing. She had loved him. She had ached to see him fight, or dance, or paint. When he had won his own badge, in the secret trials of their order, she had felt her heart swell until she thought it would break. He had been all the children, all the family she felt she would ever need.

And he had gone out into the world, and she had known that he was destined for great things. He was going to be a general, a diplomat, a man who could have forged a future.

And the Empire had come, and he had come home and gone to war, as all of them had gone to war. When she was drunk she could forget that he was dead.

That was what Eshe did not understand. He was so well meaning. He tried to keep the drink from her hands because he thought that would make things better. But when she had to remember that her student, her surrogate son, Aleth Rael was dead, it tore at her like no sword or claw ever had.

By morning the two of them were gone, she staggering off into the wilderness, Eshe silently dogging her steps, following the faded track to the next town. The cold would not take her, the wild beasts and the bandits avoided her. And so she ended up as she always ended up, seeking the oblivion of drink, because it was the only oblivion she could find.

Three days later she dragged her feet into some other no-name place with the rising sun, weary as death but still not dead. This time she did not even have the energy to beat on doors and make demands. She sat down in the cleared space that formed the centre of the village, kicking aside a detritus of spent candles and the charred ends of incense sticks.

During the war, places like this had looked to their traditions when the Wasps came. They had placed their faith in all the comforting lies and rituals inherited from generations past. It hadn't worked. Around her was the debris of a battleground where the present had slain the past.

How long she sat there in the morning chill, she could not say. Then she heard Eshe whispering her name, and a shadow fell across her. She reached for her sword, wherever she had left it, but her hands remained empty.

A boot nudged her knee none too gently. There was a stocky Dragonfly man standing before her, a cudgel in his hand. He was greying and leathery, and she guessed he must be the local Headman.

"What do you want?" she asked him.

"We want you to leave."

"Give me a drink first."

His face darkened. He could read the history of her descent in the stains of her robe. "Leave."

"Fight me." Abruptly she was on her feet, but the sword still refused to come. She had dropped it somewhere on the trail, but it would be in her hands the moment it knew she needed it. Apparently this was not one of those times.

"You want a fight?" the Headman spat, utterly disgusted. "Go to the garrison. They fight there. They fight and drink and turn our daughters into their whores. Go to the Wasps, woman. You'll fit right in."

"Sounds like paradise," she croaked sourly. "Just point the way."

"No, Weaponsmaster," Eshe whispered with a tug at her sleeve. "Not the Wasps."

"Well there'll be hunters through here within the day, asking after me," Ineskae snapped, slapping at the boy. "I wanted to fight them but you... wouldn't let me." It had been her sword and her badge, not the child, she recalled. Did the sword and badge object to her going to seek a blood match at the Wasp garrison? Apparently not. Fickle bastards, the pair of them.

The Headman was plainly glad to send her to the Empire, possibly because it would involve people he despised getting hurt either way. He said something to Eshe, too, and Ineskae thought it must have been an offer to find the boy a place.

Yes, say yes, she mouthed, but Eshe was proud. Eshe wanted to stay with her. She had no idea why. She should send him away.

With that thought, she felt a sudden cold emptiness within her, at not having the irritating child underfoot. He was no Aleth Rael, her golden protégé, but he was something. Why did she need something, in this ruin that history had made of her life? She could not say, and yet the need was there, insistent as her sword.

Where there were Imperial soldiers, there was fighting. Where there were soldiers there was drink. *I should have thought of this a long time ago.*

The garrison itself had been some noble's castle, built in the ancient days as four high walls surrounding a central courtyard. The ancient ways had not weathered well, which was why the structure was now just three walls and a low bank of rubble that the Imperial war machines had pressed down.

She took in the scene at a glance, guessing that the off-duty soldiers gathered in that space at nights, with a half-dozen big fires bleeding their warmth out at the heedless sky. There was a raised stage made of piled stone carrion from that fallen wall. There were traders and vintners who were established enough to each have a patch of wall they made their own. When Ineskae appeared, she was immediately surrounded by a sour-looking mob in black and gold who thought she looked like a beggar. When she told them with exaggerated dignity that she was a Mantis come to fight, they let her through, no questions asked.

They had several matches lined up that night. It gave her plenty of time to get in the right state of mind. When Eshe would not fetch her a drink, she was not too proud to get it herself, and when she had found a Beetle-kinden selling the harsh, cheap spirits she was fond of, she saw no reason not to sit with him and give him money. In that way, the fights preceding hers passed in a blur: men against men, a man against a big tarantula, a gang of chained criminals against a Wasp soldier.

At her side Eshe huddled miserably, jostled by every passing Wasp. "We should go," was all he would say.

"Why?" she demanded. "Look how we're all getting on! You'd think there'd never been a war."

"Weaponsmaster, if there are hunters, there's a price. The Wasps love gold as much as any," he insisted.

"Let them come," she declared loudly, turning a lot of heads. The

Beetle tapster was looking alarmed, holding off on giving her another filled bowl. She fixed him with a steel stare. "Try it, fat man. Just try and come between me and my love." When the words were out, she did not know where they had come from. They seemed abruptly pathetic.

Then someone was tugging at her sleeve again and she rounded on Eshe to snap, "I'm not leaving!" only to find it was a Wasp out of uniform. "What?"

"You said you were here to fight," he boomed over the crowd. "Your moment's here."

"About damn time." She got up, lurched, ended up clinging to him, then stumbled off into the crowd at a tangent, trying to set a course for the stone mound of the stage. When she got there, she rebounded from it painfully, and then someone unwisely tried to help her up, so she punched him to the floor.

The soldiers around her, with the exception of her bewildered victim, found this hilarious, whooping and cheering for her as she clambered up, her robe rucking about her knees. When she stood there, swaying, someone yelled out, "Did you forget something, grandma?" and another, "Where's your sword gone?"

"She drank it!" called some wit, and she only wished it were true.

She thrust a hand into the air as though calling for silence, and for once the sword knew its cue and was there. She heard the expanding ripple of surprise, a crowd of Apt soldiers – for whom a Weaponmaster's magic was just a story – hurriedly trying to rationalize what they had seen.

"Give me my fight!" she roared at them, as though expecting them to storm the stage and drag her down. "Come on, you sons of whores!"

But then someone was being shoved up to face her. Not a Wasp: somehow she had thought it would be one of their own.

It was a Dragonfly man in ragged clothes that had once been fine. She knew it was not Aleth, of course. Aleth was dead. This was some captured warrior or noble, hauled out to give the lads a bit of sport. When he stood before her, though, she could only see Aleth Rael in him. Her tear-blurred eyes would not focus on the reality. The drink betrayed her and let the memories pour in like the sea.

When he took up a stance against her, sword held high just as Aleth always preferred, she howled out her denials, staggering away but being jovially pushed back onto the stage every time.

"Come on!" her opponent yelled at her, and she knew that voice: it was the voice of desperation, of someone who wanted to die. She had heard it from her own throat often enough to recognize it now.

So she went. The sword wanted to fight. It wanted to put someone out of their misery and probably didn't care which of them. So she went with a will, with a vengeance.

Eshe hunched himself down until he had his back to the Beetle-kinden's barrels. Ineskae and her Dragonfly opponent had clashed three times, separating after each, long swords gleaming and leaping in the firelight. As always when fighting, the old woman was steady as steel: she was drunk but her sword was sober.

People thought she had taken him in for charity. They did not realise it was the other way around. He had grown up on stories of the Weaponsmasters. After the war, without family or home, those stories were all he had left of the world he had once known. Everything had been stripped from him but the dreams.

He had been begging when he saw her – that badge, unmistakeable. He had latched onto her not because she would save him, but because he might save her. He knew, miserably, that he was failing.

And then someone had sat down next to him and said, "Hello there," as naturally as anything, and he looked, and it was the Wasp woman, the one hunting Ineskae. She was here, bold as day, surrounded by men of her own kind who would rape her and put her on crossed pikes if they realized what she was.

He tried to bolt, but she had his arm in a pincer grip.

"I'm Terasta," she said conversationally. "What's your name?" Despite the roar of the crowd he heard her words clearly.

He would not say, but then her grip redoubled and he gasped out, "Eshe!"

She nodded, her eyes on the fight. "Hello, Eshe. You know we've a mutual interest? I'd say 'acquaintance,' but we've yet to be introduced. We will be, though, and very soon."

He wanted to cry out, to warn Ineskae, but there was no chance his voice would be heard and he was afraid Terasta would hurt him more.

"Look at her fight," the woman breathed, eyes gleaming as she stared at the stage. "Magnificent, isn't she?"

The duel had intensified, both of the combatants striking faster, blades scraping and rebounding from each other. Ineskae's face was set into an expressionless mask, every part of her bitter, sodden personality purged in the moments of the fight. Eshe was unhappily aware that this was what she sought, to be taken from herself. Simply being Ineskae was her own private hell.

"It looks as though things are about to become busy here," Terasta observed. She pointed out a band of Wasps who were forcing their way laboriously through the crowd. Unlike most of the off-duty audience they were in full armour, and it was obvious they were making for the stage.

"Why?" Eshe whispered, and somehow she heard him.

"The reward that has motivated my band of cutthroats is a powerful incentive to the army's more venal elements. Now..." And she was standing, dragging Eshe to his feet. "Time to get her attention."

For a blessed second her hand was gone and Eshe bunched to run, but then she had stooped and picked him up effortlessly. Almost like a proud mother, she hoisted him up into the air, holding his struggling form over the heads of the crowd.

Eshe did not think Ineskae would see. He did not think she would care. A moment later, though, she had swayed aside from a strike, failing to counterattack, and her eyes met his.

He would not cry for help. A Weaponsmaster would not. He kicked and scratched, and got nowhere, the Wasp just shifting her grip easily, anticipating every move. Then she was taking him away, and the uniformed Wasps were reaching the stage, and he did not see what happened next.

Ineskae was fighting Aleth Rael. The memory was stronger than her actual duel with the ragged Dragonfly nobleman. She had sparred with her beloved student so often, in those golden days before the fall. To relive those lost fights was far more satisfactory than to admit the truth.

Beyond the decaying vistas of her imagination, the Wasp crowd hooted and cheered as they danced, blade to blade. Who could have expected such a good show from a pair of old relics like this?

She could not know what her opponent was thinking, but when she crossed sword with him, when they tried ardently to kill each other with the razor edges of their shared steel, he played her game. It was as if she had asked him to wear her student's face, just as a favour for the woman she had once been.

And she knew it was all in her mind. She knew that she was fooling only herself. Tears drew their lines down her withered cheeks even as she fought. But while the fight went on she could pretend, and remember being happy.

And then there was a wrong note, and she fell from her killing reverie and opened her eyes.

The child: the annoying, unwanted, useless child who dogged her every footstep for no reason she could divine; the child was in trouble.

There was that Wasp woman, the hunter. She had Eshe struggling in her grip. She was taking the child. *Why was she —?*

The crowd had not noticed her distraction. Her sword had not stopped its dancing. Abruptly, though, she had somewhere else to be.

She changed her pattern and, to her joy, her opponent followed, his own sword leading him to her plan, enemy become accomplice. She went into the crowd, and he went with her.

She saw black and gold armour and heard a Wasp voice shout her name. They were arresting her. What did that mean? *Arrest means to stop,* she considered very calmly, as her sword lanced forwards. *I can't be doing with that.*

The lead Wasp, the officer, took her blade through his open mouth. By then there were already half a dozen brawls as other Wasps objected to the interruption.

Ineskae plunged into the crowd, running on heads and shoulders, hacking at arms, weaving from stingshot. Behind her, her opponent stopped and fought, buying her time though he owed her nothing.

Ahead, the Wasp woman was already out of sight, and Eshe with her.

The Wasp woman had near two-score villains assembled here, in tents and around fires. This land, a good mile from the garrison where Ineskae had been fighting, was broken and rocky. The hunter-brigands were strewn about wherever offered shelter from the cold wind. A handful were notionally on watch, and a Dragonfly man went from one to the other, kicking them if he found them asleep.

"You think they'll beat Ineskae," Eshe divined.

Terasta snorted. "They'd barely slow her down."

"Nobody can beat her. She'll kill all of you."

He expected her to slap him, or at least to sneer. Instead, her expression was thoughtful. "Could she?"

"You know the badge she wears!" Eshe snapped fiercely.

Terasta nodded. "Better than you'd believe. And I know that she has fought the desperate and the doomed in every pit across the Commonweal. And she was cut, back in Te Sora, and again in Mian Lae. Can you imagine? One of the Weaponsmasters, the ancient order, losing blood to some thug swordsman in the back of an army drinking den." She did not sound mocking, anything but.

"I hope the reward makes all your deaths worthwhile," Eshe hissed.

"Oh, my men want the reward, and we have fought off three other packs of hunters who sought it. Why else would I need scum like this? But that's not it. Not for me ..."

Then there was a yell from one of the lookouts, and a moment later the gang of villains was scrabbling for weapons, leaping up as the spitting light of a chemical lantern heralded the Imperial army.

"Time for the scum to earn their keep one last time," Terasta murmured.

The soldiers who marched up were perhaps half the strength of her hunters but their faces showed only contempt for their lessers. "Who commands here?" their officer said. Eshe guessed they were the same mob who had crashed the fight back at the garrison.

"How can I help you, Sergeant?" Terasta's hand was abruptly off Eshe's shoulder, abandoning him in the midst of her camp.

The lead Wasp raised an eyebrow at finding a woman in charge. "We want the Weaponsmaster."

Terasta nodded. "You want her; we want her."

The sergeant squared his shoulders. "We know she came this way. Don't play games."

"I never do," the woman replied, unintimidated. "I have papers authorising me to hunt fugitives from Imperial justice."

Eshe looked about him, finding that nobody seemed to be paying him all that much attention. He began a slow shuffle away from the camp's centre, edging towards the dark beyond the fires.

"I piss on your papers, woman," the Wasp sergeant snapped.

"Interesting," Terasta remarked thoughtfully. The transition from her standing there and her sword clearing its scabbard to cleave between neck and shoulder, was swifter than Eshe could follow, and yet so natural that it seemed rehearsed. The Wasp let out a gurgling yelp and went down, and then the fighting started in earnest, and Eshe ran.

He got quite far, hopping and stumbling over the broken countryside, his Dragonfly eyes wringing as much light from the waning moon as he could manage. He thought he was clear of them, the sounds of battle receding until they became someone else's problem.

Then he skidded down a scree slope, fetching up against a jutting rock hard enough to beat the breath from him, and Terasta stepped around it and took his arm again, as though she and he had been following the steps of the same dance.

Eshe struck at her with his free hand, but she twisted his arm above his head, driving him to his knees.

"I approve of your instincts, boy," she said softly. "Any other time they'd have been right on the money. But this is where I wanted you. Right here." She cocked her head, listening as the sounds of the fight were carried on the breeze.

"Your people are losing," Eshe spat at her. It was anyone's guess whether it was true.

"Probably. But they're a pack of killers, thieves and deserters fighting a squad of equally greedy soldiers. Why should we spare any tears?" She shrugged. "My scum have served their purpose, in getting me this far and fending off the others who wanted Insekae's head."

A new voice growled out, low and dangerous, "And you think you'll collect it, do you?"

Ineskae had intended to avoid the bloody skirmish between the Empire and her hunters, but somehow she had ended up going through the middle of it, her sword and the dregs of her drunkenness just drawing the shortest possible line between her and Eshe and then cutting along it. There was blood weighing down her robes, mostly other people's. Her souvenirs were a thin line of red above one eyebrow and a ragged gash across the back of her left hand.

The Wasp woman regarded her coolly. "I'm not here for any reward," she said. "I'm here for you."

"Personal, is it?" Ineskae squinted. "I don't know you." She was tensed, ready to strike, sword and mind finding her a dozen solutions to the problem: kill the woman, not the boy. Eshe's eyes were burning on her.

"I know you, Weaponsmaster," the Wasp woman told her. "I have heard more stories of you than you probably know exist. I know everything of you, your history, your victories, your provenance."

"And how?" Ineskae demanded scornfully.

"Aleth Rael." The Wasp smiled tiredly, letting go of Eshe, abruptly nothing more than a shabby mercenary in ill-fitting armour. "Aleth Rael, old woman."

Ineskae was very still. "How dare you speak his name?" she whispered.

"Because he was my teacher."

"You? A Wasp?" Her fury was automatic, and also hollow. There was something new come into Terasta's voice, an earnestness beyond her studied poise. Ineskae was practically spitting with insults, desperate to keep this confrontation as something simple: just another throat to cut. And yet no words came out. Her sword trembled in the air between them, fighting her, and her hand was stayed.

"I am Terasta of the Empire, and I was his student while he lived."

"Impossible," Ineskae got out. "Where's your badge?"

"I never had the chance to earn it," the Wasp said bitterly. "The war came. He went home to fight for his people, and against mine. And then he died."

"Yes." Something vital went out of Ineskae. Abruptly neither she nor her sword had the heart to continue their struggle.

"And I knew I should have been with him," Terasta added, "even if it meant killing my own kinden. I failed him."

"Yes," Abruptly Ineskae tottered over to a flat stone and sat down. "Yes," she said again. "But here you are."

"He left me with one thing only," the Wasp said. "He left me with his memories of you, the woman who gave him everything. He loved you."

The old Mantis looked at her bleakly. "So why are you here? To give me his fondest best wishes?" Eshe had retreated to her, half hiding behind her, and she reached up to him. His hand in hers was like a lifeline in a world that was draining away.

"I have tracked you. I have followed your path from fight to pointless fight," Terasta told her. "You are looking for death. A proper death. A Weaponmaster's death, worthy of the sword and circle badge. And you can't find it. Not here. Not any more."

"Seems that way," Ineskae grunted. "You're going to give it to me, are you?"

"If I can. Because I understand the sword and circle, even if I never earned it for myself."

The old Mantis stared at her. Wasp-kinden weren't noted for any kind of honour that the fallen Commonweal might have recognized, but she saw it in Terasta: the stillness, the calmness; a woman whose life had been given over to the sword for its own sake, and not merely for what that sharp edge might win. Something rose in her at the thought: a proper fight, a final fight, a dignified exit from a world that no longer wanted her.

Her sword and her badge desired that. She had used them badly, since the war's end. They wanted rid of her.

But she was damned if she was their plaything.

"No," she said softly.

The Wasp started in surprise. "But... all this time, what have you sought, except this?"

"I know." Ineskae closed her eyes, feeling out this new thing she had discovered within herself as though it was an arrowhead too barbed to draw out. *So I have to push it on through.* "I thought so too, until now."

"Then what changed?" Terasta demanded, bizarrely infuriated that all her good work and planning had apparently been in vain.

"You took him." Ineskae squeezed Eshe's hand gently. "And I wanted him back. It was the first time I wanted anything that wasn't a drink or a death since the war. It was meaning." She managed a brittle smile. "And you did the right thing, by Aleth Rael, by me. You were right on all counts. And if you want to draw your sword and try your luck, I don't reckon I can stop you. Only now I'm not ready to go. Now I've got other business to deal with." It was absurd, she knew. She was too old, too worn down, and yet somehow she felt younger than she had in a long time. Somewhere in that flood of feeling was the ghost of the woman she had been back before Rael died, back when she had something to care about.

Terasta was looking completely lost. She had come a long way, engineered so much, and played by all the right rules, and now what did she have? "I don't understand," she complained. "What is the boy to you, really?"

"Who knows?" Ineskae stood, feeling her joints creak. "Maybe it's time I took another student. Can't let the old ways die out just yet, can we?" She weighed the thought in her mind, feeling a tentative and probationary approval from her sword, from her badge. "I could take two, maybe." Her gaze was still red-rimmed and wild, but it was steadier than it had been in a long time.

For a long moment, Terasta stood frozen, hand partway to her sword hilt, world yanked out from under her. And Ineskae saw that the woman's hunt – her relentless pursuit of her teacher's teacher – was indistinguishable from Ineskae's own quest for self-destruction: differing strategies to deal with an identical void.

"I will fight you, old woman," the Wasp said flatly, and Ineskae sighed, waiting for the strike, but then Terasta's shoulders twitched, the smallest shrug. "But not until you are ready," she added. "Until then, it would be an honour and a privilege to learn."

Then there were voices calling amongst the rocks, the survivors of the Imperial soldiers spreading out to search for their elusive quarry. Ineskae consulted her sword and her badge, but they felt no need to go and shed more Wasp blood today. There was no hurry to go picking fights, now that she had so much else to do.

It turns out that the post-war Commonweal is a perfect setting for a Kurosawa/Eastwood sort of wandering samurai/western story, as well as my homage to David Gemmell (this story was originally published in the Gemmell tribute collection Legends*). This story, like most of its neighbours, is about picking up the pieces – the end of the war is, to some, as destructive as the war itself. Ineskae herself is equal parts Tisamon and Granny Weatherwax. Like Evandter in '*The Prince*' or Danaen in* The Sea Watch*, the Mantis-kinden archetype of the perfect warrior is more honoured in the breach than the observance.*

Idle Hands

When Gaved bundled the fugitive Sien Se into the quartermaster's office there were some subtle changes that struck him very quickly. Mostly it was that the corpulent bulk of Captain Messer had been removed, possibly with a winch, and the gaudy opulence of his office reduced to a spartan simplicity. Where the great man had lounged in his bee-fur robe, fingers glittering with resized rings, where his desk had been strewn with jewellery and miniatures, Commonweal regalia and stacks of coin, now there was a bare space of wood burdened only with neat stacks of paper, and a Fly.

True, there were a pair of soldiers there, and they, too, looked rather neater and more orderly than Messer's venal staff had been, but the Fly was plainly in charge, and that was something of note anywhere the Wasp Empire stamped its authority. He was a tidy little piece of work, pale and dark-haired with a high forehead, and he wore a rank badge but no uniform, instead favouring clothes of plain black. The rank badge said 'captain'. Gaved had never met a Fly-kinden captain before.

"So, ah…" He ended up exchanging a look with Sien Se, a lanky Grasshopper merchant who had been foolish enough to try and stint the Empire's taxes. The Empire's war to claim this slice of the Commonweal had not been overly long, but many of the locals had already become adept at properly civilized crimes like embezzlement, tax evasion and short-changing soldiers. "So, ah…"

"My staff tell me you had some business with the quartermaster," the Fly noted.

"Only, maybe it could wait until Messer's back…?" Gaved said uncertainly.

"I really don't think anyone would be willing to wait that long. Or able," the Fly told him with a tight little smile. "Perhaps I should introduce myself. I am Captain Javvi of the Rekef Inlander."

"Ock," said Gaved, or something like that. He had certainly never met a Fly-kinden from that branch of the secret service, nor had he met anyone from the Inlander who announced the fact quite so brazenly. Not until after an arrest, certainly.

Something of his thoughts must have shown on his face, because Javvi went on, "It is a constant annoyance that people forget that one duty of the Inlander is simply keeping the peace in Imperial holdings. Not the most celebrated duty, but that serves as a rather sad indictment of the times we live in, I fear. You are..." he pointedly consulted the papers before him, "ex-Sergeant Gaved, I believe. You have recently made a very lucrative living for yourself tracking down fugitives of financial substance for Captain Messer."

Gaved guessed that 'lucrative' must have a different meaning for some people, but he reckoned it wasn't a toss he was advised to argue. He assayed a very small nod.

"Captain Messer made a rather better living accepting what he laughably termed 'fines' in return for letting those fugitives go about their business," Javvi observed primly, "but then you knew that."

Gaved's eyes roamed the room as though seeking an escape. This time he shook his head. It didn't seem to help.

"These lands that we have so recently conquered," Javvi confided in him, "are somewhat lawless. You may have noticed. The Emperor, in his wisdom, has dispatched a number of Investigative Officers of the Inlander to restore the rule of law. We have been granted very wide powers, given that we are faced with territories rife with former Commonweal soldiers, bandits, profiteers, common criminals and *deserters*," and he put an unpleasant emphasis on that last word.

"I'm not a deserter," Gaved said quickly.

"You're a Wasp of eligible age and gender, and you're not in uniform and under orders. This rather begs the question."

"It's a long story-" Gaved started.

"I wouldn't dream of denying you the chance to tell it. However, as you can imagine I am rather busy assimilating Captain Messer's somewhat duplicitous records, and so I suggest you use your time in the cells to get your long story in some sort of comprehensible order."

"Hey, no, wait –!" Gaved started, but the Grasshopper merchant chose that moment to speak.

"What about me? I have a business to get to. I see Messer's gone, so fine. I can deal with you." He apparently had no idea who the Rekef

Inlander were.

Javvi smiled, the sort of brittle expression constantly on the point of shattering into points and sharp edges. "You are guilty of withholding funds from the Emperor. However, the law-abiding shall rejoice, for the rule of law is here, and *I* can deal with *you*." He nodded to his soldiers, and one of them stepped forward with a hand out.

Gaved was sharp enough to abruptly not be standing next to Sien Se. In the next second there was a crackling snap as the soldier's sting discharged, flinging the tall Grasshopper into the wall with his chest burnt out.

"You didn't have to do that," Gaved heard himself unwisely say.

Javvi looked at him blankly. "The withholding of taxes is treason, ex-Sergeant Gaved. However, your sympathy for the condemned is duly noted. Now bind his hands and lock him up until I can be bothered with him."

Messer had used the stockade at the back of his Quartermaster's shack for goods, mostly those he was waiting to sell on to his contacts back home – he had a fine line in the Commonweal war memorabilia that armchair tacticians back in the Empire were mad about. Now all that clutter was gone, and Javvi had replaced it with human chattels.

There a handful of locals were chained up there. Gaved knew the type: vagabonds, petty criminals, escaped slaves. He saw Grasshopper and Roach-kinden, and they stared at him with the big, frightened eyes they reserved for the conquering Wasps, even one who came to them with his hands strapped behind his back.

They had one cage to themselves. Gaved got the middle one next to them. On the far side, a single prisoner sat on the ground and watched him keenly. Another Wasp; *she* was a Wasp.

Wasp women didn't travel unless they were with the army, but Gaved got the impression that this specimen was neither officer's wife nor soldier's whore. Perhaps she was from one of the travelling healer bands that trailed the Imperial advance, never officially recognized but tacitly tolerated nonetheless. If so, she had plainly pushed her luck too far.

Her hands were bound as well – but in front of her. A leather thong from her wrists to the cage roof gave her enough play to roam her little slatted kingdom.

"What are you looking at, deserter?" she asked him, though her own eyes had not left him. She was a handsome woman, and in truth Gaved had not seen a good-looking female Wasp for longer than he cared to consider. She had an oval face with fierce blue eyes and a pointed chin. Someone had hacked her pale hair short into a man's cut. She wore a soldier's cast-off tunic and breeches, and she was perhaps a little more slender and boyish than he normally liked. but to Gaved she was no less a sight for sore eyes for all that. He was a man who liked women, when he could get them, and who was simultaneously too poor to pay for them, and too conscience-ridden to seek more contested opportunities. It was a difficult path to walk, for a Wasp.

"I'm not a deserter," he told her. He was well aware that he was a rough-looking character: a long face with more than one scar, stubbled and dirty, and with a conspicuous burn about his neck as a memento of the day he left the army. He still had her attention, though, and so he added, "I'm a freelancer. I hunt fugitives." Only when they were said did he consider how absurd the words sounded right now.

"Did you track yourself down and bring yourself in? I hope they gave you a reward," she remarked. She was looking him right in the eye, another thing Wasp women seldom did.

"Well I'd thought to find Captain Messer –"

"Oh, you ran into the new boy," she finished for him. Her smile invited collusion. "Messer was supposed to be getting me out of here. I paid him well enough. But then little Master Law and Order turned up, and..."

"Right." Gaved nodded grimly. "So you're... What?" Looking at her, with that bold and forthright manner, he could not guess. Had she been in the army? There had been the odd woman in the pioneers, hadn't there, or working for the Rekef? All positons that placed them outside the usual grind of the military, and the repressive structures of the Imperial hierarchy.

She drew closer, grinning, and he found himself leaning in.

"Can you keep a secret?" she whispered and, at his nod, "I'm really a master criminal."

"Of course you are," he replied, but obviously without conviction.

"Doubt all you want, but there's more than one Consortium merchant who's cursing my name. And more than one who's rejoicing now I've been caught. I'm only kicking my heels here because they want the pleasure of putting me on the pikes elsewhere, and the escort's on its way."

"You sound very proud of this," Gaved observed.

"Take your achievements where you can, deserter."

"I told you, I'm not –"

"That really matters to you, doesn't it." Her grin was still there, and it was hard for him not to match it. "You're a tough man, are you? You rough it through the wilderness on the trail of whatever poor bastard you're paid for?"

He shrugged. "I've been known to."

"You might have been sent after me," she observed thoughtfully. "Your luck's out now, though, isn't it. No cash, no freedom. And I bet *they* think you're a deserter."

"You're right there," he admitted. "You'd not credit how hard they find it to believe any red-blooded man wouldn't want to slave for the army until he dies."

"Yes, you have it really hard, you men," she observed acidly. "We women can't imagine what it's like to be forced into lives we don't want." Her smile had dropped briefly, but now she took it back up. "You're for hire, freelancer?"

"I have a feeling that, right now, you couldn't afford me."

"You haven't heard my offer. You see, I need to get out of here and across country, back to an old haunt of mine. I just happen to be on the lookout for a fellow who'll guide and guard me on the way."

He could feel his smile growing, but the direction it was going was towards incredulous contempt. "How about we pick this conversation up after we've both been sentenced and executed. I'll have plenty of time then."

"You haven't heard the pay."

"Oh?"

"One part up front on agreement, the other when we get there. First half is your freedom, tonight."

He regarded her, no longer smiling. "Is that so."

She shook her bound wrists at him, and for a moment he couldn't tell why, but then he realized that she was simply displaying the bonds. A moment later she was twisting and turning them, an exaggeratedly innocent expression on her face, but she had a hand free in moments. Deadpan, she waved it at him, and then twisted and wriggled it until she was bound once more.

"One of the things about being a thief," she told him, "is that you learn all sorts of things to do with your hands. So, do we have a deal, deserter?"

"The name's Gaved," he snapped.

"Aelta," was the name she gave him. How attached to her it really was, he could not say.

But when she put her question to him again, he nodded. He had little faith in the impartiality of the Rekef, or in any genuine attachment to justice this Javvi might harbour. And the prospect of travelling in company such as hers was hardly an argument against.

She wouldn't talk much after that, although he caught her cool eyes on him more than once. The yard outside the Quartermaster's was quiet now – a lot of Messer's people must have either been taken up or run off. The little stock of soldiers the Fly commanded patrolled regularly, though, and cast suspicious eyes over the prisoners, and over Gaved most of all. A few stayed to ogle Aelta, but no more than that. The Fly had them on a tight leash.

Only after dark did she make her move. She waited until a lone sentry had made his turn about the yard, dragging his feet somewhat, and then she stopped pretending to sleep, uncurling into a crouch and sliding her hands free.

"Second thoughts?" she murmured.

"Not me," Gaved confirmed. "So... You've a key, or...?"

"Or." And she began to twist out of her clothes right there. The soldier's tunic came off first, shrugged over her head, and then she had her britches off, a careful, minimalist ballet of economic motion. Beneath she had only a ragged shift that left very little to his imagination. Her skin gleamed pale in the wan moonlight.

"Like what you see?" she asked him.

His mouth was dry. "What are you doing?"

"What do you think? A private show, for all the fugitive deserters of the world." But she was staring at his face, trying to read him, to see what his true reaction was, body and mind. "So, you're a red-blooded soldier after all, are you? Do your duty well enough, there might be a bonus for you at the end."

With his burn scar and his low status, it wasn't the sort of offer

Gaved got often, his quick nod came without the need to think about it.

"But not before," she added, still standing there with only a little linen between his eyes and her.

"Is that right?" His voice was rough, when it came out.

She nodded flatly. "Object lesson, deserter." She gathered up her shed clothes and turned to the cage door, bundling and looping them swiftly about the lock. "For my next trick," she said softly, working her hands into the muddle of cloth.

He barely heard the stingshot, just a muffled creak and a slight rattle of hinges. All Wasps could sting, of course, women as well as men. A woman's sting was a feeble thing, though, that was the general belief. They had no chance or need to develop or practice the Art. The only reason a woman had a sting was to give it to her sons.

When she unwrapped her clothes from the door, the wood around the lock had been shattered into charcoal shards, the metal itself hanging loosely by a few splinters. She turned back to him, one white palm presented. In a man, it would have been a threat. Abruptly it was a threat from her, too.

"Easy, now," he told her.

"Not so easy as you were hoping, I'll bet." She slipped from her cell and came right up to his door. If his hands hadn't been tied behind him, he could have grabbed her through the bars. "But what can I say? I'm a miser with things of value." And the smile came back. "They have to be *earned*, Gaved."

She was pressed up against the slatted wood, half-naked and utterly stripped of the modesty and humility a Wasp woman was supposed to show. And he wanted her very much. There was a part of him telling him to seize her as soon as her back was turned, but he had fought that down before and he did so again now. Perhaps she had seen in his face that Gaved had been many bad things in his time, but never that.

She shattered the lock to his cage as quietly as she had her own, and undid his hands when he turned to present them to her. A moment later she had stepped back swiftly as he stalked out. That was the first moment where there was nothing between them but distance, and perhaps she had thought he would assert command then and there, just manhandle her away. His mind was already working on the strategy of escape, though.

"Them too," he said to her, nodding at the Commonwealer prisoners in the third cell. "Give the little maggot as much to chase as possible."

"You do it," she told him, and for a moment he felt anger rise in him: the Wasp man he had always been taught to be, denied by a woman. The pressure of time was greater, though, and anyway, all of that way of thinking seemed inextricably linked with the army life he was so desperate to get away from.

He grimaced – good coats were hard to come by – but he copied her scheme and broke the lock on the last cell, though he needed two stingshots to do so. When he turned back to her, she had her clothes on again, though they were scorched and holed, revealing as much as they concealed.

The Commonwealers were already running, scattering too, each one of them to their own path. *That should keep the little Rekef bastard busy,* but Gaved had the uncomfortable feeling that Wasp fugitives would be priority in Javvi's ordered little mind.

They cleared out quickly – surely not much time now until the next guard came to discover the wreckage. Gaved made a map in his head, and led Aelta towards the nearest stand of forest. This was good farmland they were in, but there was nowhere in these lands that was completely cleared. The Commonweal lacked the great breadbasket plains that the East-Empire boasted – too many rocks, too many trees and no modern machinery to clear them. That far, it was a fugitive's gift, but a good hunter could overcome all those advantages. Until tonight that had been Gaved's role.

He kept them on the move half the night before pausing, using their wings whenever they could, to deny the trackers. He knew all the tricks, from having foiled them. They changed direction, they followed watercourses, flitted over the great stone-walled canals. They tangled their trail in copses and straggling stands of trees.

Past midnight Aelta was slowing and, if he was honest, so was he. For some reason, running *after* someone seemed far less effort than running *away*. There was a village nearby, and he could tell at a glance that half the homes there were no longer occupied. It was a common-enough sight: casualties of war and the depredations of the Slave Corps had seen the surviving residents contract to a little knot of dwellings, like a snail drawing into its shell.

The night was cold and Aelta was certainly no longer dressed for it, but a fire would be too risky. Instead he slung his coat over her, and that was the second moment, his hands on her, the warmth of her body like a fire in itself. The contact sent a jolt through him, and for a moment he was holding on to her shoulders with a grip that had gone too hard, too possessive. She was tense, but she was a woman, and there were generations of his ancestors telling him how these things went.

If she had looked at him, if she had met his eyes with that mockery and abandon she had shown when breaking free, then he might have convinced himself it was all right. In that moment, though, she was not looking at him, not looking at anything, just drawn tight as a wire and waiting to see what he would do.

He let go and took a step back, exaggeratedly casual. He saw, then, that she'd had a hand directed at him, hidden in the shadows of his own coat. That was another thing Wasp women didn't do and perhaps she wouldn't have had the nerve. Women didn't, that was the soldier's motto, because they knew it would be so much worse for them if they did.

But he pretended he hadn't seen it, nonetheless, and just settled down, feeling the chill.

"If we head south, if we start before dawn, there's a Consortium clearing house there, it's like a tent city around some Commonwealer town with a name no one can say. Loads of people, coming in, going out. We'll head there."

Now at least she was looking at him, though rather suspiciously. "Best to avoid company altogether, no?"

He shook his head. "Problem is you can't, around here. This isn't wildlands, this is the farming heartland of half the Commonweal, for what that's worth. There are traders, herdsmen, farmers all over. Wherever we go, someone will be around to tell whoever's chasing us. So we go where there's people, lots of them. We go there, and we lose ourselves, and we spread plenty of stories about how we're off to Shev Issa or Maynes or heading north to the Steppe, wherever you like. And then we creep out to...?"

Her smile had come back, during his speech. "Well now, you appear to actually know what you're talking about. That's a nice bonus."

"I thought that was the point."

"You were just supposed to be a big chin to carry around and scare of any unsuitable suitors. But you'll do, Gaved the not-a-deserter. You pass muster, soldier. So you'll get paid."

He tried to read what she meant by that, but there was too much challenge in her face, and he knew that if he wanted to find an invitation there, his own mind would provide it. "So where are we headed, anyway?" seemed the safe response.

She grinned brightly. "Treasure."

"You're going to have to be more specific."

"You know Ash Esher?"

"Place or person?"

A place, as it turned out, and presumably one that had originally been known by some Dragonfly name too subtle for Wasp tongues. There were farms at Ash Esher, she said, and a handful of officers had settled there, the first wave of occupation, bringing their wives and servants, slaves and hangers-on, until there were enough boots and stinging hands to keep the populace properly subjugated. But what was also there was treasure.

"I'd just pulled off my biggest haul," she explained. "Some fat colonel's new-built manor, stocked with all his war loot and all the money he'd creamed off the army pay chest." Aelta's voice was surprisingly bitter, as though it was a personal affront. "But they were right on my back and I had to stash it before they caught me. It's still there. I never told them, and they'll never find it."

"Surprised they gave you the option not to tell them," Gaved pointed out.

Her smile went thin. "They were waiting for an interrogator when we stepped out."

They reached the Consortium town two days later, pushing themselves as hard as they could, and without any sign of Javvi and his men. Gaved knew his trade, though. He had a definite sense of pursuit: every time he put down a footprint he imagined it being taken up and examined within the hour.

The town was busier than he remembered, which was good. He could recall a few names: patrons and contacts, though no real friends. He made sure that he was seen there, confident that the trail would bring their pursuers to the place anyway. He spoke to people he knew had no loyalty to him, never quite disclosing any plans, but giving enough clues, in the questions he asked, to tell a sharp man where they were supposedly heading.

At first, Aelta tried to join in, but he put her in her place quickly enough.

"What are you doing?"

"It's called talking," she told him.

"Women don't do that."

She stared at him. He saw her fingers twitch.

"Listen," Gaved went on, feeling himself very patient, "what do you think they see, when they see us two? You think they see a partnership? They see me, and my woman. Probably they think I bought you somewhere, given that most of 'em wouldn't put money on me getting a girl of her own volition. And because I'm known, and I'm a Wasp, and I've had to slap down some folks around here before, they know you're not for them, not their eyes nor their hands. But you start up with that cocky act of yours and they'll get other ideas... What, why look at me like that? It's how it is."

"With you. With people like you."

He wanted to argue with that, but the precise grounds escaped him.

"All right, yes. And this town is filled with people like me."

"I managed fine on my own before."

He tried to look her in the eye, at that, but her gaze slid off him, evasive enough that he was forced to wonder, *Did you? How long were you the master thief before they took you up? Because if you knew how this worked, you'd not need me.* He wanted to say more, to hammer the point home until something broke in her. Women were owned, that was the thing. They were daughters, wives, mothers, and they were owned by fathers, husbands, and then by their own sons, widows living off the goodwill of the male children they had brought into the world. Or else they were owned by pimps and procurers, or by masters who held their chains. And these women, these owned women, they didn't talk to strangers and they didn't throw around their personalities. They were meek and mild and very, very careful about showing their virtue and fidelity. And a woman who was neither meek nor mild was likely to be judged as not virtuous, either. A Wasp man might pause before pushing himself on someone's unsullied daughter or loyal wife, but a woman once fallen was fair game for anyone

In trying to find a way to explain this to Aelta, he found himself staring into the eye of the Imperial dream, the hierarchy that gave every man the right to be the tyrant emperor over the women in his life, and it reminded him of precisely why he had got out of the army.

"Never mind," he said at last. "Just... keep it down, all right? I'm sorry, but otherwise we're going to end up fighting off every drunkard and bravo in town, because you are a very striking woman."

"That's got to be the most cack-handedly clumsy compliment I ever heard," she told him, but she met his eyes again, at least.

For his part, Gaved was finding it difficult to know where he stood with her: sometimes she flirted, sometimes it was the cold shoulder, but always there was just enough to give him hope, the door never quite closed on him. *Women*, he thought gloomily. At least he had got her some new clothes, practical to travel in and not peppered with burned holes.

They left past midnight, heading off almost at random with the intent of curving their course round until they reached Aelta's hidden trove. Certainly some eyes would have marked them, but Gaved kept a punishing pace up cross country, and then put more distance in after sunrise. Aelta just stomped on behind him, trailing him but never falling far behind. Then they found the soldiers, or at least the soldiers found them.

Not Javvi's minions, thankfully, but a young lieutenant with a dozen of the Light Airborne at his back. They were tramping about the countryside with a roving remit to scare the innards out of any locals who might be harbouring doubts about the finality of the war's outcome. They had a beetle-drawn wagon with them, loaded up with a motley of goods that they had acquired by way of freelance taxation, and they were not expecting trouble. Nor were they exepcting a somewhat shabby pair of Wasps on the road, neither of them in uniform.

The lieutenant was one Sharmen, who complained that the war had ended too soon, so that he had missed all the glory. He looked all of eighteen, and was very keen to talk about his family connections back in Capitas. Judging from the way that his men helped themselves to the wagon's contents, there were obviously worse officers to be under the command of, but Gaved found himself wondering how the youth would have fared had he actually seen a battle first hand.

Gaved would rather have given the man a salute and parted ways as swiftly as possible, but they had been heading down the same road, and suspicious behaviour stuck in the mind. Instead he invented a handful of fugitives from Imperial justice and asked if Sharmen had seen any of them, which established his credentials nicely. He made no reference to Aelta, and hoped the woman would just stay meekly in his shadow until they could go their own way.

They camped two nights with Sharmen's merry band of licensed brigands, eating well and sharing the soldiers' easy conversation. Theirs was exactly the sort of company Gaved preferred to avoid, not because it was harsh, but because they reminded him of the good times, and what he missed. He didn't want any little worm of an idea telling him he should go back.

And of course Aelta didn't stay mute, but he supposed that was inevitable. Her looks had already drawn a few admiring stares, and Gaved had firmly turned down a couple of quite profitable offers for her presumed services. Seeing that, she had taken over the situation, as apparently she had a penchant for, and cosied up to Sharmen himself, putting herself beyond the ambitions of the common soldiery. She teased the lieutenant gently and laughed at his jokes, and Gaved felt a sour jealousy come over him whenever she did. *Fool*, he told himself, but there was a hook in him and he could not deny it. He found himself recalling their journey together so far. Had there been an opportunity he had missed? Was the fear of her sting the thing that stood between her and his rightful Wasp-kinden urges? The turmoil of thoughts made him feel ill, and they would not go away.

Late on, the day after that, Sharmen found a village that he had orders to bring the joys of the Empire to, and Gaved was not sorry to take his leave of the man. That morning he had been forced to endure a particularly awkward conversation with the lieutenant, one he should have been expecting.

"This woman of yours, Gaved," Sharmen had observed, "what's the deal with her?"

"I don't know what you mean, sir."

Sharmen had cocked a sceptical eyebrow. "Come on now, she's no slave of yours, not the way she talks. And she's not yours any other way, either. Even the densest of my men have worked out she's not for sale. So, she's good family, perhaps, and you're a bodyguard? But why the nonsense about hunting runaways?" Apparently the boy lieutenant was rather sharper than Gaved had thought.

"It's not nonsense, sir," and Gaved had contrived to suggest by omission that, yes, there was more to it, but that he had been ordered to keep his mouth shut. Orders were always a good excuse.

Aelta had heard the lot, and afterwards she met Gaved's accusing frown coolly, without a hint of remorse. Soon after, with Sharmen's crew out of earshot, Gaved tried to interest her in an argument, but she just smiled at him in a way that suggested she knew full well what had got under his skin. They travelled the next half-mile in silence. That was when Javvi caught up to them.

It was all executed with creditable efficiency. Gaved and Aelta had been trudging along a stretch of road cut into a sparsely-wooded hillside. Up ahead, cover was provided by the wreckage of an Imperial war-automotive, defeated by mud and weather rather than any effort of the locals, then left to rust by the army's swift advance. Gaved's excuse was that Aelta, her conduct and her charms and the sweep of her long legs as she strode ahead of him, was too much on his mind.

There was a startled moment of blurred movement before he was bundled to the ground, a pair of soldiers dragging him down and one getting a hand to his head, warm with Wasp Art that was ready to sear.

He had a lopsided glimpse of Aelta spinning, hands coming up, and then Javvi himself stepped between them. The Rekef man had a crossbow levelled at her, quite a big piece in his small hands, and strung with two sets of arms for extra power. Weapons like that didn't care if the finger on their sensitive trigger was the child-size digit of a Fly-kinden.

"Shackle him," the Fly ordered, and the two soldiers wrestled Gaved into steel manacles, wrenching his arms behind his back.

"No burning your way out of these, deserter," one of them growled, and Gaved almost blurted out that it hadn't been him, that Aelta...

The woman was standing, as downcast and meek as he could ever have wished. Once Gaved was properly secured, one of the soldiers went over and did the same service for her: hands behind her back this time, but trussed with rope. He got a hand on her breast, as he did it, making her cry out. Gaved expected that to be the prelude to worse, but Javvi was apparently a stickler.

"None of that," the Fly snapped, and his diminutive word was law.

"Sir, they're trouble," the other soldier said sourly. "Do we need to take them back?" He had an open hand directed at Gaved, the meaning clear enough.

Javvi gave him a narrow look. "When we return them to custody I will review the evidence against them and apply the appropriate sentence, soldier. Justice will be done, exactly and to the letter. Law and justice, without which our society is nothing." Had it not been for the little man's heart-of-Empire accent, Gaved might have wondered if he had somehow wandered in from Collegium or somewhere.

"Pitch camp, now," Javvi ordered. "One of you on watch at all times. Get the deserter lashed to a tree so he doesn't get any ideas."

"What about her, sir?" The soldier's look at Aelta was full of possibilities.

Javvi scowled, a man frustrated by his own tools. Aelta herself was still being the submissive Wasp woman, her pose eloquently suggesting how she had been dragged off by fierce, lustful Gaved. *A victim*, said her stance.

"She can sleep at the front of my tent. Tie her hands to the poles and keep an eye on her," the Fly decided.

They were none too gentle with Gaved, forcing him to his knees and then twisting his arms so that they could loop a cord through his manacles and up over a tree branch. No sleep for Gaved tonight, it seemed.

He was waiting for Aelta to try something. Her cowering didn't fool him for a moment. He watched the soldier who'd drawn the short straw take the first watch, stamping and pacing about, and huddling close to the fire. Gaved's eyes skipped to the supine form of the woman from time to time, waiting for her move. Past midnight the watch changed, the second soldier yawning his way over to poke the embers and curse his predecessor for not cutting some wood. Around about then, Aelta must have gone, but Gaved missed it entirely as did the sentry. The man was so concerned with getting the fire going that he failed to notice his missing prisoner for the best part of an hour.

There was a great deal finger-pointing and blame, after that. Javvi was tight-lippedly livid, the threat of the Rekef looming large enough to make up for any deficit in his stature. In the end, though, he was forced to accept a job half done.

"We will track her down," he swore. "Come tomorrow, we'll pick up her trail. We'll follow her all the way to the Monarch's feet if we have to." He was not raging, but his anger burned in him like a furnace. "For now, at least we have the main prize."

That struck Gaved as bitterly unfair, given that he was not even a deserter, and Aelta some kind of master criminal. Javvi saw his reaction and stalked over.

"I suppose you thought we wouldn't follow this far, through all your twisting and evasion?" he demanded. "Know this: I am for law. No fugitive or criminal is safe from me, no matter how small their misdeeds, and above all, those who flee from Imperial justice. You were a man who brought in fugitives for money. I despise the fact that the Empire ever needs to rely on such. The love of the law, that is the only true motivation for a hunter of men."

Gaved could only goggle at him.

The next development came just before dawn. Gaved was snapped out of a fitful half-doze when a squad of soldiers descended on the camp with drawn blades and open hands and did to Javvi and his men what they had done unto others. Gaved watched, slack-jawed, as they secured the two soldiers and backed the indignant Fly against a tree at sting-point.

"I am a captain of the Rekef !" the little man snapped at them. "Stand down! This is treason!"

"Pipe down, maggot," and it was Lieutenant Sharmen striding into camp, an unlikely rescuing hero. "We know all about you, don't we, Captain?"

And walking past him, wearing a uniform that was only slightly ill-fitting, came Aelta. Her entire manner spoke of authority, and a particularly hard-edged kind of authority at that. She walked through the soldiers as though she owned them, and her nod to Sharmen was pure condescension.

"Impersonating a Rekef officer is the true treason, short one," she told Javvi, in a perfect balance of cruelty and amusement. "It'll be crossed pikes for you, if they can find any small enough."

Javvi's eyes bulged, and he fumbled for his rank badge, even as his gaze was drawn to the glinting object pinned to Aelta's breast. And of course the Rekef *did* have women in its ranks – the spies and the agents who would take a man's bedroom bragging and speak it back to him at his trial. A woman captain of the Rekef was at least as plausible as a Fly.

"You want us to kill him now, sir?" Sharmen asked.

For a moment Aelta regarded the defiant Javvi, and Gaved held his breath, wondering how it would go.

"Hand him over when you report in," she decided. "I am for law."

They found the key and freed Gaved, and then Sharmen and his pillagers trooped off, three prisoners in tow.

"Should have killed them," was Gaved's comment, watching them recede.

"That's what you'd have done, is it?"

"Maybe." He shrugged, then sneaked a glance at her. "Are you…?"

"Am I Rekef?" She laughed delightedly. "What do you think?"

"I think Rekef people don't laugh like that." He was still staring. "I, ah, that's a fine uniform."

"Got it from Sharmen's smallest soldier."

"Didn't look half as good on him."

Her good humour changed character subtly, but she still had a smile for him at the end. "We're not far off now," she told him. "You just hold that thought."

Another day's travel saw her words come true, and they crouched in the evening overlooking a grand estate. This had been some Commonweal noble's holding once, a fortified house and a village and field on field stretching out beyond them. Now the fortifications were scattered by war, and many of the houses just burned shells In their place stood a knot of squat two-tier buildings with flat roofs, a taste of home for the Imperials who lived there.

Most of the fields still lay fallow from the war's depredations, but there were plenty of bodies out there clearing them. Gaved knew the pattern: an organized mass of slaves with a scattering of overseers. The occasional whip-crack echoed to them even at this distance.

"This is Ash Esher," confirmed Aelta. "There's a group of officers taken up here, the sort of old men who are grabbing as much of the Commonweal as possible now the war's done. A nice little slice of retirement for them. They bring their families and servants and slaves over from Capitas, ready to make all this just another slice of Empire. I suppose you're all for that."

"I took off the uniform for a reason," Gaved murmured. He was pushed up close to her as they overlooked the village – closer than he needed to be, but she hadn't shied away. "A lot of Wasps down there," he noted. The field workers were Commonwealers, but there were plenty of pale-skinned menials around the houses themselves.

"Like I say, they bring their whole households," she agreed. "They don't trust the locals with a lot of the work. Would you want to be shaved or bathed by someone whose country you'd just invaded?"

"So where's your gold stashed?"

"See the big house there? That's the property of one Colonel Haaked, formerly of the Quartermasters' Corps and now living the dream. It's buried at the back of his home. You see the shacks there? That's where the house slaves sleep. That's where I buried it."

"That's not exactly the easiest place to go digging."

"How much time do you think I had?" She was all wide-eyed innocence. He knew even then that something was up, but that hook she had in him still tugged, in his loins and his head both.

They let darkness creep over the land, watching the industry of the estate below slowly dismantle itself, the Commonwealers crammed into pens for the night, the Wasp slaves filing dejectedly into their shacks.

"I'd never be a slave," Gaved decided, staring at them. "How can you have a sting at your command and let a man own you?"

Aelta's gaze, when he met it, was franker than he wished. "Oh you'd be surprised," she said quietly. "Live in a world that hates you, and will kill you if you try and change your place in it. Find out how much using your sting will help, if one show of defiance puts you alone and friendless against a society that *must* destroy you for your insolence. You think you're the terribly bold rebel, Gaved, because you're not a soldier. Try not being a *man* for a day, and then tell me how hard your road is."

He stared at her. There was a great weight of Wasp within him that told him he should scoff and say she didn't know what she was talking about: *you're a woman, what do you know?* But that was precisely *why* she knew. He was too honest with himself to lie.

Seeing him without words, her look softened somewhat. "And when you were a soldier, the officers told you to fight, and you fought, yes? And some of you died, and sometimes the orders were stupid, I'll bet. And you all had stings – and swords and crossbows as well! – and why not say no, right then and there? Consequences, Gaved. We all inherit the freedom to kill with our hands, men and women, soldiers and slaves, but just try using it freely. They tie our hands, Gaved. They tie our hands, and try to stop us using them. But some of us teach ourselves that there are more things these hands can do than they ever guess."

Her face was very close to his, her voice very low. He tried to make that the moment where he would just duck in a little, so that their lips met, but somehow she was never quite as close as that, and then she was up on her feet again.

"That's night enough," she decided. "Let's go."

There were lanterns lit about the estate, and a handful of guards on patrol, but they were mostly concerned with the penned Commonwealers, memories of the war still fresh in every mind. Gaved and Aelta could make their way to the back of Colonel Haaked's big house with almost leisurely unconcern: a pair of Wasps out enjoying the moonlight.

The ground before the dormitories was crossed and recrossed with tracks, with no sign of its precious hidden contents. Aelta had him keep watch while she hunted over it, skulking along the side of each hut in turn, murmuring to herself and crouching now and then to examine the earth. Every lost second seemed to weigh heavy on him, imagining a curious guard or two coming round the corner.

"Come on," he hissed. "Hurry up." They had already raided a tool store and his hands clenched and re-clenched on the haft of the shovel, ready to set to work.

She was kneeling beside a shack, head cocked as though listening to some voice only she could hear. Abruptly she stood, staring at him.

"What?" he demanded in a tense whisper. "Are we getting the goods or aren't we?"

"Yes, yes we are," and she had crossed over to a patch of earth that seemed no different to any other. "Here. Dig here."

"Right here?" There was nothing about the place that seemed to distinguish it.

"I remember it now. Straight down, right here. There's a casket you'll strike soon enough."

He grimaced, but set his spade to the earth. It was hard and wrenching labour, especially as he was forced to go slow and careful to avoid any noise. *This is not my line of work,* he decided. He was a hunter of men, not a thief, and certainly not a gravedigger.

He was down the best part of two feet, striking nothing. Cursing, he began to jab the shovel about the sides of the hole, assuming that he had just missed the mark, that she had not been as exact in her remembering as she thought.

That was where they found him. When they came in a flurry of lanterns, with Javvi at their head, he was still digging.

Colonel Haaked was a red-faced old man, his hair gone silver, and gone entirely from most of his head. He received Gaved in a room that spoke eloquently of his success during the war, in a language of gold, silver and gems. He wore a robe of Spiderlands silk that strained somewhat over the paunch that retirement was giving him; his desk was ornately carved in miniature with scenes of Imperial martial prowess, some treasured piece lugged all the way west from the old family home. Behind him was a Dragonfly war banner that probably had more weight of gold in its thread than Gaved had ever held in his hands at one time. Flanking that, two suits of mail stood silent vigil, gleaming with hues of emerald and sapphire and mother of pearl. What damage they had sustained, in being parted from their noble Commonwealer owners, had been painstakingly repaired by newly-enslaved artisans. Atop the desk, as though forming the last line of defence between Haaked and any assassin, stood a rank of twelve statues, six inches high and golden, each showing a Dragonfly-kinden engaged in some elegant activity: dancing, flying, at guard with a sword. The delicacy of the work surpassed anything Gaved had ever seen.

Of course, he had other priorities just then, beyond artistic appreciation.

"Who is this vagrant?" Haaked was demanding of Javvi. "Where's the girl?"

"Fled again." The Fly frowned, apparently taking Aelta's unwillingness to stay in one place as a personal affront. "Why she came all the way back here only to flee, I can't say."

Gaved cleared his throat, mostly to ensure that nobody hit him any more just for speaking. "The treasure," he hazarded. "It wasn't where she said to dig. She must have grabbed it while I... I could track her for you."

Haaked stared at him blankly; Javvi's look was perhaps a little pitying. "Deserter, what is this treasure?" he asked.

"That she stole," Gaved explained earnestly. "She's a thief." Still no change to their expressions. "She came back here to get... Or why was she in prison?"

Javvi looked almost embarrassed for him. "What else would I do with an escaped slave before I sent her back to her master?"

"A slave," Gaved echoed.

"Of course a slave!" Haaked bellowed. "*My* slave! One of my wife's body servants. And I want her *back*, you officious little man. And you've lost her."

"She'll be recovered," Javvi said, impervious to the insult. "And as for –" but then an old Wasp man had sidled in, head bowed, skulking over to Haaked to whisper something. Bad news apparently, for his master cuffed him savagely about the head and then turned bulging eyes on Javvi again. "She's taken one of the others!" he got out. "She has *stolen* another of my slaves!"

Javvi was the very picture of a bureaucrat whose work is never done. "Well they will be easier to track, then, two slaves with empty pockets and no friends. When I caught her, she was attempting to broker some kind of safe passage – perhaps for her and this companion. She will no doubt need to do the same again, and that is how she will be retaken. I will send the deserter back for punishment and then –"

"You will not." Haaked stared at Gaved with loathing. "He brought her here. You heard him; he came here with her intending to rob me. And I was robbed. Do you have any *idea* how expensive it is, to ship decent house-slaves out here?"

"Colonel, be that as it may –" but Javvi was destined not to finish any sentences that night, it appeared.

"You go do your job, you little maggot!" Haaked snapped at him. "This one, I'll keep. This one I'll make an example of, for the trouble he's caused me. You've ever been whipped, deserter, when you were in the army?"

Gaved faced up to those bloodshot little eyes. "Once or twice."

He thought Haaked would overturn the desk on him, statues and all, the man looked so angry. "*Sir!* You will address me as *sir!* And you have not had a whipping like the one I'll give you tomorrow. I'll put you before my house staff and show them what happens to those who dare to break the bonds between master and slave! I'll have you flogged until the flesh comes off your bones!"

"Colonel Haaked," Javvi said calmly, "this man is mine to take for Imperial justice –"

"I am justice here," Haaked said, in a voice like death. "This isn't Capitas, Captain, and you're a long way from home with only two soldiers to your name. You are not a colonel and you are not a Wasp, and you will go and do your job like a good servant and not presume to dictate to your betters."

A muscle ticced in Javvi's jaw, just the tiniest sign of anger. "May I remind you that I am –"

"Little man, I have plenty of friends in the capital," Haaked spoke over him. "Yes, and in the Rekef too. So take yourself out of my presence and bring back my slaves."

And Javvi, face meticulously devoid of expression, saluted, turned and left Gaved to his fate.

Inexplicably, Haaked had not designed his retirement home with purpose-built cells, though Gaved would not have put it past him. Instead, he found himself consigned to a root cellar, his hands tied – again! – and the shutters above him solidly barred from the outside.

It was, he had to admit, not one of his finest hours.

Come morning, he had no doubt that the Colonel would carry out his threat. Whipping a man to death in order to remind the staff of their place was almost refreshingly Imperial, a real taste of home. It put him in mind of what Aelta had said before they came to the house, and before she had abandoned him. And she had been a slave, apparently, so she had known what she was talking about. A woman and a slave, twice forbidden to use the Art within her hands, and so she had trained them to other purposes, a conjurer's miscellany of sleight of hand and escape artistry. Handy tricks for a slave, no doubt; even handier for someone trying to remain free.

He had not been a very good soldier. Right now he felt that he had been an even worse civilian. He had been played. He had even known that she was playing him, but vanity and the optimistic dictates of his groin had kept him dancing along right up until the moment that she had left him to his fate.

If I ever see her again, I'll... He wasn't sure what, to be honest. The great burning store of betrayed anger that was surely his well-earned pay for this venture was just another thing he had somehow failed to receive. Instead, he found himself hoping that annoyance with Haaked would make Javvi a less than diligent hunter, that the little man would go complain to his superiors first, and cast about for the fugitives' trail second.

There was a heavy scraping sound overhead. He had not thought dawn would come so quickly. And, indeed, when the hatch was levered open, the sky above was still a night's showcase of stars.

And her. There she was.

"Can you fly?" came her faint whisper.

"Probably not." But he called the Art up anyway, despite the awkward position of his arms, and managed a lurching hop off the ground, just enough to spring him at the open hatch. Hands snagged him and managed to get him onto the ground outside after a brief struggle. A moment later there was a sawing at his wrists, and then his arms were free.

He looked up into an open palm, a depressingly familiar sight these days. Not Aelta's, but a stocky Wasp man Gaved didn't know. He was dressed in ill-fitting but good-quality clothes – tailored for a man of around Haaked's build as it happened.

"You..." Gaved stared at him, then at Aelta. "You're who she came back for, are you?"

The man nodded. He had a sword at his belt but, unlike Aelta, there was still something of the slave in his stance.

"Come on," the woman hissed to them, and the three of them took wing, coasting until they were clear of the house, coming to rest in a nettle-strewn copse towards the edge of the estate.

There were a lot of words Gaved wanted to say to her, after that. Some were accusations, many were not. None felt appropriate now it was not just the two of them. Instead he simply stared at her, and at last she looked away and shrugged.

"Here." And she had slung something at his feet: a lumpy bag. For a mad moment he thought she had packed him some food for the journey.

But he recognized the contents, when he tugged open the drawstring. He had only got a brief look at those intricate statues, while

Haaked and Javvi had fought over him, but they had found themselves a place in his memory. Here were four of the dozen and, even sold to thieves at thieves' rates, they would keep him fed for a long time. So long as he sold them far away from here.

"So you are a thief," he said at last.

"I'm what the Empire's made me," she said. "Goodbye, Gaved."

He looked at her companion, then, trying to find out what there was in the man that had drawn her all the way back here to rescue the man. Trying to see what made her prefer *him*. Some part of him – not a small part – still wanted her, and more than ever now he understood her and had seen what she could do.

But: "You're a lucky man," he said gruffly, and managed a soldierly nod to Aelta, comrade to comrade. And so they parted, even though he carried her in his thoughts for many miles and days.

As per the note for 'Shadow Hunters', Gaved is just particularly fun to write for, but the lot of women in the Empire is a theme the novels keep coming back to - most importantly of course with Seda herself. With that social background it made for a good story to turn the 'rescued princess' plot on its head and have her rescue him. Continuing the meta-story of the Empire and the Commonweal, men like Haaken show just how the occupation is going to go – not to men like Gaved or Varmen, but to the great and the good whose blood was not the red being spent in the getting. Javvi, of course (who was supposed to be in more stories and still may be) is nothing more than a Victor Hugo tribute act at heart.

An Old Man in a Harsh Season

Sometimes, when he woke, he forgot for a moment. Lying in his windowless room in the chill of pre-dawn, he felt the desert sky's great arch over him. The hard mattress beneath (for a night on a soft one was agony to his back) became, briefly, the grittiness of sand, and he was young again.

Like scavengers to a carcase, though, the aches and pains of age came back to him one by one: his teeth, his joints, his back, his weak leg, the phantom twinge of his broken thumb-claw. Hokiak awoke. It was winter in Myna and, though the nights lacked the desert's predatory cold, the days never seemed to warm him, not even if he bowed to his years and sat dawn til dusk in the sun.

Money to be made. Work to do. He rolled awkwardly from his bed, lowering his legs over the side, clutching for his cane. *Dreaming of the old country again. More fool me.* It was not even as though they had been good times. He was not such a fool as to paint all his memories with gold. Hard, violent times, the Scorpion-kinden's endless round of raiding and stealing, killing and infighting, and if he had been the Man, when it came to pillage and savagery, where had it got him now?

No, life was better here, playing the black market in the Empire's shadow, if only he had not grown so *old* before he had worked that out.

Around him he could hear Hokiak's Exchange already bustling. Gryllis, the emaciated Spider he had taken on as a business partner, was an early riser, and the man made sure that his staff kept to the same clock. Even now their band of young wastrels would be cataloguing the most recent imports, or boxing the next round of goods to be smuggled out, and if they were not then Gryllis would be reminding them that Hokiak still held their papers, and juvenile slaves were hardly a rare commodity anywhere under Imperial rule.

Hokiak grunted, dragging on a pair of loose breeches and an open fronted robe. He scratched at his sagging, wrinkled belly with the curved claws of one hand. *And have these claws not torn the guts from a*

215

challenger, and let his blood soak into the sand? Nowadays the thought was dismal to him, if only because of the *mess.*

A half-hour later found him in his back room, breaking his unenthusiastic fast on a bowl of porridge garnished with chopped dates. Some bastard somewhere was frying cricket meat with lemons, the scent leaching in from the outside, past the Exchange's front door, sneaking by Gryllis and his underage labourers to creep into Hokiak's slit-like nostrils and make his mouth water. *And last time I gave in to* that *I lost a tooth*, he reminded himself. He was wealthier as a merchant in Myna than he ever had been raiding up and down the Dryclaw, but the more money he had, the less there was left in the world that he could profitably spend it on. Hokiak gave his porridge a snaggle-toothed scowl.

Few were desperate enough to disturb his repast. So far, apart from the band of Fly contrabandists who were kicking their heels until Gryllis had packed their shipment, he had spotted one of the local players, midway between criminal and resistance fighter, who was probably selling pilfered Wasp goods, and the unwelcome sight of another Scorpion, a squat, pug-faced tracker of fugitives that Hokiak had reluctantly done business with a few times. Neither of them seemed inclined to trouble him while he was eating, so he set to his bowl without enthusiasm. He had a couple of Mynans on watch and, three mouthfuls in, one of them stood up and moved closer to his table, indicating a visitor he wasn't sure of. Hokiak glanced up balefully, noted the newcomer, and waved his employee back. He was in a foul mood this morning, and it would do him good to ruin someone else's day.

The man who sat down opposite him was Wasp-kinden, a solid-built, broad-shouldered example of Myna's new masters, dark hair cropped shorter than usual, which Hokiak knew was a practice of the Slave Corps, because the full-face helms they wore could swelter in hot weather. There was a distinct edge to the Wasp, a nervous tightness about the eyes, that suggest this master of Myna was losing his grip on things.

"Sergeant Mordrec," Hokiak noted. "Third time in a tenday. Don't tell me your luck's run even further out? You'd need a glass to see it."

The Wasp's face twitched but he manfully banished all irritation from it. Begging favours from a 'lesser race' was something that many

Wasps would rather die than do, but the Slave Corps men had always been monstrous pragmatists. Hokiak knew, almost to the last coin, the burden that was on Mordrec's back.

"Hokiak. I've... got a business proposition."

The old Scorpion-kinden treated Mordrec to the full glory of his jagged and blackened smile. "Well, always willing to listen to business, son."

"The new territories, Hokiak, the principalities. You must be keen to set up trade contacts there," the Wasp said, meaning those Commonweal lands that had been signed over to the Empire at the end of their war. "You know me. I've been all over there, last three years."

Hokiak made a noncommittal noise.

"How's about it? I'll do good business there. I'll pass it all back to you. You know me, Hokiak. I'm reliable."

"You're a liability, you mean," the old man rumbled. "And in return all I'd have to do is get you across the border, is that it? Now why would a strapping young Wasp like you need my help for that? Just hop on the next slaver caravan headed that way, I would." Seeing the little twitch of a snarl that came to the Wasps's face he chuckled. "Only I hear something about debts, Sergeant. Dice not being kind to you? Only two days back there was two slaver sergeants and a Consortium captain in here, asking if I'd seen one Sergeant Mordrec, absent without leave and owing more than his year's pay to all and sundry? Now, Mordrec's not so rare a name that maybe they meant someone else...?"

Mordrec held very still, save for his eyes which flicked at the almost-empty room around them, fighting to see if Hokiak's men were about to jump him. "Hokiak..." he murmured, with a slight tremble in his voice.

"Now they were making *demands*," Hokiak went on amiably. "I don't take to them that give me demands. So I ain't telling them nothing." Seeing the Wasp relax he added, "Not unless'n they come asking nicely."

"Hokiak, listen to me," Mordrec hissed. "It's the crossed pikes for me unless I get *out* of here. I owe..."

"Three-hundred and seventeen gold Imperials to Captain Lyker," Hokiak finished. "Oh a load more than that, but I guess by now you've worked out that Lyker's not just your regular-type creditor?"

The word *Rekef* hung between them, unspoken.

Hokiak shook his head. "You want out? Use your feet and hope they can take you somewhere that Lyker can't reach you. Or you want my help over the border, you come up with some payment in *advance*, Sergeant. Any man who eats promises goes hungry, and your history ain't inspiring me to extend you any credit."

Mordrec opened his mouth to argue but Hokiak was no longer paying the sergeant any attention. He struggled to his feet all of a sudden, cane almost snapping as his weight bore on it. The Wasp kicked back out of his chair, as if sure that the old man was going to attack him, but the Scorpion's red-rimmed eyes were elsewhere.

Three men had pushed their way into the backroom as if they owned it. The leader held Gryllis off the ground by his collar, and now dumped the spindly Spider-kinden to one side without a glance. The other two spread out, one either side: Scorpion-kinden, all three of them, massively built, bald heads brushing the ceiling. Piecemeal armour of chain and chitin and leather bulked them out further, and they were all armed with double-handed swords or axes, massive weapons almost as tall as they were. They radiated fierce strength, the jut of their fanged underbites, the talons that curved like knives from each thumb and forefinger, the waxy paleness of their skins, all spoke of a world beyond these seedy backstreets. Hokiak felt ten years older just seeing them, and his withered heart sank and stuttered in his chest.

Ah no, not now. Couldn't they wait a decade more? I'd he gone then, and they'd not need to trouble themselves. And he hadn't thought they would. Despite it all. Despite all he'd done to hold his place amongst them, to keep his rivals down, he'd thought that the desert would burn out their memory of him soon enough. But no.

Their leader had fixed his yellow eyes on the old man, and the disgust and disdain on his face cut deeper than years. *So that is what I look like to them.* Those few of his own kind he had been forced to deal with, like the man who had been waiting for him that morning, had at least needed his goodwill and covered up their revulsion, but here it was, naked and plain to wound him. On their faces was written in a large script: *you should have died before you became as this.*

Hokiak lent on his cane for a moment, husbanding his strength, and then hobbled forwards, eyes narrowed as though against a glaring light. "What do you want?" The words had formed with all the illicit authority he wielded in Myna, as a buyer, a seller, an arranger of things, but they came out as an ancient's rattle.

"You know," spoke the lead Scorpion, not loud, but his deep voice was robust with life and health.

"Who was it then?" Hokiak pressed. "Your father? An uncle? Did I cut the head off your family and not come back to finish the job? Who?"

"Father? You might have done for my *grand*father, for all it matters," the huge Scorpion replied, "But I'd not come so far north for him, nor just to trade slaves with the Wasps, for all their gold flows like sand. You *fled*, old man, when you owed us all a death. Every wrinkle in your rotting face cries out to me. '*Bring an end to me, Ecta,*' it begs. I've come to set things right. You owe a death and I hold your marker."

Hokiak's Mynan guards were standing uncertainly, hands to sword-hilts, but the Scorpion-kinden would make short work of them, sure enough. And the mention of the Empire showed that the three were here with imperial sanction, no mere trespassers to be arrested or enslaved. As for their words…

Hokiak felt himself shrivelling before the thought of his homeland, the harsh sands, the harsher people: men and women who lived by strength, who took what others could not deny them, who cared nothing for laws or empires, who lived in freedom and blood until their limbs faltered and their deeds caught up with them, then died at the hands of those that would take their place. There had been a day when Hokiak had driven his band of raiders across the sands and known no master, and killed with his mighty clawed hands any who would challenge his will.

That was thirty years before, and for the last five years of his rule he had relied on reputation more than action to hold his place.

He had left it all behind. When he saw he could not hold them, he had fled them. He had left their world of brutal simplicity for the shadowsand allowed himself to forget. Now here were the scions of his old life of strength and battle, fired with their right to his blood. He had broken a chain of generations of murder when he fled, and here came the smiths to reforge it.

"There's a market a dozen streets from here, off Seldom Street. Wasps've got a stage there, to sell slaves off. Nice place," the Scorpion told him relentlessly. "Two days' time, they're done with their selling. Come meet us there then, after dusk. Come pay your debt."

"Or?" That one word was the worst admission of weakness Hokiak had heard in his long life, but the mere presence of these, his people, his successors, was draining him. The fugitive decades that they had brought with them were laid like timbers across his back.

"Or we come for you, and all of yours," the uncompromising voice assured him. "You, him," the hand picked out Gryllis before taking in the whole exchange, "this. We'll burn you out, old man. We're time and we've caught up with you. Two days." The big man turned on his heel, his companions giving the room a flaying glare before following him.

For a moment, as alone as a man can possibly be, Hokiak lent on his stick, feeling it tremble beneath him, or perhaps just feeling himself tremble against its support. All eyes were on him.

"Get out," he whispered, barely to be heard, and then, "*Get out!*" at them all, the petitioners, the smugglers, his own people, even Gryllis. "All of you! Out!"

"Hokiak, listen –!" Mordrec started, and the other Scorpion, the tracker, was on his feet as well, but Hokiak summoned all his strength, that had been whipped into cowering by the presence of his kinsmen, and bellowed at them hoarsely, shouting them down until the sheer senile fury of him had driven them, and everyone, out of the door.

Then, unwatched, Hokiak let himself sag onto a chair, his cane clattering to the floor.

There were two Wasp soldiers amongst those passing by the front of Hokiak's Exchange, but they were staring after the departing Scorpion-kinden and Mordrec made good his exit, heading away from the centre of Myna towards those parts where he would be less likely to meet with other servants of the Empire. Two turns later, though, he heard footsteps behind him, and saw the Scorpion who had been his fellow petitioner before Hokiak. The man regarded him narrowly, pausing to see if Mordrec was going to be a problem. He was short for a Scorpion, broad across the chest, wearing the metal-inland leather hauberk of a Commonweal brigand. There was a crossbow slung over one shoulder.

In a moment of mutual scrutiny each man sized up the other, trying to cast him as a threat, then:

"I see nobody's doing business with Hokiak today," the Scorpion said. His voice, against all odds, was ridiculously cultured, his accent definitely from somewhere far from wherever either Hokiak or his

Tales of the Apt Volume 1: The Spoils of War

three antagonists had come from.

"Possibly ever," Mordrec said shortly and then, drawn from a well of bitterness, "when they chop him into wrinkled bloody segments."

The Scorpion shrugged. "Who knows? I take it you're not just buying and selling, slaver?"

At the word, Mordrec flinched, only then remembering that his colours marked out his allegience and station. With a snarl he dragged his barred tunic off, exposing the stained arming jacket beneath. "What do you want?"

The Scorpion grimaced toothily. "Out. Saving that, a drink."

"Fine, lead on."

"The place I'm drinking doesn't like Wasps, Wasp."

"All the better. Se- Mordrec." With difficulty he bit off the rank that had preceded his every introduction for years.

"Barad Ygor," the Scorpion returned, his fluid accent running the words together.

"And where's Barad, when it's at home," asked Mordrec, who knew a little of Scorpion naming customs.

"Further south than you've ever been, I'll bet. Come on, let's see if you get lynched by the mob."

Mordrec had guessed at some den of the locals, filled with surly, unruly Mynan Beetle-kinden, or rather the local pack of grey-blue-skinned malcontents that passed as Beetles if you had no better. Instead, Ygor led him to what had been someone's home once: a flat-roofed house with boarded-up windows. From outside, nothing suggested it was a taverna save the faint murmur of voices but, when they got inside, the dim interior had a dozen or so drinkers, and a halfbreed local sat on the floor at the back, filling clay bowls from the cask beside him.

The drinkers were, to a man, Grasshopper-kinden: tall, lean men and women wearing imperial colours, auxillians drafted in from some conquered Commonweal province to perform those civic tasks too menial for the proud Wasp army. Not surprisingly, none of them looked on Mordrec with much love, but his lack of uniform apparently earned him a stay of execution.

Ygor scanned the room as he walked to the barrel. "Where's Soul?" he asked its tender, but the man just spread his hands. The Scorpion scowled briefly but secured a couple of bowls, and he and

Modrec found themselves alone at a table for the simple reason that the other drinkers would not share one with a Wasp.

"You're in trouble, then?" the Scorpion suggested.

Mordrec sipped what turned out to be the thinnest honeydew mead he had ever been exposed to. "Debts," he admitted. "You?"

"Heheh." Ygor's expression was awkward and evasive. "Worse than debts, me. Imperial debts, yours?"

The Wasp nodded glumly. "And yours, Imperial worse-than-debts?"

"Hmm, well, let's just say that a friend and I did a real big *service* for your lot, after your lot had conspicuously failed to do it."

Mordrec regarded him for a moment, translating. "So everyone else hates you for what you did, and the Empire hates you because you're not a Wasp and you made them look like fools."

Barad Ygor's smile was a nightmare snarl of fangs. "In one," he agreed. "Soul and I, we need to disappear quietly from Myna before one side or the other decides that they'd rather we disappeared noisily. You're trying to ride out on the same beetle, I take it?"

Mordrec nodded, but not the sullen bob of the head of a moment before. "Can you meet Hokiak's price?" he added.

"Academic," Ygor told him dismissively, but when pressed he added, "I've no idea. I never got that far. You can't?"

"That depends on the currency." Modrec frowned. "Those Scorpions came up to sell slaves. That puts them somewhere near the market and the Corps barracks. It's more than my neck if I'm spotted there. But you..."

"Go spy on the Scorpions," Ygor said carefully. "As a prelude to...?"

"Hokiak wants payment up front, he said. I reckon we've found a new currency."

Gryllis crept into the empty backroom as though he was burgling it. Hokiak glanced balefully up at him. "Well?"

"Well you're lucky your fellows like the big public song and dance, old claw," the Spider told him softly. "If my bad memories caught up with *me* the first I'd know would be finding myself tied upside down in a cellar somewhere, surrounded by lads with razors. None of this showmanship." Under the Scorpion's yellow gaze he shrugged his bony shoulders. "But I see what they did, yes. Clever. Easy to look into a mug like theirs and think they're stupid, but I see." He stilted over and took a seat on the next nearest table to his business partner. "You're going to fight?"

"The word's out. If I ignore 'em, everyone in Myna will know it," Hokiak growled. "Then it'll start: people stop paying their debts. People start pushing me for terms. Before you know it, some bastard local or Skater or someone has decided he can run my business better than I can."

"And they're sitting with the Slave Corps, under the Empire's wings," Gryllis noted. "So you can't just do them in without losing all that goodwill we've worked so hard on." But there was a speculative expression on his face. "Old claw, I'll risk that. Old men together. Let's face it: you'd not be able to best that big fellow if you had a repeating ballista."

Hokiak's gaze dropped to the table, where his broken-clawed hand lay like a dead thing. "Once..." he rasped.

"We can neither of us live on 'once'." The Spider let out a sigh altogether too big for his narrow frame.

"When I roamed the length of the Dryclaw," Hokiak whispered, "nothing could stop me. I was like a flame, burning. Any who stood against me were ash, just ash on the wind." The words came unwillingly, as though drawn from him by wires. "So much heat and fury. But the sands never stop, do they?"

"They don't," murmured Gryllis, in heartfelt agreement.

"And I cooled, year on year, then month on month, then each day a little cooler, and I saw that I was guttering, and the next man who braved me would snuff me like a candle. But I had sold my loot all the way up the silk road to the Empire's edge, and all the little cities in between, and I hauled my embers off and thought that the others'd forget, that they'd overlook, this once, one of their own leaving the table with a handful of his winnings. I was sure that nobody cared."

"Well, touching as their sentiment is, what's it to be?" Gryllis prompted. "Broadswords at dusk? Honourable clash of two barbarian princes?"

Hokiak's hand clenched, and he stabbed his finger-claw at the table, another scratch amongst dozens. "We Scorpions," he snapped, "we don't do *honour*. Not me, not them. We fight. They came to *my* city. We fight my way."

When Barad Ygor rejoined Mordrec it was with a savage welt across the side of his head. He entered the auxillian drinking den with another of the long, lean Grasshopper-kinden behind him, and the murmur of the drinkers went quiet for a moment. Mordrec felt a wave of disapproval, an utter back-turning on the part of the auxillians. Whatever disdain they felt for the Wasp in their midst, or the Scorpion mercenary, it was as nothing to what they reserved for this one of their own.

Ygor dropped into the seat across from Mordrec, his lanky companion standing behind the chair and ignoring his kin.

"Well, there's good news and there's bad news," the Scorpion declared. "The good news is, I got a good look at them. In fact I offered to take up with them."

Mordrec looked sour. "Well it's good that one of us has options."

"Listen, I know we all look the same to *you*," Ygor snapped, clearly put out, "but they're Aktaians and I'm an Aranai, and that means they wouldn't have me, and I wouldn't take up with savages like them. Still, it let me get close and sound them out. Got me this as well." He gave a bristling grimace, indicated his lacerated scalp. "Bad news time: there are nine of the sods. Our three were just the bait."

"But they were calling Hokiak out. A duel, wasn't it?"

Ygor snorted. "Listen. I know you Wasps love the idea of battle-honour, soldier's codes, noble savages. Forget all that. They want him dead because he used to be a Big Name back in the Dryclaw, and your man Ecta there wants to be the man to have killed him. Nothing to do with dead grandfathers and honour. Forget all about honour – mine, Ecta's or Hokiak's for that matter."

"And they're in tight with the Slave Corps, so... The only chance we'll get to do anything about them is when they move out for Hokiak," Mordrec mused. "So they'll set an ambush?"

"I'd guess so."

"We can't do it with two," Mordrec decided.

"Nor three," Ygor agreed. "Modrec, formerly of the Empire, meet Soul Je, formerly of the auxillians."

The Grasshopper nodded. He was the leanest, most angular man of his kind that Mordrec had ever seen, lantern-jawed and with his hair gathered back in a tail.

"You're in whatever trouble he's in?" the Wasp asked.

"Bad career decisions," said the Grasshopper quietly. The hostility of his fellows was palpable but he shrugged it off coolly. "Three of us, nine of them. Hokiak might thank us for evening the odds, but he'd be thanking our corpses. We need more help."

"Well the locals hate us and the Empire hates him," Ygor pointed out, "and because of that we can't trust freelancers."

Mordrec put his head in his hands, not despairing but building his courage. "Right, listen," he said at last. "There's one group of clowns who'd do anything to get out of the city, and who aren't going to have any better offers."

The other two looked at him blankly

"I don't know what the Corps have in their stockade right now, but some of them are bound to be fighters," the former slaver explained.

"I thought you didn't want to show your face there," Ygor pointed out.

"I'll wear my helm. He has a uniform, and they're used to Scorpions around the place. We'd go by night. We'd be quick."

"Freeing slaves is a little more than just desertion or bad debts, Mordrec," Ygor pointed out. "You're an Empire man, still."

Mordrec stared into his mead-bowl moodily. "I've pissed off the Rekef. I owe what I can't pay. It's slavery for me at best. Any idea how well a Slave Corps sergeant does, when they put the shackles on him? It'll be the arena, if some other slave doesn't do for me. I need *out*, Ygor, some way that they can't trace and they can't follow."

The Scorpion exechanged a look with Soul Je. "Well we managed to overachieve to the extent that nobody likes us and we're on the same road as you. So..."

"Three of us, nine of them." Modrec threw his hands up. "A day and a half, now, to get it done. It must be tonight. Then tomorrow we bring every cursed thing we have down on Ecta and his mates."

"Just so we're clear, I'm going in as a freelance slaver," Barad Ygor hissed, as they neared the stockade. "Only, I knew a man who had the bright idea that he'd get snuck in to a place like this done up as a slave. Did twenty years down a mine, he did."

"Relax." Mordrec's voice sounded hollow and anything but relaxed. The full-faced Slave Corps helms were designed to give their wearers an intimidating facelessness, to strike fear into the hearts of slaves. Now, for the first time, Mordrec felt it restricting and close.

The three of them approached the Slave Corps depot with all nonchalance. There were a couple of the Corps on watch at the outer wall but they took no great notice of their visitors, just nodding to whoever they imagined was behind the helm. Inside was a Mynan townhouse that the Corps had converted into a barracks, and a warehouse that held their stock in trade, a constant flux of human traffic that was a link in the great Imperial chain.

To Mordrec it felt as though every eye must be upon them, these three patent intruders trespassing on sacrosanct imperial soil. Ygor was right about one thing: people who visited the Corps unlooked-for were usually invited to stay. However the handful of Wasp-kinden present paid them no heed, and the bulk of the slavers were clearly in the barracks. With all appearances of confidence, Mordrec led the others into the converted warehouse, where there would be a hundred likely slaves worth the freeing.

Except there were not.

He had to force himself to complete his journey inside, rather than just stopping dead in the doorway and letting the other two run into him. There were no slaves. Every cage was empty. They had come at the worst possible time. Either some grand buyer had just cleaned them out, or a Corps caravan had set off for the inner Empire earlier that very day.

He could feel the accusing stares of the others on him. The helm, which had been his companion for seven years, began to feel like a prison.

"Him." Soul Je was striding past him, stalking towards the back of the barred space. One man: the Grasshopper's eyes had spotted one man remaining. A tug of warning jerked through Mordrec: *Why was he left?* But they had come here with a purpose and it wasn't as if they had any better options.

The man was a Commonwealer, a Dragonfly-kinden, a little stockier than they usually were, a good few years Mordrec's senior with the faintest peppering of grey in his hair. He regarded the trio impassively.

Mordrec looked the man over: he looked capable. "Show me your hands," he directed. Sourly, the Dragonfly jammed a palm towards him, mimicking the threat of a Wasp's sting. It showed the calluses that Mordrec had been looking for, though. "Archer," he noted. "You want out of here?"

The Dragonfly said nothing, but shrugged.

"Out of this city," Ygor prompted in a low voice. "All the way home, if you want it. Willing to kill for it?"

"*And what are you doing with my prisoner?*"

There was a Wasp in the warehouse doorway, a tall, smooth-looking man with fair hair. He held himself with an utter certainty as he strode towards them, as though swords and stings meant nothing to him. Modrec's heart lurched and a chill rash ofsweat broke over him. It was Lyker, the holder of Modrec's gambling debts: Lyker of the Rekef. That was why the Dragonfly had been left behind. He was being saved for Rekef questioning.

For the moment, Lyker was ignoring the helmed slaver, staring instead at Igor and Soul Je. "He's not for sale, Scorpion," he snapped. "Now get back to your rabble of friends before I see what price your waxy hide might fetch. You," he directed at Mordrec, "why'd you ever bring him in..." And then the dreadful moment came, Lyker's eyes narrowing. "Name, soldier."

There were dozens of Slave Corps soldiers just a shout away, and Lyker *would* shout. Mordrec's former comrades would be all too happy to turn on one of their own. The slavers bred no great loyalty amongst their number, only cruelty and greed. *Perhaps that's why I'm in this mess, because I never really fit in*, Mordrec considered. *Or perhaps I'm just a rotten gambler.*

"Mordrec...?" Lyker growled and Mordrec felt his palm flash with fire, without even consciously deciding on it. The flare of his Art lashed between them, taking the other Wasp directly in the chest. Lyker was without armour, and the distance was mere feet.

A silence followed, save for the sound of the men in the barracks laughing and drinking.

Well there's no going back now, Mordrec thought numbly. He reached for his keys and unlocked the Dragonfly's cage, his hands performing their tasks by long habit, without the need for thought. None of them spoke as they exited the warehouse. The slaver stockade was as before, and nobody was paying them any attention. The dead Rekef man was a secret that the night still kept, for all that Mordrec felt the corpse behind him like a hot iron against his back.

There was a sudden blur of sound and motion beside them, and the Dragonfly was gone, his Art-conjured wings taking him straight up into the night. Mordrec started after him, and it was a good thing that helm hid his utter chagrin from his fellows.

They left the slaver compound as quickly as possible, and trailed their way back to the nameless auxillian drinking hole. Few words were exchanged until, at the door, Ygor gave a great sigh and said, "Well, three against nine. Maybe we'll be very lucky. I have a trick or two."

Mordrec opened his mouth to reply and there was a sudden scuff of feet behind them that had all three whirling. The Dragonfly stood there, arms folded.

"Out of the city, you said," he reminded them. "Killing, you said. Fine. I'll need a bow. The name's Dal Arche."

In the still of the night, Hokiak drank and waited. The stuff in his bowl bore the same relationship to wine as a rusty saw blade did to a rapier. Hokiak, whose cellar had all manner of delicate vintages, had gone back to the drink of his youth, a vitriol his people called sak, although proper sak was traditionally drunk from a helm or a skull. There was no great mystery in that: it showed the drinker had triumphed over the world for another day. Hokiak had once heard a Beetle scholar expound on how the Scorpion-kinden lived in *harmony* with the rhythms of the desert. Hokiak's people had never lived in harmony with anything. They fought the land around them and they fought everyone else and they fought each other.

It was past midnight now, and past time, in Hokiak's estimation. The Exchange was silent around him. There were lamps lit still, in the shop front, but little light spilled into the backroom. Scorpion-kinden eyes were adapatable, from sun's glare to the dark of the moon, but these days Hokiak's own were failing. He saw best at dusk, and dusk was long gone.

At last it began. He heard a rattling, just long enough to check the door was locked, and then an explosion of shattered wood. His people were not known for subtlety. They struck hard and fast and were gone.

He sat there, sipping his sak and scratching at the tabletop with one claw as the fighting started, letting the individual details of it wash over him: the clash of steel, smash of wood, crossbows' clack and the hoarse yelling of the wounded. If things went unexpectedly badly then Ecta's people would burst into his backroom in a moment and do for him. Otherwise...

In under a minute the skirmish was played out, the only voice remaining was the strained swearing of one of Hokiak's Mynan employees. It had been hard to muster any number of guards, once Ecta had bearded him. The local resistance was in an uproar over their recent reversal, the Empire disdained to lend a hand. He had fallen back on the local gangs, freelancers, mercenaries, men unreliable and untested. Still, it seemed that his precautions had been enough.

Gryllis came in, dusting his hands off theatrically. "Well, old claw, I'll keep the lads on watch, but I reckon that's the lot."

"What damage?" Hokiak asked him.

"Three came in. One of our lads got ripped up badly. One of theirs is dead. The other two made their exit when they saw we were ready for them." The Spider-kinden's face twisted. "Only thing is, the Scorpions that came in tonight weren't any of them the fellows who were with your friend Ecta yesterday."

Hokiak nodded safely. "These tonight will be his youngest, the least experienced. He'll have set them a challenge to win his respect. Or perhaps it was even their own idea, to steal the glory of taking my head. So much for whatever their plans were, then. But Ecta won't weep. All he'll care is that I've been sent a message. No quiet nights until this is over."

"Lovely," said Gryllis drily. "You're still going ahead with this tomorrow?"

The old Scorpion nodded. "Oh to be sure," he said, with a trace of iron in his voice. "After all, any more of this and I'll start taking it personally. We'll pay the men a bonus, for tonight, and tell them to spread the word."

Gryllis nodded. "And I'll get a better door put in."

The next day Mordrec, weighed at one side with a lumpy package wrapped in oilcloth, crept his way to the drinking den. The small hours had seen him turning up, unannounced and unfriendly, at a Consortium merchant's door: The Beetle-kinden man had obviously heard that people wanted to speak to his former associate but Mordrec gave him no time to raise the alarm. Instead, keeping the palm of his hand almost in the panicking man's face at all times, he retrieved what he had put by in the man's care during better times. Thus fortified with a purse of money, a little pilfered jewellery and his heavy burden, he made a quick escape to the skies before the Consortium man could fetch help.

The Dragonfly Dal Arche had been hidden by the Auxillians who apparently approved of his rescue, although not so far as to change their dislike of Modrec or their absolute despite of Soul Je. It was quite an education, in fact, for Mordrec to discover just how much the conscripts got up to behind the backs of their Wasp masters. When he rejoined them, Dal and Soul both had a bow: man-high, recurved pieces of elegance that Mordrec remembered from the war.

Dal had strung his, and was running his hands down the sculpted lines, the lethality inherant in the tensioned wood. His face had a thoughtful expression to it. "To think, some master bowyer spent months to craft this for the hand of a prince, perhaps, and now it's war loot. You can see where the gold inlay's been pried out."

"Your sort of bow, then?" Mordrec said cautiously, unsure where this man had been while the Empire pillaged his Commonweal.

"Me?" Dal Arche gave a hard smile. "Not a bit of it. Give me a brigand's shortbow any time. This'll have to do, though. Where's your Scorpion got to?"

Mordrec shrugged. "He should be here."

"He's coming now," Soul Je stated with a nod. "Brought a friend."

Glancing past the shutters, Mordrec saw that someone resembling the Scorpion was indeed approaching, but swathed in an enormous cloak, considerably bulkier and inexplicably affecting a pronounced hunchback.

"Is he in disguise?" he murmured.

Soul Je had a slightly amused look. "He's bringing everything he's got to the table, gambler," he replied softly.

Barad Ygor stumbled through the doorway and descended heavily onto a bench, which barely survived the experience. "Right," he announced. "I'm ready."

"Armour?" Mordrec asked him, baffled.

The Scorpion-kinden glanced left and right conspiratorially, before slinging his cloak back.

"Light's fire!" Dal Arche spat, and Mordrec leapt back from him, almost tripping backwards. Ygor had come with a friend: it was coiled about him, eight legs clasping his chest and stomach, burnished pincers resting on his collarbones like hideously oversized jewellery, and about his waist the segmented tail, with its needle-tipped stinger nestling companionably over his navel. Mordrec had seen big scorpions before, of course. They were popular in the arenas, a good match for a handful of badly-armed slaves or one skilled fighter, but to have such a dangerous animal loose within a city was unthinkable. To have one just across the table made him sweat and, as for having one actually draped, all claws and tail over someone's body...

"You're mad," he told Ygor flatly. "Even that brute Ecta would say you're mad."

"Let him," Ygor replied. "Scutts and I understand each other." He put a hand on one of the beast's fierce pincers, which shifted slightly under his touch. "Back home, the speaking Art isn't so rare as around here. You can't even get to be a proper Stalker unless you can take a wife."

"A *wife?* You're ill. What if it..."

"She," Ygor corrected. "And consider her one of us, our fifth. Now what have you brought?" He shrugged the cloak on again and nodded to Mordrec's parcel.

"Ah well." Slightly shamefaced afer his outburst, Mordrec drew back the cloth to reveal an ugly, lumpy weapon as long as his arm, something like an armless crossbow but with a boxy mechanism over the trigger lever.

"Right," Ygor said levelly. "And *I'm* mad, am I?"

"What is it?" Dal Arche asked blankly.

"It's part of my winnings from an eighteen-hour game of toppers with an Engineering Corps captain, who must have had a lot of explaining to do the next day. We call them nailbows. They're quite new."

"And quite *loud*," Ygor pointed out. "Do you even know how to use that thing?"

"As I understand, it's mostly a matter of pointing it in the right direction and waiting for the noise to stop," Mordrec said blithely.

"Well it'll give Ecta a shock, as well as most of the city," Ygor decided philosophically.

The marketplace Ecta had picked out was mostly abandoned some time before dusk. Those traders who had intended to remain were soon discouraged by a band of big, heavily-armed Scorpion-kinden, at first by means of a few words, and then with broken stalls and goods. The Empire, which might have been expected to take an interest in this lawlessness, was conspicuous in its absence. It was clear to Mordrec that the Scorpions had made a donation to Slave Corps coffers, and they in turn had leant on the auxillian militia, Soul Je's kindred, to keep away. Soon enough, even before the sun was falling behind Myna's city wall, the place was deserted save for Ecta's people. At a signal from their leader the Scorpions broke up, each finding cover amongst the stalls, spreading out through the deserted lanes of the market. Mordrec saw, then, that Ygor had been right about his own people. This was no matter of honour. Ecta might be standing out in his full glory, leaning on his man-high sword like a noble barbarian prince, but the others had fanned out into a pincer ambush, fingering their axes and blades. They hid well, too, for big men. Soon only Ecta was left, but the jaws of the trap were trembling, waiting for one old man.

Soul Je had used his Auxillian status to install them in the upper room of a wayhouse at the edge of the market. From its small window they had done their best to keep track of where Ecta's followers had *gone*, but in the end at least half of the Scorpions had vanished entirely.

"Time to move," Mordrec decided. "Hokiak'll be here any moment." He looked at his allies doubtfully. "We'll have to hunt them."

"We'll strike when the old man turns up," Dal Arche stated. "You want him to be impressed, yes?"

"Yes," Mordrec agreed, heartfelt. He glanced from face to face: the grizzled Dragonfly-kinden; Soul Je with his long, unreadable face; squat and broad Barad Ygor with his lethal pet, Scutts, coiled about his feet. The former slaver hefted the weight of his nailbow. "Let's move."

The Slave Corps were not known for subtlety, but Mordrec had fought in the Twelve-year War and had his own memories of playing stalking games with Dragonfly Mercers and assassins. He had served the Corps as scout and spotter, in the air and on the ground, and he entered the hushed market noiselessly, the bulk of the nailbow cocked back over his shoulder to keep it from rattling against anything, his free hand palm out, ready to unleash his sting in case someone else was stalking *him*.

Of his allies, Dal Arche and Soul Je had vanished utterly, not a sound or scent of them. The maze of vacant stalls did not admit to their presence in any way. Barad Ygor was hanging back, not the stealthiest of men, crouched by a derelict potter's with his crossbow cradled, string taut, in his arms. His venomous friend was gone, though, and Modrec imagined the creature creeping, belly to the ground, beneath the awnings and the wooden stands, hunting out the enemy on Ygor's behalf.

It was dusk now, and Wasp eyes were not at their best. Mordrec took his progress step by step, working his way towards the centre. He was in sight of the cleared space, edging round to get an angle on Ecta himself, when he realised that, only a few yards away, one of the other Scorpions was crouched, clawed hands on the haft of a crescent-headed axe. Mordrec froze, but the man's attention was wholly inward. With painstaking care the ex-slaver canted the heavy nailbow from his shoulder and brought the machined barrel round.

The Scorpion twitched, and very nearly died for it, as Mordrec's nerves were stretched to snapping. A newcomer was shuffling a slow progress out into the open space at the market's heart.

Hokiak lent on his cane with each step, breathing heavily as though the mere walk from his Exchange had worn him down. He glanced around him, plainly suspecting that Ecta's confederates were nearby, and then stopped a dozen yards from the bigger Scorpion, both hands on the head of his stick. Ecta's stance had changed when the old man made his entrance: the greatsword's length and weight now hanging easily in one fist. For a moment it seemed that he was expecting something special: for Hokiak to leap into the air and reveal himself as some great combat master whose edge could never be dulled by mere time. The ancient renegade just hunched there, though, a sack of bones and yellowed skin and rheumy, watering eyes.

You had better be bloody grateful for this, Mordrec thought to himself. *You had better not have come here* wanting *to die, you wrinkled bastard.*

Ecta had apparently understood that there was nothing more than this: an old man at the end of his times. With a disappointed grunt, clearly audible against the sound of so many people being silent, he hefted his blade.

Now. And Mordrec's finger twitched on the lever, and the nailbow roared in his hands, all but jumping out of his grip. He had intended to put a neat hole in the back of the man before him, but he emptied a half-dozen bolts in a wild arc amidst the sound of firepowder and thunder. Two bolts struck home, more by luck than anything else, slamming the man forwards hard enough to overturn his hiding place. Then a second Scorpion had arisen from a few feet to Mordrec's left, lifting a halberd with a roar of fury, and everything started to happen at once.

Ecta was single-minded and he went for Hokiak still, trusting to his men to deal with the noise. He changed his mind when an arrow clipped his shoulder, signing a narrow line of blood against his dead white skin. Turning, he saw a Dragonfly drop to the ground across the market square, already reaching for another shaft. Ecta was at him, though, covering the intervening ground with startling swiftness, the greatsword's blade blurring between them. Dal Arche's wings flickered in and out of sight, landing him ten feet back, but the string of his borrowed bow snapped as he tried to get his second shot off, whipping across his face.

As the halberd came for him, Mordrec loosed his sting, the golden energy flashing from his palm to scorch across the Scorpion's flank. The man snarled and hacked for him, and the Wasp let his wings cast him sideways between two stalls, nailbow dragging in his wake. He almost barrelled straight into another man who was rushing towards the noise. For a moment he was caught between them, stumbling aside from the newcomer's scything claws. The halberd came down again and Mordrec bounced the haft bruisingly from his forearm, waiting for the claws to come in. Instead, the second man went down with a howl, and Mordrec tripped over him. He landed half on something hard and lumpy, and rolled off with a yell when he saw that it was Scutts' segmented back, the sting poised above him like a stiletto.

Mordrec twisted urgently to one side, seeing a brief glimpse of the creature's claws clasped about his fallen opponent's knee. Then the needle point of the sting lashed down into the luckless man's groin. The halberdier roared and raised the heavy blade of his weapon to strike, and Mordrec emptied the nailbow into him in an explosive judder of finger-long bolts.

When he looked round, Scutts had made herself scarce amongst the stalls. *And I hope that bloody Ygor keeps her on a firm leash.*

Dal Arche had a Wasp-issue shortsword out now, looking like a butter-knife compared to Ecta's greatsword. He could have flown away without difficulty but Hokiak still stood there, staring pop-eyed at the spectacle of a Commonwealer rushing to his defence, and so he led the Scorpion chieftain a chase about the market square, keeping out of the broad reach of that massive blade. Initially he had hoped to be able to feign his way past the Scorpion's guard for a swift strike, but Ecta was both fast and skilled. Twice now he had almost caught Dal Arche with a sudden burst of speed, or an unexpected leap forwards that extended the man's reach four feet. Every time Dal tried to turn the assault, the sweep of the greatsword almost had him, every time he fell back Ecta drove for Hokiak. *Where are the others?*

Mordrec was heading for the market's centre when a couple of fighters crashed through a stall immediately in front of him. For a moment he saw only two Scorpions fighting, but then he spotted the shorter one as Ygor. The Wasp barked out a shout, the sort the Corps used to stop running slaves in their tracks. With a supreme effort, Ygor's adversary cast him down to the ground and stared at Mordrec, obviously unsure whose side he was on. With a hard grin the Wasp levelled the nailbow at him and pulled the lever.

Of course, I should probably have reloaded the cursed thing...

The backhand blow of the Scorpion's clawed fist knocked Mordrec entirely off his feet, his head ringing with the force of it. For a moment his enemy stood over him, hand raised to drive those Art claws down like daggers, then the man was running, seemingly without transition, and a moment later Scutts bounded past, pincers wide and body a sinuous curve. Ygor had recovered his crossbow from somewhere and got off a bolt that flew a good eight feet wide of the fleeing man, but a moment later a long arrow appeared like magic through the running Scorpion's neck, stopping him for a moment, upright and dead still, before he collapsed.

Without a word, Modrec and Ygor ran for the central square with Scutts pursuing them excitedly.

Dal was running out of options. He was relying on his wings more and more to keep him out of Ecta's way, and the Art was draining him slowly of his strength. The Scorpion seemed indefatiguable and had found a rhythm now, was even giving the retreating Dragonfly a fang-bristling smile.

"About time!" Dal shouted, as Modrec and Ygor pounded into sight. "You get the rest?" Then he kicked high into the air, passing entirely over Ecta's bald head to land in a crouch, rasping for breath, behind him. When the big man turned he saw three human opponents and a barely-restrained animal facing him.

He seemed utterly undaunted. He was barely breathing hard, they saw. "Oh this is good," he murmured. "Hokiak, you amuse me."

Mordrec had his hand out, fingers spread, ready to sting, and Ygor had reloaded his crossbow, dragging the string back with one notched thumb-claw. Ecta barely seemed to care.

"Come forth, my warriors," he bellowed. Mordrec was frantically counting in his head. He had done for two, and Scutts had stung another, and presumably removed him from the fight. Dal Arche had gone straight for Ecta, as they had planned. Had Ygor killed any others? That still left...

None. Apparently that left none. Nobody came forward to answer Ecta's summons. The Scorpion chieftain shrugged, looking from the newcomers to Hokiak. It seemed he would say something, some threat or piece of defiance, but then he launched himself at the old man, sword drawn back, an unstoppable, unheralded charge. Ygor loosed and missed, and Mordrec held off his sting for fear of striking Hokiak himself.

Ecta fell at Hokiak's feet. The slender shaft of a longbow arrow stood between his shoulder-blades like a standard. For a moment nobody moved, waiting, and then a tall, angular shadow moved amongst the stalls, and Soul Je stepped out, almost apologetically, nodding briefly to his allies.

Hokiak stared at them for a long while. He had barely moved throughout the whole skirmish, still leaning on his stick as though he was just an old veteran enjoying clement weather. Eventually, and in tones that were hard to analyse, he said, "You clowns."

Mordrec exchanged looks with his allies, save for Dal Arche who was mopping gingerly at the red weal that his bowstring had left across his face.

"Oh you utter clowns," the old man repeated, but there was a chuckle recognisable in his tone now. "All right lads, out you come."

And out they came, more than a dozen of them: Mynan Beetle-kinden with levelled crossbows emerging from either side of the withered Scorpion, all of them staring at Mordrec and his fellows as though waiting for the order to shoot.

"You..." Mordrec started uncertainly. "But I though that..."

"I *told* you Scorpions don't care about honour," Ygor reminded him in a murmur.

"And there's another two dozen ready to come in," Hokiak said slowly. "I called in a lot of favours. What do you clowns *want?*"

"Out," the Wasp replied promptly. "Safe travel out of the Empire. Papers, transport, whatever it takes to be out of the reach of the Rekef." He glanced at Dal Arche. "The Commonweal's nice, this time of year."

For a moment Hokiak regarding him disdainfully. "I hear Lyker got himself dead."

"That was... careless of him," Mordrec managed.

The old Scorpion could hold his face still no longer. He shook his head to hide it, but there was a grin somewhere amongst the yellowing stumps of his hutting teeth. "Myna's better off without you," he spat, and then held a hand out swiftly in case any of his followers took this as an order. "You're fools, all of you, to do this on credit, but I'm feeling generous all of a sudden. Come back to the Exchnge and I'll see what I can do."

He lent on his stick less, they saw, as he hobbled off back towards his den, and despite his years there was a decided new spring in his step.

Characterisation in Shadows *is often a case of playing against the type I've given a particular kinden, and Hokiak is surely the most extreme example: the most important Scorpion character in the series is, at the same time, the least Scorpion of them all. Here we have conquered Myna shortly before the events of* Empire, *with the Twelve Year War consigned to history and Myna as just a stopover for the loot funnelling out of the Commonweal. Speaking of that, Dal, Soul, Ygor and Mordrec all have their day in court in* Heirs of the Blade, *which draws a lot of loose threads together. The only other major character from the novels whom this story touches is unnamed here, but it doesn't take much to work out just what major blow the Mynan resistance has suffered, and just why Soul and Ygor are* persona non grata *with the locals.*

Brass Mantis

Helleron, city of smoke and iron; a good city for bad times. Oh, perhaps the rich magnates there lived swaddled in wealth and luxury, but then it never seemed to be Helleron that they lived in. Their lives of palatial townhouses, of elegant waste and barbed entertainments, belonged to some other city that the rest of the populace could only observe as through grimy glass.

For the Apt, those whose birthright was machinery and the ability to understand it, Helleron exercised a powerful attraction. Its countless forges and workshops and factories were always hungry for bodies. There was a living to be had there, slotted into a tiny mould, performing one restrictive function over and over, making a lifelong profession of being a miniscule cog. Helleron was a vast machine that consumed lives and produced everything else. It was the industrial heart of the Insect-kinden's world, beating oil and gear trains and the hissing strength of steam.

What, then, for the Inapt? For those to whom machines were a mystery that could never be parsed, choked by their mystic superstitions that the Apt laughed at in scorn, what could Helleron possibly offer? And yet they came, and the answer seemed to be nothing more than dissolution. There were Moth-kinden begging on the streets whose ancestors had been great magicians back in an age nobody could quite remember any more. There were Dragonflies starving in the gutters who had donned glittering armour to ride against the mechanized hosts of the Wasps, and lose. There were renegade Spider-kinden in the tavernas and the whorehouses, stalking death one sin at a time.

There was a Mantis-kinden Weaponsmaster that nobody could kill.

He was a lean, deadly man, Tisamon his name, and he had drifted about the eastern Lowlands, cutting wherever he touched, until he drew too close to the hungry pull of Helleron. People whispered about his past. Certainly he seemed to have little to live for. The only thing keeping him alive looked to be pride. They said his brooch, a sword crossing a circle, was the mark of an ancient, forgotten order of warrior mystics. They said he was seeking death, but it was not in him to bare steel with any intent save to win.

Tisamon fought two kinds of matches. Publicly, he was a prizefighter. Such clashes were never overtly to the death. The pretence, at least, was of a clash of skill, two professionals meeting with respect and elegance to the delight of an informed crowd. Standing on that bloodied sand, listening to the drunken jeering, the bustle and babble, Tisamon felt the artistry of his trade corroding, as though the caustic air that hung about the factories could etch and eat at a man's soul.

He preferred the other sort of match, staged for nobody's entertainment. Much of Helleron was held by a patchwork of gangs, the Fiefs, who existed under and alongside and sometimes in the pocket of the great industrial magnates. There was always a fight brewing amongst the Fiefs. There was always a street or a gambling den changing hands. There was always blood. It was almost reassuring how there was always blood.

Tisamon admitted to no Fief, acknowledged no masters, but there was always a brisk trade in skilled freelancers on the hard streets of Helleron. There, to no applause and to the death, he plied his trade. He had a reputation.

It was a Fief turf war that brought him to the artificer Ellery Mainler.

A disagreement had arisen over a particularly choice establishment, conjoined brothel and gambling den – specifically, who had the right to protect these establishments from the woes of the world, for a modest fee. The players were the Seven Clocks, native Beetle-kinden muscling in from the nearby factories, against Fabrus Brothers Union, close-knit Ant-kinden exiles from some place in the Empire. The Fabrus boys were noted brawlers but the Clocks had the wherewithal to call in a few independents. Their factor tapped the Beetle woman who served as Tisamon's agent, and she gave him a time and a place.

Supposedly it was going to be just a friendly piece of leaning, the Clock lads swaggering over to take in the sights and put the Ants in their place, with Tisamon for backup. The Fabrus caught wind of it, got the wrong idea, and did their level best to turn a minor incursion into a war. Tisamon had to earn his keep. Whilst the grandees from Seven

Clocks decided the game had gone sour and beat a retreat, the Mantis had a busy few minutes dancing and stepping through a shifting net of Ant swords and knifes, leaving bloody writing everywhere he went and getting a guided tour of most of the establishment along the way.

He particularly remembered a tight spot when three knife-men had him penned up in a small room in the brothel, whilst the original occupant and his patron cowered underneath the bed. Tisamon's claw – the gauntlet with its metal blade that jutting down the line of his fingers – had been busy fending off their furious lunges and, whilst he left them plenty of shallow wounds to remember him by, the Ants fought together well, and he had begun to wonder if *this*, this tawdry little business, might be *it*. Then one of them lunged too strongly, and Tisamon took the man's arm and flung him through the wall, so that the entire brawling pack of them spilled out into the gambling den next door.

With a little more space at his command he was able to teach the Fabrus boys that the game was not worth the stakes, and once he had killed one and bloodied the rest they vanished away, leaving him standing on a card table with a stunned audience of gamblers.

There was one woman there, who did not seem the type. A Beetle-kinden, like most of the Helleren, but dressed too well and looking too clean. She had been staring up open-mouthed with the rest at this bloody interruption to the game. Unlike the rest, who got out of his way as though he had the plague, she trailed him to the doorway and offered to buy him a drink.

Tisamon did not want a drink, particularly. He wanted to track down the Seven Clocks and get the balance of his fee. However, he saw the way that some of the woman's gaming partners looked at her – as though they had already tallied up the worth of her clothes and decided that they were too valuable to be allowed to leave with their current owner. In the hope of a new fight, he agreed.

She named herself Ellery Mainler. She spoke with an educated precision he recognized, a graduate of distant Collegium. She was young, monied, intense. She kept unfolding her spectacles to look at him closely, the lenses flashing with reflected gaslight against her dark skin, then tucking them away again.

"You fight beautifully," she told him. They were at a taverna well out of the reach of the Fabrus Brothers.

Tisamon looked her over, trying to work out what she wanted. Her expression was still lit from within as though witnessing the bloodshed had set a fire there.

"I'm a connoisseur," she confided to him, "of the fight."

She must have read his reaction – the haughty disdain felt by the master of the ancient tradition for the presumptuous amateur – and was instantly trying to disabuse him.

"It's not like that! I don't just bet on the matches. I'm not one of *those*," and, seeing that the distance between them was only growing, "I'll show you. Come to my home. It's not far."

Tisamon shook his head, drained his wine, stood to go. Instantly she'd reached for his sleeve, almost bloodying her fingers on the sharp spines that ran down his forearm, a manifestation of the Mantis-kinden Art, that made him what he was.

"Come with me!" she insisted and, when he turned to go, she shouted after him, "I need you to see! I'm not just some sad spectator. I'm a scholar of the fight. Mantis, I have my honour!"

In the taverna's doorway, Tisamon turned.

"I have my honour," she repeated. "I won't be... dismissed, misinterpreted, like that. At least let me show you." There was something naked in her face, not need but needs, intertwined. He knew then that she was trouble but, in his circles, everyone was trouble of one kind or another.

"Show me," thus he committed himself.

Her home was mostly a workshop. She lived in the small upper rooms, she said, but artifice was her life, and where her money went. The building was expansive and in a good area, redolent of inherited wealth.

"Why risk yourself gambling, if you have this?" he challenged her.

"Because my research is expensive," she explained tersely, as she unlocked the door.

"Gambling is a good way of losing what little you have."

"Not for me. I never lose." Her eyes glinted as she turned the lamps up, the light spreading out across a great open space that was most of the ground floor. "Nobody realizes what you can do with cards, if you've a perfect memory and a good head for figures. Of course, I have to move about a bit. People don't like to bet against me twice."

"You'll get yourself killed."

She shrugged, crossing to some kind of machine that stood in the centre of the floor, the focus of the room. It was a pillar a little over man-height, a mass of interlocking components that Tisamon's Inapt eyes skipped over. All machines were incomprehensible to him.

"Look." She led his eyes to the walls, where the light guttered fitfully over sketches of the human body. He saw what seemed at first to be a view from a torture chamber: figures with bones laid bare, flayed men, women who were strung with bared sinews, all annotated in minute script. And all in motion, each sketch catching the mangled body in mid-strike. Ellery's studies of the fight. This was what she had meant.

Her expression was calm, focused enough to cut steel. "I know. I'm Apt. What can I know of your great and noble mystery? That's it, isn't it?" And, when he just looked at her, "But I do understand. I know everything of the fighter's art save how to fight. I know the leverage and the fulcrums, all there is about balance and joints, extension and angle. I have anatomized the fight."

She was young, unskilled, built to that Beetle-kinden frame that produced solid, compact, slightly overfull bodies, but her intensity intimidated him more than a drawn blade. "To what purpose?" he asked her.

"To reproduce it," and she threw a lever on the machine and then stepped back.

He heard the hiss of steam, the floor beneath him quivering with the motion of buried engines, and then the thing unfolded its blade, a length of razored steel on an arm with three joints. There was nothing human – nothing natural – in the way it brandished the weapon.

"I will pay you," Ellery Mainler told him. "I want to watch you fight. I want you to fight it."

"How can it be fought?" Tisamon demanded. "It's a *thing*."

"You won't know what I mean by a ratiocinator," she told him. "They're new. Nobody's done anything like this with one. It lets my duellist think – or calculate anyway. If you approach it now, it will know where you are, from sound, from vibration. This leads into a cascade of gear trains that tell it how best to kill you. So fight, Mantis." Her eyes were very wide. "I will pay you. I have money. Fight for me."

He should have walked away, he knew. She was unbalanced, and this was no use of his skills, to attack an object. That should have ended it. He was going to do just that.

One step towards the door and he made the mistake of looking back at her, seeing her tremble at the rejection. Poor Apt girl, wealthy beyond counting in the world she had been born into, and yet without a single coin in his. He saw how long she had been working on this joke of a thing, how very badly she wanted to achieve... what? Perhaps even she was not sure.

He turned back, and now his clawed gauntlet was on his hand.

"You want me to destroy this thing."

"I want you to try."

He stepped towards the machine cautiously, watching that crooked blade. As he neared, parts of it moved, sliding and spinning, and abruptly its single arm flicked out, so that he leant back to avoid its reach. He circled, step by step, seeing the band that held the arm revolve with him. He had no sense that he was facing a living enemy.

He feinted twice, watching the machine follow his movements, feeling out the delay in its response, and then struck, batting aside the blade with his own, following through, stepping around it and then driving the point of his claw three, four times into the workings. A moment later he was pacing back, weapon raised between him and it, anticipating the mechanical arm spinning to lash after him. It was frozen, though, locked where he had parried it. Whatever damage he had done had returned the mechanism to the world of the inanimate.

He cocked his head at Ellery, surprising a wealth of expressions there as she fought to master herself. Very few of them made sense to him: perhaps these were Apt expressions, interpretable only by those who understood gear trains and calculus.

The Seven Clocks and the Fabrus Union had worked out their differences, but there was always another fight. Tisamon drifted from one to the next, but nothing pushed him, and the sense of purposeless despair that was never far away began to loom large in his life. Then came a challenger from the South, a Spider-kinden who called him out. Tisamon's loathing for the Spiders was legendary, and his opponent seemed to return the sentiment in equal measure. They fought, and though the man had no sword and circle badge, he was good enough to have earned one. Afficionados of the duel said that it was best they'd seen in years, and Tisamon was bleeding from a handful of shallow wounds by the time he cut the Spider down, finding himself standing over the body, feeling oddly bereft that the man was dead.

Looking up, his gaze lit on Ellery Mainler, wide eyes fixed on him. He could read desire there, that possessive kind that rich Beetles specialized in. When he met her gaze, he felt the same physical shock he had when he had looked at the Spider down the length of the man's steel.

She sought him out, of course she did. "Come and fight for me," she told him.

"Your machine, again?"

"I've improved it." And of course that was what the Apt did. While the old world of magic, that Tisamon had been born to, had sprung into being in the height of its power and only declined since, the Apt were always improving. "I can pay you," Ellery added, and "Please."

The machine, when he laid eyes on it again, had changed. He had made some comments before leaving the last time, concerning how such a thing could never be what she wanted it to be. She had taken the details to heart and discarded the body of the message.

There was a webwork of rails patterning the ceiling, crossing everywhere in the room, and the machine was no longer just a pillar fixed to the floor. "It must move," Tisamon had said. Now, the lumpy, part-armoured cylinder of its body was suspended between the rails and four articulated legs. It had two arms, the familiar blade and a twin that ended in the bronze disc of a buckler. It still resembled nothing living and, even when she threw the lever and it juddered into motion, it remained a dead thing to him.

"You must fight it," she told him, and he saw the articulated legs pick their way sideways, not supporting the machine's weight but just guiding its progress, so that it seemed to glide over the floor like a crab over the seabed. When Ellergy spoke, the machine stopped and turned towards her.

"What if I leave?" he asked her. "Can you make it stop?" And he had its faceless attention once more.

"I don't know," she told him. He remembered her in the gambling den, amongst men and women who would have murdered her for her shoes. A Beetle girl, yes, born to money and education, and not satisfied, never satisfied. A warrior's heart in the body of a dilettante.

He approached the machine at a rush.

It reacted more swiftly than the previous incarnation, lashing towards him with sword and buckler together, dominating the mid-line like a real swordsman. Still, it was slower than flesh. Still the movements were that fraction of a second late, a hand's span off, as it tried to keep up with where he was. He led it around the room, getting a feel for this new mobility, fending the blade off when it came in range. The machine pursued him relentlessly, snorting steam, the massed ranks of clockwork within it sounding like grinding teeth.

He struck three times, watching the machine move shield and blade into place, understanding its rhythms. A moment later he had dropped beneath its next swing, putting a boot into its torso that set it swinging on the rails. An upwards blow locked the sword arm rigid where it met the body, brass housings bent into a firm clasp. He had no way of telling its weak points, but he let his blade drive into those parts that seemed less armoured, and finally it stopped chattering and hissing, the last of its steam escaping in a long, disappointed breath.

"It's still nothing but a thing," he told Ellery. Her stare was disconcerting, acquisitive. He took his fee and left.

Tisamon's agent was a pragmatic Beetle woman named Rowen Palasso, and she became very familiar with Ellery Mainler over the next month. Business was slow, and Mainler paid over the odds – indeed it seemed she would pay whatever Palasso asked. Three times more, Tisamon trudged to her workshops to demolish the latest incarnation of her machine. She never seemed to run out of money, though he wondered that there was anyone left in Helleron who would bet against her. More, she never ran out of whatever drove her. She watched him fight with an avid hunger that he felt every moment. She sketched him, not clad as he presented himself, but stripped – to the skin, to the muscle, to the bone, intimate beyond the dreams of pornography. Tisamon knew obsession when he saw it. He had been its victim, in his time. What he did not know was how to cure it.

The machine was still lacking. Even as he engaged it, it failed to engage him. It remained a thing.

After that last clash, third of this series, fifth overall, she asked him to stay with her. Given how much she was paying Palasso, he felt he owed that to her, and she poured out a little wine and asked him questions. At first these were the expected: technique, distancing, balance, a façade of professionalism, as though all she cared about was her pointless, useless fighting automaton. Once the wine had loosened them both a little she segued into darker territories. She asked him about his upbringing, his training, his badge. She asked him a dozen questions about what his fighting *meant* to him, the Inapt Weaponsmaster, and he did his best for her. His answers slid away from her, just as hers would baffle him if he asked her to explain the workings of her machine. They were from different worlds, and he was bewildered that she, the inheritrix of all that was new and strong and dominant in the world, should yet find herself jealous of the old, pining for a world of uncertainties that she could never be a part of.

He imagined her as she staked her fortune at the card tables, pitting the gleaming steel of her wits against the risk of losing everything. What would her face look like, in the moment before the cards turned? Would he recognize that expression from the fighting ring, from the swordsman caught at the height of his skill, letting his blade bear the weight of a life?

She met his gaze, and he realized that he had been staring at her for some time.

"I will make it better," she told him. "Come back to me."

To Palasso's annoyance, he began to turn down commissions. He did not need the money – though perhaps she did – and he felt off balance, incomplete and without his unassailable focus. He was waiting for Ellery's word.

When he dreamt, he did not see Ellery but he heard as she worked invisibly about the craft that he could not imagine, as though she was tunnelling through the walls of his dream. Instead, what he saw was the machine stalking through the halls of his mind to challenge him. In her workshop he had faced it boldly, but in the dreams it was a thing of terror and he fled rather than see its face. He awoke ashamed, sweat-stained, feverish.

If Ellery had been a magician, he would have understood, but she was Apt, an artificer, as far from magic as a kinden could go. He had bewitched himself.

Then the call came, at last, and he went to her like a warrior to his last battle, but gladly.

She met him at the door of her workshop. There was a terrible excitement bubbling in her face.

"It's finished," she told him. "It's ready for you. Nobody has ever built such a thing as I have. I took all you told me of yourself, and I have measured it and calculated and trapped it in metal. I am the greatest artificer in the world. Fight my champion, Tisamon. I challenge you. Like a Mantis, I challenge you." Just as her machines were not life, but could feign, so she was not Inapt, and yet she had listened to him enough to know what words to say.

He stepped into the workshop with Ellery at his back. The machine was ready for him, gears wound, steam hissing softly from its joints as it waited. She had given it two legs, and it no longer hung from the ceiling tracks like a murderous marionette. The arms still had a joint too many, and its shape was hunchbacked and inhuman to accommodate the burgeoning intricacy of the workings, but it had a head now. His face, cast in brass, as perfect and devoid of expression as a death mask.

Tisamon fell into his stance, the blade of his claw unfolded to lie between them. When the machine smoothly adopted a mirror stance, he stared into that familiar face and felt the shock of contact that had never come before.

He could no more back down from this challenge than he could have refused the Spider-kinden. He would leave her workshop victorious or dead.

He stepped in, expecting to hold the initiative, but his movements triggered a sudden whirling rush by the machine. Its footing was still slightly slow and awkward, but its attacks were fast and not limited by the arcs of human joints, and abruptly Tisamon was on the defensive.

He could keep clear of its reach, but the workshop space – that had seemed huge when he first saw it – was abruptly constricting, with the machine constantly sidestepping to herd him towards the walls. Each time he backed up, the machine followed further, faster. That razor edge whirled in from unexpected directions as it tested out his guard.

He changed stance, trying to get closer, within its reach, but ducking past and through swiftly when he saw that its loose-hinged arms could just fold straight back on themselves. As he passed, he struck back, and felt a scraping impact of his blade on the thing's armoured body. Then he was rolling below a counterattack as it stepped heavily after him.

He caught a glimpse of Ellery, of her face, mouth slightly open, eyes very wide, watching her champion defend her honour.

At the far end of the room, he paused and watched the machine slow as it ceased to hear him or detect his motion. He had thought that it would stop, then, blind as it was, but it began methodically stalking forwards, sweeping left and right, knowing to an inch the dimensions of the space around it.

With the greatest care, Tisamon bunched himself to spring, a foot against the back wall for more purchase, seeing the automaton grow closer; unhurried, assured of finding him.

He waited until it had committed to its next exploratory sweep before kicking off, catching that blade-arm in his off hand and slamming into the thing's body before its shield came up. He felt the device begin to topple, but it took three clumsy steps backwards, adjusting to his weight, and the blade was pivoting on the end of the arm, slicing back towards his fingers.

He kicked away again, shifting his hand to dig into the edge of its armour, throwing his full weight against it, driving his blade in. A moment later he found himself tumbling across the floor, staggering a little as he found his feet.

The automaton had turned for him again, but his claw had struck true, finding the gap he had wrenched in its plating. There was a rupture of steam venting there, half-obscuring the thing's impassive face.

He had left a smear of blood on the floor, he saw. It had cut him twice as he left, two long, shallow lines, outer thigh and back.

The automaton was coming for him again. He was breathing heavily, and he glanced at Ellery, to see an expression of fierce passion on her face. "Finish it!" she demanded, of him, of *it*, and in that moment she had truly understood the fight, as the Inapt knew it: the fight that is a gamble where neither player can limit the stake.

He threw himself at the machine. It lunged at him, slowed by its injuries, and he was able to take the blade and fend it off, grab the shield as it came in, and use the machine's own strength to lift him above its guard. Driving down into that same gaping gash he had cut, he felt the delicate structures of its innards part, and the machine died.

Even then, it cut him, laying a line of blood down his forearm, and he staggered back from the steaming automaton as it slowly froze into statue-stillness, heart pounding but alive, so very alive.

He looked on his opponent now and it was nothing but a thing, but while he had fought it, it had lived. This was like magic, the sort of magic the world no longer held.

Ellery was beside him before he remembered her, reaching out a hand and painting one fingertip with red from his sleeve.

"And you thought I did not understand you," she whispered. "Magnificent, beautiful, and yet I have bound your mystery in brass and steel. I have challenged you, my fierce Mantis."

"Your machine –"

"No, not the machine! *I*! I have taken the weapon of my choosing, and I have called you forth, and bloodied you. I am the world's greatest artificer, but now I have proved myself in your world too. Can you deny me?"

Her hand fell on his gashed forearm and then clasped, hard enough to make him wince, her fingers curling about his spines. She was looking up at him, this girl who had everything in the world save one thing, and who had coveted and desired until that, too, was within her grasp.

"I have won you," she told him, and her other hand was reaching to cup his head and draw him down to her lips, but he twitched away, stepped from her grip as though he was smoke.

"No," he told her.

"No?" she demanded. "You can't say 'no'. I know how it is, for your kinden. I have researched you, ransacked every library for your secrets. I have seen you fight. I have understood you as no other can! And I have challenged you, and proved myself worthy. I *know* how this works."

He felt the bonds of his honour pull taut, seeing that pride in her and knowing that everything she said was true, so that when she threw at him, "Because of my kinden? Is that it? You dare to judge me only for that?" he could only shake his head.

"There was another," he said.

She would not accept it. "Liar! I know you! I have watched you. I have paid your agent for morsels of your life. No other have you looked at, here in Helleron. No whore, no magnate's wife, no swordsmistress."

"Because there was another."

"No! Because nobody has challenged you, before now!" Ellery insisted desperately.

He had no way to tell her save the hard way, the true way. "A long time ago, there was a woman. Just the one. For my people, there is only ever the one. Then she betrayed me and left me with nothing but ashes. Why else would I be living this life in Helleron, save to blot out that?"

She had started to shake, just a little. "Nobody lives that storybook life, not even you. There is never just the one. There is no destined love. So there was another, and she is dead or gone, left or abandoned or betrayed you. *I* am here, Tisamon!"

At that moment he bitterly wanted to be anything but what he was, standing there with his honour rising in his throat to choke him. For a moment he saw himself through Apt eyes, bent beneath a burden of his own making, ridiculous in his assumed gravitas, the clown that thinks he's king.

But if he unbent from that load, if he cast off the chains that shackled him, then he would not be what she had set her heart on any more. He would be one with the grime and the graft of the Helleron streets, just an exotic thug with a penchant for murder. The thing she desired was what stood between them.

He wanted to reach out to her. He wanted to beg forgiveness. Most of all he wanted to not be who he was, and yet give her what she wanted, but those were opposing poles, and he could not make them meet.

A month later, when his agent, Palasso, told him that Ellery had paid for his time, he sought within himself for how he felt, and found something hollow and hard, as though he had been the automaton all the time.

The treacherous thought: *Perhaps it's not too late,* though he did not know whether he meant her, or the next iteration of the deadly machine.

It was too late, nonetheless. When she did not open the workshop door to his knock he pushed it inwards, and saw the ruin the device had made of Ellery Mainler.

He could never know if she had been repairing it, or improving it, or just winding its springs, stoking its fires. When its blade had ripped into her, it had finished with one of those boneless flourishes he remembered, doubling back along the length of its own arm to pin her to its metal body, her arms encircling the cold plating of its trunk. Over her shoulder, his own face cast in brass seemed to smile at him.

So we travel from the Commonweal, by way of occupied Myna, to Helleron to set the stage for what comes next, and at this point in time, Helleron is the personal hell Tisamon is putting himself through, just as Ineskae seeks redemption in the Commonweal. Tisamon, Atryssa (his betrayer/lover) and even Rowen Palasso have their role to play in Shadows, *but, although Ellery Mainler's story ends here, her work lives on in the books. Her ratiocinator – the clockwork difference engine which gives her fighting machine a semblance of conscious thought, will see a lot of use when the Empire gets hold of it in* The Air War *and beyond. Although much of the journey through these stories has been through the shadowy world of the Inapt, therefore, we end, as we began, with* Aptitude, *and not the Wasp Empire's brutal militarism but Beetle-kinden imagination. Lial Morless conquered the sky. Ellery Mainler set out to conquer something far more nebulous, and if she had not died at the hands of her own obsession she'd have given Drephos and Totho a run for their money.*

About the Author

Adrian Tchaikovsky was born in Woodhall Spa, Lincolnshire before heading off to Reading to study psychology and zoology. He subsequently ended up in law and has worked as a legal executive in both Reading and Leeds, where he now lives. Married, he is a keen live role-player and has trained in stage-fighting and historical combat. He maintains a keen interest in history and the biological sciences especially entomology.

Adrian is the author of the acclaimed ten-book Shadows of the Apt series starting with *Empire in Black and Gold* published by Tor UK. His other works for Tor UK include standalone novels *Guns of the Dawn* and *Children of Time* and the new series Echoes of the Fall starting with *The Tiger and the Wolf.* Other major works include short story collection *Feast and Famine* for Newcon Press and novellas *The Bloody Deluge* (in *Journal of the Plague* Year) and *Even in the Cannon's Mouth* (in *Monstrous Little Voices*) for Abaddon. He has also written numerous short stories and been shortlisted for the David Gemmell Legend Award, the British Fantasy Award and the Arthur C Clarke Award.

Coming Soon from NewCon Press

TALES OF THE APT

Volume 2
A Time of Grief

Cover art by Jon Sullivan

Continuing the companion series to the best-selling *Shadows of the Apt.*

Praise for the Shadows of the Apt books:
"The whole Shadows of the Apt series has been one of the most original creations in modern fantasy" – *Upcoming4.me*

"A page-turning ride to its superb finale" – *FantasyBookCritic*

"Tchaikovsky makes a good and enjoyable mix between a medieval looking world and the presence of technology" – *Starburst Magazine*

Due September 2016

Now We Are Ten

The Sister Volume to

Crises and Conflicts

Celebrating the first ten years of NewCon Press
With sixteen original stories written especially for this book

Contents:
Introduction by Ian Whates
The Final Path – Genevieve Cogman
Women's Christmas – Ian McDonald
Pyramid – Nancy Kress
Liberty Bird – Jaine Fenn
Zanzara Island – Rachel Armstrong
Ten Sisters – Eric Brown
Licorice – Jack Skillingstead
The Time Travellers' Ball (A Story in
Ten Words) – Rose Biggin
Dress Rehearsal – Adrian Tchaikovsky
The Tenth Man – Bryony Pearce
Rare as a Harpy's Tear – Neil
Williamson
How to Grow Silence from Seed –
Tricia Sullivan
Utopia +10 – JA Christy
Ten Love Songs to Change the World
– Peter F Hamilton
Ten Days – Nina Allan
Front Row Seat to the End of the World – EJ Swift

Cover art by Ben Baldwin

Available as a signed limited edition hardback, paperback,
and eBook

www.newconpress.co.uk

Crises and Conflicts
The Sister Volume to
Now We Are Ten

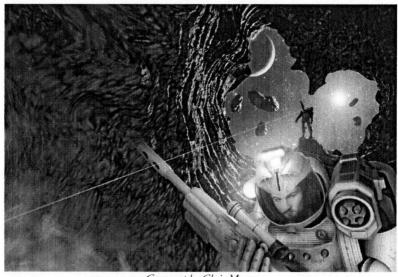

Cover art by Chris Moore

Fifteen tales of space opera and military science fiction from:

Nik Abnett * Amy DuBoff * Michael Brookes
Janet Edwards * Una McCormack * Christopher Nuttall
Mercurio D. Rivera * Adam Roberts * Robert Sharp
Gavin Smith * Allen Stroud * Tim C. Taylor
Tade Thompson * Ian Whates * Jo Zebedee

Available now as a signed limited edition hardback, paperback,
and eBook.

www.newconpress.co.uk

Lightning Source UK Ltd.
Milton Keynes UK
UKOW02f0350210616

276753UK00003B/52/P